W9-BRW-397

Praise For
Annette Appollo
and
The Last One Home

"Appollo blends vividly realized characters with startling plot twists in this tumultuous comic novel. . . . Appollo confronts difficult issues with forthrightness and satirical bite."

—*Library Journal*

"Dust off your catechism, dig up your pasta machine, and prepare to be completely enveloped in the Italian Catholic culture of Annette Appollo's *The Last One Home*. Appollo's carefully developed characters and authentic touches bring this world to life, where quirky details and surreal moments prevent the danger of suffocation by nostalgia—and some predictable and not-so-predictable twists capture the reader's attention and heart."

—Amazon.com Reviews

HarperChoice

THE LAST ONE HOME

A NOVEL

ANNETTE APPOLLO

HarperPaperbacks

A Division of HarperCollins*Publishers*

♜ **HarperPaperbacks**
A Division of HarperCollins*Publishers*
10 East 53rd Street, New York, NY 10022-5299

ISBN 0-06-109721-7

Cover design © 1999 by Honi Werner

A hardcover edition of this book was published in 1999 by HarperCollins*Publishers*.

First HarperPaperbacks printing: January 2000

Printed in the United States of America

Visit HarperPaperbacks on the World Wide Web at
http://www.harpercollins.com

❖ 10 9 8 7 6 5 4 3 2 1

FOR
HELEN P. BROWN
GOD'S PROTOTYPE FOR A FRIEND

THE GREATER PART OF WHAT MY
NEIGHBORS CALL GOOD I BELIEVE
IN MY SOUL TO BE BAD, AND IF I REPENT OF
ANY THING, IT IS VERY LIKELY TO BE MY
GOOD BEHAVIOR. WHAT DEMON POSSESSED
ME THAT I BEHAVED SO WELL?

—Henry David Thoreau, *Walden*

ACKNOWLEDGMENTS

A long time ago, Darryl Ponicsan, Harry Stein and Priscilla Turner encouraged me to write. For their loving support, I say thank you. Deborah C. Schneider believed, believes, and makes all things possible for me. She started as an agent, became a friend, and ended up as the love of my life. I can never thank her enough.

Marjorie Braman took a chance, taught me how to be a writer, and, along the way, gave me some pointers on friendship and love. She is the bravest woman I know. She is a wonderful gift.

Cathy Gleason and Jeffery McGraw have smoothed this new road for me in more ways than I can count, and they did it with grace and style.

And Oscar H. Wiygul, Jr., just keeps holding on to me, for which I'm eternally grateful.

PROLOGUE

In the dark, the pain doesn't seem real. The old man doesn't even have to close his eyes to believe that this is only a dream, only a dream. The morphine helps, he knows. It makes his disbelief possible, but he is a man who built his life on disbelief. He scoffed at the others, the ones who clung to faith or to God or to the mystical certainty of a higher power; he has believed only in himself and his loved ones all his long life, and now that that life is ending, Tony Scarpino also believes in morphine.

He is hugely amused by the fact that there is a Catholic priest in the dark room with him. The priest won't go away, no matter how many times the dying man tells him to leave; even as a boy, Willie Cunningham stayed, but thirty-five years ago he wasn't a priest, only a boy looking for a girl, a woman now, who is tonight thousands of miles away from the dark room where the old man is dying as the younger man sits beside his bed.

"When are you going to call her?" the priest asks the old man.

"Tonight," he answers slowly. "I'll call her tonight."

Gia Scarpino sits alone in her dim office, watching the bloody red sun sink into the Pacific Ocean. After all her years in San Francisco, she has never been able to take for granted the magnificence of these West Coast sunsets; in Pennsylvania, in her small hometown, the sun disappeared early behind low mountains stripped clean of their soft coal, dug under by anthracite miners. When she left that town, three and a half decades ago, the green sprouts of reclamation were just beginning to show on the barren gray hills where she and her friends had played their children's games.

Tonight, she waits for the phone to ring, her lawyer's desk covered with the messy filings of the many divorces she shepherds through the courts. Tonight, she knows that she is a very good lawyer, but tonight, as she sits waiting for her stepdaughter to return the call placed early in the day, she also knows that the young woman will not return the call, and again Gia Scarpino will dine alone.

She begins to gather files, sliding them off the desktop into her briefcase. It is, she tells herself, just another night. But it isn't. It's Nancy's twenty-first birthday; Gia has sent her flowers and a card, but there has been no response. There rarely is, but still Gia calls, still she tries, because it is always possible, she honestly believes, to rectify mistakes of inexperience and grief. As long as there is life, there is time and there is hope. She honestly believes this, but as she turns out the lights and picks up her briefcase, she knows that this will not be the evening to set it right with her late husband's younger child.

When the phone rings, she is almost at the door, and she drops the briefcase and grabs the receiver, straining to hold down her breathlessness, as she starts to say, "Hello," but hears instead a ghost of a familiar voice, softly saying, "*Vieni qua. Ora.*"

Hearing the whispered words, she feels her world, so carefully structured to shut out the sharp pain of closeness and intimacy, the world she shapes and reinforces every day, begin to fall down, as she hears the man she has loved her whole life tell her to come home.

It was how he summoned her when it was getting dark, darking, the little girl called it, and it was time to run to the safety of his arms, when he would hold her tightly to him and young Gianna knew then that she would be safe forever in the arms of the man, her godfather, her uncle Tony, who loved her with a ferocity that has protected her even to this day.

This day she knew would come, but it is too soon, and she's not ready. Even if it was another forty years from now, it would be too soon.

There will be no cuckolded husband tomorrow. Her clients will have to destroy their lives without her counsel. There will be no tomorrow. Time has stopped. The smallest things have become huge. After Gia calls the airline, and leaves messages for her stepchildren, telling them what has happened and where she is going, she realizes that she has to concentrate on taking each breath, that the simple autonomic exercise of breathing is no longer available to her, that she must concentrate on inhaling and exhaling, or else she will end up smothered by the weight of the words she just heard him say, the words for which she thought she was ready, but, as we all find out, for which there is no preparation. There is nothing to be done but to concentrate on breathing in and breathing out, and Gia does this with great determination, as if she were breathing for two, as if the air flowing into her lungs will keep alive the man who told her a year ago that he was dying.

Vieni qua, he said.

Come here. Now.

Barbara Arminavage Eckroat tops off the glass almost filled with cheap vodka and lemonade from a paper carton, and continues with what will occupy her for the rest of the night. She'll keep the drink close to her as she cleans the house. While her children sleep, she will vacuum; they long ago learned to sleep through her nocturnal racket. Her husband won't be home until after dawn, and by that time she'll be unconscious, dead to the world, thanks to fatigue and a steady infusion of vodka and lemonade as she scrubs and scours, wipes and rinses, thinking all the while that Shakespeare was right: no amount of scrubbing will ever make it clean again.

But she will sing while she cleans, and by the time she crawls, clothed and sweaty, into her lonely bed, she will be almost certain that she has a happy life.

Or, in any event, the life she deserves. Barbara remembers the first prayer the nuns taught them: Now I lay me down to sleep, I pray the Lord my soul to keep; if I should die before I wake, I pray the Lord my soul to take. The prayer used to terrify her, as it would any normal child confronted with the notion of dying in her sleep, but now she finds it comforting. To die in her sleep. That would be all right.

As she fades out of the small consciousness she has left, she sees an old picture in her mind: her and Gia Scarpino, two little girls who used to visit funeral homes. In their parochial school uniforms of navy blue jumpers and white blouses, blue knee socks and saddle oxfords, they would go, solemnly respectful, to all the wakes that were being held. In those days the dead were laid out for two or three days before the funeral, to give distant relatives time to get there. Very often the wakes were held in the front parlors of the decedent's home, the only use to which those rooms were ever put. So specialized were these parlors that some of them had windows that came out of their frames, the easier to get the casket in and out of the house.

Barbara and Gia would enter the wake, be it in a funeral home or a private home, go to the bier, kneel, bless themselves, say earnest and lengthy prayers, all the while studying the corpse, looking for a movement, a twitch that would enable them to stand and announce, "He's alive!", thereby securing their places as heroines in their community. Instead, they would turn to the family and offer their condolences: "He was a nice man, missus," or "She was nice, mister." Then they headed for the kitchen, where there was usually a pretty good selection of cakes and cookies. By the time they returned to their respective homes, they were stuffed, ready to do their homework and eat supper, happy in the knowledge that the dead had not been lonely, at least for a little while, and that they would see each other after the dishes were done.

We were good girlfriends, Barbara thinks as the long-ago children slip away from her, and her consciousness deserts her just before she wonders why she is thinking of someone she hasn't seen for thirty-five years.

Yozo's wife nudges him awake. "It's your turn," she mumbles, and he wonders if he can fake her out, so he stays very still, regulating his breathing, deep, even breaths that don't fool her for one second. "So get the fuck up," she hisses.

He walks the baby boy for a while, then pops a bottle into the microwave and stretches out in his recliner while he feeds his only grandchild. "You're a good kid, Joey," he tells the baby. "Your mother and father are assholes, but you're a good kid." Upstairs, his son, the baby's father, sleeps soundly, the thick, uncomplicated sleep of a boy barely out of adolescence, a boy who hasn't the years or the experience to know that he is screwing up his life, and the lives of those around him, in ways he can't even begin to understand. Someday, when the boy is my age, Yozo thinks, he'll be sorry. And with that thought comes a pain in his heart that he once thought was the beginning of cardiac trouble, but which extensive medical testing proved to be nothing more than the pain that comes to middle-aged men in the middle of the night when they realize that, no matter how successful they have been, they will live the rest of their lives with regrets.

He holds the baby closer to him and, after a long, productive burp, cradles him on his chest as they fall into a sleep that will last for the rest of the night. When Yozo awakens, the pain in his heart will be gone, and he will be happy for the rest of the day because his grandson will be smiling at him when he opens his eyes.

FIRST DAY

*T*his is what he remembers about the Senior Prom: she wore a dress in the style of Jackie Kennedy, who was enjoying her last spring as First Lady. The frock was strapless, with lacy blue embroidery on the bodice and a straight white skirt. With her dark brown hair teased into a bubble and her elbow-length white gloves, he thought he would lose his breath and die when he saw her. Her grandfather slipped him twenty dollars after he tucked her into the new Cadillac his mother let him use that night, and her uncle put his heavy hand on the back of his neck and said, "She comes home the way she leaves."

But what he remembers best is her bare back, that moment in the dimly lit, guilelessly decorated gym, with the aluminum foil Eiffel Tower, when they came together for their first slow dance. He can't remember the music—he wishes he knew what song was playing—but he can so clearly, in his mind, recreate the sensation he felt when his hand touched that delicate winglike bone below her shoulder, the scapula. She was so thin, the flesh seemed to have nothing between it and that bone, and the delicacy of that moment stays with him, has always stayed with him, and still there are times, not so frequent now, when the simple recollection of his young man's hand innocently resting on her naked back, her oh-so-naked back, can bring him almost to a swoon.

She is seated at a cafeteria table, staring down into a styrofoam coffee cup, looking as though she might spit into it. Her hair is no longer a mahogany *bubble, but now a tangled mass of graying curls. As a young girl she was not vain, and that seems not to have changed. While her girlfriends were experimenting with makeup and powder, foundation and eye shadow, she remained shiny and clean, with sometimes a hint of mascara, not even rouge or lipstick, so sure she seemed to be that her own beauty was quite enough for the world to deal with. Even now, the pallor of her overnight plane trip and sixty-mile drive haven't made her look as any other middle-aged woman might. She glances his way, but she doesn't see him. She is seeing her own thoughts.*

The slenderness is gone, though. When he watched her go through the food line, and then look around for the most remote and unoccupied table, he could see, even though she was carrying a heavy trench coat, that she had developed into a finely built woman. Not for her, and he is not surprised, would be the aerobicizing and toning and surgical interventions that seem to have come upon so many of their contemporaries; she has an incipient double chin and a more than generous chest. Ah, what he wouldn't have given for her to have had that shape when they spent nights parked in his mother's car, hidden away in St. Canisius's Cemetery, overlooking the lights of the town.

She seems taller, even sitting down. Perhaps her life has given her stature, perhaps her professional accomplishments? Perhaps he has grown smaller next to her. She scared him when they were young together; she knew about passion in ways that are still unrevealed to him. Not just the physical part of

*the passion, but the willingness to embrace life, to
go forth into the world, and to seek out everything
that might hurt or pleasure her. They whispered the
promises of youngsters, but even then he knew that
they were not to be lived.*

*She was too much even then, and now, as he
watches this handsome woman she has become, at
this terrible time in her life, his heart is pounding,
more than it has in years, and he would like nothing more than to run out of this hospital cafeteria,
out of the situation that has brought them both
here early this morning, but he has nowhere else to
go, and he wants to be with her. After all these
years, nay, decades, he wants to see what she has
become. He wants to see that the passage of time
has not dulled the sharpness that once danced in
her dark eyes. He wants to know that the sweet
shining girl he once loved lives on in the woman
drinking coffee under the painfully artificial lights
in this busy place. He wants to recall the joy of loving her, as he did the moment he first saw her, on
the first day of ninth grade when she leaned across
the aisle as the roll was called, and said, "Cunningham, William, is that you?"*

"Yeah."

"You Irish?"

"Yeah."

*She gave him a heartbreakingly broad grin and
said, "You're cute, Cunningham, but you can't come
to my house. My grandfather kills Irishmen and
keeps their ears for souvenirs. You have nice ears."*

He fell in love.

• • •

And now, intact ears ringing, he approaches her
table, remembering that they are exactly the same
age, but feeling like a young boy, helpless at the feet
of the queen. She glances up at him and then gives
him a slow up-and-down look, something he doesn't
ever recall seeing done in such a deliberate and
unstudied manner. She isn't the slightest bit self-
conscious about her curiosity, and when her eyes
return to his, he sees, with some relief and even
more joy, that they are the same sparkling, clear,
deep brown eyes. She doesn't recognize him, and he
is reluctant to have to introduce himself to the only
woman he has ever loved.

Then her eyebrows shoot up, and her generous
mouth does an elaborate serpentine as she looks
him over, more quickly, and after all these years, his
beloved speaks:

"It's fucking Halloween, right?"

"You still have that mouth on you, don't you?"
And then, because the young man doesn't ever really
leave the older man, he leans across the plastic table,
and grabs her face with both hands and kisses her in
a way that leaves the ladies in the cafeteria staring,
then staring some more, and then leaning and whispering and using their elbows ever so gently on each
other, while Father Cunningham lays the kiss of his
life on the strange woman sitting over in the corner.
Tonight the supper tables will crackle with talk of
the priest and the lady he kissed and the town will
not hold it against him, but the women will begin
wondering about him in ways they never did before,

and the men will wink at him and smile and no one will ever say a word about it.

When he pulls back from her, he says, "Yeah, that same mouth." And she, Gianna Scarpino, who, after flying all night, has just spent the longest hour of her life sitting beside the bed of her sleeping, dying godfather, Gianna Scarpino, who made her fortune with her smart mouth, that same mouth, is finally speechless.

From the fall of 1960 until late spring 1963, there was not one blowjob performed in the United States. Gia knows this because her girlfriends told her that no one ever really did such a disgusting thing. They were in tenth, eleventh, and twelfth grades, and no one, no one, those girls assured her, would ever do that.

They were lying sows, every one of them. But Gia believed them, and so she and Willie spent their every spare moment trying to get away from everybody else, to find a safe and warm place, and to let their exploding hormones have their way with them. There were things to be learned then, places to find, places to be touched, secrets to tell, hands guided, lips bruised and swollen and bitten, and always, always, the wanting of more. At the end of one of their nights, wet in places that until then had been dry, she would smooth her hair, her clothes, and steal a glance at the boy in the driver's seat who was sitting, just staring ahead through the windshield, at what, Gia did not know. He would stay silent for a long time, and when he finally turned to her, he would have such an agonized look on his face. Now, a grown woman, she knows that look. It is longing, but, as little more than a child then, she did not know.

The things they did together. Willie taking her hand and showing her what power it gave her over him, at the same time giving him pleasure. Her shorts coming down for him, and then his eyes, just his smiling Irish eyes, that was all she could see, as she went faster and faster down that wonderful slide and his mouth made sounds that were funny and thrilling at the same time. She never thought to ask him how he knew about that. She thought it was all magic, and now, years later, many men, maybe too many men later, she still does.

They did it all, except the final thing, because Gia was a good girl, Willie was a frightened boy too in love ever to force the issue, and because it was 1963, and she honestly thought no one else was doing it. Just like blowjobs. She was never going to do that, she and her girlfriends agreed that it was just too gross, and no matter how Willie begged, it never happened. He was probably the only guy in their class not getting head, but Gia didn't know that. Everything else was good, though, and they couldn't wait to get themselves alone in his mother's car, or stretched out on the grass in one of the cemeteries that overlooked the town, or on the banks of the town's water supply, listening to the water slapping the side of the concrete dam. They did it almost everywhere, and she didn't know enough then to wonder how the poor boy ever made it home. Gia

had Uncle Tony and Pop waiting for her, and she is
sure now that they knew exactly what the two ado-
lescents were up to, but they never said a word to
her. Willie was in absolute fear of both of them, Gia
knew that. He was a smart kid.

So the boy she grew up with, the boy who showed
her such lovely things, the boy who trembled when
he held her, that boy has grown up, and now he has
Gia's face in his hands, he has just taken his mouth
from hers, he is smiling at her, the pretty boy who
has grown up to be a big, handsome man with a
wide swatch of white cutting through his thick
black hair, his blue Irish eyes still pierce, and his
nose, she doesn't remember that great hawk thing
that now sits in the middle of his face, but he is smiling at her, and she puts her hands over his, and right
now she is very, very tired, she is frightened, and it is
such a great comfort to see a friendly face in this
strange place, even though it is the hospital where
they both were born, and Willie Cunningham,
whose naked body she once knew better than she
knew her own, is wearing a black suit and a Roman
collar.

Gia remembers Tony telling her, well over a year
ago, that Willie Cunningham had come back home,
that he was a Catholic priest. It was in the same
conversation that her uncle told her that he had lung
cancer, and that he had decided to forgo the radia-
tion and chemotherapy offered to him, sure as he
was in his knowledge that his life had run its course.
The news of her old boyfriend's vocation had been

eclipsed by Tony's crisp and inarguable announcement: "I'm gonna die," he had instructed her, "and I'll call you to come to me when I need you."

"Ever been French-kissed by a priest, Gia? Did you like it? Do you want me to do it again?" He's laughing, he does it very easily. She thinks Willie might have become an extraordinarily charming man.

"A priest," she repeats.

"Yeah, I join them together and you put them apart. Aren't we a matched set? I'll bet you thought God doesn't have a sense of humor." He kisses her again, softer this time, friendlier, and then he just presses his cheek to hers, an unspeakably tender gesture. "Hello, Gia, hello. Come, let's sit. Do you want more coffee? Have you eaten? You must be tired." He pulls two molded plastic chairs together, and gently pushes her down into one of them, draping himself casually onto the other. His head is enormous, and his longish hair accentuates it. Gia thinks of movie actors she has met, and they always have huge heads, too.

Willie has grown up to be a hunk. A hunk who has taken vows of poverty, chastity, and obedience.

God's not as funny as Willie thinks He is.

"My godfather." Gia points at the ceiling. "He's here. He's very sick, Willie. You remember my Uncle Tony?"

"I've been seeing him, Gia. He's very sick, yes."

"He lets you in his room dressed like that?"

"We don't pray. I've tried to give him the opportunity to make his confession, but . . ." Willie shrugs, still smiling.

"He bites you?"

"Yes, he's done that. Last time, though, he kissed me."

She leans back. "He's mellowing."

"No, he's just suckering me. If I try it again, he'll bite me again."

"He's just like my grandfather."

"Your grandfather was an atheist, I remember that."

"Yeah, but when the priest wasn't wearing his cassock, they were good friends. I remember falling asleep on summer nights in my bedroom above the store, hearing them argue in Italian on the bench in front of the store, drinking wine my grandfather had made from grapes he had shipped from California in railroad boxcars. God, Willie, that was such a long time ago, wasn't it? Do you remember any of it, or is it only me?"

And then she starts to cry. Not a big howling cry, just silent tears running from her eyes. "Ah, Gia," Willie reaches for her, "sweet Gia. I know how hard this is for you. I know what he is to you."

"My *Padrino*, Willie, my godfather," she croaks, and his big arms are around her, holding her against his chest, ever so softly rocking her like the large child she has just become, and here is her old boyfriend, the priest, comforting her. "This is too complicated."

"What's that?"

"Tony's upstairs dying, you're down here being a priest, and I'm in the middle. I don't get it. Is this some kind of joke?"

"You've got to admit, this is a good one, don't you think?"

"*Quel che spute in cielo, lo receve nel'la faccia.*" She quotes her grandfather's favorite observation of the world as she pulls herself out of the good father's embrace.

"'When you spit up in the air, it lands in your face,'" Willie translates perfectly. "Yes, I think you might be feeling like that, yeah, I can understand that, but, Gia, I didn't take orders just to upset you."

She yanks herself out of his embrace. "When did you learn to speak Italian?"

When he says, "I spent six years at the Vatican," Gia thinks that she has arrived at the Gates of Hell, and that the easy times are over.

"What order?" she asks.

"Jesuit."

"The ones called 'the soldiers of Christ.'"

Nodding, he says, "We enjoy that reputation in some quarters, yes."

"Willie, I'm a Jesuit-trained lawyer. I went to Loyola, Los Angeles."

"Gia, I'm a Jesuit-trained philosopher. I went to Georgetown."

"You guys are the toughest people in the world. I've been up against murderers and rapists and child molesters and, even worse, women whose husbands have come out of the closet to them, but I've never encountered anything like you guys. I once represented a Ranger, and they're supposed to be superhuman, but he wasn't anything; he was a pussy compared to some Jesuits I've known. Willie, you?"

"I never actually philosophized. All the good spots in the *agora* were taken, so I went to Rome and did research in ecclesiastical philosophy. A lot of book work. I found that I was quite suited to the academic life. You, of course, would find yourself in the thick of it. I think perhaps you might be tougher than someone as mortal as, say, a Jesuit."

"I think I might be getting set up."

He blushes. "You're still your grandfather's kid." He shakes his head as though this is hard for him to believe. "You haven't become the easygoing California type, have you?"

"Did you expect that?"

For a moment his wide-open face looks even more vulnerable, and the boy is back, just for an instant. "I expected nothing," he says quietly. "I deplore the reasons for your being here, and I have been praying for him and for you, but the truth is, I'm so very happy to see you again, Gianna."

That, naturally, makes her cry again. "I can't go back," she says to herself, but the words come out anyway, and Willie quickly says, "Oh, Gia, please, I expect nothing. I'm just happy to be with you, that's all."

"No, no, Willie, I didn't mean you, don't, please, no."

"What?" He looks into her face. Gia has visions of old ladies coming to Father Cunningham, pouring out their stories, him listening intently, nodding, holding their hands, praying over them, comforting them, burying them. She doesn't know him, she

can't know him, he lives in a world she has long
since renounced and abandoned, and that is his
whole world, his very life.

"I think I have to go back to the house now. I'm
tired."

"Of course you are. Can I drive you?"

"I have a car. I flew into Philadelphia, rented it
there."

"I know, but you're tired. I could pick you up
later, we could come back here, you could visit with
your uncle, get your car. How about it, Gia?"

"He sleeps during the day, the nurses told me,
and his friend the priest stays with him at night. I
didn't realize it was you, Willie. Why?"

"The truth?"

"Do priests lie?"

"Better than lawyers." He grips her hand. His
hands are big and soft and dry. They are not the
hands of a working man. "Your uncle sleeps all day
because he says his pain is worse in the daylight. In
fact, I think it's his way of avoiding your aunts. I don't
mean to offend, Gia, but they are an odd bunch. At
night he seems to believe that the pain medication is
more effective. If he thinks it is, then it is."

"The Angels of Death, sure, they'd drive him
nuts, even while he's dying. That figures."

"Have you seen them yet?"

"No." The immutability of what awaits her lies
heavily across the back of her mind. "They weren't
around when I got to his house. I just had a cup of
coffee with Tony's wife. She was praying at her
shrine when I arrived. Francie has a statue of the

Blessed Mother in her bedroom, Willie. She has flowers and candles and all kinds of shit like that around it. It's a regular Wop grotto."

"I know." He grins. "I bless it every year."

Gia thinks this over. "You do?"

He nods.

"You do the blessing of the houses? You?"

"Yeah."

"Willie, which one's your parish?"

"Gianna, Our Lady of Mercy."

"My old church. The one all the Italians went to. The Italian church."

"Yes."

"It's where I went through First Holy Communion. Confirmation."

"You were baptized there, too. You should come over and look through the old records with me. They're wonderful. Fascinating. You'd like it."

"No, wait, wait, Willie, stay with me on this. I've been away a long time. You're telling me that you're the pastor of the Italian church? The Italian church has an Irish priest?"

"Welcome home, Gia."

"You better give me that ride home now. I can't drive. I can't even think anymore."

They rise, and it's the most natural thing in the world for her to slide her arm through his as they depart the cafeteria. Outside, it has become a day, she can't remember which one, but she looks up at the sky and realizes that her sleeping godfather is one day closer to death and she is here to help him. Willie squeezes her arm tightly against his side.

In the parking lot, Willie doesn't know why, but he stops walking and takes his old girlfriend into his arms. She comes to his embrace so simply, as if she were still that lovely young girl at the Senior Prom. He holds her close, his hand rests lightly, ever so lightly, on her back, and for an instant he knows that they are again those beautiful children, regardless of the truth that the harsh, muted sunlight shows on their faces this early morning.

Because children dance, he sweeps her along in the beginning steps of a slow dance, and his heart shivers with happiness when she moves with him. For a few moments Gia's tears stop, she laughs, and Willie, Willie the priest is Willie the boy, who has wanted nothing more in the past thirty-five years than to dance with Gia one more time. She tilts her head back and looks at him, smiling with the mouth he once lived to kiss, and he realizes that he is happier than he has been in years, that her glistening eyes are looking at him with love.

He leads her away in a lingering slow dance, in the shadow of the hospital where death waits to break both their hearts.

Lately Yozo smells garbage at the oddest times. Sometimes it seems to cling to the people he meets; sometimes it just seems to drift somewhere around him. He wonders if he's growing a brain tumor, or are people rotting and only he can smell it? Yozo has harbored, for much of his life, although time and the world have pretty much disabused him of it, the notion that he just might be the Messiah. He's not sure, though, that smelling garbage is any kind of divine gift, but what if it was a metaphor for the decay that's running rampant through our world?

And then Willie Cunningham opens his door and strolls in, wearing a grin that Yozo hasn't seen on him since 1963, a leer that means only one thing:

"You got tit?" Yozo inquires genially.

Willie sits down in the one other chair in Yozo's office, which is in a small building separate from the larger one in front that houses the impossibly successful auto-repair business he opened twenty-five years ago. "I pray for you, Joe. Did you know that? Every morning I pray for your miserable, wretched soul."

"You didn't get tit?"

Willie looks at him. "I'll add evenings."

"How come you look so happy? Why the hell are you so happy? You're a priest. I'm the one who should be happy. I'm rich, and I can get it anytime I want it."

"No, you can't. Remember, you told me how Christine said you were both too old to do it."

"That was in confidence. You ought to be ashamed."

"I didn't tell anyone else."

"Yeah," Yozo rubs the back of his head, "I think I have a brain tumor."

"I think," Willie rubs his neck, "I have polio. You know this place smells like, what, garbage?"

Yozo sits upright. "You smell it, too?"

"How can you miss it? Jesus, Yozo, maybe you better have the pool guy come in, check it out.

Algae or something." Next to his small and efficient, computer-loaded, windowless office, Joseph "Yozo" Walenticonis has an exercise pool in its own solar-powered enclosure, ten feet wide and fifty feet long. Adjoining it is his small driving range, his poolroom, and the tiny bedroom for the nights when Christine is so pissed that it's better to stay away.

He picks up his phone and speed-dials the pool maintenance people, who tell him that they'll have someone there before the end of the day. He turns to his oldest friend. "So, you got tit, yes or no?"

Willie is grinning as he begins to talk, and soon Yozo is grinning, too, even though neither of them got tit.

When he finishes telling Yozo about Gia's return, leaving out the dancing, Willie is flushed. Yozo watches his oldest best friend's face. He still loves her, Yozo thinks.

"I told her I'd pick her up after she got some rest, and I'm going to take her to the hospital," Willie continues. "Maybe we can get together after she visits with Tony?"

"I'll go with you when you pick her up," Yozo offers.

"No, that's all right." Willie eases his oldest best friend away. "Maybe we can have dinner or something."

"Why don't you call Barbara?"

"Barbara? Yes, that would be good, wouldn't it? You call her."

Yozo shrugs. "Yeah. No. You call her."

"You're sitting here," Willie gestures, "doing nothing. Sniffing, that's all you're doing."

"Here." Yozo kicks the phone over to him. "Call her if you're so hot to talk to her. Go on."

Willie looks at him.

It's like looking in the mirror, Yozo thinks, except all I see are my mistakes looking back at me.

"You call her." Willie rises. "I've got to get back to the rectory."

"No, you don't. Wanna go get a beer?"

"Yes."

"Some priest. Drinking in the daytime." Yozo pulls on his baseball jacket, pulls a cap over his bald head. "Life's good, isn't it?"

"Today, yes," Willie says.

Barbara wakes up just before one o'clock. A Marlboro and a Diet Coke are her traditional breakfast, although her hands are shaking more than usual. She stands, in fuzzy, scuffy slippers and a shiny lightweight nightgown and robe, at her kitchen sink, smoking, sipping soda, looking out the window at her backyard, noticing that another summer has slipped by. She had bought a lot of little flowers that she had intended to plant, but somehow the time got away from her. She had left the flats out in the garage; they're probably dead by now, she thinks.

In fact, her husband, Eddie, threw them out before the Fourth of July, but Barbara Eckroat will never know that. Her husband cleans up a lot of her never-begun projects. Barbara has three children, two teenage boys, both in high school, and the oldest, a married daughter with a daughter of her own. In all the lives of her kids, she has never gotten up to fix them breakfast or to see them off to school. Eddie, who has always worked the night shift at the plastics plant, took care of them.

She won't be here when her boys come home from school today, because she's due to go to her father's house, the house in which she grew up, where Tom Arminavage lives alone since her mother died more than a decade ago. Once a week she cleans his house, top to bottom, and cooks him as many meals as she can. She never seems to cook enough, no matter how much she packs into his freezer, because her father still has dinner at her house almost every night. She understands his loneliness. It is her loneliness, too, and sometimes, usually while watching the Philadelphia Eagles in the fall, on TV, it seems far away. Barbara still feels her absolute best and happiest when she and her father are tossing back the Yuengling beers, sitting side by side in the family room with the TV blaring, oblivious to the gorgeous autumn taking place right outside the glass doors, when her father loves her, she is just so sure of it.

When the phone rings, she jumps, and ashes and Coke fall into the sink. She half turns, scowling at the instrument on the wall. It couldn't be Eddie, who is asleep on the couch downstairs. It could be her daughter, looking for a baby-sitter, or for money, or for refuge because her husband hit her again. It could be the school telling her that one of her sons was in trouble again, or sick, or not there. All of the possibilities are too troubling to think about. She reaches over and slides the ringer switch to Off, and then she lights another cigarette.

Gianna Scarpino was born to an Italian war bride whose husband had sent her to America to live with his family just a couple of months before he was killed when his jeep flew off a mountain road in Sicily. When Gia was little more than a year old, her mother was hit by a bus when she stepped off the sidewalk against a red light while on a shopping trip in Philadelphia with her sisters-in-law. At the age of one, Gia was an orphan, but her paternal grandfather and her godfather, her uncle Tony, stepped in to take care of the little girl. She grew up without the touch of a mother's or father's hand on her shoulder, but she always knew the strong feel of her grandfather's love and the security of her uncle's embrace.

A female child born into a household of women, Gia was, in her formative years, treated as a threat. Her mother had been a stranger, and her father the most beloved older son. Gia's very being in that house was a constant reminder of what had been lost. A son, in effect, traded for another girl. Gia used to stare at a photograph of her father that hung on the wall of the living room and wonder how he could have died without waiting for her to be born.

Occasionally, one of the aunts would find her standing there, a small girl looking at the face of the father she had never known, the face that would, in her middle age, find its way onto her own; their responses to her silent vigil were telling—Angelina, the cold, efficient one, would order her, without touching her, to stop it and to go outside and play; Rosa, the frightened one, would tell her that she shouldn't be doing that; and Mella, the oldest, the one who had been closest to Gia's father, would mock her. "Whaddya think," Mella would say to that little, little girl, "do you think he can see you?"

Well, yes. Of all the Angels of Death to have guessed Gia's secret, it was Mella who made her blush with the embarrassment of having been found out, but Mella, with her husband and two healthy children, never looked closely enough at the kid to see that she really had caught the little girl trying to see if her dead father could see her.

She thrived under the protection of the men, her grandfather and her uncle, staying out of the reach of her older cousins, Peter and Tessa, although Peter, being six years older, wasn't very interested in the little girl; Tessa, however, tortured the child every chance she got.

Tessa pushed her too far the day she took the little girl into the garage and demanded she pull down her pants. Gia shouted that she was telling, and when she began to run away, Tessa grabbed her and gave her a dime, telling her never to tell. Gia never did, and Tessa soon moved into the world of junior high school, leaving her little victim behind. Whenever Gia wanted a dime, though, she wasn't above reminding her cousin what she had done. That was when the incipient lawyer learned that bullying can work both ways, if done properly.

When she was a very little girl, she remembers walking with her aunt Mella. The moment is incandescent in Gia's memory. They were passing Aleshefsky's hardware store, and Gia was prattling, something about her mother, someone the little girl discussed with her uncle Tony and her grandfather quite regularly. Gia had never told Mella what she knew, but on this day it popped out. "When my mommy comes back," the child began, and the grown woman never even let the kid finish.

Gia can still see the display in the store window, lightbulbs stacked up in their boxes, forming a lovely yellow and blue pyramid. She can still see the slant of the sidewalk, and the cracks in the concrete rectangles. She can still feel the summer sun on her small face as her aunt sternly lectured her, all the while gripping a small hand, "Your mother's not coming back. When you're dead, you're dead. There's no coming back."

Gia never told her grandfather or Uncle Tony about what Mella told her on Reading Street in front of the hardware store. And they never talked about her mother again. Something went away that day: the hope and faith of childhood. The little girl didn't have anything wonderful to wait for anymore, so she simply went on. Her father's death was an abstraction to her, a lot of stories attached to a black-and-white photograph of a smiling young man with lots of curly black hair, sleeves rolled up, arms folded across his slender chest. But she still remembered her mother. Rather, she remembered a moment with her.

Her mother was bending over her as the baby girl lay on a big bed, and she was smiling and tickling her and they were both laughing. It was the only memory Gia had of her mother. Until Mella told her the mean, hard truth, she had prayed every night for God to hurry up and send her mother back. That night she sat upright in her bed and realized that there was nothing left to pray for.

She never prayed again. Even during First Holy Communion and Confirmation, she faked it.

Mella's truth telling was, for Gia Scarpino, the beginning of what good Catholics would call "loss of the faith."

Looking back on that incident now, almost a half century later, she realizes that her reaction was odd in a number of ways. It never occurred to her to doubt what Mella had told her, maybe because Gia halfway knew it herself, somewhere inside. And she was never angry with Pop and Tony for lying to her. The nuns at Sunday school taught her that it was a *mortal sin* to tell a lie, yet Pop and Tony had lied to her and Zia Mella had told the truth. If the truth hurt so much and a lie felt so good, something was wrong with the Church's rules.

It was also the beginning of fear for Gia. The acknowledgment that death was irreversible and final, an empty, dark place to which she, and her miserable mortal soul, would one day be consigned, knocked everything out of her.

Gia was five years old, and convinced that she was doomed for all eternity, no matter what.

● ● ●

After a short nap, Gia stands in the kitchen doorway, freshly showered, dressed, and ready for the deathwatch that has already begun.

Tony and Francie's kitchen has a couple of sofas, a large table, a fifty-four-inch color television, as well as a smaller set under the cabinets, four ski poles propped in a corner, and a dress dummy with a broom stuck down her neck. The TV apparently is never turned off, and right now it's tuned to the twenty-four-hour Weather Channel.

Francie is sitting at the big round table with her husband's sisters Angelina and Mella. The third sister, Rosa, is cleaning out the refrigerator; she seems to have been doing that since Gia arrived at the house earlier in the day. The man Rosa was going to marry all those years ago had dropped dead on a subway in Boston, and she never married. She still wore his engagement ring, and taught commercial subjects at the local high school. She has lived with Tony and Francie since her fiancé died; Gia thinks there is some unwritten rule in Italian families that at least one sister must remain a spinster and she must live with the brother and his wife. Rosa never got over the idea that she constantly had to earn her way. She was the perfect slave. If her presence in the house had been a burden to Francie, it didn't show. They got along well, more like sisters than sisters-in-law.

Mella, that vast, icy juggernaut that was the oldest aunt, sits across the table from Francie. She had arrived sputtering, pissed off that Tony wasn't dying right. "He sleeps all day and he's up at night, what the hell is that?" is her greeting to Gia, who hasn't seen her in five years. Mella's only son, Peter, died in Vietnam. Her husband followed his son not long after.

Angelina, the nurse who married the German veterinarian, and who chose to raise whippets instead of children, rises to embrace Gia. She looks exactly as she did when Gia was a little girl, although her husband, Gar, appears to have become an old, old man as he barely lifts his hand to wave to Gia, and winks at her.

Lenny, Tony and Francie's older son, stands and opens his arms to his cousin Gia. He has shoulder-length black curly hair, the look of a Renaissance prince. After Gia embraces him, she turns to his younger brother, Joey, who is his father in every aspect, and hugs him, then sits beside Tony's wife.

"Did you see him?" Francie asks.

"Yeah, he was sleeping, so I didn't stay. I'm gonna go back tonight," Gia reports.

"You know it's not too late for the surgery," Carmella tells her.

"He doesn't want it, Mella," Lenny speaks up.

"Well," Angelina opens her hands, examines her palms, and folds them.

"You want some coffee, honey?" Rosa appears behind her right shoulder.

"I'll get it," Gia says, but Rosa is already at the counter. Gia calculates that all the aunts are in their mid- to late seventies, but Rosa moves with astonishing speed and the others have smooth faces and clear eyes. Only their hands, spotted and crepey, give them away. She glances at her own hands, makes a fist to erase what she sees.

"You should talk to him," Mella tells Gia.

"About what?"

"Tell him to have the surgery."

"I can't do that."

"He doesn't want it," Francie says.

"Then he's gonna die," Mella announces.

Gia is sure that this conversation has taken place at least a dozen times before her arrival.

Rosa places a cup and saucer in front of Gia. "You want some rolls, honey, or bacon and eggs? You want a sandwich? Some sauce and bread?"

"This is fine, Ro." Gia smiles at her elderly aunt.

Angelina says, "I'm concerned with the amount of morphine he's getting."

"Yeah," Joey quietly notes. "He's addicted."

"So?" Lenny gives his brother a look.

"I just said," Joey defends himself.

"He's so groggy," Francie says, clutching her ever present rosary and handkerchief. "If he has the surgery, he could possibly feel better," Francie wishes out loud.

Lenny is lovely with his mother. He takes her hand, presses it to his mouth, and quietly says, "He's real sick, Mom."

"They opened him up and they closed him," says Gar, who, in spite of his years in the family, doesn't really understand that none of these women, including his wife, will pay any attention to anything he says. "Why put the poor guy through more surgery?"

Rosa, meanwhile, is doing something Gia has never seen before: she has attached a nozzle to her Dustbuster, and she's sucking out the crumbs from the toaster. Gia glances at Lenny, who says, "Don't worry. The toaster's unplugged."

Gia shrugs and furrows her brow, and he knows how to answer his cousin's unspoken question.

"Dust," he says.

"If it gives my brother another day," Mella intones, "I say we go ahead."

"Major surgery?" Gia says. "Anytime you open up the chest, you're talking about a major, major procedure. With all due respect, if Tony has said he doesn't want it, you can't even think about overriding his wishes."

"He's so doped up, he doesn't know what he's saying," Mella counters. "Have you talked to him?"

"No, he was asleep when I stopped by this morning."

"Well, you talk to him. I think that dope has him thinking crazy thoughts."

"What, like not wanting somebody to put him under, cut open his chest again, and fool around with his insides? You think that's nuts? I read his chart when I was there. The cancer has spread everywhere. The only thing we can do is make sure he's comfortable," Gia argues.

Francie's brown eyes are clear and questioning as she looks across the table at her husband's godchild. She looks frightened. Gia feels like the headlight Francie must face. After all these years Gia still remembers so clearly her uncle's phone call during her senior year of college. "Hey, I'm getting married. She's Polish, but she's nice."

Gia shakes her head and finds herself making the same hand gesture she saw Angelina make a few minutes earlier. "When did anyone ever tell Tony what to do?"

"Yeah," his older son smiles, "now he'll change, right?"

"You can do something," Mella instructs Gia.

"Like what?"

"You're a big-time lawyer now, so get a court order or something."

Gia laughs. "You watch too much TV," she answers.

When the doorbell rings, Rosa jumps faster than Gia thought an old woman could move, and scampers to the door. Gia leans over and kisses each of her cousins, Lenny and Joey, on the cheek as the aunts rise and follow Rosa to see who is visiting. "You're good kids. Your father always says you're bums," she says with a smile, "but I think you're good kids."

"Naw," Lenny smiles back at her, "we're bums."

"Gia," Rosa calls, "you have company."

When she enters the foyer, she finds Francie kneeling before Willie, who is standing there, big and handsome, and Gia thinks that maybe he became a priest just so he could wear black all the time.

She doesn't know why her aunt is on her knees in front of her old boyfriend, but she's hoping it's nothing more than a blowjob.

It's much worse than that. Francie is kissing

Willie's hand, and he's embarrassed, trying simultaneously to get her to unstick her lips and to stand up. He has one hand at her mouth and the other in her armpit. He says to Gia, "You look great."

That lifts Francie to her feet; she turns and glowers at her niece. The mood swings around here can be timed in nanoseconds, Gia notes.

"Hi, Willie." Mella and Angelina have taken up their positions on either side of him, flanking him like wizened guardian angels. Lenny tilts back in his chair at the table and waves his hand gracefully. Rosa holds her broom at attention. Gia closes her eyes. This is her family. These are the ones she came from. These are what she will become.

"I figured you'd be going to the hospital, I thought I'd give you a ride over." Willie addresses Gia while, she notices, he keeps his arm around Francie, who still holds his hand.

"She has a car," Mella chimes in.

"Oh, I know, but," Willie has such a fine smile, "it's been a long time since my girlfriend and I had a date. You can't blame me for wanting to be with her, can you? Just look at her."

"Father Bill!" Francie admonishes him.

"Would you like some cake?" Rosa inquires.

"Where'd you get those boots?" Lenny asks.

"I heard you already had quite a date in the hospital cafeteria early this morning," Mella says.

"Ah, Carmella," Willie tilts his head toward her, "that was just foreplay."

While the Angels are frozen in shock, and Lenny and Joey howl, Willie and Gia make their escape.

• • •

He holds the door open for her, just like in high school, and she slides into the big black Ford. As he adjusts his seat belt, she says, "They're crazier than they used to be."

"No, they're not. You've lost your tolerance."

"Does she kiss your hand every time?"

"Yeah, she thinks I'm a cardinal."

"Oh, God." Gia rubs her eyes. "Wait. Did we arrange this?"

"No, but I figured you'd be going over about now. I was right, wasn't I?"

"Don't you have priest stuff to do?"

"I did it. The rest I'll do later."

"This is a priest car," she observes.

"The diocese provides it. My personal car is a Porsche."

Willie's grandfather was very wealthy. Gia's grandfather always maintained that Willie's grandfather had made his money as a bootlegger, which was probably the truth. Her own grandfather's hands hadn't been so clean; there had always been men in suits, men with hats, who came into the Italian grocery store he owned, men who spoke with her grandfather, and who then got back into their dark, shiny cars and left. Gia remembered that as soon as they entered the store, they took off their hats and addressed him as "*Padrone*," which means "owner," and Gia found out years later that he was also in the business of bringing immigrants over from the Old Country, a place which always puzzled her, since she could never find it on the map. He got them here, arranged for housing and work in the mines, for which he was paid by others, she doesn't know who, probably the mine owners. Gia never asked, it was none of her business, it didn't matter.

Some days, when the idea of being a divorce lawyer makes her feel especially soiled, she finds strange and strong comfort in the fact that her grandfather was a white slaver.

Willie's grandfather's sin, in her grandfather's eyes, was being born in Ireland, and that was a transgression for which there was no penance.

"It's black, isn't it?"

"No. Red."

"Ah, you're full of surprises." She looks out the window. "Full of them." It feels so good to be sitting beside Willie in his car, she thinks. For one moment she realizes how much she has missed the simple act of being able to say to another person, "Where are we going?" or "What do you think we should do?" Gia is suddenly aware of how alone she is in her life.

"He's thrilled that you're here," Willie says.

"You've been over there already?"

"I've got a few parishioners in the hospital. I was just visiting. I do it every day." Because she thinks she should, Gia tries, in one thought, to comprehend what Father Bill Cunningham's life must be like, and she fails. She fails miserably, because when she glances over at the man driving this priest car, she still sees the boy.

The Angels of Death are old women now, she and Willie are gray and middle-aged, and she sees only the boy. Just as she's sure he sees only the girl. This is a dangerous kind of magic trick we're pulling here, she thinks.

He never takes his eyes off the road when she unbuckles her seat belt and slides next to him. All he does is put his arm around her shoulder and pull her even closer to him, and whisper, with his eyes still on the road, "Don't worry. I'll drive safely."

"Do you recognize this place?" They are stopped at a small stadium with a huge parking lot. At one end of the field, a football team is practicing, the sound of whistles carries to the hurricane fence where they are standing, and at the far end, a band with majorettes is performing something, she thinks, from *Cats*. In the late afternoon sun, it is a pretty American picture. "This was our old field, Gia. Imagine."

Their old football field, when they were in high school, was a hundred yards of dirt, with ten rows of wooden bleachers on each side. No fancy concession stand, no press box, no Astroturf, all of which this behemoth has. "So," she's watching the players, "they're our latter-day Red Demons?"

"No, our school merged with a group of area schools a long time ago. It's a very large complex now, about fifteen miles from here. But they still play here. The town floated a bond issue to build this thing, so the pols wouldn't let the athletics go. It's worked out pretty well."

"So all our old traditional rivals . . ." she starts.

"They're classmates now," Willie finishes for her, and she jumps when she hears the screaming. High-pitched, hysterical, loud, it seems to be coming from his car.

"The hell was that, Willie?"

He turns quickly toward the car and then back to her. "Shit. Um, Gia, I've got to . . ." His hands are in the air, and then they slip into his pockets, and he looks evenly and unsmilingly at her. "Gia, you've gone away from the Church, haven't you?"

"Yeah. So? Willie, somebody's screaming in your trunk." She starts toward the car, and he grabs her arm.

"Gia, there have been changes in the Mass, in the ritual. There are certain things that must be done at certain times of the year. You remember, Lent, Advent."

"Yeah?"

"Well, things have changed. We have special participants in special Masses. There's one at midnight tonight, but I thought she'd, well, never mind. I'll take care of it. You stay here."

"What are you talking about?"

He is calm, soothing, as he still grips her arm and speaks. "You're not of the Church anymore, Gianna. It doesn't matter. There are things you don't need to know."

"Give me the fucking keys, Willie."

"I'm sorry, I can't do that. Wait here."

She's right behind him as he approaches the car and inserts the key in the trunk. Before he opens it, he says, "Gia, are you sure you want to see this? There'll be no turning back."

She feels this bad, empty feeling. Willie was, of

course, too good to be true, and now he's going to show her something freaky and twisted and sick, and she's never going to be able to tell anybody. She hates her life, she hates her family, she hates her hometown, she hates her godfather for getting sick, and, most of all, she hates Willie for having grown up to be someone who lives in a world unknown to her.

"Willie, whatever's going on, I'm going to the cops. I have to."

"Separation of church and state, Gia. It won't get you anywhere." He moves closer to her. "This is a Catholic town, remember?"

This is a bad movie, she decides, and she's looking around for the best escape route when Willie pops open the trunk lid, and a bald, slender, wide-eyed man in a Yankees jacket is lying there, screaming and laughing.

She looks at Willie, who takes a step backward.

"Yozo," Gia says, "you're bald."

"I have my hair at home, in a box. I'll show it to you. You have tits. Are they real?"

Before he can sit up, she closes the trunk lid. Her heart is pounding, and without any warning she bursts into tears. Yozo is still laughing when Willie lets him out, and Gia can't stop crying as the three of them fall against the black priest Ford, holding on to each other.

Gia's entire world changed the day a pissed-off nun armed herself with a bucket of water. Until then the little girl had been touched only by loving hands, had never known physical fear, had grown accustomed to loud voices and shouting matches, but that was how her family talked, it wasn't anything to be afraid of. She was in third grade, an excellent student, and she and her best friend Barbara Arminavage were favored by the nuns, those ominous, omnipotent, swirling figures in black and white who let them stay after school to wash the blackboards. Clapping the erasers was left to the boys, it being physically much more demanding, or so went the theory. Also, it was done outside. Two little girls couldn't be trusted with those felt and wooden things out of doors.

Joseph Walenticonis, Jr., was an undistinguished, dirty-blonde boy with a bit of an overbite and curious eyes that were sometimes brown, sometimes hazel, sometimes green. He used to lean against the playground fence during recess and watch the girls jump rope, he and the other boys. They lacked only smoldering cigarettes to make their drugstore cowboy personae complete, but that would come in a few years. When they were in third grade, Joey, "Yozo" for reasons that were never explained, was just another boy in school. He didn't come home with Gia, they never played, although sometimes he would let her watch him while he stared at the sun and didn't blink, a feat which, even today, she finds impressive. When the nuns called on him, he fumbled through his reading, labored at the blackboard with his arithmetic problems, but usually came up with the right pronunciation, the right answer. Gia remembers his fine light-colored hair falling over his forehead as he bent before his spelling book.

On a quiet day, a school day like all the ones that had come before, Sister Mary Dominic of the Holy Family, their third-grade homeroom teacher, a gray-faced woman who all but clicked her heels together when she stood at attention, called on Yozo for something, Gia doesn't remember what. He didn't answer immediately, he never did, and she shouted at him as she marched, habit fluttering, down the aisle to his seat. "Joseph Walenticonis, are you chewing gum?"

"No, Sister," the little boy said, just as she caught the shortest part of his haircut between her thumb and forefinger and began to twist, bringing him up out of his seat, while his arms struggled to keep his hands down, to keep them from swatting her away. Tears squirted from his eyes.

"Don't you lie to me!" she snarled. "Spit it out!" She snapped his head against his desk, and Yozo did the next best thing: he threw up.

That flipped Sister Mary Dominic out so badly that she dragged him to the front of the room, where a bucket of water sat on the radiator along the wall, waiting for the blackboard cleaning that would come at the end of the day. With her hand still entwined in Yozo's hair, she grabbed the bucket and smashed it down onto her desk, and without a wasted motion—this nun was smooth—she shoved his head into the water and held it there while he struggled, a small eight-year-old boy.

Gia still can't remember whether anybody laughed or even made a sound. She was so horrified by what *was happening, she can only remember how her whole body felt like it was blushing. When the nun finally let him up, he was ready for her: he brought up a mouthful of water and let it go, in a strong and steady spray, right into her nun's face.*

Then she hit him. Hard. With her fist.

Yozo went flying, falling backward over the teacher's chair behind the desk, and before Gia knew it, she was all over that great big nun, smacking her everywhere she could, yelling at her to leave him alone. She still remembers the strange stiffness of the black material that was her habit; she had never touched a nun's habit before. Hasn't since.

She backhanded Gia right into the blackboard, and the little girl took off, running out of that classroom, out of that school, and all the way down Reading Street, a good six or seven blocks, all the way home, and she didn't stop running until she reached the store. Her grandfather and Uncle Tony were talking to some of the old men who hung out there when Gia arrived, breathless, crying, legs pumping, and Tony scooped her up and held her while she sobbed, "Sister hit me!"

Her grandfather already had his hat on when Tony stopped him. He didn't put his niece down, he held her so tightly, he took his father's handkerchief and wiped her face, and when Gia's grandmother came out from the kitchen in back of the store to find out what the ruckus was, he sent her away. "Shhhhhh, Gianna, shhhhhhh, bambina, *it's all right."*

Ever since that moment, all Gia has ever wanted was someone to tell her that it's all right. Lots of people have, but she's never believed them the way she believed her godfather that day.

"Now," Tony set her down in Nonno's chair behind the counter, the one from which he watched everyone walk by the big windows overlooking the street, "drink this," he gave her a sip of his wine, it being just before lunchtime, "and tell me what happened."

The warm, familiar red feeling of the wine made her feel safe again, and she told him, with hiccups and sniffles, about the nun's attack on the boy. The men stood nearby, speaking softly in Italian while she told her story, and she knew she was all right when they nodded and winked at her, and one of them, a kindly man she remembers only as ChiChi, gave her his pocketknife to hold, a gesture that she found strangely comforting. He and Gia used to spend summer afternoons sitting on a wooden bench in front of the store playing mumblety-peg, and only now does it strike Gia as odd and wonderful that an old immigrant Italian man spent his time teaching a little girl how to play with a sharp knife. No one ever stopped them.

Her grandfather stood apart from the other men, and when she finished telling her story and handed the green glass back to Tony, he said something sharp in Italian that Gia didn't understand. Tony, who was kneeling before her, with his hands on her knees, half turned his head, and said, "I'll do it." To Gia, he said, "I'm gonna go talk to your teacher and to your principal. Do you want to come with me?"

No, she didn't. She was afraid of what Sister

Mary Dominic might do to her, but she didn't tell
Tony that.

"You don't wanna go, all right. But I want you to
come with me, so will you do it for me?"

She nodded.

"We have to go take care of this," he said. "We
have to take care of your friend, too."

"He's not my friend," Gia piped up.

Tony looked at her for a long time. Pop smiled,
the old men nodded, but Tony didn't move, and she
began to wonder if she had done something wrong.
"You stuck up for him even if he wasn't your friend.
That's very good, Gia. You did the right thing."

He went into the back of the store, passing
through their living quarters, and Pop opened one
of the jars of olives and everyone ate olives until
Tony returned, wearing a fresh shirt and a hat. Pop
pressed a quarter into her hand, and she slipped it
into her pocket. She returned ChiChi's knife as,
holding Tony's hand, she began her long return to
the place where she had first defended someone
accused of wrongdoing.

Yozo was siting outside, on the curb, mostly in the
gutter, crying, when Gia and her godfather walked
up to him. "Are you Joey?" her uncle asked him,
looming over him the way adults do to kids.

Yozo looked at her. "It's okay, Yozo. This is my
uncle Tony. I told him what happened. He's not
mad."

"I'm expelled," the little boy said, and the snot
coming out of his nose just got longer and longer

*until her uncle crouched down and wiped his face
with a fresh handkerchief.*

"That's nothing, Joey. We'll take care of that.
Does that hurt?" Tony tenderly touched the blue-
green bruise on the boy's forehead. "You got a real
goozie there, kid." Yozo stared, wide-eyed. "I know
your dad. Come on, kid." He lifted Yozo up and,
taking each of them by the hand, said, "Show me
where this nun is."

"His father is at work, and his mother works in the
dress factory," her uncle said to Sister Mary
Sebastian, the principal, "so I'll be the adult for
both these kids here now. I'll talk to his parents
later, and if they don't like what I do, they can come
and talk to you themselves."

"Mr. Scarpino, we'll allow your niece to return to
class after she spends a certain amount of time con-
templating her transgressions today. She's an excellent student, and after she apologizes, we can go on
as though none of this ever happened."

Oh, God. They were going to make her wash
windows in the convent. Gia had heard about girls
who were bad who got sent to do that, and the nuns
made them cut off all their hair, and when they got
finished, they had big things growing on their faces
and they were ugly and no one ever liked them
again. And they wore big black shoes because, she
had heard, the nuns did something to their feet, but
she was never really clear about that part.

"Mmmmmm, Sister, I'm sorry," her uncle said.
"I didn't make myself clear when I said I was here

to discuss what happened. She's not coming back here. Neither is he." He pointed at the two children, sitting side by side on a wooden bench in the principal's office while Tony had taken a chair and carried it, quite collegially, as close to the principal's chair as he could get. From where the kids sat, they could see the nun's face, but they could only see the back of Gia's uncle's head. She was carefully not looking at the little boy and girl through her wire-rimmed nun's glasses that made her blue eyes seem lemur-sized.

"Joseph's return is out of the question."

"Good," Tony said, "then we don't disagree. You decide that he can't come back, I decide that she won't. But I want to tell you, her family, we do not like what was done to her, and I think you better talk to your sisters about manhandling the children that we bring to them."

"Your niece struck a nun," Sister Mary Sebastian said, as righteous as she could be in the face of Uncle Tony's anger.

"The nun was beating up a little kid. Sister, with all due respect, if that sister had stuck my niece's head in a bucket of water, I would kill her. I am telling you the truth."

"This is a brutish conversation, Mr. Scarpino, and," she stood up, and Yozo, trembling, reached for Gia's hand, "it is over. It would be best if you took your niece and Master Walenticonis and left now."

Tony, in a stunning act of disrespect, carefully adjusted his hat in the window behind Sister Mary

Sebastian of the Holy Family. "Okay," he said. *Turning to the children, he asked,* "Did you leave anything in that classroom?"

"My book bag," *Gia said, and Yozo said,* "My pencil case."

"Gia," *Tony turned away from the desk,* "show me where the room is, and Joey and I'll wait outside while you go in and get the stuff," *he instructed,* "and, Sister," *he looked over his shoulder at her, for she was already an afterthought to him,* "we'll leave then."

"She's getting their stuff," *Tony called to a damp and red-faced Sister Mary Dominic as Gia slithered into the classroom and grabbed her book bag, quickly emptying the school's books into the desk and grabbing her pencils. Yozo's desk was two rows over, and she went to the rear of the room to cross over as Yozo stood behind her uncle Tony.*

"Gianna Scarpino, get out of this room immediately!" *the nun snorted, and the small girl froze. Tony sidled up to her and, turning his back to the class but not removing his hat, said something to the nun. Her face got very white, and she said,* "You may remove Joseph's personal possessions," *in a quiet voice. Barbara was gaping at Gia, who whispered to Joanne Fadule to tell Barbara to come to her house after school.*

She gave Yozo his pencil case outside as Tony, standing by the curb, lit up a Pall Mall. "I heard what he said to Sister Mary Dominic," *Yozo whispered.*

"What?"

"He said that if she ever even looked at you again, he'd find her and he'd kill her."

"To Sister he said that?"

"Uh-huh," Yozo answered, and then her uncle took their hands to walk them across the street.

"You hungry?" he asked the little boy on his right, and when the boy nodded, he said, "Come on, let's go home."

They are all shoved into the front seat of the priest Ford, Gia in the middle, just like in high school, and each of the men has an arm stretched across the back of the bench seat, that simple and arrogant gesture of male ownership that thrilled her in high school and, she is surprised to discover, still pleases her.

"You really are a couple of assholes."

"Nice language. Seriously, are they implants or what?" Yozo asks.

"Unbelievable," she says.

"Like time stood still, isn't it?" Willie asks.

"Will you show them to me?" Yozo asks.

"You'll see the deep interior of Hell long before you ever see my breasts."

He touches the back of her head. "I like your hair, that silver, it's nice."

"Hair and tits, is that it?" she asks Willie.

"Everything he never had."

"Guess what?" Yozo leans past her, talking to Willie. "Bald guys have more testosterone, you know that? You know why? Because we don't waste our male hormones growing hair. We use it for what matters, not that you'd know what I'm talking about, Father. He never gets laid, you know." This last sentence to Gia.

"Neither does he," Willie says.

"Oh, that's real nice. I told him that in confidence."

"Really, you're not getting any?" Gia asks. "Who'd you marry, anyway?"

"Christine Velanowski. Remember her sister, Carol Ann, she was in our class?"

"Carol Ann Velanowski, no, oh, yeah. Quiet girl, brown hair, nice girl."

"Yeah, I married the other one. The one on the broom. Did he tell you I was rich?"

"Is he?"

Willie shrugs, driving one-handed, taking turns wide and lazy and slowly. "He tells me he is and he lives like he is, but we won't find out until he dies."

Yozo nudges me. "I have a grandson."

"How many kids do you have?"

"One. He's a bum. Luckiest sonofabitch ever born."

"He's just like his old man," Willie tells Gia.

"What's his name?"

"Joey. Didn't you notice, everybody in this town is named Joey. Except my wife. She's Chris. Chris the fuck."

"This is a good marriage?" she asks Willie, who's smiling. He shrugs. "Did you marry them?"

"Please."

"Why's your kid lucky?"

"Couple of years ago, he's out in Snowmass, skiing—imagine that, I got a kid that skis. We used to walk through those huge snowfalls to get to school, we never got snow days, do you remember, and my son straps thousand-dollar pieces of fiberglass to his feet so he can go sliding down a mountain real fast. All that progress in one generation, huh? Anyway, he was out there and he got hit by a car. Busted him up pretty bad, but he's okay now."

"That's lucky, Yoz?"

He holds up four fingers. "Four nuns. Church car. Nun driver. Kid got so much money in the settlement, he'll never have to work. He's a bum. He just rented out the house he built and moved back in with us. His mother worships him. His girlfriend had a kid because he wanted one, and now I'm getting up in the night with the kid."

"He sounds just like you," she says.

"Fuck you. I worked hard. He'll never even know what hard work is." He sighs heavily and sinks back into the seat, squeezing her to him. "I go to see Tony every day. Whatever you want, okay? I'll take care of everything."

"I don't know. I don't know anything. I'll stay as long as I have to."

"Well, you got us," Willie assures her, rubbing her right shoulder. "The old crew hangs together, even after all these years."

"Did you call Barbara?" Willie asks Yozo.

"There was no answer," he says. "No machine. We'll go over there later."

She turns to Yozo, who says, "What?"

"Tell me about Barbara," Gia commands him.

"She's got some kids, a grandkid. She married this guy from Jersey, they lived over there for a while, but then they moved back here. She keeps to herself," Yozo says.

"Don't you ever see her? Don't you ever get together?"

"Gia, there are a lot of our classmates who never left this town, we see each other all the time, and a lot of the time we never even say hello," Yozo says. "I guess it's kind of sad, but that's how it is."

"Well, find her, tell her I'm here. Let's get together, please, okay? I'd love that."

"Why didn't you come to the twenty-fifth reunion?" Yozo asks. "It was fun. I'm not the only bald guy, you should see. All the girls had the same color blonde hair, isn't that amazing? Why didn't you come?"

"I was in Japan on vacation."

"Excuse the fuck out of me," Yozo says.

They pull up in front of the red brick hospital where they all drew their first breath more than a half century ago. Willie turns off the ignition and reaches under the front seat. "I arranged to have a cot brought into your uncle's room, in case you decide to catch a nap and you don't want to leave him. And I got you some things you might need." He hands her a paper bag. Yozo is getting out, holding the door open for Gia so she can slide out of the priest Ford.

"Here's my cell phone number. This is Yozo's. Anytime you want us, just call us, anytime at all.

Call when you want to go home." Willie kisses her neatly and quickly.

Yozo hugs her and whispers, "They feel great," just before she slaps him. They drive away, waving and smiling and looking back at her.

She is left standing on the front steps of the hospital where she was born, where Tony will die. Inside the bag Willie has given her are toothpaste, a toothbrush, floss (that he has even thought of such an item is a sure sign that they are middle-aged), a combination comb and brush, deodorant, and the last item, the one that breaks her heart, a jar of Noxzema, what she used in high school.

The daylight is fading, and so is the time she can spend with Tony. She turns and goes inside.

"She looks older than I expected, don't you think?"

"Oh, for Christ's loving sake, Yoz, you're bald, I'm fat, Barbara is wasted. What do you expect?"

"This is gonna be some kind of reunion."

Willie turns right onto the road leading down into the town. "We'll go to her house first. If she's not there, she's probably over at her father's house."

Gia stands in the doorway of her uncle Tony's hospital room and marvels at how tiny this place has become. As a child, she was brought here her share of times, with sprains and cuts and other kid incidents, but that was a very long time ago, and now the hospital has shrunk to a little small-town hospital, which is, after all, just what it has always been.

His illness has made Tony an old, old man, and

she didn't expect that, either. He's lost a lot of weight, so his body is simply a slight presence under the light blanket and sheet that cover him. Too many tubes run in and out of him, and she closes her eyes at the bag that is collecting his urine. Some things are too close, should remain private. She stands over him while he sleeps.

"You sonofabitch," she coos. "If you think you're going to die and leave me alone with those witches, I'm here to tell you that you're wrong. You don't do this. You just don't. I'm not going to get stuck with them. I'll chew my own leg off if I have to to get away from them."

His eyes stay closed, but a smile comes to his mouth. She waits for him to say something, but the smile fades, and she thinks he hasn't really awakened at all, but only reacted to her voice. Maybe that's all she can do for him now. Maybe he only needs to know she's there. She looks around for a chair, and quietly carries it to his bedside. She is almost afraid to take his hand, which is thin and spidery and wrinkled.

"You're not alone," she speaks softly to the man who raised her. "If you've been waiting for me to get here, you don't have to wait anymore. If it hurts, go ahead. I don't want you to go, I don't want you to, but if it's too hard, you go on." She covers his hand with hers.

His eyes don't even flutter, but his voice is steady. "That's that California bullshit I been hearing on television. What's it, permission to die? When did I need anybody's permission to do anything? Who do you think you're talking to, huh?" His hand moves quicker than she would have thought, and he is holding onto hers, tightly, strongly, the way he held her hand when they crossed the street together.

"You're an old goat, you know?" Tears come and go in her eyes, tears of gratitude.

"California bullshit," he repeats. "I got to listen to my wife praying over me, and my sisters, my sisters, ah, my sisters. Your aunts, huh?"

"I was here last night."

"I know. I tried to say something to you, but I think I took a little too much of that stuff, I couldn't talk. You know, sometimes this stuff maybe works too good."

"What's this about surgery? You said no, right? Or do you want surgery?"

"Damn the doctors. Damn your *zia* Mella. I'm dying nice here, the nurses are nice, you're here now, Lenny comes, Francie, Joey. This morphine, it works, what the hell else do I need?"

Gia sighs, stroking his hand. It's good to hear his voice.

"I'll tell you what I need," he goes on. "To get these tubes out. To go sit in the yard, in the sun, that's what I need. Remember how Pop used to put his hands in the dirt, remember how he smiled when he did that? I know why he did it, Gia. It feels good. That's what I wanna do. Can you get me out of here? Just to have a glass of wine, to feel some dirt." His pale eyes are clear but too shiny, junkie eyes, and right this minute, Gia would cut off her right arm to give him a glass of wine in his very own garden, in the sun, embracing the soil.

"Take me out of here, Gia. Just for a little while."

"Tony, I can't. You're weak. You could get hurt."

"*Cordarda!*" He pulls his hand away from hers.

"I'm not a coward. I care about your not getting hurt. That's not cowardly. *Spaccone!*" she spits back at him.

He smiles. "You remember your Italian, that's good. You can call me a bully. You have to use it, remember that. All the old guys I used to talk Italian to, they're gone now. They go, then the language goes, eh?"

"I'll see if I can take you out, all right? I'll see."

He puts his fingers to his lips, kisses them, and places his fingers on her cheek. "Your old boyfriend, he's all excited that you're here. What are you gonna do to him?" His narcotized eyes are glistening with more than drugs.

"He's been sweet to me, *Padrino*. He brought Joe Walenticonis to see me. They come to see you, don't they?"

"They're nice kids. The Collar, he wants more than he has. Joey, he's the same kid, you know? He's good." Her godfather pulls her hand, and her, closer to him. She rises from her chair and leans over him. "It's Yozo, eh, who's going to be your best friend. He has *lealta*, that man. He'll be with you. Willie, no, his loyalty is somewhere else. Not where his heart is, I don't think, but his loyalty. *Lealta*, Gianna, that's all that matters."

"I know, *Padrino*."

"Yozo, he's been like another son to me all these years. He's a good man."

"I know."

He looks at her with eyes she recognizes as her own grown old. "You made a promise to me." His grip on her hand stays strong.

"Oh, son of a bitch, you had to bring that up, didn't you?"

"You promised."

"Tony, please. Don't." She holds up her free hand.

"You gonna renege on a promise? Nice." His mouth turns downward in that inimitable Italian expression that tells the recipient that he or she is too stupid to stay in the company of the frowner.

"Not renege. That's just insane, what you asked me to do."

"I asked you to have me cremated. What's so bad about that?"

"First of all, your sisters, and probably your wife, don't want you to be cremated."

"What the hell do I care what they want? It's my body. I can do what I want with it."

She is just about to tell her uncle that his survivors would be comforted by having a grave to visit, but she catches herself. "Tony, please."

"I want to be cremated."

"Did you tell them?" she asks.

"You tell them," he counters.

"Oh, beautiful. You tell them."

"No, you tell them. It's part of your promise to me."

"I never promised that."

"Yes, you did. You just forgot. And then you have to get that big water pistol, like I told you. I have one in my office at the house. It's in the safe. Lenny or Joey'll open it for you."

Her godfather, during the conversation they had when he had first voiced his final wishes to his godchild thirty years earlier, had instructed her to take his ashes, mix half of them with a goodly amount of water, fill a water pistol with the solution, and then write the family name on the front windows of certain Irish families who had treated her grandfather badly when he had first come to the United States. The other half of his ashes were to be sprinkled on the graves of his mother and father.

At the time Gia attributed the mad conversation to the very fine Montepulciano they were both drinking in a hotel bar in Rome during a family vacation celebrating her college graduation.

"Then I'll be at peace, when you do that."

"You old extortionist."

"Yeah, yeah, you promised."

"Tony."

"If you don't do it, I'll never be at peace. And, no church funeral. You tell them that."

"You tell them that!" she almost shouts. "Are you nuts? They're never gonna let you out of here without a church service. Tony, they're all devout, you know that."

"I'm an atheist, like your grandfather, and I'm proud of it." He points a skinny finger at her. "No church. Cremation. Water pistol." He shrugs, just slightly, and his eyes close. "It's easy for you. You do this." He touches her face. "It's better now that you're here," he mumbles, and she sees that his other hand is administering morphine. The catheter taped to his forearm guides the drug slowly into his system.

He is still holding her hand when he drifts off to sleep, and she stands there, leaning uncomfortably over his bed, watching him sleep, and there is nowhere else on earth that she would rather be.

"That's her!" Yozo yells when a maroon Oldsmobile comes toward them on the narrow tertiary highway that leads back into the town. "She's coming back from her old man's house. Make a yooey, go ahead."

As Willie slides into the turn, he says, "What's the hurry? She's probably on her way home, we can see her there."

Yozo is reaching into the glove compartment, where he flips a switch Willie has never seen before. "I want to see if these work. They should."

"What? What're you doing?" Willie asks, just as the interior lights start flashing on and off. "What the hell is that?"

"Last time you had the car in for servicing, I had them install grille lights. Cop lights. See? They work. Look, she's pulling over."

"This car has cop stuff on it?" Willie is incredulous. Just when he's sure Yozo won't pull another one on him, he does. "Will this ever end?"

"Yeah, if you pull it over, it'll end. Here." Yozo points.

"She's gonna fucking kill us."

"Naw, she'll be so happy we're not cops, she'll be glad to see us," Yozo assures him, and then asks, "Won't she? Or will she fucking kill us?"

"This is Barbara," Willie reminds him. "Remember? She doesn't get mad."

"Yeah, right." Yozo gets out of the car, and Willie follows.

In her rearview mirror, she sees the black Ford make a fast and dusty U-turn, and when it starts bearing down on her with flashing lights, she drops her cigarette in her lap and shouts the universal prayer of everyone who has ever seen those blue lights pursuing them: "Sonofabitchbastardgoddammit!" She retrieves the cigarette and, with shaking hands, dusts off her slacks, pulls over to the shoulder, and reaches for the glove compartment.

"OhGodOhGod," she chants, drops the registration on the seat, and starts going through her purse, looking for her license. She sees that the Ford has parked behind her, and, getting out, smiling, are not the Pennsylvania state troopers she expected, but two men, two men she has known forever, and they are more frightening to her than any cops. She checks her face in the mirror, and sees that her smile looks real. Then she gets out of the car.

"Hi, guys!" Barbara's relief shows in her face as happiness, and both men think she is happy to see them, which is not so. "You playing cops and robbers now? I would've held up the A&P if I had known."

"Barbara, the lights aren't my fault. You probably had some kind of coronary incident." Willie tilts his head at the other man. "He did it. It's his fault."

Barbara touches Willie's arm in a familiar and friendly way, although she is feeling neither of those things, but these men are, after all, old friends, from a time back when she had friends. "Just one thing, Will. Could you just give me absolution for all the dirty words I said when I saw those lights in my rearview mirror?"

Willie, who has never taken his calling lightly, extends his right hand over Barbara's head, quickly and quietly whispers the words of belief: "I absolve you from your sins in the name of the Father, and of the Son, and of the Holy Spirit."

She stands still, staring at him. "That was a joke, Willie."

He shrugs. "Consider yourself forgiven. You've probably done other bad stuff."

Yozo says, "Gia's back."

Barbara is lighting up a Marlboro. She sucks the smoke in so deeply that for a second both Yozo and Willie, although they'll never admit it, wish that they smoked. "What's the occasion?"

"Her uncle Tony is in the hospital," Yozo says.

"Jesus, is he still alive? He must be a hundred."

"He's in his seventies, Barbara, but he's got lung cancer." Yozo suddenly no longer wants a cigarette, recalling the racking coughs that echo in his brain for hours after he visits Gia's godfather. "He's dying, that's why she came home. She wants us all to get together."

"That's gonna be rough," she says, already finished with her cigarette, grinding it into the dirt on the road's shoulder. "I've just gotten the kids back to school, and my daughter's little one is only in preschool, so there's just not a lot of time."

Willie is looking directly at her, unsmiling, when he says, "We haven't been together for almost thirty-five years, Barbara. This is a time you just can't miss. Don't you want to see your old best friend?"

"Well, sure, of course I want to see you all, but Eddie's on the night shift, and it's hard to get away."

Yozo, who knows everything, says, "We'll come over to your house, then."

"Oh, my God, the place is such a mess. I don't want my own family to come over. We should meet somewhere. When? How about tonight? Tonight?" she asks Willie. "How about tonight?"

"Get the hell out of my room, you Vatican wolverine," Tony Scarpino says to Father William Cunningham, who has just entered his room, tiptoeing so as not to awaken Gia, who sleeps in the chair beside her uncle's bed.

"Shhhhh," Willie holds his finger up to his mouth, "we're not even supposed to be in here. The new supervisor is trying to enforce visiting hours."

"Hey, Tony, how's it going?" Yozo calls out, and Gia jumps, awake.

"What? Jesus, I fell asleep."

"You know, you snore," her godfather tells her.

"I do not."

"It's a cute little snore. You used to do that when you were a little girl. I thought when you got your tonsils out you'd stop it, but I guess you didn't."

"What time is it?"

"It's only nine-thirty," Willie says, "but we thought you'd like to come with us. If that's all right with you, Tony."

"You kids wanna go out. What's new?"

"Don't worry, Tony," Yozo says. "We're taking her to a bar."

"That's good. Go." He looks at his niece. "Go, have a good time. Come back tomorrow."

She's rubbing her eyes and running her hands through her hair. "I thought you were sleeping all day."

"Naw, now that you're here, you can protect me from them. Except for that wolverine who got in here. Get him the hell out of here. Take him and get him drunk. He's Irish. All he has to do is smell it. Get outta here. Come back tomorrow."

She bends to kiss her godfather, and his grin is demonic. "Get him in trouble," he whispers.

"I think I already have," she whispers back, kissing him.

"Good. That's good."

Yozo stays behind when Willie and Gia leave. "You doing all right?" he asks the old man. "You want anything?"

"Go with them," he says. "Tell me what they do."

Yozo laughs. "Like the old days, Tony, huh? Am

I still your spy?" He realizes he can hear the raspy, ragged breathing of the dying man louder tonight than the other nights. "I could stay here," he offers.

"For what? You go. I'm all right."

No, you're not, Yozo thinks. You're dying. I don't want to go.

Turning his head to look at the younger man, Tony tells him, "I want something."

"What? Tell me."

"I wanna sit in the yard, in the sun, and drink wine."

"All right." Yozo doesn't hesitate. "I'll take you tomorrow."

"Gia's afraid, she won't do it. When did she get so scared?"

"She's not scared. She just wants you to be taken care of."

"So when did she forget what was good? You tell her, all right? You make sure she finds out what's good." Tony shakes his head just so slightly. "Hell of a thing, to forget what's good."

Yozo puts his hand on the old man's forehead, which is feverish. He's not gonna die from the cancer, Yozo thinks. He's gonna burn out, like a star exploding.

Tony closes his eyes. "Go," he says again. "Don't leave that poor Irish sap alone with her too much."

Yozo laughs and bends over Tony, kisses his cheek. "He's a priest, Tony."

"Yeah, a priest," the old man whispers. Before Yozo can answer, Tony is asleep again, and so he leaves the room quietly, stopping at the door to look back at the man who has been his father for as long as he can remember.

"Don't die tonight, Tony," Yozo whispers, and then he leaves.

Their hometown was a great place to grow up, and an even better place to leave. In its heyday, it had been a major coal mining center, prosperous and crowded. More than fifteen thousand people had once resided in this one square mile. By the time the class of 1963 graduated, the population had dwindled to fewer than five thousand. Now, as they drive through the town, Gia sees familiar structures, wooden row houses where some of her other classmates once lived. Many of them are now empty hovels, no glass in the windows, crumbling front porches, dark, deserted houses that were once homes which welcomed her and her young friends.

"Who left these behind?" she asks the two men.

"There's not much work here," Yozo answers, "but a lot of migrant workers came here anyway. They're illegals, and they squat until they get chased. In the meantime, they trash the places."

"But why were they abandoned in the first place?" she persists.

"Because the old people died," Willie tells her, "and usually the taxes were unpaid for a long time. The heirs don't live here, so they took the money and said the hell with the houses. Even if they tried to sell them, there's no one to buy."

I could live like a queen here, she thinks. But I could never live here.

When her senior year began, she approached her uncle with the idea of her going to Penn State. He would have none of it. "You're going to Italy for a year," he reminded her, "and when you come back, you'll go to college."

"I'll just go to Penn State then," she said.

"No, you're going out of state. You have to go away, Gia."

"Why? I don't want to go away. I want to be able to come home on weekends."

"To what?" he questioned her. "Your friends? They won't be here. They're leaving. There's nothing in the future for this town, *cara*. It's not anything anymore. When I was young," he shrugged, "there was coal, there were factories, there were stores. Now you look." His hand rose from the desk for a moment, then fell. "They're gonna build a mall up on the mountain. That's gonna close down the stores on Main Street within a couple of years, 'cause the owners won't be able to compete with the big stores, and everyone's gonna wanna go to the mall. You'll be all right. You're going to your cousins in Rome, you'll be a sophisticated woman when you come back."

She was at the age when the word *woman* still embarrassed her, young as she was, still a little uncomfortable with her new body, her new thoughts, her new desires.

I want to stay, she thought, but she never told

him, and he turned away from her to his desk, and
she left his study that day, counting the days she had
left to be with her three best friends, sure as only a
sixteen-year-old can be that she will never again
have such friends.

"So this is what happened to our hometown?"
she sighs. "It deserved better."

"It's not a bad place," Willie says. "There are
some interesting people here; it's starting to get a
reputation as a good far suburb of Philadelphia."

"People commute to Philadelphia? That's a two-
hour drive," she observes.

"Watch," Yozo says. "In ten years I'll have devel-
opments on each end of Reading Street and Water
Street." He refers to the two primary thoroughfares.
"They'll be sold out, too."

Gia looks at him.

"He will," Willie agrees. "He tried to buy the
football field a while back."

"That was gonna be a health club." Yozo sounds
a little dreamy. "Oh, man, I had plans for that piece
of land."

"Jesus," Gia says. "You're for real, aren't you?"

"Hey, the Poconos are only forty-five minutes
away, don't forget. I have a nice place near
Stroudsburg, if you ever want a vacation. On a
lake. It's real nice."

To Willie she says, with a nudge, "Our own little
entrepreneur."

"Capitalist pig." Willie smiles.

"I love being rich," Yozo says. "I fucking love it."

"I wanted to stay here," she confesses.

"Ha!" Willie laughs. "What would you have done here?"

She shrugs. "I don't know, teach maybe, or even be a lawyer."

"Be a wino, is more like it," Yozo says. "You would never have survived here. Tony knew we had to get out, at least for a while."

"He told you?" she asks Yozo, who nods. "You?" she asks Willie.

"He was one of my references for Villanova," Willie answers.

"You never told me that," she says.

"We never talked about it, remember?" Yozo says. "We never said good-bye. We were all coming back."

"We were?" Gia is perplexed. "I'm old. I don't remember that."

"You didn't remember it when you were young, either," Willie says.

"Huh?"

"Nothing. Forget it. This place look familiar?" He pulls into an angle parking space on Water Street.

"There was a newsstand here, and that restaurant where we used to go. Remember, I got food poisoning there twice."

"Twice?" Yozo says. "You're dumber than I thought."

The buildings are empty now. "Nothing," she says. "There's nothing."

"An insurance agency is moving in here, as soon as it gets fixed up," Yozo tells her.

"You own this, too?" she asks.

"No. Piece of crap property."

The three of them walk to the corner and turn down a dark, deserted alley.

"I know this place." Gia is surprised at her recollection. "These are the backs of the stores that used to front on Coal Street. Roseanne Carpenter, remember her, she was with us in sixth grade and then she moved away? She lived up there, over the Sharp Dress Shop, with her mother and her sister, and there, over there, Elaine Wunder, remember, the first girl with tits in, what, seventh grade? She lived in that little dark place up there with her family, she moved away, too. What is this place, Cardinal Street?"

"Columbus Street," Yozo says. "You remember that place?" He tilts his head.

A single bulb burns, dimly, above a narrow recessed door with two stained concrete steps leading up to it. "No. What is it?"

"Let me refresh your memory," Willie says. "My brand-new sharkskin suit jacket with sloe gin and 7-Up all over the lining. Tenth grade."

"The Palace! The first place we ever drank indoors? Is that it? We went into such a scary-looking place? It looks like something they'd warn tourists away from in Marseilles."

"Fourteen years old," Willie muses.

"But we looked twelve," Yozo adds.

"We had cash," Gia recalls. "How did they get away with serving us?"

"Guess." Yozo rubs his thumb and fingertips together.

"Are we going in there tonight? It's pretty scary."

"What we did at fourteen scares you now?" Willie asks.

"Lots of things we did at that age scare me now."

"All you have to do is wrap most of them in rubber," Yozo observes. "The Palace is a magnificent relic. We should be grateful that it's still here."

"Will they serve us?" she asks. "Aren't we too old?"

"Ask the owner." Willie nods at Yozo.

"You own this place?"

"Yeah, and I didn't change a fucking thing."

"You serve kids?"

"They dropped the drinking age, Gia. I serve everybody. Come on." He takes her elbow, and she is seized, in all her menopausal, middle-aged glory, with the sudden, irrational, and self-aggrandizing fear of being carded.

It is dark and small and smoky, but it is familiar, that unforgettable scent of stale beer and cigarettes that, no matter how long she lives, will make her ache for the days of adolescent camaraderie, lost evenings acting grown-up, wasting time when they didn't know they'd have the rest of their lives to be grown-ups, blowing smoke rings into the dark bar air, watching the old winos standing at the railing sometimes make it to the men's room, sometimes not. Drinking sloe gin and 7-Up, and being sure that it was simply the most sophisticated thing to order. The boys, of course, drank Seven and Seven, not much of an improvement. While Gia's eyes adjust to the dark, she hears something.

The music is the same, which, for some reason, makes her dizzy. "This Is Dedicated to the One I Love." Making out in the booths, stumbling to the car where they could go, not all the way, but a bit further.

"I put in a jukebox with all the oldies on CD. It's the only music I'll ever have in here," Yozo whispers to her. "Want to look around?"

"Is the ladies' room still downstairs? It was what, like dug out of dirt?"

"No, I fixed that up. I wouldn't recommend it anyway. I haven't seen it for a while."

And then Gia sees her.

They sent her off to kindergarten when everything at home was just fine, except for her recent introduction to eternal death, thanks to Mella, and she struggled with the notion of having to get up every morning and go to a funny-smelling place every day. It was almost more than she could bear, except that she met another little girl who was as exotic to Gia as Gia was to her. Her name was Barbara, she was blonde and blue-eyed, and when Gia didn't have the milk money they had been told to bring, Barbara Arminavage came over to where Gianna Scarpino sat, milkless, and offered to share hers with the small, dark-haired girl. Gia refused, because she hadn't forgotten the nickel; she had deliberately said nothing because she suspected her school milk might be poisoned.

Barbara sat with her anyway, and drank her milk while Gia watched. Gia started bringing Barbara home with her at noon, and Barbara thought the store was the best place she had ever seen. When she saw the play school Gia had set up in the back room, where the desk was a huge, uncut provolone, she announced that they would be friends. Gia liked the idea, and they sealed their vow with a small brown paper bag of freshly grated Locatelli, a plate of cured olives, some warm bread, and lime soda.

When her grandfather found out Gia wasn't getting any milk during the mid-morning break, he asked her why. She told him she didn't want any. That seemed to be all the answer he needed. Until ten-fifteen the next morning, when, as her classmates were slipping their straws into the milk bottles, a gentle knock came on the kindergarten door, and when Sister Mary Frances opened it, there stood her grandfather, hat in hand, bowing and nodding, and speaking softly to the teacher. He handed her something, looked into the room, smiled and waved to his granddaughter, and slipped away.

Every day, for the rest of kindergarten, her grandfather, sometimes her uncle, brought her milk. And then, somehow, she was no longer afraid of dying.

After more than thirty years, Gia would know her anywhere. She feels herself flying backward through time, away from Willie and Yozo, with only her best girlfriend, and they are hiding out in Barbara's bedroom, hanging out the windows, smoking; they are locked in the upstairs bathroom, trying to make sense out of the Kotex box Gia found in her aunt's room; they are sliding in and out of Woolworth's after school, and meeting around the corner to compare what they have shoplifted; they are standing, hands seductively draped on their nonexistent hips, modeling their first bras in Gia's bedroom mirror; Barbara is getting on a bus to go to New Jersey, where her sister lives, and has gotten her a job as a clerk-typist at Johns-Manville, and Gia will be leaving for Italy in a few days, and the last thing she sees of Barbara Arminavage is her crying face, her outstretched hand, her cry of "I'll write every week!" Of course she didn't, neither did Gia, and now, more than three decades later, they are walking across a crummy bar's dance floor with their arms out toward each other, and Gia can hear only her laughter, her light, lovely laughter, and Barbara is someone Gia hasn't thought about in all these years, except in passing, but now she is filled with a surge of love that she almost doesn't recognize, for that little girl who came to share her milk with her.

She was always a petite thing, but she seems even more fragile in Gia's arms now. They are hugging hard and laughing and pulling back to look at each other's faces closeup, unself-conscious as they can be only with those who know each other well from a long time ago, while each examines the lines in the face, the gray in the hair. "You look exactly the same!" Gia exclaims, and it is not simply the right thing to say.

"You look like something out of an Italian fashion magazine. When did you start looking so Italian?"

"When I was born, asshole, remember? I am Italian."

"No, you've changed, Gia. You look terrific. Come on, let's let the boys into this. C'mere." She gestures to Willie and Yozo, who have been standing on the edge of the dance floor, leaving the moment to the girls they once were.

Gia is about to say something characteristically witty about sailors on shore leave when she sees that Willie has removed his collar. He's now just a guy in a black suit and a black T-shirt. Yozo is wearing a dark turtleneck and a baseball jacket and jeans, and he is smiling at them, a smile that makes everything around him glow. Willie isn't smiling, though, just looking at the women so intently Gia is tempted to look down to see what is hanging out.

The last time we were all here together, she calculates, those men, those men over there, their fathers might have looked like that. But their fathers then would have been younger than those men over there.

Barbara is leading her to a table where a cigarette is burning in the ashtray and a coffee mug sits at her place. She slides into her chair and pulls Gia down to sit beside her. "I was going to order you a sloe gin and 7-Up, but I wasn't sure Willie here would appreciate the dry-cleaning bill."

"After all these years, all you can do is rag me about throwing up on my date's jacket? That's all we have to talk about?" Gia is entertained.

"Oh, no," Yozo seats himself on Barbara's left, while Willie is to Gia's right, "that wasn't what you call throwing up. No, that was an eruption, that was an act of God, that was something they've written songs about. I think there's a fresco of it in the Vatican. It's something that's never been duplicated, Gia. That was a moment in history like Neil Armstrong walking on the moon. In this town, they only speak of it between noon and three P.M. on Good Fridays."

"Remember how the spaghetti came out of your nose?" Barbara reminds her. "It was all in one strand."

"A real mark of greatness. I once saw a guy puke in Korea," Yozo goes on, "a shrimp came out of his nose, intact, too, but that was nothing. Spaghetti, unbroken, that's something they write operas about."

"Shut up, Yozo." Gia puts her arm around her girlfriend. "Your hair is darker. You were a blonde kid."

"Pregnancy," she says. "Each kid, it got darker."

"How many kids?"

"Three. Andrea is twenty-seven, married with a little girl, Greg is sixteen, a junior, and Jamie is fourteen, a freshman."

Gia puts her hands over her eyes, although she's not sure why. "You're a grandmother. You're a grandfather," she nods at Yozo. "You're a priest. This is a lot."

"Did you have kids?" Barbara asks.

She tells them about her stepchildren. "I adopted them legally as soon as I could get the paperwork done after their father died. They're mine."

"Giving birth is the least of it," Barbara tells her.

"I can't even imagine you pregnant," Gia says.

She laughs and lights another Marlboro. "Why don't we order? I want some of those rancid peanuts you serve, Yozo, and how about a ginger ale? Gia?"

She looks good, fresh and bright and smooth and pretty, with just some fine lines around her eyes and her mouth, but her neck is too lean, and the flesh there is thin and delicate and trembling. Her hand is in Gia's, and Gia can feel the trembling that she knows owes nothing to her presence. Barbara drinks coffee in a bar and then switches to ginger ale and she shakes. Gia remembers sitting in her bedroom, drinking out of quart bottles of some hideous local brew. She never especially cared for beer, but Barbara always whipped through their stash and never wobbled. Now she shakes, and Gia hopes she's missing something. Maybe there's just too much going on. Maybe all the senses and instincts she's relied on for so many years are just worn down on this day of days.

Barbara squeezes her hand as Yozo puts a tray down on their table, and she is looking Gia straight in the eye, clear, level, unblinking, calm. "I forgot that I could feel this happy," she tells her.

"You see her tits?" Yozo is nudging Barbara.

"Look at her," Barbara says. "The hair, the skin, that face, she's a big-city lawyer, and she has a chest. Life is unfair. All I got were stretch marks and facial hair."

"Facial hair?" Willie winces.

"Every time I was pregnant, I grew a beard. It fell out right after I delivered, but it happened every time."

"Did you do natural childbirth?" Gia is wondering exactly how much separates them now. Once they were so much alike.

"Are you crazy? I screamed for painkillers as soon as my water broke. I'm not even sure the kids are mine. I was unconscious when they were born, so they could be anybody's. All I know, though, is that the hospital makes you take them home with you. I was kind of shocked by that. I'm not sure my daughter's mine. I think my real daughter might be at Harvard Medical School, and the one they gave me is some kind of spawn of Satan. So, Scarpino, are you married?"

"I got married, right out of law school, to a classmate. It was just one of those really hot things, flush with passing the bar and all that, I think. It only lasted a few years, and then I managed to date just about every man in Los Angeles, so when there was no one left to date, I moved to San Francisco and hooked up in a law practice with some other classmates. There I met the love of my life. He died early in the eighties. The kids I have, Cameron and Nancy, they were his. Their mom had died when Nancy was just a little girl, so I adopted them."

"No man?" Barbara asks.

"There are some men I know, but for anything, you know, substantial or long-term, hell, I'm just not very good at it. I've been alone for a long time, and I'm not the easiest person to live with, I know that."

"You've not changed." Willie clicks his beer against Gia's, and for an instant there is an icy pink edge in his voice. "You weren't the easiest girlfriend to have."

"Not that you ever had me," Gia snaps back, reflexively, shocked at the quick anger she feels in the midst of so much cheer.

"See?" Yozo observes. "See how it is? No matter how old we get, no matter how much money we have, no matter how much education we get, it stays tenth grade. We never get any further than that. You two sound exactly like you did in high school."

Barbara laughs. "He's right. You do."

Gia smiles at Willie, who smiles back, and she can't remember the last time she ducked a fight.

"Are we going to show pictures of our kids?" Barbara asks.

"I didn't bring any," Gia says.

"You'll meet mine," Yozo says. "We don't try to photograph him anymore, since we kept getting blank film, the little vampire. But my grandson, him, I have videos. We'll watch all of them."

"Yeah, right," Barbara says. "Since we have that nastiness out of the way, I think we should get down to the real meat here," and she hauls out a red and white yearbook, the class of 1963. "You didn't make it to the reunion, so I figured you'd like to get an update." She smiles wicked!y.

"I told her about the blonde hair," Yozo says.

"What blonde hair?"

"How every girl had the same color hair at the reunion."

"Right." To Gia she says, "It wasn't blonde. It was brown, deep, dark, mahogany brown. Even if they were all twelve years old, it would have looked phony. Miss Clairol made a fortune that night."

"Remember when all we wanted to do was to dye our hair?" Gia reminds her.

"Remember when we went blonde, in seventh grade? I thought your grandfather was gonna have a stroke," Barbara begins, and the old best girl-friends are launched on an ocean of recollections refreshed, astonished laughter, and sudden embraces.

Yozo nudges Willie. "I gotta check in back. Come with me," he says.

Willie sits silently, smiling at the women across the table.

"They don't even know you're here." Yozo leans into Willie and whispers in his ear. "Leave them alone. Come on."

Willie settles himself on a stool at the bar, and orders a beer. He greets the man to his right. "Frank, how are you?"

"Father," the old man replies, "can I ask you a question?"

"Sure."

"When you drink, you ever see things coming out of the walls? Snakes and shit like that, excuse me, Father?"

"No, Frank," Willie shakes his head and lifts the glass, "can't say that I've ever had that much to drink."

"See?" The man slaps the bar. "See? I don't, either."

"Well, that's good, then," Willie says.

"It's when I stop drinking that I start seeing them. So I start drinking again, and my wife starts up all over again. She don't believe me."

Willie sips his beer and smiles at the man's reflection in the bar mirror. "Oh, I believe you, Frank."

"Do you, Father?" He claps the priest on the back. "Will you tell that banshee of a wife of mine that?"

Willie laughs, and the man says again, "She don't believe me."

Willie is watching Gia and Barbara in the mirror when Yozo comes out from the office behind the bar. "Move down, Frank," he tells the drunk, who obliges without spilling his drink. Yozo nods at the bartender, tilts his head at Frank, and the drunk gets one on the house.

"Look at them," Willie says.

"Yeah," Yozo agrees. "They don't even need a spotlight. They're throwing off their own light. They look good. They look happy."

"What are they talking about, do you think?"

"Not us, friend," Yozo sighs, signaling the bartender. "Anything but us."

"I wish they were," Willie admits.

"Never stopped, did it, for you?" Yozo asks.

"No."

"You surprised?"

Willie almost laughs. "Yeah."

"What are you gonna do?"

Willie sips beer, and carefully puts the glass down on the bar. "For now, I'm gonna watch her."

"What are you gonna do tomorrow?"

He closes his eyes. "I don't know."

Yozo puts his hand on Willie's forearm. "Don't be stupid, okay? I don't think she likes stupidity."

"You know what's funny, Yoz? For the first time in years, I'm not really concerned with what someone else likes. Now. After all this time. When I should care, I should really care about what she thinks of me, now here I am, and all I want is as much of her as I can get, because she's going to be gone again, and I know she'll never come back. How's that for perverse?"

"You never got over her, that's the problem."

"I never wanted to."

"Love of God?"

"Love of God is real, Yozo. So is love of Gia."

"God versus Gia. Mothra versus Godzilla. Which big one will win?"

Willie puts his empty glass down. "You're a blasphemous swine, you know."

"I may be, that's true. But I'd still put my money on Gia. And Godzilla."

Willie looks at him. "Let's go get the girls."

"You've been dying to say that, haven't you?"

Willie leaves him alone at the bar, and Yozo stays there, just for a moment, watching his best friend approach the women. Gia reaches up and touches Willie's chest, resting her hand on it in that most proprietary gesture. Barbara is laughing. Yozo goes over to the table, because he knows that there is something wonderful happening, and in that moment he cannot bear to be apart from whatever it is. He has spent his life outside, he believes, and it never mattered, but with them, these three, he must be there.

Gia says to Barbara, when the men sit down, "You're still a chain-smoker. Did you ever try to stop?"

She shakes her head.

"While you were pregnant?"

She shakes her head again. "I think if I quit, I'll die. I think there's something in cigarettes that's good for me."

"We all started smoking together," Yozo reminds them. "You," he says to Willie, "you were never really into it, were you?"

"Even when you all thought it was glamorous and adult, I thought it was dirty. Now it seems as though the rest of society has caught up with my thinking."

Barbara looks at him. "I'll bet you say 'chair' instead of 'chairman.'"

"I remember kissing you, Gia, after you had a cigarette. It wasn't pleasant."

"Gee, Willie, you should have told me. I would have given it up sooner. As it is, I smoked for another twenty years. You could have saved me from myself." She turns to Barbara and asks, "When he got the collar, did he also get a license to become a righteous prig, or had he already made the transition all by himself?"

"Are all our memories simply to be fluff," he retorts, "or are we allowed to tell the truth here?"

"I came home to help my godfather die. I don't feel like helping you work out whatever teenage angst you're still carrying around with you. I want the fluff."

"Here's to fluff, bullshit, and tenth grade." Yozo hefts his glass. "Who's hungry? Guess where we're going now?"

"Oh, God," Barbara moans, "do we have to?"

"Yeah," Yozo says, "tonight's the night. Let's walk."

"Where?" Gia asks. "Where are we going?"

"You really don't know, do you?" Yozo asks.

"No."

"Then you deserve what you're about to get," Willie says to her, and he takes her hand. His touch signifies a temporary truce, for which Gia is thankful, because when she goes to stand up, she realizes how drunk she is. "Come on," he says to her, clutching her hand and putting his arm around her, steadying her, just as he always did whenever they left this place.

Nothing ever changes, Barbara thinks as she watches her old friend throw up behind the high school. Yozo is holding Gia by the back of her jacket as she sways, tiptoe, over the railroad tracks. Barbara and Willie are standing back, leaning on the hood of the priest Ford.

"When she starts crying, she's done," Barbara calls to Yozo, who nods without turning around or loosening his grip. "Do you think this is the first time she's done this since the last time we were here?" she asks Willie.

"It would be nice to think so, but I expect she's done this in all sorts of exotic locales. She never understood her own capacity. She always did everything a little too much."

Yes, that's a good description of my friend, Barbara muses. I used to be afraid of her, how she'd yell sometimes, how angry she'd get about things that I didn't even notice. My mother told me it was because she was Eyetalian. She said that those people were loud and rude. But I always envied her. Whatever went through her head showed up right away on her face, and came out of her mouth. Sort of like what she's doing right now, only with words instead of those nasty burgers with hot sauce and the fries we just sucked down.

"I think going to Rudy's was a big mistake," she says.

"It's always a mistake. When the waitress asked us if we really wanted the fries, since they're going to change the oil tomorrow, we should have been smart. She was trying to warn us off."

"Goddamn, though, Will, they were good, weren't they? I just can't believe we ate lunch there every day for four years."

He rests his hand over his belt buckle. "The truth is that I'm not that far from doing what she's doing," he says, and swallows.

Barbara turns around and looks up at the boarded windows, the shattered iron gate, the crumbling stone building that was their high school. "They're just going to let it rot away, aren't they?"

"We met in there. Room Eleven. Remember?"

"I was so happy to get the hell out of sister school. Those fucking nuns, excuse me, Will, but you know how vicious they were. Don't you?"

"They're different now. Younger. Calmer. I think the reasons women take the veil today are very different than when we were kids."

"I wish we could go inside. I wonder what it's like."

"Stripped. Our pal there bought up all the desks and chairs. The clocks, too. He shipped them up to antique dealers in New England. Made a bundle. He may have bought the building, too. I'm not sure."

She stomps out a cigarette and moves closer to him. "He was such a nothing kid. He just went along, never did anything outstanding. Look at him today. He's a real success story."

"Aren't we all, Barbara?"

"Did you get what you wanted, Willie? Has it turned out like you thought it would?" She follows his gaze and sees that his eyes haven't left Gia, who is still heaving.

"Once I entered seminary, I never thought it would be any different. I didn't plan on coming back here, though, but it's just how I want it now."

"What about her? You were so crazy about her."

"She was gone," he says quietly. "I knew she wouldn't come back."

"And now that she's back, what?" Barbara knows she's probably causing some kind of pain to this black-clad priest, but she persists, maybe because she knows that no man, anywhere, will ever talk about her with that same sound in his voice.

"She's exactly the same, and she's completely different. I know her and I've never met her. She's still the most complicated human being I've ever met. Just when I think I can settle down around her, she does something and I want to smack her."

"You know, I know exactly what you're talking about. I remember, one time I made the honor roll, and my parents didn't think it was such a big deal— I mean, I wasn't going to college or anything—and Gia came over and said something to my father like, 'Aren't you proud of your daughter?', or something like that, and he said it didn't really matter, and she flipped out, went up to Daniels' Leather Goods store and bought me a manicure set, had it gift-wrapped, and gave it to me. I still have it. I've used it all these years, but every time I look at it, it pisses me off because it reminds me, well, you know? I just wish she hadn't done it. But she said somebody had to do something."

Willie turns and looks at her. "But you still have it. You kept it all these years, and you thought of her. I don't think you wanted to hit her very hard. Or maybe it wasn't Gia you wanted to smack."

"Father, Father, this isn't the confessional."

"The world is a confessional. Sometimes it's official, sometimes it's not, that's all. Is she crying yet?"

he calls to Yozo, who shakes his head. "Did you ever get your youngest one baptized, Barbara?"

"No, it just got away from me. With three kids, things get pretty complicated."

"You can bring him in anytime."

"He's a walking hormone, Will. I don't think his interest lies in being sprinkled with Holy Water."

"I guess not," he agrees, smiling. "Did we have a good time tonight?"

Barbara, who is already worried about driving herself home because she's not used to being on the road at night, is trying not to think about how relieved she's going to be to get inside her house tonight. The kids will be asleep, or at least in their rooms, and she'll pour herself a tall one and watch the soaps she's taped the previous week. She will not think about this evening.

"Yeah, we had a real good time, Willie."

"She's crying," Yozo calls, and they watch as Gia pulls herself upright, with Yozo's assistance, and with his arm wrapped firmly around her, she slogs slowly back to the car.

"Do you people do this all the time?" she asks in a pitiful voice. "Don't you ever sleep?"

Barbara watches the two men help Gia Scarpino into the backseat of the priest Ford. They handle her as though she were made of old lace. Willie looks across the top of the door and says to Barbara, "You'll ride with us to her uncle's house, and then we'll drive you back to your car, all right?"

"Will you follow me home? I'm a little nervous about driving in the dark."

"Sure," and then he turns to minister to Gia, who, for reasons Barbara will never know, has begun crying again.

Nothing ever changes, she thinks.

They stay in the driveway, lights shining on the porch until she gets inside Tony and Francie's house, and then she watches the headlights leave a trail across the kitchen wall, hears the crunch of the gravel as the priest Ford departs. She is as wasted as she's ever been. Marathon sex sessions, too much marijuana, acid, coke, booze, preparing for trial, nothing has ever left her as totally turned out as have the last twenty-four hours.

She leans on the sink, running the cold water, holding on tight, trying to remember exactly how long she's been here. It couldn't be the several years it feels like. And, with the last bit of sentient being she possesses, she is trying to remember exactly why she is in this house when a noise comes from the doorway, and she turns in the darkened kitchen to find herself staring at herself. Except that her other self is much younger, her hair is still dark, and she seems to be taller.

I left a ghost here, she thinks. Except she never lived in this house. Tony and Francie built it long after Gia moved to California.

Okay, she's hallucinating. That happens. She is a child of the sixties. Hallucinations are an acceptable explanation for strange happenings. Her other self looks so young and unmarked. Maybe I'm looking at the face of who I used to be? she wonders.

God, she's cute.

But the voice isn't hers when it says, "Gia, I've been waiting for you." It's softer, slower, more New York. It's a pleasant voice.

Gia draws a tall glass of water, decides against drinking anything else tonight, and feels a strange sense of peace when she realizes that she is Death, come for her. How about that? Death looks just like me. She is filled with wonder. She guesses that everybody's Death looks like them. She bends over the sink, her face close to the cool stainless steel, and marvels at the efficiency of such a system.

"Are you all right?" Death asks.

"If I said I wasn't, would you leave me alone?" Is that any way to escape Death? To tell her that you just aren't in any shape to die?

"I'm sorry," Death stammers. "I was just really looking forward to seeing you again."

Again? She's never met Death before, has she? Oh, there have been the rain-slicked roads, the lightning striking the plane, the deeply dissatisfied client who opened fire in the law offices two floors above theirs, but no, there haven't been any real close encounters.

Unless Death was too canny to let Gia know she was standing close by.

Death, she concludes, is a tricky broad. It's going to take a lot to outsmart her, but Gia always had this secret feeling that she would be the one who would never die. Too bad she's too drunk tonight to think straight.

Whoa. Don't be rude to Death. "No, I'm glad to

see you. It's just that I've been throwing up for a long time now, and I'm really not at my best." Her face is still very close to the stainless steel sink, and the feeling is very much like the comfort of the inside of the toilet bowl in which her head has so often found itself.

"Do you know who I am?" Death asks.

Gia swallows, a dry and painful exercise. She won't do that again. "Yes," she whispers.

"No, you don't."

"You're Death, and you've come to take me. Why don't you take my aunt Mella instead? She's really old and she's mean."

Death laughs and laughs, an oddly familiar sound. It is Gia's laugh. This is all too much for her, and she feels herself passing out. Or away.

Her face slides across the bottom of the sink, up over the counter edge, down the cabinet doors, pausing only to snag her upper lip on the handle, and she is just about facedown and unconscious on the kitchen floor when Death catches her and effortlessly pulls her semi-upright. Gia's battered and weary head snaps back, and the last thing she hears Death say is: "I haven't seen you since I was five years old. I'm your cousin Mia. Your cousin Tessa is my mother."

SECOND DAY

He knocks on the door, which, he notes, badly needs painting, and a small girl, maybe three years of age, opens it and, smiling, lets him inside. There is not an adult in sight.

"Where's your mommy?" he asks the girl, who runs away from him, down the stairs he knows go to the family room, from which he hears booming cartoons. "Fucking great," he mutters.

He goes up another set of stairs, in this suburban split-level single-family dwelling which is slowly falling apart, and goes into a darkened bedroom, which has a musty, beery smell, a room in which one can hear the deep, unlabored breathing of a person sprawled across the king-size bed in which only one person at a time now sleeps, thanks to third shift.

He sits down in an ersatz Queen Anne chair and crosses his legs. He would like to rip down the heavy brocade drapes, throw open the windows, let out this foul air, and let in the clean October sunshine against which this entire house seems to have barricaded itself. He rubs his ankle and wonders why he keeps coming back. Even after all these years, he keeps coming back.

Loyalty runs deep in him. It is the thing he cherishes most; it is what he thought about at seven o'clock Mass this morning, when he prayed for help in finding the right thing to do. He isn't sure if he should do anything, but still, here he is, in this familiar house, sitting in a darkened bedroom, and not even knowing for sure what he's going to do next. He thinks that he should do something about that little girl, who is essentially alone in this house, but

he knows, perhaps better than most, that God pro-
tects children and fools. There is a child downstairs,
and the woman softly snoring on the bed is a fool.

"Barbara!" he shouts, an explosive bark designed
to wake her from where he sits, since he has, in the
past, had the distasteful experience of shaking her
awake, and smelling the alcohol oozing out of her
pores combined with the cigarette smoke and,
worst of all, the perfume she uses to cover it up.
"Barbara!"

She rouses, slightly, and sinks deeper, it seems. He
sighs, uncrosses his legs, gets up, and goes to the
bed, doing the very thing he doesn't want to do.
He touches the back of her shoulder—she is facedown—and shakes her. "Barbara, wake up. It's
time." He would like—he is surprised by this
thought—to touch her hair, but he is afraid of how
it would feel. He still remembers kissing his dead
mother's hair before the coffin was closed, and it is
something he will never forget and always regret.

She rises up, faster than Lazarus, her eyes wide
open, clearing her throat of the deep phlegm that
has made a home there, and smiles, a smile which, if
he didn't know her, would make him think that she
meant it.

When she smiles, he thinks, she has such a sweet
face. The thought pierces his heart. He wishes, for
an instant, that Gia Scarpino had never come back.

"Your granddaughter is here. She probably needs
to be fed," he tells her.

Barbara reaches for the Marlboros sitting on the
nightstand, and Yozo retreats, not wanting to be

caught in the cloud of smoke that will, he knows, puff up around her in a few seconds.

"She's all right," Barbara mutters around the cigarette she holds to a pink Bic lighter.

"She's alone, isn't she?"

"She's watching TV. She's fine."

"Aw, shit," he says, and goes downstairs into the kitchen, which is surprisingly clean, except for an orangeade carton on the counter and a wrapper from a raspberry Pop-Tart which missed the trash container. He reaches down and stuffs the wrapper into the green Rubbermaid receptacle which is peeking out from the cabinet under the sink. Here, in the kitchen, the sun streams through the window above the sink. He looks outside, into the backyard, and sees Eddie, Barbara's husband, asleep in a chaise longue on the patio. How does that poor sonofabitch put up with all this? he wonders. He's never heard any gossip about Eddie running around on Barbara. Is that what love is, he wonders, you put up with anything? I'll be fucked if Christine would ever get away with anything like this. Yeah, he snickers, like she'd ever pull this. He thinks about his taut, aerobicized, facialed, manicured, hair-woven wife, a poor girl from a large Polish family who married the boy who knocked her up only to discover that the boy had more burning ambition than she had ever suspected, and she stayed with him, with their son, while he worked harder and harder, took more and more chances, and emerged a prosperous and influential businessman in their hometown, a place she had always wanted to leave, but in which she now prevailed as a rich man's wife.

He reaches into the refrigerator, finds a carton of milk, opens and sniffs it, then pours some into a small plastic cup he finds in one of the upper cabinets. It is a measure of his distrust and familiarity with this house that he looks inside the cup before he fills it. He looks through some other cupboards, finds a box of Rice Krispies, pours some in a bowl, pours the milk from the cup over the cereal, sprinkles just a little sugar on it, and then, spying a banana in a bowl on the kitchen table, he slices part of that onto the cereal and eats the rest himself. He has not eaten this morning, still preferring, in the old-fashioned way of the Catholic Church before Pope John XXIII, to fast from the night before so as to take Communion on an empty stomach. He finds that the emptiness enables him to focus much more intently on the miracle of the Transubstantiation that he witnesses every day except Sunday, the one day he is obligated, as a Catholic, to attend Mass. His own personal perversity keeps him home in bed on Sunday mornings, surrounded by Philadelphia and New York newspapers, and Washington talk shows on TV. Yozo has never listened to anyone's music but his own, and he still, after more than a half century, finds it a pleasant, albeit sometimes discordant, tune.

He goes down to the family room, where the child is sitting directly in front of the television set. He scoops her up, and she goes, uncomplaining, as he deposits her on a chair on the kitchen table and tucks a napkin into the neckline of her already stained T-shirt. "Can you feed yourself?" he asks her. She seizes the spoon and, dripping milk and cereal from the bowl to her mouth, shows him, with a knowing look from her big hazel eyes, that she can indeed feed herself.

"Good girl." He has no hesitation about tousling her hair, this sweet little girl who lets a stranger into the house while the adults who should be minding her are sleeping off their respective demons.

As he turns to go back to the bedroom, Barbara comes in, showered and damp, in a pink robe, carrying another cigarette. Her hair drips down her neck, and he has a sudden image of his tongue running along that wet path. She reaches into the refrigerator for a Caffeine-Free Diet Coke, and pops the top with her free hand. "Are you my new live-in houseboy? I've always wanted one of those."

He looks at her for a long time, a look she unblinkingly returns. "She was hungry," he says.

"So you came over to feed her. How nice."

"What's going on with you?" He leads her by the elbow into the living room, which is never used, and he notes that it is furnished in much the same way Barbara's mother kept her living room. They sit, side by side, on a flowered sofa. "You have fun last night?"

"Yeah, it was nice to see everybody."

She starts to go through a newspaper scattered on a coffee table in front of the sofa.

"No, did you?" He puts his hand on hers, stopping her. "I know you said all the right things to Gia when you saw her, and all that, about looking good and all, but you didn't want to be there, did you?"

She smiles and laughs. "You found me, remember? You invited me. What is wrong with you? We had a great time. The old foursome, right?"

He says nothing.

"I had fun. I'm sorry you didn't. Maybe the old gang just isn't what it used to be." She pulls her feet up under her, settling into her end of the sofa, farther away from Yozo. "Joe, I've got a lot of things to do today. If you're finished, why don't you go?"

"Doesn't any of this matter to you, Barbara? Isn't the past worth anything, even a little bit?"

"Why do you want to go back so badly? What's wrong with now?"

"It was just a simple evening of old friends getting together, that's all. I thought it would be different."

She stares at him for what seems like a long time but really isn't, since she's never been good at eye contact. "You thought we'd be the same old kids. You're so sentimental. I never knew that about you."

"Yes, you did. You just didn't like it."

"What do you want me to do, apologize or something? To Gia?"

"No. No apology." He reaches for her hand. "I wanted," he starts, "I wanted us to have fun."

She shakes her head but doesn't pull her hand away. "You're so soft," she says. "You, of all people."

"It's a gorgeous day," he says, "and Tony wants to sit in his garden."

"I thought he was in the hospital."

"He is, but this is what he wants, so I promised him we'd take him."

"You're gonna just take him out of the hospital?"

He looks at her. "Tony wants to sit in his garden. He's gonna sit in his garden."

"Will the good Father be one of us?"

"Yeah," Yozo says, "he's driving. I guess I should call and tell him."

Maybe Willie was right. Maybe God has a hell of a sense of humor. Her torturing cousin Tessa's only child is a dead ringer for Gia.

"My mother showed me your baby pictures. Even when I was little, I looked like you," the young woman is telling Gia, who is propped up in one of the twin beds in the guest room in Tony's house, sipping a Coke with all the fizz stirred out of it. Mia Lentini had gently awakened Gia with the news that Yozo was on the phone. Gia took the call, which was classic Yozo.

"He's going to the garden," he told her.

"He's practically on life support," she answered, and then grimaced from the pain in her head. She mouthed the word "Coke" to Mia, and then covered the mouthpiece of the phone, and instructed her on how to get rid of those damn noisy bubbles before it was served to her.

"He wants this," Yozo said. "We're taking him."

"We?"

"Yeah, the four of us. I'm at Barbara's, we'll go get Will, and pick you up last. You still puking?"

"You can't take him out of the hospital, Yoz. There's all sorts of liability there, and he's really frail."

There was a silence, and then Yozo said, "You've been gone too long, Gia."

"What does that mean?"

"I'll tell you later," he promised, and then he hung up.

"Who's Yozo?" the pretty girl with the still-new dark eyes asks.

"A lunatic I grew up with. God, you look just like me!"

"I know." Mia has the same smile.

"Have we ever met?" Gia asks.

"Once, a long time ago, at my uncle's funeral. I was real little, but I remember you. And your husband, John. He was nice. He gave me twenty dollars."

"Yes," Gia says, realizing it's time to get out of bed. "He was nice." She puts one foot on the floor, checks to see that neither the floor nor the ceiling is spinning, and puts the other foot down. "Is your mother here?" Gia thinks to ask, suddenly nauseated.

"She's at my grandma's house. You don't like my grandmother, do you?"

"Mella? Oh, honey, she doesn't like me, so, right, I don't like her. Sorry."

"That's okay. I think I understand. She's kind of, you know, difficult."

"Yeah, difficult," Gia says.

"You want me to help you?" the young woman asks.

"No, I can stand by myself." Gia is trying to convince herself, but she's still sitting on the edge of the bed.

"I'm a nurse," Mia says. "I do this for a living."

Gia turns her head and smiles at her cousin's kid, the innocent, who smiles back. "Do you have any plans for this afternoon?" she asks the youngster.

Willie Cunningham stands on the lowest step of the altar, right behind the communion railing, and looks out over the almost empty church. Margie is kneeling in the second row, her head bowed, forehead resting on the back of the pew in front of her, rosary working spastically in her hands as she reads the beads, as she has done every day since he became pastor of Our Lady of Mercy, as she has done, he's been briefed, every day for the past twenty-two years. If she's not praying, she's scrubbing—floors, wainscoting, kneelers, baptismal font, anything that can tolerate her hands and Pine Sol. Willie used to savor the scent of the incense used in the Consecration of the Host, but now everything smells like his mother's bathroom, and his heart gives a little lurch for his loss. As long as Margie is around, he's never going to have his church the way he wants it, and he has surrendered to that fact, although—and he laments this daily in his conversations with God—he resents her for it.

"Margie, go home, your family needs you," he says, uncoupling the railing gate and stepping into the main aisle, carefully latching the gate behind him. A GIFT FROM THE CUGUSI FAMILY, 1952, the plaque on the gate reads. There are no more Cugusis in the parish, not even grandchildren.

"The Mass was inspiring, Father. I felt His presence very near this morning." Margie Sherpinsky Glodecki lifts her naked face to glance his way. He always expects some sort of glow to emanate from her, as if she really does have a track to the Almighty, but all he ever gets back from her is the older, worn face of the girl he went to school with, the one who, for reasons that will forever remain obscure, had all her teeth pulled in tenth grade, was fitted with the same dentures she now wears, which, after years of marriage and the births of six children, have receded in her narrow mouth, giving her the look, prematurely, of a crone. She would have achieved that look eventually, Willie suspects, but it's still just a little too early. She has a bad perm, fanning out her thinning hair in a mad harridan's nest, and she has taken to dyeing it black, an unfortunate choice. She still has the blue eyes he always loved looking at; he remembers sixth grade in Annunciation School, when she was seated all the way across the room from him in arithmetic class, and how her eyes shone when she stood to recite. They are duller now, but they are still striking. If she got some rest, he thinks, she could look a lot better.

He's kidding himself, he knows. Zealots just never look good.

"That's good, Margie, but God wants you to serve Him in your home, as a wife and mother. With your children, that's where you can do the most good," he counsels her, sliding easily in her pew, although he seats himself at the far end from where she is still kneeling.

"I feel Jesus with me all the time, Father, but I feel closest to Him when I'm here."

"That's 'cause you're nuts, Sherpie," Yozo calls as he and Barbara come through the swinging doors at the rear of the church. The whole place is so small that whispered conversations in one corner can easily be heard at the holy water fonts in the foyer, behind the heavy wooden doors which are still slapping at air as Barbara and Yozo make their way up the main aisle. Yozo genuflects, makes a quick sign of the cross, and sits behind Willie. Barbara stands behind him, neither sitting nor blessing herself, looking amused as she nods and smiles at Margie, who takes on the feral look of a mother hyena whose den, filled with newborn pups, has just been invaded.

"Hiya doin', Margie?" Barbara waves and winks.

Yozo pokes Willie's shoulder. "You working today? We need you to go with us."

"I've got confessions at four. That's all for today. There's a CYO meeting tonight, I have to be there for the invocation."

"Good, then you're coming with us. Margie, you wanna go with us, do an honest-to-God Christian act of charity, or you gonna stay here and rattle those beads some more? How many rosaries have you gone through since we graduated? Do they wear out?"

Margie is busily concluding her prayers, and she

stuffs the beads into the pocket of her colorless jacket; everything about her seems to be colorless, except for those eyes and that scary hair, and with the practiced ease of a woman who's spent most of her adult life on her knees, slithers out of the pew, goes to the altar railing, makes a great show of the sign of the cross, genuflects, and joins her classmates, standing almost nose to nose with Barbara. Yozo takes this in, recalling when the girls were both cheerleaders, brazenly and openly competitive, all that teased hair, those jumps, those silken crotches, those naked legs, and thinks: It's always tenth grade. Here we go again.

"Barbara." Margie lays a hand on her old classmate's forearm, the gesture of a gracious hostess. This is, after all, her church. "Ronnie and I are having a special Mass said next month for our anniversary. We're going to renew our vows. I hope you can join us."

"Jesus, Margie, you three months' pregnant again?" Barbara sweetly smiles as Margie Sherpinsky Glodecki hurries out of the church.

"That was mean," Willie says. "She's harmless."

"She's a little Nazi." Barbara sniffs. "She's always been so holier than thou."

"Good one, Barbara," Yozo encourages her, and she smiles, a real smile, one of genuine surprise. "Remember when you were going for captain of the cheerleaders?"

"That stuff about the basketball team, at the dance, in the stairwell?" Willie looks from Yozo to Barbara. "Is that what you're talking about?"

"That really happened, you know," Barbara says. "But it wasn't me. It was Beverly Adamavage."

"I know," Yozo concurs. "I was on student council. I was supposed to check the exit doors, and I found her doing the team just when Mr. Gazan came by. He wanted to know what was going on in the stairwell. What was I gonna do? Tell him Beverly Adamavage was blowing the basketball team? I stalled him as long as I could, but he went around me and pushed the door open. Sonofabitch, it was empty. Everybody had taken off. I still don't know how they knew to go."

"You were on the basketball team," Barbara reminds him.

"I know. But I didn't get a blowjob." He shrugs. "I should have known then that was going to be the story of my life."

"This is God's house," Father William Cunningham, S.J., reminds his friends, but makes no move to get up.

"Who do you think invented blowjobs, Will?" Barbara asks him.

"Guess what we're going to do today?" Yozo asks him.

"Dear God, help me," Willie says, eyes turned toward the altar as his old friends lead him out of the church.

"Here, now," Willie says softly, "here, hold it, can you hold it, there, just a little bit, there."

"More." Tony nudges the wineglass at the bottle Willie holds to the glass's lip.

"All the refills you want, Tony, just for now, that much, so you don't spill it."

"I have to be able to smell it," Tony chides him. "Even with this schnozz of mine, there's not enough there for me to get a good smell."

"Pour more," Yozo tells Willie, who complies. "There're worse things than spilled wine."

"Blood," Barbara says.

"Mercury," Mia says. With her along, it was easy to take Tony out of the hospital this bright October afternoon, his IV still connected, tended by his very own nurse, his very own lawyer, his very own priest, to sit here, in the warmth of the sun, in his very own garden, the plot of land where Gia's grandfather, Tony's father, tended his tomatoes, his peonies, the long broad beans, the lettuce, and, best of all, the grapes that rose and climbed up to the small arbor he had built. The vines are gone, the shaded haven under which Gia and her grandfather used to sit on an old wooden bench is no longer there. But this small acre or so, whatever it is, hasn't changed much. Across the street, Scarpino's Market, the nice shiny supermarket that replaced the small store opened by Tony's father, with the apartments in back and upstairs, where the whole family lived, where Gia grew up, looms large and new and prosperous. When she dreams about the store, she sees only the old one. This is where I learned to cross the street, she thinks.

The small pen in the back of the yard, where Gia can vaguely recall chickens and a rooster whose crowing woke her every morning, but which she remembers mainly as a home for her bunny, is gone, too, just as the bunny disappeared one day, when her grandfather assured her that Mrs. Bunny had come by looking for her baby and so Bun had gone with his mommy. Gia doesn't recall being upset at the time about the rabbit's sudden disappearance, but today she feels something.

Willie and Barbara, looking for all the world like a priest and an altar boy dispensing Communion, give the others glasses, and then fill them with the zinfandel Yozo has supplied. It's a light touch, a perfect wine to drink on this sparkling autumn day while Tony says good-bye to the piece of earth where he has been happiest in his life.

"Toast, anyone?" Yozo asks, holding up his glass.

"I will," Barbara says. "To friends who are family and," she nods at Tony and Mia, "to family who are friends."

"Oh," Tony begins to weep, "that's nice. That's so nice. How'd you know such nice words?"

"Somebody said them at my wedding," Barbara confesses.

"It's good they get said once every thirty years," Yozo says.

Mia is wiping Tony's face. She holds a handkerchief to his nose, and his hand reaches up and covers hers. Gia stands very still, expecting to feel, irrationally, a pang of jealousy, but what she feels is a deep comfort. She is not alone in her almost violent love for this old man. The youngster loves him, too.

She wonders how much longer he will live.

"Remember the store?" Yozo leans into her. "Remember eating the grated cheese out of the big jar he had behind the counter?"

"Dried figs," Barbara says. "That was the first place I ever saw dried figs. I thought they only came in Newtons."

"I grew up there," Gia says. "And it's not even there anymore."

"Gia," Tony calls. "Let's go for a walk." He looks up at Mia. "Take these out."

"Tony." The young woman hesitates. Her hair, in the sun, is redder than Gia's ever was, but, yes, she still looks an awful lot like her. "I won't be able to put them back in until we get back to the hospital, and you could have a lot of pain by then."

"I don't care about pain. I'll take more dope. But I want to walk in the dirt one more time. With her." He points at Gia. His finger is steady. "With her," he says again, in case anyone harbored any plans to come with them.

"Can you stand?" Yozo is on one side of him, Willie on the other, as they raise him up. Mia pulls the one large needle from the feeder in the back of his left hand, and Tony is free. He has slippers on his feet, slippers high in the back with toes almost curling up. Leprechaun shoes, she used to call them when she was a kid, when her grandfather wore the exact same soft brown leather footwear.

"She's gonna be my crutch. Come here," he tells her, and Gia slides under his right arm while Yozo and Willie slowly let go of him. "See?" Tony looks delighted. "I used to hold your arms while you were learning to walk. I used to hold you up, and now you're holding me up. See how it goes?"

She is swallowing her tears as the others back away, and Tony and Gia go into the working part of the garden, where, even a month ago, tomatoes were on the now dead vines. "I should have cleaned this up before I went into the hospital."

"I'll do it," she promises him, and she knows she will keep this promise. "Don't worry about it. The ground will be all right."

"Remember coming in here with Grandpop? Do you?" he asks her.

"I was always afraid to touch the plants. I thought there'd be bugs on them. So Grandpop would pick a couple of the Italian tomatoes and we'd go over there," she tilts her head toward where the grape arbor had been, "and sit on the bench. He'd take a salt shaker out of his vest pocket, and a knife, and we'd eat those tomatoes, still warm from the sun. They were so good. Tony, do you remember the golf course you made for me?"

"Over there, after the peonies flowered. We dug holes all over the place, and you had your little stick and a ball, and we used to play golf. Jesus, you remember that? You couldn't have been more than three. Four." His right hand is rubbing her shoulder, and it is no effort, no effort at all, to hold up this dying old man who weighs much less than she expected. Willie carried him to the car from the hospital, picking him up as easily as one might scoop up a kitten. "What do you remember best? What's the best thing?"

It might be the hardest question anyone will ever ask her.

"Your beard." This is it, she understands, this is the memory that, after you're gone, is going to lay me flat out on the floor while I cry my heart out. This will be the memory I won't be able to allow myself to remember. "You used to come and get me when you came home from work, and you needed a shave, and you'd grab me and rub my cheek up against your face. Not so you'd hurt me, just enough to get my attention. Tony, it tickled, and I remember laughing while you held me. Laughing. While you held me. That's the best thing."

His grin is wide in his thin, lined face. His teeth look so big. "You know what I like to remember about? You and Grandpop, in the parlor. He'd have Caruso records on the Victrola, and you'd be standing on the top step of the landing going up the stairs. There's the two of you. He's sitting there, smoking a cigar, and you have a towel tied around your neck, like a cape, and you got a butter knife in your hand. He has the sound turned all the way up, and it's Caruso singing 'Vesti la guibba' from Pagliacci, and you're singing at the top of your lungs, all about 'Petey Pagliacci.' You thought that was what Caruso was singing, you thought that that was the clown's name. You loved that aria, especially where he laughs, and you used to sing along with it, and then, when it was over, for some reason you used to collapse, dead, on the floor. Then Grandpop would clap, and he'd get up and move the phonograph needle back, and the two of you would do it all over again. You could do that for hours, and he'd sit right there with you. Aw, come on, don't do that. Don't. I didn't mean to make you cry."

"Yeah, you did. It's okay. I never said thank you, Tony. I never thanked you for all you gave me. You gave me life, *Padrino*. Thank you." She rubs her face against his rough woolen jacket, and, just a little, it feels like his beard used to on her young face.

"You were the light from the sun, Gianna. You were ours. Eh, you know that. Take me over there, over there, by the fence."

She leads him to a spot just a few feet from where they stand, and helps him move his arm from around her shoulders as she steadies him against the rough wood. "Can you do this?" she asks him.

"I can do this," he assures her. "Now you're gonna do what I can't do anymore. Go scoop up a bunch of that dirt. Bring it to me."

When she presents it to him, he runs first his right hand, then his left hand, through the rich, dark earth that was first cultivated by his father more than seventy years earlier. Tony closes his eyes as he works the soil through his fingers, and he asks her to get more when the first batch loses its warmth. She brings him more, and she would gladly fetch him dirt forever if it would keep him alive and free from pain. But some things resist even the sweetest steps backward, and it isn't long before Yozo and Willie carefully slip the wheelchair under her godfather, and they are all silent in the car as they drive back to the hospital, only Tony's sighs and moans punctuating the stillness.

• • •

"Va fa in culo!"

It's astonishing how quickly Gia's facile Italian returns as she tells her aunt Mella to go fuck herself up her ass. Willie, whose Italian is probably better than hers, but whose classical education at the Vatican did not include the finer points of the language, such as phrases necessary to put rampaging relatives in their respective places, grabs her arm and pulls her away as Mella's hand flies to her mouth, effectively covering and silencing that powerful orifice. Gia once read something about a supermassive black hole out in space, more than fifty million light-years away, whose gravitational pull was so great that nothing, not even light, once it's been sucked in, can ever come out again. It made her think of Mella's mouth, that mouth that Gia's time-honored Italian vulgarity has just closed, for which the entire world should be grateful. But all Gia gets is yanked away.

Everyone is at the hospital when they return, and everyone is mad at them. Except for Joey, Tony's younger son, who is upset because they didn't include him. "I was across the street, in the store. You could have just yelled."

Tony is in a great deal of pain by the time Yozo carries him to his bed, and the physician attending him, some snotnose whose nameplate means nothing to Gia, demands to know how dare they remove his patient without his permission. Yozo stands very close to the young man and explains:

"Because it was what Mr. Scarpino wanted, and

we do what Mr. Scarpino wants. Any more questions?"

"You know, his medical insurance could cancel him because of this," the young man threatens.

"Cancel this." Yozo gives his crotch an affectionate squeeze.

Mella started screaming at Gia, only Gia, as soon as they came up on Tony's floor, and Gia waited until she paused for breath—she's getting older—before she uttered her curse.

Francie, Tony's wife, stands at his bedside as a medical team ministers to him. Her sons are beside her, and Mia is on the other side of the bed, assisting the doctor. With an angry wave of her hand, Francie orders everyone else to get out. Lenny, Tony's older son, slips outside.

"Is he worse?" the son asks. "Is he worse or does he just need morphine?"

Willie is soothing as he tells the young man, "Right now he's in pain, but that's going to go away in a minute. Len, the trip did him more good than harm, believe me."

"Why the hell weren't you here with your father?" Mella attacks the kid.

"Why the hell are you here?" Gia steps in front of Tony's boy. "Leave him alone. Stop this."

"He needs surgery." She points toward Tony's room. "He could get some help."

Angelina, who has been lurking in the background in Mella's very big shadow, emerges to say, "I don't think so, Carmella. I don't think he could tolerate any procedure."

"You had to take him, didn't you?" Mella doesn't let up on Gia. Willie's hand is still on his old girl-friend's arm. Yozo has wandered off somewhere, and Barbara is outside, smoking.

"Yes," Willie answers for Gia, squeezing her arm as a caution to remain silent, "we did. He had to go there. Can you understand that, Carmella?"

"I don't understand anything since she came here. Mia! Get out here!" she bellows, and the hospital walls vibrate.

Gia looks at Willie. "She's worse than ever," she says, and someone in Tony's room, Gia doesn't know who, gently closes the door.

"Come." Willie leads Gia to the elevator. "Let's get some coffee."

"You can't go back there tonight," Yozo says, after Willie tells him about the scene upstairs with Mella. "Come to my house, or, there's a little apartment at the store, you can stay there."

"I'm not going to let her drive me out of a house that's not even hers," Gia protests. "She's railroaded everyone all her life, just by brute force, and it's going to stop now."

"Do you really think now is the time to strike a philosophical stance?" Willie asks.

"Get her, Gia." Barbara has a wicked smile on her face. "That old bat's been flapping her wings ever since I've known you. Yes," she says to Willie, "it is exactly the right time to strike, as you put it, a philosophical stance. What did they teach you at the seminary? Make peace all the time? Sometimes you have to fight back, Willie. Sometimes you just have to stop them. You can stay at my house if you want, Gia, but I personally think you ought to go to Tony's house. He wouldn't want you anyplace else, would he?"

"No. God." Gia pushes her cup and saucer away. They are all seated in the hospital cafeteria. Yozo, for some reason, has gathered one of each dessert available, and their table, not counting coffee cups and Barbara's Diet Pepsi, is covered with gelatinous rice pudding compositions, multicolored Jell-O cubes, pies of indeterminate identity, strange layered cakes, and slabs of ice cream wrapped in white paper. "I always try to believe that crisis ennobles people, but the pricks just keep being pricks." She stretches her arms above her head. "Am I the only one who feels like shit? Or do you people just not react to greasy food and too much drinking?"

"You need to work out," Yozo tells her. Barbara shudders. Willie announces that he has to get to the church by four P.M. in order to hear confessions, and asks Barbara if she wants to come along.

"Only if I can sit on your side of the confessional." She gives him a crazed smile.

"That wasn't quite what I had in mind," Willie demurs, but holds her chair for her as she rises, and takes her hand as they leave the cafeteria.

"You're coming to my house for dinner tonight," Yozo informs Gia. "I'll cook some steaks, we can sit in peace. My wife told me she wants no part of old home week, so she won't bother us."

"Actually, I'd like to see Chris. I kind of remember her, but I want to see what kind of woman would actually sleep with you. Over a period of years."

"What makes you think she sleeps with me?" Yozo cracks, and stands up. "You feel like a swim? Would that make you feel better? I think it would. Come on."

And, following him as she never did before, she leaves the cafeteria, the hospital, and her birth family, gathered up on the third floor, doing only God knows what to each other with words and looks and dangerous silences.

He walks her through it all in a very low-key way, but she knows that he's proud. Gia is amazed. Everything has happened so quickly since she arrived back in this town, it has all been so emotionally loaded, so dense, she hasn't taken a moment to wonder what Yozo's life is like, and now, as he quietly shows some of it, the professional part, to her, it is nothing that she would have expected. He told her, when they first picked her up, that he was rich, but Willie made light of his boast, and Gia made fun of it, and now she knows that he was telling her a fact. He is rich. Very, very rich. And very, very happy about it.

First they drive around town and he shows her the different rental properties he owns. There are more, but he gets restless, and Gia's questions about the people she remembers, the ones who are all gone away now, make him uneasy. In spite of his success, Yozo doesn't like to be reminded that everyone left while he came back. "I'm a big fish in a shitty creek," he tells her.

"I think making it is making it, no matter where," she counters.

"It's easy to make it here."

"No, not in a place this depressed, not like you've done it. It's harder. How did you do all this, Yoz?"

"I got drafted. In 1964, a year after we graduated high school. It was before Vietnam, so that wasn't any concern, but they sent me to, Jesus Christ, Korea, Pusan, right outside. Fuck, it was cold, Christine had had Joey, and I didn't even find out about it for a week after he was born; that's how primitive communications were then. Found some amazing women there, though. They did things I haven't seen since. Anyway, remember Charlie Vinsko, our economics teacher our senior year? He had said to me, wise up, kid, and stop being such an asshole. You're a smart kid, but if you don't quit fucking around, you're gonna spend your life digging a ditch. So, there I am, in 1965, winter in Korea, freezing my nuts off, and what am I doing? I'm digging a ditch.

"Sonofabitch, I say, Mr. Vinsko was right. So I came back to the States, reenlisted when they promised they'd give me some training, learned how to fix cars, some helicopters, too, although when the Army offered me the chance to learn more about chopper repair in Southeast Asia, I declined and left the service. Came back here from Texas, where I was stationed, and you can't believe the screeching my wife made about coming back—she only screamed for about a year. That's part of the reason

why we only had the one kid. Anyway, I got a job
fixing cars with Connie Lukasik, remember him, the
one they used to call Deadman? Even pronounced
his name "Lookasick." He took me on, we moved
in with Christine's mother, that was a trip, and I was
with him for about three years when he had a
stroke, and his wife offered me the business.

"I went up to the Merchants' Bank, borrowed
twenty thousand dollars, which looked like the
biggest fucking amount of money in history, I nearly
peed myself, but remember Zoo Smetana, he was a
year behind us, he was the manager of the basketball team? Well, he was the loan officer of the bank,
and he gave me the money just like that. Christine
screamed for another year, and her mother died.
Zoo died not long after that, he got some kind of
weird leukemia, took him away in just a couple of
weeks. I was one of his pallbearers.

"So, Christine inherited the house, along with her
sister, whose marriage had broken up, so she moved
back in with her two kids, and that was a pretty
good incentive for me to stay at work even longer.
Chris was happy, she had someone to scream with,
and pretty soon I was back at the bank, borrowing
to build a new garage, and then I expanded it, and
hooked up with the Vo-Tech program at the local
high school. You can't believe the tax credits I get
for taking these kids on, and they do really good
work. A lot of them come to work for me after they
graduate, and I help them buy their tools from the
Snap-On guy, and it's all worked out pretty much
like that.

"What I didn't realize was that there are people in this area who had been waiting for someone to open a place that promised good service, loaners, rides, pickups, whatever. Along with doughnuts, cable in the waiting room, and a phone where they all come to make their long-distance calls, even when they're not having their cars worked on, although those calls aren't very long, they're afraid of getting caught. It costs me about three hundred bucks a month in long-distance charges, but I write it off to good community relations. I started advertising on the local radio shows, and got busy with the American Legion and the VFW and the Kiwanis and the Elks and all that other stuff, and after the first few years it just took off. Now we've got a reputation, we get the cars fixed on the first try, I pay my men top dollar, and everyone in the county knows that I'll refund your money if you think you got a bad deal. You know how many refunds I've made in twenty years? One. And he was a psycho, it was worth the money just to get him out of the store.

"So, while all this is going on, Chris is getting tired of screaming, and the kid has grown up—I think he started going out at night when he was about five—and she wants to give the house to her sister, who's getting married again, this time to Blackie Starzinsky, remember him? The one with the really good job collecting tickets at the Capitol movie theater, the one that's not there anymore? So, my wife wants to buy a house. I bought her a house on Jardin Street, do you remember Jardin Street?"

"We're on Jardin Street." She looks out the Rover's windows. "My piano teacher was in that house. Esther Marasco. Is she still alive?"

"Naw, she died a long time ago. Jesus, Gia, she was an old lady when we were kids. This was the street where all the rich people lived, the doctors, the dentists, the old Irish politicians. I bought this house, and she stopped screaming. For a while, anyway."

This was the fanciest street in their town. Old oak trees lined the wide sidewalks. The houses would now be called town houses, with hulking stone porches and steps and walkways. They were magnificent inside. Soaring, elaborately carved, fourteen-foot ceilings, huge rooms, leaded windows of beveled glass, three and four stories, set far back from the sidewalk, and so well built that sound never moved horizontally from one home to the next. There were huge backyards, too. Gia and Barbara and Yozo used to run through the alley behind those yards and look in at the rich people. Gia's family wasn't poor, they were quite comfortable, but they were Italian, and they lived in a different part of town.

"You made it to Jardin Street." She smiles. "You made it, Yozo."

"We closed on this house on my thirty-third birthday," he tells her. "And then I got in bed and couldn't think of a reason to get up. Stayed there for about six months. Scared the living fuck out of my wife. Myself, too. She finally brought a doctor to see me, a shrink from Philadelphia. Pretty nice guy, we got along. The second time he came he brought beer, and the third time we went out for beer, so I guess his treatment was successful."

"You ever figure it out?"

"Sure. I knew it the first time I pulled the covers over my head. I had scared myself. I had done even better than I had planned. I was shitty little Yozo, the kid whose old man died in the mines, the kid whose mother ran a sewing machine in the dress factory. You know, she used to run needles from that machine through her finger, through her nail, but she went to work every time there was work, and she stood in line at the unemployment office to sign up when there wasn't any. God, she worked hard, and she never lived long enough to see what I did.

"So, there I was, thirty-three years old with a wife and kid who was almost a teenager, and I had my own business and I just bought one of the biggest old houses on Jardin Street. Wouldn't you be scared? I had everything, and that meant that all I could do was lose it. The shrink told me I might think about doing other things, let the garage run itself, take on new challenges, and I thought it over and decided to go to college.

"I enrolled at the Penn State extension here, and spent a couple of years there, and then went up to the University Park campus and finished up in a little over a year. I came home on weekends, but nobody noticed, and got a degree in business administration."

"You son of a bitch, you're a college graduate!"

"Yeah." For the first time in this narrative he looks very pleased with himself.

"Well, then, I have to give you a gift."

"You're gonna show them to me, aren't you?"

"You have a way of spoiling the nicest moments."

"If you showed them to me, that would be a very nice moment, I promise you."

"I was thinking more along the lines of a Cross pen."

"Yeah," he laughs, "you can get me a Cross pen."

They are still parked in front of the Jardin Street house. "You grew up to be a very interesting man."

He lifts his baseball cap and runs his hand over his skull. "Lost my hair, though."

"You want to know something, Yozo? Your hair, when you were a kid, was so fine and blonde, you looked bald. It's not really that much of a difference, the way you are now. Also, bald men are very attractive. Sean Connery. I rest my case."

He looks at her for a long time. The sun is going down, and she is getting chilled. "You don't know what to do here, do you?" he asks.

"I'm a stranger. I don't live here anymore. I don't belong here, especially in Tony's house. I don't know anything. Back in San Francisco I have it all in order, things go pretty much the way I make them. Sometimes I have to bend stuff, but mostly they fall in place. Here, it's all different. I feel like a cork on the ocean—only the ocean isn't salt water, it's hydrochloric acid."

"What happened to your husband, the one who died?"

"He was shot." It's the short answer, so she gives him the longer one. "It was an accident, and he got shot."

"How old were you when it happened?"

"Thirty-five. Nineteen eighty-one. I turned thirty-six not long after his funeral."

"And the kids?"

"They were young. It was hard on them. Their mother had died right after the girl was born, so they really needed their dad. One of the first things I did after he died was to adopt them. They needed a mom, and I needed them. We moved to Los Angeles, I quit work, and that was in the days when the beaches weren't polluted, so we spent a lot of time in the sun, mostly because the shadows were so scary. Sometimes we went to a shrink, sometimes we didn't, and after a few years we moved back to San Francisco. This time I bought a house in the city. Before we had lived in Marin county, but they had become city kids in Los Angeles, and it was time to turn them loose. They thrived. I went back to my law firm, and the kids grew up."

"What was his name?"

"John."

"He was the love of your life." It is not a question.

She thinks about it. "It's been such a long time, Yozo. Sometimes days go by and I don't even think of him, and when I realize that I haven't thought of him, I feel ashamed of myself. But it's true what they say, time takes care of it."

"It doesn't heal, though, does it?"

"No. It's like how it must be not having a right hand. It's a drag, but you get by, and I guess you don't notice a lot of the time that you don't have a right hand."

"What kind of shooting was it?" Only someone who feels very close to her, someone like this man she's sitting with, would ask her this question.

She looks straight ahead.

"You don't want to tell me?"

She is silent because she doesn't know what to do. There are not many people in her world today who would be this direct with her.

"Okay, I'm sorry." Yozo starts the car. "I guess I overstepped. You mad at me?"

"No. No."

"You know what we need? We need to sit in a Jacuzzi, take a sauna, drink some nice wine, and talk to each other, just talk about whatever comes into our heads. Let's go do that, all right?"

"Where?"

"There's a place. I'll show you."

Father Cunningham sits in the confessional, watching what little light seeps through the wooden slats grow faint. He listens for the sounds of people still saying their penances, and thinks about what he saw today. When I'm old and sick, he wonders, who will be there to take care of me? A bunch of young priests? Not bloody likely, he decides. Not the way it's going today. Maybe some nuns. Maybe no one.

Where would I want to go if I were dying? Tony knew that he wanted to be in his garden, to drink wine, to touch the earth one last time. It was a sacred afternoon, Willie knows, and he is grateful that he was blessed to participate. He whispers a quick prayer for Tony, that his suffering should not be great, that it should not be long, and then, surprising even himself, he says another prayer, slowly this time, and he prays: Dear Father in Heaven above all, keep us safe from one another. Let us remember that once we loved each other. Let us love each other again.

He came back here, to this town, because it was finally safe. After all those years in the Vatican, all those years watching people pass by, husbands and wives, lovers, families, all those years out in the world he knew he could never join, he came back to his hometown when a parish opened up—her old church, for God's sake—because he knew he could hide here. His mother and father had died long ago, there was no family left. He had sold their house, and the furnishings had been given away to the poor. He had kept some small items, a chair in which his father had always sat to read the evening paper, his mother's needlework, and that picture of him and Gia at their prom, the one that had sat on his mother's piano until the day she died. The chair is in his bedroom now, he had some of the needlework framed, and it hangs throughout the rectory, and Gia's photograph is hidden away in a drawer with his socks and shorts.

There have been women who came close to him throughout his life, women, he knew, who were attracted to him, and he felt the stirrings, but he always turned them away, never letting them know that he was even aware of their seductions. Amazing the number of women who find priests so challenging and desirable, he recalls. Perhaps, he thinks now, if he had gone with one of them, perhaps it wouldn't be so complicated now. Perhaps if he had had someone in his life, he would not want her so much now.

Perhaps, he thinks, God is no longer enough. The thought fills him with terror. He is no longer of the world, he knows, and the idea of forsaking his identity, his very being, leaves him chilled. Her return has brought into sharp focus something he has been able to push away. The question hangs there now, though, as a sinner recites his transgressions on the other side of the thatched screen: Do you believe, William? Do you believe, or are you willing to forsake it all for a woman who just appeared and who will just as easily disappear? What will she leave you, William? If not your Church, what will you have when she leaves? And she will leave, of that you must have no doubt. She will leave you again.

But Father Cunningham is only a man, as he would be the first to tell you, and he throws a postscript onto his prayer for himself and his old friends: Let her remember that she once loved me, and let her love me again. Please, God.

He was right about the swim, although when he offered it, if Gia had given it a second thought, she would have guessed that health spas, workout palaces, Gold's Gym, had made it into the mountain areas of eastern Pennsylvania.

Well, they might have, but that is of no import to Yozo. He has built his own retreat, and that is where they are, where she has just spent she doesn't know how long swimming facedown against a current machine, the one he has installed in his one-lane pool behind his business, the hideaway with the skylights, the electronic everything, the basketball half-court for his mechanics to work off their aggressions, the most luxurious car-repair shop she's ever seen. Yozo has made his employees a part of his natural family, and, judging from the photographs in his office, they have taken him into theirs, too. He's holding babies, he has his arms around young women with lots of hair, he is at picnics, poolsides, Christmas parties.

He pulls a plain black tank suit from a locker, gives it to her, tags still attached. "I always have hope," he tells her, grinning, handing it over. "It should fit. You can adjust the pressure." He shows her the control panel for the exercise pool. "You can set it for how long you want to swim here. I'll just set it for an hour. It'll turn itself off, but if you want to quit before then, you can just leave it running. I'll be in my office, you can call me on that intercom over there if you want company. Otherwise, you know where the sauna is, there's the fridge, there's the microwave, here are the robes and towels, you do whatever you have to do." Then he kisses her cheek, turns away, turns back, pulls her into a long, hard embrace, and leaves.

At first the swimming is hard, and after a couple of minutes she's thinking about getting out, getting a beer and going right into the sauna, which Yozo has fired up, but something happens, and soon it's not as hard. In fact, it's easy, and her stroke is even—this gizmo is great because she doesn't have to think about hitting walls, turning, other swimmers, anything. It's Gia and the water, and then it's Gia and someone else, and she swims furiously, crying, crying, crying where no one can see her, sobbing where no one can hear her, grieving for what is to come, for the loss she's about to endure. She is, she understands, feeling very sorry for herself, and she makes a vow in the churning, noisy water that this is the one time she will do this. After this there will be no more self-pity. After this it will all be outside her.

Before she's ready to quit, just when she's finished crying, just when the motion and strain are starting to feel good, the water stops. Someone has turned off the machine. Gia stands in the waist-deep pool and pulls off her goggles. Yozo is kneeling at poolside.

"Barbara's in the emergency room. Willie's with her. She's been hurt. Come on." He holds his hand out to Gia. She takes it, and he pulls her up.

Willie is dressed in civvies, a navy blue polo shirt, jeans, sneakers. He is waiting for them in the entrance when Yozo pulls up and parks in the no-parking lane. "She's not in any danger," he says, "but she's suffered a concussion, and they're going to keep her for observation."

"What happened?" Yozo goes past Gia as she questions Willie, and he goes down the hallway, looking for a doctor, or for Barbara.

"She fell. No one was home, she drove herself here. They found a broken rib and a bruised kidney. She cracked her head pretty good, too; that's where the concussion comes in. She's got a sprained wrist. She slipped on the stairs going down to the family room.

"I called the house. Only her younger son was home, he got home after she went to the hospital, so I sent a guy to take him over to the grandfather's house. Eddie, that's her husband, he's at work. You want to see her?"

"He hit her," Gia says.

Willie stops, holding the entrance door half open. "It's not the first time she's been hurt, Gia. Before you flip out, just remember, right now all Barbara needs is her friends, all right? Just like she was with you this afternoon, you must be with her right now. If you can't do that, I think it would be better if you waited out here."

"She's been getting beat up and you've known about it and nothing's been done. I'm gonna kill that sonofabitch." She starts to enter the hospital, but he stops her.

"Gia, she's been hurt before, but no one knows what really happens. Right now she needs your love. Not the burden of your anger or your righteousness or your condemnation. Can you do that? Because if you can't, you'll do everyone a favor by staying in the car."

"Does Yozo know?"

"He's come here like this before, yes. So have I."

He holds the door open all the way for her, and

she entertains a brief fantasy of driving around the town, finding Barbara's husband, and, bare-fisted, beating the living shit out of him. But when Gia realizes that she's never met him, doesn't even know what he looks like, her fantasy fades, and she passes through Willie's open door, looking for her oldest best friend.

"I guess I just can't stay away from this place." Barbara smiles at them from her hospital bed. She's sitting up, in a regulation gown of some faded festive print, and she looks better than Gia expected. It's only when she coughs—the pain comes on her, her face pales, and Gia realizes that her broken rib, taped now, and her sprained wrist, thickly wrapped in an Ace bandage, are still hurting her, in spite of the painkillers she must have been given.

Gia kisses her. Her face is warm but unmarked. The cocksucker doesn't hit her where anyone can see it. She feels her own face flush, but she keeps silent. Willie's eyes are on her, she knows. "For an old cheerleader," Gia tells Barbara, "you take a fall like a *bapci*." She uses the Polish word for grandmother, the one Barbara taught her a lifetime ago, and Barbara laughs, then seizes her side.

"Don't make me laugh," she groans.

"What happened?" It seems like the most normal thing to say, she figures, and she is striving for normalcy. It is a stretch. Gia has met clients in emergency rooms, women who have been raped and beaten by the men they chose, and she has never before had to pretend. It is surprisingly easy. She loves Barbara, and she did not love her clients; it is more important that Barbara not be hurt anymore, especially by her friends. Gia is struck by the wisdom of Willie's counsel. She turns and looks at him; he's studying Barbara's chart at the foot of the bed. He glances up at Gia, winks, and goes back to the chart.

"I was doing too many things at once, and I didn't watch where I was going. I wanted to get some laundry done, and fix something for Eddie to eat, and check on the kids, it was all just too crazy, and I slipped."

"Yeah, in the old days you just would have done a 'Hit him again, harder' cheer and landed in a split." Gia realizes that her choice of old cheers is probably not the best, but it was the first that came to mind.

"A split?" Barbara shudders. "I don't even want to think about that."

"Oh, I don't know," Gia teases her, "I do some of my best work from that position."

"Hussy," she teases back.

"Ladies," Willie cautions, smiling.

"Where?" Barbara makes an attempt to look around, but her head hurts, and she moves only her eyes. They dart around the room, and her wisecrack isn't funny when Gia watches her eyes, because they are frightened eyes.

"Asshole." Yozo enters the room. "Clumsy fucking asshole." He is carrying a stuffed pig, big enough to require both his arms to hold it. "This is for you. It represents the four of us."

"Where'd you get that?" Gia asks.

"The gift shop is still open. If you're gonna be in the hospital, you might as well get a gift."

"This joins a collection," Barbara says as Yozo positions the pig on the dresser. "He brought me one every time I had a kid," she tells Gia.

"Pigs?" Gia asks.

"No, one was a walrus, one was a panda, and what was the other one?"

"I don't remember," Yozo says, leaning against the dresser.

Willie replaces the chart, and goes to the other side of Barbara's bed. "What do you need us to do, Barbara?"

"Oh, nothing. You don't even have to be here. I panicked, Willie, I'm sorry. I didn't, when they asked me, I couldn't think of who to call. I didn't want to call my dad, he couldn't take the excitement, and they wanted to call someone."

"No, don't think about it. You should," he stutters, and Gia thinks she sees the first crack in the priestly veneer, "you should always know that I'll come to you when this happens. I'll always come to you."

And once again his smoothness trips up Gia. He's just told Barbara, in his own code, that he understands her secret.

Barbara gives away nothing. "I did all this with carpeted stairs, can you imagine?"

"You might want to get the walls carpeted," Yozo says dryly. "For the next time."

They are both letting her know that they know,

but Barbara gives no sign that she has received their messages. "God, I need a cigarette."

"It's a hospital," Gia says. "You can't smoke in here."

"Just open that window, and help me get over there," she directs Gia. "You two, turn your heads," she tells the men.

When she's seated beside the open window, Gia gives her the cigarettes and lighter she's dug out of Barbara's purse, crushed down in the nightstand drawer. She doesn't inhale as deeply as before. The rib is giving her trouble. "Is that broken rib anywhere near a lung?" Gia asks her.

"It's only cracked," she says. "It's no big deal."

Gia looks out at the darkness. Here she is, back in the hospital where they all began life, where her godfather lies dying a floor above them, beside her oldest best girlfriend whose husband has just beaten her, and the two women are being watched from the other side of the room by the two men who, perhaps, love these women better than anyone has ever loved them in their lives.

They are all silent, watching Barbara smoke, watching the night, and Gia puts her hand lightly on Barbara's shoulder. She doesn't look up, but she puts her hand over Gia's, and then Gia feels Willie's hand on her left shoulder, Yozo's hand on her right, and Willie is cupping Barbara's face in a gentle embrace while silent tears run out of her eyes, and they stand there, the four of them, watching the night.

• • •

With the keys to Yozo's Range Rover rattling in her pocket, and the directions to Barbara's house fixed in her head, she takes the fire stairs two at a time to the third floor, to see how her godfather is getting through the night, after this exhausting day. Gia finds his room darkened, but he is awake.

She thinks he is running a fever, but it is hard to tell.

"You're a bad girl," he whispers. "Everybody is mad at you for taking me out today."

"Everybody's always mad at me." She sits carefully beside him on the bed. "They're mad at you, too. Did you like it, did you like today?"

He dips his chin in a tiny nod. "I can die now."

"No, no, no, that's not why we did it."

"Yes." He looks directly at her. Even in this darkened room, with only the faint light from the hallway falling into the partially closed door, she can see his eyes. "Yes, Gianna, that's why we did it. You knew that."

Yes, she did. But she hadn't planned on hearing it said out loud. Ah, Tony, you never left anything to doubt, she thinks. I have learned so well from you. Tonight I understand better than I ever have before that I am your legacy. My deeds in this world are what you will leave behind.

Finally, when she can trust her voice, she softly answers. "I did. I know. How do you feel?"

"It doesn't hurt, but I'm tired." This is the first time she's heard him say that, and something has gone out of his voice. It is an old man's voice now, and she closes her eyes against the darkness, not the room's darkness but the one that is soon to come. "I'm tired, Gianna."

"Do you want me to stay with you tonight?" Barbara's beating suddenly seems so unimportant. Shit, she's been getting whacked all these years, what's one more night?

"I'm not gonna die tonight," he tells her. "You come back tomorrow night."

"You sure?"

"No." She hears the shrug in his voice. "I guess I could die tonight, but it doesn't seem like I will."

She can't resist. "How can you tell?"

"Because I always knew that when I was gonna die, I'd dream about Grandpop and your father. I've been dreaming about Grandmom but not about them. I think they're the ones who are gonna come for me, so maybe I'll dream about them tonight. But I don't think so."

"Then I'll go."

"You going home now?"

"First, I have to go somewhere and beat the shit out of a guy. Barbara's husband hit her. He's been hitting her for a long time."

"Oh, that's no good. You use something. Take a baseball bat. He won't be able to get close to you if you keep swinging it. And don't get caught."

She bends to kiss him good night, and she is filled to bursting with how much she loves him, how much he has given her, how strong his spirit is, how much she still wants to be like him. She is not ready to say good-bye to her godfather, but for the first time in her life, she realizes that they both have read-

ied the way, that nothing is left unsaid, that he has
been perfect in her life, that she has indeed become
the woman he wanted her to be, and that, perhaps
more than savoring her own successes, that thought
gives her peace and pleasure in a place within that
belongs only to her and to the old man she loves.

The priest Ford is parked behind a hedge and some
big plastic trash cans a few houses up and across
the street from Barbara and Eddie Eckroat's house
on the east edge of town. The two grown men
crouching down between the hedge and the car are
watching the woman knock at the Eckroats' front
door, ring the bell more than once, knock again,
then pound with her left fist on the door. Nothing
inside the house changes, no lights go on, nothing.
She looks at her watch and crosses the dried-out
lawn, the spotty driveway, the next-door neighbor's lawn, and, stepping up to that front door,
rings the bell, this time like a normal person.
    Rosemary Dunzilla, Barbara's neighbor for more
than twenty years, answers the door in a burgundy
velour robe with a narrow pink stripe down the
middle. The optical illusion does nothing to dimin-
ish her massive size. She was a year behind Gia and
Barbara in school. The two hiding men watch the
women converse, Gia offering her hand, Rosemary
tentatively accepting it, and then, as Gia gestures at
Barbara's house, Rosemary grows more animated,
pointing behind her, into her house, nodding her
head, and then, stepping out onto the brick and concrete stoop which is identical to the one on the

house next door, except Rosemary's isn't crumbling, she points at the rear of her house, and Gia nods, apparently understanding. They shake hands again, Rosemary says something and points again inside her house, Gia shakes her head in a smiling refusal, and Rosemary closes the door to her visitor with a smile and a wave. Gia stands facing the Eckroats' house for a second, and then scrambles down the steps and disappears into the darkness between the two houses.

"She's gonna try to get into the house through the back, from the deck," Yozo tells Willie.

"He's at work, it's after midnight," he answers. "The boys are with her father." The two men had called before leaving the hospital to make sure that Barbara's older son, Greg, had joined the fourteen-year-old Jamie at their grandfather's house for the night while their mother recovered and their father worked the third shift at the plastics plant. Neither of the men had thought to call Eddie.

"She doesn't know where the plant is," Yozo says. "She didn't ask, she doesn't know his hours. She'd go there if she knew."

"Yeah, wait, what's she got?"

"A broom? Maybe she'll just fly away?" Yozo hopes. They are both whispering.

"It's a bat, is it a bat? What's she gonna do with a, oh, don't tell me she's gonna beat down the door, oh, Christ!" Willie laments.

"He doesn't have a lock on that garage door," Yozo observes as Gia easily lifts the white overhead door, the only one on the block with peeling paint.

She disappears inside the garage which holds Eddie Eckroat's prized 1955 Packard Clipper, a shiny black one, the one he has lovingly restored and maintained for the past twenty-one years, after he found it down at Connie Lukasik's garage, abandoned by its owner, an old Italian gentleman who had run a fireworks business but who was retiring and moving to Naples, Florida, where his son lived, and which the old Italian gentleman would soon learn bore no resemblance to the one in the Old Country.

Yozo and Willie look at each other, their gazes locking even in the darkness. "Oh, no," Yozo whispers just as the first crashing sound of breaking glass and twisting metal shatters the black night. There is another one, then another, and then the crashes are coming so fast it is not possible to differentiate one from the other.

"We ought to stop her," Willie says.

"She has a baseball bat, and she's pissed. You want to go in there?"

"What's she gonna do next?" Willie asks.

Yozo doesn't take his eyes from the garage. "She'll go home. It's late, she's tired, and that," he tilts his head, "that'll keep her calm until she wakes up tomorrow. Then she's gonna start all over again."

"I have three Masses tomorrow. I can't get away until noon."

"Yeah, well," Yozo goes around to the passenger side of the priest Ford and opens the door, "say them all for Eddie Eckroat, because she's gonna go looking for him tomorrow, and I think she's gonna find him. Come on. We're going to the plastics plant."

She gets back into Yozo's car and hunches behind the steering wheel, her arms across her chest, her throbbing hands squeezed in her armpits. "Fuck, fuck, fuck, fuck." She never dreamed that killing a car would be so painful. The sharp stabs pulse up her forearms, into her biceps and shoulders and neck. It seems as though her head is still vibrating with each hit she put on that Packard.

It felt great.

She thinks about how much better it would have been, albeit with far more serious legal conse-quences, if she had been able to do it to Eddie Eckroat, that weasel prick.

A light in the rearview mirror catches her eye. The taillights of the priest Ford betray Willie and Yozo making their getaway. She watches as the car rolls down the hill behind her, away from Barbara's house. Punks are afraid to turn their lights on, she thinks, but Willie couldn't keep his foot off the brake. Squid.

Then another thought seizes her.

Throbbing hands and all, she manages to turn on the ignition, to make a hard U-turn on the once again silent, sleeping street, and, without headlights, to follow the priest Ford.

They're going to him, she wagers, and so am I. She glances, and then smiles, at the baseball bat leaning on the passenger's seat. She makes a left turn, the bat rolls toward her, and she puts a hand on its narrow neck to steady it. Then she runs her hand affectionately along the grain, stroking it, patting it. It is now her best friend.

Didn't this used to be a baseball field? Gia wonders as the Range Rover slithers down the last lane of the parking lot at Zagon Plastics. Yozo and Willie have parked in front, and she has circled around to the back, and then up along the north side of the big cement-block building, just to the turn, from which she can see them ringing the night bell, but they can't see her, hidden as the Rover is by other parked cars and trucks.

They have no idea she's followed them to what must be Eddie Eckroat's workplace. The door opens, and the two men stand talking, and then she can see a man's arm opening the door wider, Willie smiles at the arm's owner, and they disappear inside. For the first time she wonders what she should do next. She doesn't know Eckroat, couldn't pick him out of a lineup, and now, with the warning that he's about to get, he'll probably be on the lookout for her. And, Gia hates this, he'll know exactly who to look for.

Punks. They're warning a wife beater. They should be beating the living fuck out of him. She eyes the baseball bat again but doesn't touch it. She pulls on the parking brake, but leaves the motor running and opens the driver's-side window.

"She's what?" Eddie Eckroat shouts. Yozo looks steadily at him as Willie recites Barbara's injuries to

Eddie, who is a tall, solidly built man with a face that was probably very handsome in youth but who spent too much time in the sun, or perhaps squinting through the cigarette smoke that has always blanketed his home with Barbara, and now he is weathered beyond his fifty-four years. He is a man who has gone to work every day of his adult life, including his four years with the army, and who has always done as he was told. His children are strangers, as well as a mystery, to him, and his wife, who, he will tell you honestly, he once loved, has slipped away from him over the years, lost in an alcoholic fog and, during the times when she wasn't drunk, acting as though nothing was wrong. Eddie has often thought about going to AA or Al-Anon or one of those places, but he has never found the time, and when he might have gone, he's been too tired. That might be what it will say on Eddie Eckroat's tombstone: He was tired.

"You think I did it, don't you?" Eddie smirks, and at that moment Yozo understands Gia's desire to smash the shit out of the guy. "Man, if you thought I did it, why didn't you send the cops? I've been here since before three o'clock. I'm double-shifting this weekend. I'm going hunting up in New York next week, so I'm working a double shift. Double time on Saturdays. I get four days' pay for two shifts here today. So, it wasn't me. I was here. You can ask all these guys." He gestures at the three-story assembly line that turns out hangers, shoe boxes, trash containers, and all those things that will be here thousands of years after man has ceased to inhabit the earth. Eddie Eckroat will leave his legacy, but it won't be through the children he has sired; it will be a pink plastic coat hanger.

"You didn't go home at all?" Yozo inquires.

"No, Columbo, I've been here. So Barbara banged herself up again. Well, guess what? She's a drunk. She gets drunk, she falls over. Do you know how many times I've had to pick her up and put her to bed before the kids found her, huh? And now the kids find her. They step over her, that's what they do. Nice way to grow up, huh? You care so much about your old friend, where have you been all these years? How would you like to watch her trying to fix dinner for three little kids while she's smashed, and she's trying to cut up an onion, and she cuts herself, and then starts waving the bloody knife around. That's what the kids got from their mother. So, no, I didn't hit her. She fucking beats herself up."

"Why do you stay?" Yozo asks.

"What the fuck is it to you? I don't even know you. And if I did, I wouldn't tell you anyway. It's my life, she's my wife, I'll go to her now, so just get the fuck out of our business."

"She needs help, Ed," Willie softly says.

"Everybody needs help, Father. You're so devoted to her, how come you haven't done anything? You don't know anything. You know dick. You think you know. You know shit." Eddie Eckroat pulls off his long rubber gloves, his blue apron, his paper cap, and stuffs everything into a plastic hamper. "You know shit," he says again as he departs.

Yozo and Willie silently watch him leave. "He has a point," Willie says.

"Maybe. But he has her outside waiting for him, and he has a Packard in his garage, and you know what? Now I'm glad she did it."

"It's a bloody night, Joe," Willie says. "A bad, bloody night."

"They all are, Willie. You've just been sleeping through them."

Eddie Eckroat gets into his pickup truck and drives out of the parking lot, unaware that the woman who has been waiting for him has fallen asleep behind the wheel of a car she borrowed from a friend earlier that night, when her anger gave her strength, when the sky was still dark, when everything, as awful as it was, seemed so much simpler.

"She's asleep." Yozo stands on tiptoe and sees Gia slumped over the wheel. "Or she's dead. I can't tell from here."

"Whatever," Willie answers. "We're delivered. Come on. I'll take you home."

"You think we ought to wake her up?"

Willie looks at Yozo for a long time, and then the two men get into the priest Ford, and they drive away, not afraid this time to turn on the ignition and the lights.

So much hair. He has so much hair, thick, curly black hair, just like mine used to be. My little brother, my *fratello*, Gianni, looks so young. Your daughter, he tries to tell the young man, but there are no words coming out, your daughter is older than you are now.

Then, just as silently as his brother appeared in the dream, he fades, and Tony Scarpino sleeps on, drugged and dying. When he awakens, and he will awaken again, he will not remember seeing his only brother for the first time in more than fifty years, but he will instead be left with the calm certainty that death will come to him as a friend, and that new knowledge will leave him feeling what others might call peace as he prepares for his last, longest journey.

THIRD DAY

She's too old to stay out all night, she sees that pronouncement in her aunt Rosa's face just as the old woman's lips touch Gia's cheek. "You want some coffee, honey?" she asks, as if every fifty-something niece of hers showed up in rumpled clothes, with a wrinkled face. The imprint of the Range Rover's steering wheel is still on Gia's face, no matter how hard she rubbed it when she woke up in the plastic plant's parking lot well after sunrise.

"Coffee, yeah," she answers. The four women sitting at the kitchen table all resemble Gia to some extent—the youngest one could be her clone, young Mia—and when the middle-aged one rises, smiling too broadly, and lifts her arms to Gia, she recognizes her dreaded cousin Tessa, Mia's mother. Mella, Tessa's mother, is seated on the other side of the table, dunking chunks of plain Italian bread into a large cup of black coffee.

"We've been waiting for you," Tessa greets her, wrapping Gia in her embrace. Gia does not even hug her back, her nose buried in Tessa's armpit.

"Yeah, well, you go out with a priest, you never know what's gonna happen." She winks at Mia, who grins and gets up, offering Gia her chair. "Thanks, Mia. Nice kid you got here. What the hell happened to your face?" she asks her cousin.

"What? Nothing." Tessa has an odd, wide-eyed look. Gia, who has lived in California for most of her adult life, thinks, Botox, face-lift, collagen lips.

"You look good," Gia says.

"You look like hell," Tessa answers.

"Ah," Gia sips the hot black coffee Rosa has set

before her, "I had forgotten what a charmer you are."

"We've been waiting for you."

"Why?"

"I think we ought to go start making funeral arrangements," Tessa announces. Mella still doesn't look up. Gia is looking from one to the other. This isn't how it's supposed to be, she thinks. Mella quiet?

"Who died?" Gia asks, and feels Mia's finger poking her from behind, where the young woman sits on a stool.

"Don't be cute. We have to do this."

"I can't help being cute, Tess, but what's the hurry? I think maybe Francie and the boys might want to take care of that. When the time comes." She emphasizes the last sentence.

"We can save them the trouble."

It's not yet eight A.M., and Gia notices that her cousin is wearing full and heavy makeup, is perfectly put together in what she knows is a St. John's suit, with a full set of false nails and a suspiciously curvy chest. Not a gray hair on her auburn head, which is, of course, perfectly and fashionably cut, albeit for a woman twenty-five years younger.

"You're efficient, huh?" Gia asks, smiling in spite of herself at her old jeans, cowboy boots, cable-knit sweater, and tousled, graying hair.

"It's gonna have to be done," Tessa observes. Even her voice sounds fake, Gia thinks. High-pitched, with just an edge of desperation in it.

"You ought to talk to Francie," Gia says. "He's her husband. How's your husband, Tess?"

"He's fine," she says. "He's working, he couldn't come." Mia pokes Gia again. Tessa married a quiet man, an Italian carpenter who earned a very good living, but who, from their first days of marriage, had avoided Scarpino family gatherings.

Gia is still waiting for Mella to say something, maybe something nasty, to her or to Tessa, or just to the kitchen in general. But the old woman doesn't look up.

"Keep eating that bread, Ma," Tessa says to Mella. "Get even fatter, why don't you? That'll be good for your blood pressure."

My God, Gia thinks. There is justice, after all. Or maybe just balance in the universe. Mella's daughter is worse than Mella ever was.

Suddenly, she's not as tired, her head doesn't hurt as much as it did when she first walked into this house, and everything seems just a little brighter.

And then Gia says something she never, never in her most bizarre daydreams thought she would ever say: "Back off, Tess. Leave your mother alone. That's rude. We don't need any meanness in this house. Not now, not with what we're facing."

"She has high blood pressure," Tessa starts.

"I don't give a shit if she's sprouting wings," Gia interrupts her. "Behave."

Mella's head comes up, and she looks at her niece. Her eyes are almost soft and loving, Gia thinks. "It's only bread," she says.

"The staff of life," Gia says.

"Fine. Dig your grave with your mouth," Tessa says, a little too loudly for Gia's liking.

Gia stands and bends over her older cousin, their noses almost touching. Tessa, to her credit, Gia notes, does not lean away. "Back off," Gia hisses. "I'm sure your daughter would love to hear the story of you and me in the garage, you pervert. Just shut up." She sits back down, a little dizzy. "You owe your mom an apology," Gia continues.

Tessa looks at her, a fine flush covering her smooth features.

Gia nods. "Go ahead."

"I guess I'm a little tense, with Tony so sick," Tessa begins.

"I didn't ask you for an emotional update," Gia says. She tilts her head at Mella. "Apologize."

"I'm sorry for snapping at you, Mom," Tessa mutters, her head turned stiffly away from Gia.

"That was nice," Gia observes. And then she does something she doesn't ever recall doing before. Her aunt glances at her, and Gia winks and smiles. Mella smiles back, and Gia now sees the tired old lady who will soon, Gia suspects, follow her beloved son and husband. She's an old lady who won't live long, she thinks, once her brother dies.

"Was that hard?" Gia asks Tessa.

Tessa says nothing.

"I liked it. If I were, say, a bully, I'd make you apologize again, but I'm really nice, so I'm just gonna let it go. Did I tell you that I grew up to be a really nice person?"

"Jesus Christ," Mella says, and Gia relaxes, knowing that things are normal again.

"I gotta shower." Gia rises. "It's been lovely."

"Father Cunningham called here for you a little while ago," Rosa chirps from the other end of the kitchen. "He said for you to come by the rectory, that if the police showed up, just to tell them that it was all a mistake."

"Police?" Mia asks.

"Ah, you know how nuts these priests are when you take them out on an all-nighter," Gia says as she heads off to her room.

"Can I come with you?" Mia calls, and just as Gia is about to say yes, her mother snaps, "You're staying here."

Gia stops, turns around, and asks the young woman, "You want to have dinner with me and my friends tonight?"

The kid doesn't even look at her mother, which cheers Gia, when she says, "I'd love that."

"Fine," Gia answers. "You stay with your mom and your grandmom today. We'll go out tonight, all right?"

She sees Tessa's shoulders stiffening, but she says not a word. Not a word. Gia cannot believe that the demons of her childhood have been vanquished so easily.

They were bullies then, she thinks, and they're bullies now. They just never bet on that little kid growing up.

"So, what are you gonna do?" Mella asks her daughter.

"You wanna go up the mall?" Tessa answers, and Gia walks out of the kitchen, invisible again, as she was when she was just a little girl, surrounded by these bullies, but now she has extended a momentary hand to her most loathed aunt, and she has seen the old woman look at her with gratitude in her eyes.

There's something to be said for this growing-up business, Gia thinks, but then her aching arms and Willie's cryptic message about the police remind her of what she did last night, and she remembers that she has not grown up all that much. Not in this town, at least.

Gia stands at the foot of what used to be the longest, steepest steps in the world. They are small steps, sloping easily up to the church's entrance, and they are not dangerous, not at all as she has carried them in her mind these many years.

It all comes back to her: they used to line us up there, at the left, along the wide concrete balustrade worn paintless and smooth by the tiny hands that gripped it as the nuns marched their helpless little charges into Our Lady of Mercy Church, up the aisle, to the front rows, right before the altar, where they taught her from that dreaded dark blue book, the Baltimore Catechism.

"Who made you?" was the first question that was to be memorized, then answered by the second line:

"God made us."

"Why did God make you?"

And there her memory fails. She never got beyond that third line simply because the second one was a much greater leap of faith than she was able to make, even at the tender age of six.

She also never learned to say the rosary, and she honestly believes that she was absent from school the day they taught it. She wonders if Willie could show her, and then she has a sudden, clear vision of the rosary going up in smoke and flames. Since she's come this far without knowing, she quits the vision.

This is the church where her mother's and father's funerals took place. This is where she was christened, where Tony and Maria, her long-dead aunt, held her over the baptismal font and promised to take care of her. They were just kids then, and they made that promise, that huge promise. Could they have imagined what was going to happen? The baby's father was already dead—they named her after him—and her mother had only a dozen months to live.

She lowers her head and turns away, walks along the grassy path that goes to the right of the church, opening into a narrow alley, and then she turns left, following the narrow brick path to four enclosed steps leading up to the rectory, the place where Willie Cunningham now dwells as pastor of the church where Gia was baptized.

She rings the bell, and quickly, almost as soon as she removes her finger, the door opens, and Gia sees the woman who was Father Pietro's housekeeper when she was a child. Mrs. Miller, who was an old lady then, a very nice one, is still an old lady, except that she hasn't changed one bit, with not even a stoop, another wrinkle, a clouding of her friendly blue eyes, or a yellowing of her white, carefully permed hair.

"Mrs. Miller?" Gia asks, her voice soft, as if to speak loudly would cause this old lady to dry up and fly away.

The housekeeper squints at the younger woman and then steps back, smiling, holding the door wide open. "Gianna Scarpino, Father said you might be by. Come in, please." She holds out her hand in a sweetly welcoming gesture.

"Mrs. Miller?"

"Oh, honey," the old lady laughs, her hand flying to her mouth, "you've been gone such a long time. I'm Julia Stabinsky. You remember me? I was Bobby's mom. Mrs. Miller was my mother."

"Bobby's mom. Oh, Lord, Mrs. Stabinsky." Gia steps across the threshold and bends to kiss her. "You look just like your mother."

"So do you." The old lady looks up at her. "You look like your father, a little bit, too. He died so young." She shakes her head. "I'm sorry about your uncle. Father said he's not doing too well."

"No, he's not."

Her shining eyes don't leave Gia's face. Gia is reluctant to break the moment, but she must. "Is Willie, Father Cunningham, around?"

"He's in the church. He has one more Mass today, at six-thirty."

"Should he not be disturbed?"

"Oh, just go ahead." She squeezes Gia's hand and leans into her arm. "He sits in the confessional booth. I think he just likes to sit there by himself."

"Maybe I shouldn't bother him."

"He told me you'd call or come by, and that you should just go in. Go on," she waves her down the steps, "make a confession. It'll be good for you." And then she lets go of Gia's hand.

Do I look like a sinner? Gia wonders as she retraces her steps back to the churchyard and Bobby's mom closes the rectory door.

After she pulls the dark wooden door shut, its fragile latch sealing her inside this womblike place, with its simple oak bench, its unadorned leather kneeler below her, the thick wooden screen shielding the penitent from the gaze of the priest who sits only inches away from her, she waits for her eyes to grow accustomed to the sudden dark, so complete, so perfect, even on this sunny October afternoon. The lessons come back to her: you are to sit here and to contemplate your sins, examine your transgressions, speak them out loud to the man on the other side of the screen, and then wait for him to tell you that you are forgiven, and to give you a penance. Father Pietro always gave the best penances in town, which was why his four P.M. Saturday confessions always had two waiting lines. Three Hail Marys, whether you had wiped out your family with a machete the previous night or simply taken the Lord's name in vain. When she was preparing for her first Holy Communion, she asked her Pop, an outspoken nonbeliever who nonetheless sent his beloved granddaughter to parochial school, what she should say for her first confession; the old man told her not to worry, it didn't matter what she said, she'd be forgiven. So, when the six-year-old granddaughter of his old friend confessed to Father Pietro that she had committed murder and adultery, the priest gave her three Hail Marys, and little Gia marveled at how much her Pop knew.

Gia wonders for a moment what kinds of penances Willie hands out. She has absolutely no idea. She doesn't know the priest. She doesn't even know the man.

She listens to his steady breathing on the other side of this black confessional, and thinks of all the other men beside whom she has lain in darkened places, listening to their breathing. She thinks that thought just might qualify as a sin.

It smells like church even in here, she notices.

"Of all the Commandments," Willie says, "how many do you think you haven't broken?"

"How'd you know it was me?"

"I saw you. This place isn't airtight, you know."

She is silent. "I never coveted my neighbor's wife," she finally answers.

"You killed?"

"Yeah. I once had to vacuum up one of my kid's pet mice. It got into the cashmere sweaters. Does that count?"

"No. Only human life counts."

"Oh. Well, two then. I've never killed anyone."

"You got all the other eight?"

"I think so. I can't remember what they are, exactly."

"How about the seven deadly sins?"

"I don't remember all those, but I'm pretty sure I've nailed all of them. Sneezy, Grumpy, Doc, Sleepy, right?"

He says nothing for a long time. She doesn't care for his silence. "Bite me, Father, I haven't sinned."

"You really are your uncle's child."

"Yeah, I really am. That's why you called the house? That's what you wanted to tell me?"

"No, I wanted to tell you that Eddie Eckroat called the cops and Yozo went down to the station to take care of it."

"How does he know it was me? Did you tell?"

"The neighbor lady told them you had been there. Apparently, you took care to introduce yourself to her."

"Well, you ring someone's doorbell in the middle of the night, the least you can do is identify yourself. Besides, we went to school with her brother-in-law."

"Jesus Christ, Gia, we went to school with fucking everybody in this town if you scratch long enough. The fact is, you wrecked Eddie's Packard, and he's pissed."

She is grinning, and it sounds in her voice as she tells him, "I can't believe how good life is these days. I just got to listen to a priest swear in the confessional. I can die happy now."

"I live to make your dreams come true, no matter how sacrilegious they might be."

"Thank you, Father. Why haven't you done something about how Barbara's husband's been whacking her around? What's the matter with you?"

"He's pressing charges against you."

"Fuck him. I'll pay him. That always shuts them up."

"You have experience in this sort of thing?"

"I'm a lawyer, Willie, remember?"

"I could scarcely forget. Do things like this happen wherever you go?"

"Do I need to remind you that I came upon this? Barbara wasn't hurt for the first time yesterday, and you and Yozo both know it. Who else knows it? Doesn't anybody in this goddamn town have any balls? Does a man get to beat up his wife without anybody saying anything? And," she hears him inhale, preparatory to saying something, and she cuts him off, "don't tell me that things are different here. Nobody knows that better than I do. Willie, what are you going to tell yourself when he kills her? How are you going to rationalize your guilt away then? You gonna preside over her funeral and say what a shame it is? Are you, huh?"

"What do you think I should have done?" His voice sounds pinched, like he really wants to shout but doesn't dare.

It was the one question she hadn't anticipated. Gia spends much of her time gearing up for argument; she is, of course, caught completely off guard when someone simply turns reasonable. She doesn't think this sort of behavior is fair, and she doesn't like it. Then she remembers that he is a Jesuit.

"What do you think you should have done? Or rather, what should you do now? It's not too late."

"The Socratic method was not lost on you, was it, Gianna?"

She shakes her head. "Dueling wits and educations, even while our old friend is getting hurt. Doesn't ego ever play second with you?"

"Or you?"

"Me? No. The world revolves around me, and what I do, and what I want. I can't function any other way. Can you? Your pious posturing, Willie, it probably works really well here, where people don't know any better, but this is me you're talking to. I know you. You've taken up a calling, but you're still you. And you're still a center-stage kind of guy. Jesuits are, in spite of all their coy protestations."

"And we are their product, you and I."

"Well, wouldn't Saint Ignatius be proud?"

"You know, I can hear everything you two are saying in there, but I'll be fucked if I can figure out what you're talking about," Yozo calls from the last pew, where he sits, arm draped across the varnished back of the seat, his baseball cap in his lap. "Gia, you owe me five grand. That's what it cost to shut Eddie Eckroat up. He's not pressing charges. And while you're in there, would you mind reciting your confession for the last thirty years, and could you speak up, please?"

She hears Willie exit his side of the confessional. Toad, she thinks, you choked. "Five thousand dollars?" she says out loud. "That much?"

"I thought it would be more like ten, but he said five. Gia, I even got him to sign a waiver. Are you proud of me? Are you proud of yourself, you slap-happy dickwad?"

"Fuck you." She decides to stay inside the confessional. She's comfortable, and she's just not ready to face the two of them.

"She's overcome with gratitude," Yozo says to Willie. Quieter, he says, "Are you all right? What's the matter?"

"She's right," Willie says. "We should have done something for Barbara. We shouldn't have let it go on this long."

Yozo scratches his chin. He hasn't shaved today, it being Sunday. "Gia, come on out." He lowers his voice again. "Did she confess anything to you before I got here?"

"You're scum, you know that?" she tells him as she opens the door.

"You heard that?"

"You raise kids, you grow bat ears. When you paid the creep off, did you say anything to him about beating his wife, or are you a gutless wonder, too?"

Yozo sighs. "We talked to him at the plastics plant last night, this morning. He was at work. He couldn't have done it. He doesn't hit her, Gia. She gets drunk and falls down. Our old pal is a drunk, all right? We've all known it, we've all seen it, and we've all stayed quiet about it because if you know anything about drunks, you know that you can't get them to do anything they don't want to do. She's been an alkie since high school, all right?"

She slides into the other end of the pew, opposite Yozo. "That's good for you, isn't it, to believe that? It's so easy, it's so neat, it's so out of your hands.

Bullshit, boys. He's using her drinking as a cover. He hits her. He hits her. You don't get hurt like that falling down a couple of carpeted steps. I've been a lawyer for a long time, and I've seen the inside of way too many emergency room cubicles, and I know what it looks like when a woman gets beat up. I saw that on Barbara the other night, and you two don't have to believe it, I'm sure you won't, and your tiny, little selfish lives can just go on after I leave, and you don't even have to think about it, much less do something about it. The guy tells you, so you believe it. Man, I wish I had had more like you on my juries. Totally unthinking toads. He hits her, and nothing you tell me is going to change my mind. Staying out of this, Willie, letting her get hurt over and over again, is that your idea of Christian charity?"

They both look at her silently for a long time. "I know she drinks. I'm sure she has for a lot of years," Gia says. "But that's not the biggest problem she has." They are all silent. She closes her eyes. We'll sit here forever, she realizes, saying nothing, because they believe the husband. "Five grand," she finally says.

"Yeah," Yozo answers.

"You understand, I'm not at all sorry about what I did."

"You seemed to really want to do it," Yozo says.

"It was a beautiful car."

"Yeah."

"Five grand."

"Yeah."

"It should have been him," she says. "So, can I get a receipt?"

"Get out of my church," Willie says, and walks toward the altar, genuflects after he closes the railing behind him, and disappears into the sacristy.

"He's mad at me," she says.

"Yeah."

"You mad at me, too? What, the sin is saying it out loud?"

"I'm not mad at you."

"So, what's his problem?"

"Did you ever have sex with him?"

"No."

"That's it."

"I just haven't had time since I got here." She is amused.

"I don't mean now."

"You mean back then?"

"Yeah."

"He's been mad for, what, thirty-five years?"

"Not mad, he just doesn't know what he missed out on. Or he does, in which case he's really mad."

"Has he ever?"

Yozo shrugs. "I don't know."

"You never asked him?"

"No."

"You have asked to see my breasts about twelve times since I got here, but in all the years you and Willie have been friends, you've never asked him if he's been with a woman?"

"Right."

"What's the difference?"

He turns and looks at her. "I really want to see your tits."

"You elude me. You really do."

"That's because I tell the truth. You're too used to looking for subtexts, hidden agendas, immoral motives. Your time in the big city has jaded you. Life here is just much simpler than you're used to."

"This is the craziest place on earth, Yozo."

"I know. It might be something in the water. Oh, yeah, that's right, did anybody tell you not to drink the water out of the tap?"

"No, what?"

"Something about contamination. Some bacteria. You can't drink it."

"This place used to be famous for its water. What happened?"

"Remember those underground mine fires out by Centralia? Remember those?"

They were scenes out of Hades. Right along the highway, smoke rose out of the ground, an underground fire burning for as long as anyone can remember, burning acres of unseen veins of anthracite. Sometimes flames made it to the surface, but usually, it was just a roadside attraction of white-hot ash, thick smoke, and a sulfurous odor that carried for miles. Summer and winter, the ground was on fire, and it was just another part of growing up.

"Yeah."

"You know they're still burning?"

"Really?"

"Yeah, nobody knows how to extinguish them.

They've pretty much evacuated the town. The government bought up the houses, like Love Canal, and the people relocated. Of course, some stayed. Some always stay. But it's fucked up the water supply. It'll never be the same."

"Remember swimming in the Greenie? Remember walking through the woods, how far was it in from the road, a mile, two?"

"Tony used to drive us up the mountain, and we'd have lunches packed, and we'd walk in. It was far, maybe it was a couple of miles. I don't think I could do it, but do you remember what the water was like? You could see all the way down to the bottom. And cold! Christ, it was cold."

"At six o'clock he'd be there in the car on the shoulder of the road, waiting to take us home."

"The light," he says. "It was so clear then. Sunlight's not like that anymore."

"Or our eyes can't see it. It might still look that way to kids that age."

"Yeah," Yozo says. "I hope it does."

After a while, she says, "Five thousand dollars. Why didn't you stop me?"

"Yeah, right. Hey, I gotta ask you something."

"Hmmmm."

"Tony told me. I know what you're gonna have to do after he dies."

"What?"

"About cremating him. I'll help you. I know talking to your aunts and to Francie, that's not gonna be easy, but I've been around them a lot, and I think they'll listen to me."

"Are you fucking crazy?" Gia shouts. "You think you know them? How many years you been hanging out with them, thirty, thirty-five? Guess what? You don't know them at all. They've been on their best behavior because you're not one of them! They're not gonna fucking listen to you, oh, man, you are so delusional!"

Yozo laughs and laughs, the sound ringing through the church, off the golden candlesticks, the thickly leaded stained-glass windows, the high varnished pews, the stone floor. All those Sunday mornings she sat in this church not understanding anything of what was going on except that it was lovely to watch the altar boys light the candles before Mass started, and then the priest appeared and the choir sang and incense burned and that gorgeous sonorous Latin rolled across her.

When he stops laughing, he asks her, "You're gonna do it, aren't you?"

"You're as crazy as he is. Did he tell you the part about the water pistol?"

"I can handle that," he says. "You gonna tell him you're not gonna do it?"

"Why don't you mind your own business?"

"You know he still holds you to it."

"I don't want to think about it."

"You're gonna go back on a promise to your *padrino*? Whoa, that's not you. Is it?"

"It's not your family, Joe. Back off."

"Ah," he folds his hands across his lap, "that was a crack worthy of your aunt Mella. I guess blood is thicker than, what, gutless bitch wonders?"

"I'm sorry," Gia softly says. "That wasn't right. You're closer to him than I am, I know that. He talked about you all the time. I should have called you years ago, Yoz. We should have stayed in touch." She suddenly remembers her god-mother, Maria, holding the little Gia in her lap as the choir sang, and the middle-aged Gia is watching the beautiful colors of the stained-glass windows, watching them move as the leaves of the trees outside rustle in the wind. She blinks at the sudden intensity of the long-forgotten scene.

"So, who was your first?"

"My first what?"

"Your first lover. Who was he?"

"I don't believe you. What's it to you?"

"I thought it was Willie. Now I find out you two did everything but."

"What do you mean, everything but? What are you talking about? What did he tell you?"

"Ah, he never told me anything. You know how he was, still is, the perfect gentleman. Jesus, even when we were all bragging and lying about what we were getting, he stayed quiet."

"So, what are you talking about? You making a good guess?"

"I used to follow you."

"You what?"

"Your grandfather paid me to follow you when you went out with him. I used to follow you."

She sits back, momentarily breathless and speech-less. "You watched us?"

"Only up to a point. Then I didn't watch. Respect, you know? Now I wish I had watched, but I doubt that I'd be able to remember it. My memory isn't as good as it used to be. I find myself standing somewhere, wondering how I got there, you know? That happens to me a lot. I don't know if I'm just doing too many things, or if I'm starting to lose it. I wonder if you can tell, when it happens to you. Do you think you know you're losing it while you're losing it, or does losing it carry with it the implication that you don't have the slightest idea of what's happening to you? What? Why are you looking at me that way?"

"You watched." She is aghast and embarrassed about something that happened thirty-five years ago. She is as flushed as if he had come upon her and Willie just as her jeans slid down.

"No. I didn't. And I never told."

"How much?"

"Ten bucks. Your grandfather was no cheap man. He knew how to buy a boy's loyalty."

Lealta, Tony had told her. Loyalty. He said Yozo would be the one who was loyal.

"Tony know you were doing this?"

"Yeah."

"Does Willie know?"

"No."

She kneels then and buries her face in her hands. He kneels beside her and puts his arm around her shoulders. "I never told, Gia. It was always us, you know, just the four of us. I never told."

She lifts her head. "I used to follow you and the girls you took out."

He jumps back onto the pew. "You what?"

"Yeah. I followed you when you used to go down to the old baseball field. Into the dugout. I followed you."

He stares at her.

"I did it for free. Nobody paid me. And I did something you didn't do, Yozo."

"Ah, no," he whines.

"Yeah. I watched."

A frazzled young woman who isn't going to look young very much longer is leaving Barbara's hospital room as Gia walks down the corridor. For an instant she thinks of introducing herself; she can see Barbara's jawline and mouth on the blonde, sort of frowzy girl who is berating a little girl for moving too slowly through the doorway, so it would be a safe guess that this damsel is Barbara's daughter. Eddie Eckroat must be fair, Gia thinks. The little girl is darker, with hair that used to be called dirty blonde. Then it hits her:

She is looking at Barbara's grandchild.

Even the thought seems impossible. We were only a little older than this kid, she measures, when we met in kindergarten. She crouches down, in the kid's path, and smiles at her. "Hey, what's your name, beauty?"

Her mother grabs the little girl's upper arm and steers her around Gia, this strange woman who just tried to talk to her kid. Gia stands upright, wonders about the world, and watches the young woman, the one with the already worn look about her, drag her whining daughter down the hospital corridor. Her jeans are too tight, Gia notes, and her hair is that overprocessed, dry, frizzy mass that prevailed in Los Angeles more than a decade ago. What the hell, the receptionist she just passed on her way in, the one with the beehive and the original cats' eye glasses, is probably considered the height of fashion here.

"Hey, you still here?" Gia greets her friend as casually as she can. Barbara's forearm is wrapped in a small Ace bandage now, a sign of healing, and her eyes are bright, undimmed by painkillers or booze. "How are you feeling?"

"A whole lot better. The doctor said I can check out anytime."

"So why are you still here?"

"Well, Eddie's at work, he's leaving for New York straight from work, he's going hunting, and my daughter, that was Andrea. She just left. Did you pass her on your way in?"

"The blonde, with the kid?"

"That was my granddaughter, Megan. Andrea brought her to see her Mammy."

"Mammy? That's what she calls you, Mammy?"

Barbara laughs, and then her face is as pretty as when she was a kid. She used to laugh a lot when they were kids.

"She couldn't say Granny."

Gia sits heavily on the bed. She thinks about stretching out on the other, unoccupied bed in this semi-private room. "Granny."

"Yeah, kid, that's me."

"How long have I been back, Barb? Did you know that time in this town isn't like time in the real world?" Gia lays her head in Barbara's lap as she reclines in her hospital bed.

"Time catching up with you, is it?" Barbara asks.

"No. I just don't know what happened to my life. One day you and I were Megan's age, and the next day here we are, and I don't remember much in between."

"Born. Graduate. Marry. Kids. Die. Did I miss anything?"

"I think you got it all."

"You ever wish you had kids?" Barbara asks.

"I do have kids. They're my kids, as much as if I had birthed them myself. Except that I didn't have to do the actual physical labor. That's pretty much been my lot in life. I've never been one to get my hands dirty."

"Didn't you ever want to have one, though?"

"John and I talked about it. If he had lived, I think we might have had one. But it didn't happen that way."

"Does it bother you?"

"Sometimes. Yeah, sometimes it does. With John it would have been a beautiful child. He was a looker, he was. Real easy on the eyes. Tall, dark, and handsome." Gia smiles. "And rich. And an orphan. Both his parents were dead. The only way he could have been more perfect would have been if he had been mute. We used to have some prodigious fights."

Barbara is stroking her hair. "Ah, even if he couldn't talk, he would have had his fingers in your face all the time," she says, and then she bends over Gia, embracing her, as Gia's arm goes around her waist and they are two young girls again, laughing and laughing at the folly of men and women, but this time, in this real time, they are also laughing with relief, that they have lived long enough to share this laugh.

"So," Gia sits up, still chuckling, "how come you're not on your way home?"

"Andrea's hassled. She has to go to work and she can't find anyone to watch Megan."

"She brought the kid here, here? Did she think you were going to watch her here?"

"Gia, my daughter married a man who can't even hold a job. Do you think I understand anything about her?"

"Why does she stay?"

"I don't know." Barbara's eyes look away from hers. "I don't know why she's pregnant again, either. She just told me."

"Is he working now?"

"He drives a tow truck. How's that for a thriving nineties kind of career? They live in a trailer."

"How old is she?"

"Twenty-eight."

"Ah," Gia wants to make this better, at least for the duration of the conversation, "at twenty-eight I still knew everything, didn't you? In fact, it's only recently that I've discovered that I don't know anything. That everything I was ever certain of was wrong. It's a curiously liberating feeling. Of course, that could just be a function of being back in my hometown. I could be brain dead."

"That helps, if you're going to live here."

"How have you done it, all these years?" Gia asks, but she knows the answer: You drank.

"It's not a bad place. It's still an all-right place for kids, and Eddie and I, well, he's been third shift for so long, we never even see each other. When Greg and Jamie graduate from high school, well, maybe Eddie and I'll buy a place up in the Poconos. He'll be close to retirement by then. Maybe that's what we'll do."

"Retirement? Grandchildren?" Gia's head seems to be filling up with snakes. "We're our parents, you know that?"

"My dad still comes over every Sunday to watch the Eagles games. He still lives in the house. Takes care of himself. He even drives, Gia, and he doesn't drive like an old man yet. When he turns into the guy with the hat, you know which one I mean, he'll probably have to come and live with us."

"What about your sister? Where's she?"

"She's a nun," Barbara tells Gia from her hospital bed. "She entered the Sisters of Saint Cyprian in sixty-six, and she hasn't been out since."

Gia considers this piece of news. It's as nuts as anything else she's heard since she came East.

"Mary Ann is a cloistered nun? She taught us how to shoplift."

"Yep. We visit her once a year. I don't know what there is to steal in a convent. Or where she puts it when she steals it."

"After you visit her," Gia asks, "is your pocket-book usually lighter?"

Barbara looks at her. "Will you take me home? I don't have anybody to give me a ride, and I don't want to spend another night here."

Gia stands up. "Barbara, I'll always take you anywhere you want to go," she tells her as she starts folding the robe, and Barbara slides out of bed and heads for the closet that holds her civilian clothes.

"So then I took her home, and she went in her house, and I watched until some lights went on inside, and then I came here. Tony, I couldn't say anything to her. I wanted to, and I couldn't."

"Whyn't you just say it?"

Gia rubs her face and her tired eyes. "I don't know. She's so fragile, I don't want to hurt her. Or maybe I don't want to piss her off."

"You're afraid of Barbara?"

"Not like that. I can't just show up and dis-rupt her life, no matter how rotten I think her life might be."

"Why can't you? She's hurting herself, you're her friend, you have to help her."

"What can I do?"

"Eh, don't wreck any more of her husband's

cars." He chuckles, and a thin line of saliva runs along the corner of his mouth. Gia uses a tissue to dry it, and Tony doesn't even seem to notice. It's not very late, but it is dark now—it is getting darker earlier, even Gia has noticed it in the few days that she's been here. The sun sinks behind the mountains that ring the town, and a strange and beautiful twilight appears, lasting just a few moments, but it is a light unlike any she's seen anywhere in the world. The light in Scotland was pretty good, but it wasn't as good as it is here.

Of course, in Scotland she is sure you can still drink the water.

"I didn't tell her," Gia confesses. "I don't know if she knows about the car."

"She knows. You think her husband didn't tell her?" He turns his head and looks at his niece. "You don't believe that drunk story, do you?"

"He hits her. And she didn't say anything about it to me, so I couldn't bring it up." Gia shifts uncomfortably in her chair. Tony reaches to her face and gently touches her cheek. His fingers feel like feathers.

"I don't know what to do about Barbara."

"Maybe you could just love her." Willie glides to the other side of Tony's bed. "Maybe that's all you can do."

"Why don't you just kill him?" Tony asks, not unreasonably. "The Collar's here. Protect me."

"Protect me more," Willie says. "How are you feeling?"

"I'm not gonna die tonight," Tony announces.

"That's good," Willie says.

"I don't know," Tony muses. "I'm getting ready. I think I dreamed about your father last night. I think maybe I did."

"My father?" Willie asks. "Did you know him?"

"Yeah, I knew him. Her father." He squeezes Gia's face, the face his hand has not left.

She covers his hand with hers. "Not tonight, Tony," is all she can say.

"Your father," he says to Willie, "you're just like him."

"How's that?"

"Dreamer. He was a dreamer. So are you."

Gia has never heard anyone say anything about Willie's father. He just wasn't there very much when they were growing up; Willie had his mother, his brother, his maiden aunts, and that was all he seemed to need. The children certainly never noticed Mr. Cunningham's absence. And then Willie became a priest, a surefire way of having a man around the house, so to speak, forever, and a pretty good guarantee that there would never be another woman around to provide any kind of competition or distraction. She looks at Willie, and for the first time she has some idea of what his demons might be. He is looking across her godfather, at her, and he is not smiling. His face has an expression she remembers, that look of longing.

Tony, who doesn't miss anything, closes his eyes, releases Gia's face, and says, "It's not late. Why don't you go somewhere? Come back, all right? Eh?"

"Buy you a coffee?" Willie asks.

"Remember when that was such a grown-up

thing to do, go for coffee? Now it's just another little Starbuck's on the corner."

"Starbuck's?" Willie looks blank, and she remembers that they are, truly, hidden away in the mountains.

"We'll come back," she tells her uncle as she bends to kiss his warm cheek.

They move around each other awkwardly, as if the very act of bumping into the other will cause a burn, or bleeding. The kitchen never seemed so small. When Barbara and Eddie bought this house, they intended to remodel. They had so many plans, but they never got around to any of them, so the kitchen is still the same outdated room it was when they moved in more than twenty-five years ago.

"You want me to pack you some sandwiches?" she asks. "There's lunch meat, and I could make some tuna, if you want. Or hoagies."

"Naw, we'll stop. It'll be for a break. I don't want Greg driving at night."

"You could have been there already." Barbara's hospital stay has delayed Eddie's annual hunting trip to New York state with his sons by more than twelve hours. "It's my fault."

"It's my own damn fault," he says, standing in front of the open refrigerator, not really looking for anything, but it is a place to stand where he doesn't have to look at his wife. "I shouldn't have come back that time. We should have split up a long time ago." He closes the door. "Why do you stay here?"

She laughs, a tight, nervous sound. "Why would I go? It's my home."

"It's nobody's home, Barb." He sounds so tired. "Look around. You have a house with stuff in it. There's no home here. You could put these boys anywhere, they'd act like nothing happened. There's nothing here."

"We have a family," she protests quietly.

"We have kids. They raised themselves. We just had them, that's all, and I don't even know why we did that."

She shrugs. "Accidents happen, Eddie, all the time."

"Those boys weren't accidents. Those boys were your insurance policy. You had them to nail me down. You think I didn't know that? How stupid do you think I am?"

She knows. She has always known that he wasn't fooled by her unexpected pregnancy. He had come back after they had separated for a couple of months. She had been frantic with fear, her alone with an eleven-year-old daughter who was already seeking out the company of boys. They had gotten along that first night, even having wine with dinner, and then, before Eddie could tell her that he had met someone else during those two months living in a town five miles away, Barbara was telling him that she was pregnant.

Things quieted down during her pregnancy. She wasn't as young as she had been with the first one, so Eddie gave up the woman he had met and moved back home. Even Andrea calmed down, thrilled with the idea of a new brother or sister. After Greg was born, though, things started to fall apart. Andrea wasn't interested in taking care of a baby, not when there were boys outside, calling softly to her from old cars on dark nights. Eddie loved his son, was thrilled with the baby boy, but soon found himself thinking of the woman, and it was while he was thinking of the woman that Jamie was conceived, just before Greg's first birthday.

After that Eddie stopped thinking about the woman, because he knew he would never see her again.

"They're our children. You want to think of them as insurance policies, go ahead," Barbara says.

"You know, you're right. They're old enough to know who they want to live with. I don't want to keep living like this. I'm gonna come home some morning, and you're gonna be laying there dead with a broken neck or something. I don't wanna have to wait for that. I don't want the kids to see that. Goddamn, they've seen enough."

She turns and opens a cabinet on the wall above the counter. "Maybe the boys want peanut butter and jelly sandwiches."

"They don't want anything from you. Don't you understand? I've waited all these years for you to do something, get help or something. I don't know what to do, Barbara. I don't know what the hell makes you drink like that. I thought, you know, with the kids you'd change. But you hide, that's all you do, you hide. They know. Who do you think you're fooling? They know. Andrea knows. They know. They know their mother's a drunk. Why'd you let them grow up like that?"

She doesn't turn around to face him. She stares at the jars and cans on the shelves. "I need to reline these shelves," she says. "I'll do it while you're gone."

"I loved you so much," he quietly says. "I loved you so much, I used to cry in bed, while you were sleeping, because I was so afraid you'd die. That's how much I loved you."

"I still love you," she says, not turning around.

"No, you don't. Maybe you did when we first got married, but I don't know what happened. I'm just the sucker you got. The one who pays the bills. No more, Barbara. No more. When I come back, I'm getting a lawyer. And I'm taking the boys."

She is thinking of the bottle of vodka she has in the trunk of her car. There is powdered lemonade mix in one of the cabinets. She has an extra carton of cigarettes in the freezer. When he leaves—will he ever leave?—she'll be fine. She's just not fine right now, thinking of all that she has to do. The downstairs bathroom needs cleaning, the boys' bathroom is always a mess. This would be a good time to go through their closets and get rid of all their outgrown clothes.

She always fills a big trash bag with old clothes to take to the Salvation Army, but she also always gets confused, and leaves that bag with the others, out in the garage, or sometimes in the middle of the living room, and someone, Eddie, or one of the boys, always comes along and puts it with the other trash that gets picked up by the municipal garbage truck that comes along on Monday mornings, late in the morning, around eleven, while Barbara is still unconscious from getting drunk the night before. If you asked her, she would tell you that she takes those old clothes to the Salvation Army. She honestly believes that she does.

"Did you hear what I said?" Eddie Eckroat asks his wife.

She turns and smiles at him.

Even after he leaves, slamming the door, she is still standing there, smiling.

"Beats coffee." Gia is looking out over the town. The mountains on the horizon are black against the dark blue sky, with only occasional light showing on them as one or another lonely car makes its way along the serpentine tertiary road that was once used as a testing ground for General Motors cars. Her uncle, long before she was old enough even to have a learner's permit, used to have her drive, in his Buick with a stick shift, along those roads, where she learned to navigate blind curves with sheer drops on her side, where she learned to back up and turn the car around with certain obliteration waiting for them over the side of the road that was beautifully free of guardrails which might at least have slowed their sudden death. Tony never got out of the car to watch her turn it around; he stayed with her, and that did more for her confidence than any external cheering or coaching might have. She could do it because he knew she could do it, and she would not let him down.

"It's ironic, isn't it, that the most beautiful real estate in this place is taken up by dead people?" Willie says.

They are standing on the edge of Cicada Mountain, the top of which, the great plateau, really, is all cemeteries. Just as all the churches have their own parishioners, their own elementary schools, their own languages, so too do they have their own cemeteries. Right now they have parked the priest Ford at the entrance to the Annunciation Cemetery, the Irish one. Naturally.

"They're nicer to the dead than they are to the living," she says.

"Most people are." He surveys the cemetery behind them. It is a cool evening, and the leaves are beginning to crunch. "Remember the sticky buns?"

There was a bakery on the corner, across the street, right outside the cemetery gates. Late on Friday nights they used to put their sticky buns out on racks to cool, and the four teenage friends, cruising, drinking beer out of quarts, happy to be together out in the dark, away from the adults, they would park in the cemetery, sneak down to the back of the bakery, where the aroma of those buns would intoxicate them even more, and they would swipe handfuls of the gummy, gooey treasures. They would sit on gravestones, eat warm, sweet buns, drink beer, and tell each other their dreams.

There was that one time Barbara fell into an open grave—no moon that night—but they got her out pretty quickly and she was able to speak again by the following day.

"Why did we come here?" It seems like such an obvious question, but Gia really doesn't remember.

"There was no place else. We had Schiavone's. That was the best hangout." A tiny joint across the street from the high school, with pinball machines and burgers and Cokes and fries and high booths where you could neck if the need came upon you and a loud jukebox and rock 'n' roll and a back room where you could dance if you couldn't neck. Mr. and Mrs. Schiavone, a pair of saints who honestly liked young people, ran the place. She asks Willie, but she really doesn't want to hear the answer.

"They're both gone. Not long after we graduated he died, and she followed him. Pretty much like you might have expected."

"They were good to us," she says.

"They were lovely people, weren't they?"

"We weren't bad kids."

"No," he looks up at the star-driven sky, "the world was a lot less complicated then. It was easier to know what was right and what was wrong. We knew what the rules were."

"I'm not used to feeling this useless, Willie. Tits on a boar, that's how I feel. I can't do anything about anything here. My uncle, that's out of my hands. Barbara, she's an alcoholic whose husband clubs her around, I don't care what you say, and I can't do anything. She shakes, have you noticed that?"

"She shook in high school, Gia, and I have to tell you, her mother had Parkinson's."

That piece of information comes into her like a large, flat black spacecraft landing on top of her brain. "Does she have it?" she finally asks.

"I don't know. I don't think she knows."

They are talking now about how one of them might die, and it is not such a strange subject.

"We're getting old, aren't we, Willie?"

He is still looking out at the town, but she can see his smile and his slight nod. Then he says, "It's not so bad." He has never looked as handsome as he does tonight. She's back in the cemetery with Willie. But this time they have thousands of nights behind them, and the last time they were here, they could still count the nights they had had. Now the numbers are too high. The stakes are beyond her vision. Gia doesn't play games she has no chance of winning.

And then he turns to her and takes her in his arms and kisses her, as any old boyfriend, given this setting and this time, would. He is still possessed of a remarkably gifted tongue, and Gia is, somewhere in the back of what is left of her mind, aroused and loosening and leaning into the big chest of the man in whose arms she is now safe.

"Ah, Will," she whispers, their lips barely apart.

There's that old, familiar thing pressing against her, and she is suddenly struck by an odd nostalgia: her first hard-on.

She jumps backward, just before the lightning

strikes, she's sure, and Willie is left standing alone, with his arms outstretched, like a song from the sixties.

"Was it that unbearable?" he quietly asks as he lowers his empty arms.

"It was gorgeous," she tells him, and her voice surprises her. She is angry. "That was on its way to being the best kiss I ever had."

"Then why?"

"Because it's you. And I don't, I can't."

He watches her, so she decides she has to keep talking, because if she doesn't, she'll move back into those strange and familiar arms, and she will lift her mouth to his, and she will put her hands into those graying curls, and she will feel the two of them pushing against each other, like the two parts of the one puzzle that they made when they were young, when they knew what they wanted, but, more important, when they knew what was forbidden.

"When I left my first husband, I made up some rules for myself, since I was back in the dating game. It was the seventies, I was newly single, and I thought a girl needed standards. So, I made some up for myself: no activity that might draw blood, nothing that had been dead for more than an hour, and no married men."

He says nothing, just stands there, looking simultaneously helpless and dangerous, and licks his lips, as though he's still tasting her mouth. She doesn't know if he knows that he's doing it. If he does, then he's simply dangerous.

"Willie, you're a married man. You're the most married man I've ever known. You also are, right now, maybe the most irresistible man I've ever seen, but I've made all the mistakes and you are not going to be one of them."

"I waited for you. I waited."

"And now I'm here, but not the way you planned. I'm sorry."

He keeps looking at her, and then he smiles. "In 1964 I waited for you. You were supposed to come back from Europe. I waited for you. You went to California. You didn't come back."

Gia is puzzled. She remembers none of this.

"I had finished my freshman year at Villanova. You were going to go to Penn, we were going to get pinned, then engaged."

She opens her mouth and then closes it. What's the use? She might as well be hearing about someone else's life. "I don't remember, Will."

"Did you know that I was a pallbearer for your grandmother and your grandfather?" he asks.

"No, I didn't know that."

"You were in Italy. It felt close to you to help carry their caskets."

"Willie, we had it bad. I know."

"Why didn't you come back?" His voice is steady and measured, with his priest's silkiness and softness gone. She is standing on top of a mountain in the dark, talking to a man who once loved her, who just kissed her, and who now wants to know why she left him.

"I don't know. It was time to get on with growing up. And away. My grandparents were gone, I had to go to school."

"In California?" he shouts. "You were supposed to come to Philadelphia! We were supposed to be together!"

"Willie, I can't remember any of that." She holds out her hands in sweet supplication. "We were kids. Kids make plans, and adults talk about why the plans fell through. That's life, Will. That's life."

"I loved you so much. I loved you for years." He takes a step toward her, and she fights down the urge to back up. If she's going to die up here tonight, she's not going to do it in retreat.

"We were beautiful young kids. Let's not do anything stupid that might erase that memory, Willie. There are some things that even confession won't ease." She is now pretty sure that the last part of her to die, when the time comes, will be her mouth.

He laughs, a brittle, unhappy sound. "I've confessed you too many times, Gia. I don't even list you anymore. You're just one of my General Absolution sins."

Gia falls silent, completely perplexed by that admission, which was either a slur or a compliment. She stands still, and self-control overpowers her body, the one that wants to merge with the one opposite her, the one she had once known so well, the new one, the one she wants to find out about, completely, again, on this dark night in the cemetery.

"Come here, Gia," he says, with frightening timing, and she goes to him, because there are too many years between them, too many firsts, and there will never be another night like this.

When he holds out his arms to her this time, she knows that she will enter them and stay there, and there will be no pulling away, and even as they sink to the ground, as someone's grave is about to become their ultimate marriage bed, she hears the Devil whispering in her ear. "Yes," the Devil says, and for a second her eyes fly open, fully expecting to see a demon in red standing over them, or at the very least, given his penchant for trailing, Yozo.

But there is no one. There is only Willie and Gia, just as it was all those years ago, when they were new, and it was new, and it was scary then, but that fear was nothing compared to the terror she is feeling now, even as she is slipping into an embrace that feels like the one she has been in all her life. For a second Willie's big head, his handsome face, hangs over her, and then he lowers his face to hers, and, as she knew she would, she slides her hands into his curls, and he whispers her name just before his lips touch hers.

His hands slide over her, and she is loving what is happening. Gia does not wear a bra, and when his hands find bare flesh he gasps, he honestly gasps, such is his surprise and delight, and then he is in familiar territory, as is she, and he is, she's sure, remembering the girl, and she knows the boy, and they are lost in each other, in ways that even God would embrace.

"Oh, yes," he whispers when she pulls his sweater over his head and tosses it, and unbuttons his shirt. He starts to unzip his pants, stops, and reaches for her all over again.

"You are my dream," he whispers to her. "You have been my dream for my whole life."

"Dreams should come true," Gia murmurs.

"No," he says, still holding her.

"What?" she gasps.

The moment slips by, along with whatever remained of her youth.

"I can't," he whispers, his mouth still on hers, warm and soft.

Sure you can, she wants to say, but she doesn't. His hands leave her, then his mouth, then he stands up and turns away from her, heading for the tombstone that caught his sweater. Gia pulls her clothes together and sits up.

His back to her, he stands, holding his sweater. She swears she can hear his heart beating, or is that hers?

"I love you, Gianna. I will go to my death loving you. I want you to know that. I hope it's not a burden to you."

"Love's not a burden," she says, still sitting on a grave.

"That's enough for me." He turns toward her, and all she can see is the corona that the lights of the town behind and below him make of his curly hair. She is ashamed to notice such a patently symbolic and frightening detail. "I've dreamed of having you. I've dreamed of this night, but I can live with the dream. That's enough for me. I'm sorry. I didn't mean to lead you on. I hope you're not angry."

"Isn't that my line?" Not that she's ever used it.

"I love something more than I love you," he says simply, and he is, with that utterance, the most desirable man she has ever encountered, and she knows, with a strange bump in her heartbeat, that she'll never kiss him again, that he'll hold her, but only in the ways that keep them both safe and sure of each other, and she realizes that her old friend is her old friend. They have come through the fire, and they are still standing, they are standing closer together than ever before.

"Willie, that's good. That's right where you ought to be."

"Yeah," he nods, and his brightly lit curls shimmer while he holds his hand out to her. "Come're."

When he kisses her, it is on the mouth, but it is different. It is cool, they are safe, the fire is out, and the night around them is not as dark as it was before, the night that envelops them as they stand holding each other as tightly as ever, in the cemetery of their youth.

Yozo watches.

Sometimes it seems as though he has spent his life watching others, but then, sometimes it seems to him as though whenever he wasn't watching, he just got into lots and lots of trouble.

Trouble that most people never even know about. They never will.

I'm doing what I'm best at, he thinks, watching the house, hoping that he'll see lights go on and off, but knowing, in his heart of hearts, that the lights will stay on all night, like they always do, while Barbara gets boozed up. Her sons have gone hunting with their father, and her daughter's car isn't out front.

She's alone in there. He gets out of his car, which is parked across the street from the house, goes to her door, tries it, finds it unlocked, as he always does, and enters.

At the kitchen table, slumped over, her head resting on her bandaged wrist, a bottle of vodka on the table beside her, Barbara has passed out. He picks up the blue plastic tumbler and sniffs what little liquid remains. He winces. Straight vodka, not even the usual lemonade or orange juice or iced tea. If he were the kind of man who spits indoors, he would do so now.

Instead, he lifts her up and throws her over his shoulder, paying no mind to her injured rib or forearm. She can't feel anything anyway, he thinks as he carries her to her bedroom, as he has done so many nights before, which no one knows about, not even Barbara, and, balancing her on his shoulder, his right hand wrapped around her skinny hips, he pulls back the bedspread, then the blanket, then the sheet, and, carefully now, he lays her down, his left hand cupping the back of her head, as if a newborn's. Then he kneels beside the bed and sets about unlacing her sneakers. They are plain white Keds, the kind that have just come back into fashion, the kind she wore in high school. Her ankles are so thin, he notes. So thin. He touches the sharp bone with his forefinger, as if it were the most delicate ice sculpture that would melt with his touch. Then he bends to kiss her ankle. And then he rests his head on her knee, and he cries, all the while holding her foot that is still in its Ked, the kind she wore in high school.

Mom, look at me. Mom, look.

She turns her head, and he sees that long braid, wrapped into a tight bun at the back of her head, where the hair never quite turned completely gray. She is sitting on a wooden bench, like the one in front of Pop's old store, and she is holding a peony for her little granddaughter to smell. The child is looking into the flower and making a face, there must be a bug in there, and the old woman is looking at the child, she is looking down at the child of her young dead son.

Mom.

She looks up from the little girl, into Tony's camera, and she closes her eyes.

Mom, look at me.

No. Not yet.

Tony Scarpino falls into a deeper sleep, and when Gia and Willie enter his room, with the one small light burning at his bedside, they tiptoe. Willie silently moves a chair to the bed and motions for Gia to sit. She sits, Willie stands behind her.

They watch the old man sleeping. He smiles in his sleep, and that makes Gia cry.

When he opens his eyes and sees them waiting for him, he is almost disappointed. "I saw your *Nonna*," he tells his godchild, the middle-aged one with the graying hair, hair that will soon be like her grandmother's. "She was giving you a flower."

"That's a picture. You took a picture of me and her like that. On the bench in front of Pop's store."

He thinks about this. "Yeah, yeah, you're right. So I wasn't dreaming about her."

"You were dreaming about a picture of her, Tony," Gia whispers.

"I guess I won't die tonight." He seems to slip back into sleep, but then his eyes open again, and he asks, "How come you're back already?"

"We were gone a long time," Willie says. "You fell asleep."

The old man looks at his teary niece. She threw him back, he thinks. He looks at the priest standing behind her.

No, he let her go. He sees that they are holding hands. Sonofabitch, he thinks. Sonofabitch. You never know shit with these kids, do you?

"Where'd you go?" he asks.

"For coffee," Willie says, and Tony, drugged though he might be, isn't too stoned to miss the sight of the priest's hand squeezing Gia's. She knows that Tony has spotted the untruth, but she stays quiet, knowing that her godfather is perfectly happy to be in the same room with a priest who has just told a lie.

She leans over his bed and whispers in his ear, "Today, I made him curse in church."

He closes his eyes again, still and silent, smiling. She has just made him even happier.

No one notices when Yozo appears in the doorway. "How is he?" he asks, baseball cap in hand. Then he shoves it in the back pocket of his jeans.

"It's a quiet night," the nurse tells him as she passes him on her way out.

"He's okay," Gia says softly.

She looks awful, Yozo thinks, and how the hell come Willie looks so good? Something happened. He sniffs the air around his head, as if to divine from their scent what might have taken place.

"He's usually awake this late," Yozo observes.

She shoots him a sharp, rebuking look. This is a night like any other, her look tells him. Don't even think to say that Tony might be slipping. Don't. It's just another night.

He stands at the foot of the bed. "Can I stay with you?"

"Can I come in?" a small voice asks from out in the hall.

Gia glances at the doorway. "Mia, honey, come on in here. What are you doing here?"

"There's so much noise at the house, and everybody is yelling, and you weren't there, and I knew you were here, and I didn't want you to be alone."

"You're a good kid." Gia reaches out and hugs the young woman, who wraps her arms around her mother's cousin.

Willie watches them for a moment, then circles the women, heads for the door, and says to Yozo, "Come on. It's time for us to go."

Yozo obediently follows his oldest friend out of

the hospital room where the women are still standing close to each other, whispering things he can't hear. He thinks he might have to get his hearing checked.

"That's a cute kid. She looks a lot like Gia, doesn't she?"

Willie sighs. "Yeah, she does."

"You were with her tonight?"

Willie nods.

"So? You get lucky?"

Willie nods again.

"You did?"

Willie looks at him.

Yozo goes to the nurses' station and quietly asks the night nurse, "Could you please help me? I think my heart has stopped. Could you check it for me?"

The woman begins to rise, reaching for the stethoscope around her neck, saying, "Are you having any pain? Shortness of breath?" when Willie grabs Yozo by the arm.

"Don't," Willie warns him, "it's not funny."

"Sorry, miss." Yozo is instantly contrite. "I was making a bad joke. I didn't mean to upset you."

"Very fucking funny," she says.

"You're a real charmer, aint'cha?" Yozo notes while Willie, who hasn't released his arm, drags him away.

"You can be a real pain in the ass, you know that?" Willie scolds him.

"For a guy who just got his jollies, you're in a bitchin' mood."

When Willie slams him against the corridor wall, Yozo reacts automatically and raises his fist, but he pulls his punch and stands, shaken, against the wall, looking at Willie's red face. "What the fuck is going on here? What's with you? What the hell?"

Willie wraps his big hand around Yozo's neck and pulls him to him. "I'm sorry," he says, and lets go. "It's been a long day. Night, I guess. What time is it?"

"I don't know." Yozo glances at the nurses' station, where the charmer still sits, glaring at him. If I had a heart attack now, he thinks, she'd let me die. "Ten after two. It's early. I'm sorry, too. You don't have to tell me anything."

"You're going to ask her."

"Yeah. She'll tell me."

"No, she won't."

"Big fucking secret. Right?"

"Like you said, I got lucky."

"What's that supposed to mean?" Yozo follows Willie out into the parking lot.

"Why don't you go home, Joe? Christine might welcome her husband into her bed tonight."

"You never said anything like that to me, in all the years we've been catting around." He looks at Willie for a hard moment, and then reaches for his baseball cap and pulls it over his head. He notes that the night is getting chilly. It's gonna be winter soon, he thinks. Another winter.

Willie is walking away from him, toward his priest Ford. It's over, Yozo thinks. They finally finished it up between them, and he's sad. He looks around for his car, because he can't quite remember where he parked it. Willie's car pulls swiftly out of the lot, with no flashes of the high beams, no toot of the horn, no wave. Willie just leaves, and Yozo suddenly understands why his old friend is sad, and then, because loyalty runs deeper in him than anything else, he is sad, too.

Down the road that leads to the town, Willie pulls over to the side of the road, onto the shoulder, because he has started laughing, and he is laughing so hard, he knows how giddy he is, that he can't see to drive in the darkness. He laughs and laughs, and then he is crying, and he tries to laugh again, but there's no going back. He cries, and there is no going back.

"You'll stay with him?" she asks the young woman. Since Mia is an R.N., Gia feels less guilty about surrendering to the bone-shattering fatigue that has settled on her. She kisses Tony, then Mia again, and leaves the hospital.

It isn't until she reaches the front door and steps down onto the stone walkway that she realizes the dawn will soon break; she sucks deeply the clean, cool, autumn air, savoring its sweetness. The night before seems like a very long time ago. "It was winter," she says out loud. "We came out of the winter."

Yozo sits on the sign that advertises the hospital's name and the entrance to the emergency room and watches Gia lift her face to the brightening sky, watches her bend over as though to stretch her tired back, and then watches her straighten and walk slowly to her rental car.

It's time to go home, he thinks as he slides off the sign.

FOURTH DAY

Because of how it was in her grandfather's house, the house in which she was raised, she is never surprised. Nothing surprises her. Nothing.

This was a typical occurrence at the table in her grandfather's house:

A summer evening. It is still bright sunshine outside. They eat supper early, around six, so that Grandpop will have time to work in his garden after the sun goes down. Later, when it is dark, and hot, he and Gia will water all the plants, something they don't do during the day because, he has taught her, the sun will turn the water on the leaves into a magnifying glass and it will burn the plants. The smell of damp earth on a hot, dark night, a scent one does not frequently encounter, can still set her reeling.

They are sitting around the kitchen table, and they are eating watermelon for dessert. "This is a great melon," one of the Angels proclaims, and everyone agrees. It is superlative, sweet, red, just a touch sugary, and juicy, so juicy they are all slobbering over their plates. The others spit out their seeds; Gia and her Grandpop, side by side as always, chew them up and swallow, their own little acts of rebellion. They also like the taste.

"It's good," Grandpop nods. "Where did you get it?" he asks *Nonna*.

"Angelo Spagolio came to the door with one this morning. He was giving them away. He said if we want another one, he has lots."

Her grandfather nods, not looking up from his watermelon. "He hijacked the wrong truck," he says. "He was supposed to get the one with the television sets."

That is why nothing surprises her. Watermelons can appear before you, watermelons that should have been television sets. Things happen.

She wakes up in the narrow twin bed in her uncle Tony's guest room, when the room is bright with midday sun. She stretches slowly, luxuriously, deeply, as if she were a warm oil slick; she slides off the bed and stretches again before the glowing window.

"I never gave it much thought, but you've got a beautiful ass." Yozo's voice comes from the doorway behind her. She turns without thinking and remembers, too late, that she sleeps in the raw. His face reddens, and his mouth snaps shut. Not for Gia Scarpino the indignity of the shameful, pathetic, futile attempt to cover any part of herself. Besides, she doesn't know what to cover first, and anyway, she doesn't have enough arms. She stands brazenly before Yozo, whose eyes are bigger than she has ever seen on a human, and she wonders if they'll ever go back to their normal size. But, curiously, she notices that she is not surprised by his being there.

"Your dream," she says slowly, "has come true. Now, get out."

He nods but doesn't move. What the hell, she figures, and turns to pull the comforter off her bed. "How did you get in?"

"Tony gave me keys a long time ago. I tried calling you, but I got the machine, so I came over. You want some coffee? You wanna give me that blanket?" he asks.

"Get out," she tells him again, and this time he goes.

"Coffee?" Yozo asks, standing outside the bedroom door, to the side, so she can't see him and he can't see her.

"Coffee," she says. "Yeah."

"People come and go," she says to Yozo, "talking of undertakers."

"It makes sense," he shrugs. "You know?"

"I walked in here yesterday morning, and they were planning his funeral. He's not dead yet, you know?"

Yozo rubs an invisible spot on his jeans leg. They are sitting in the warm sunshine on the deck, the remains of the scrambled eggs and toast he fixed for her on the table between them. He shrugs again, and he doesn't look at her.

"What?" she asks. "You saw me naked and now you can't look at me?"

When he looks up, his mouth is trying to smile, but his eyes are wet. "What?" she asks again.

"He's been like my father, like the one I didn't have. You don't know. He's been like a father to me."

"All this time," she nods. "Sure."

"I never made a move without talking it over with him first. He never told me I couldn't do it, so I did it. The only time he left me alone was when I couldn't get out of bed that time. Later, he told me that I had to figure that one out by myself. He was right. Tony was always right."

She feels a small stab of jealousy, and she is instantly ashamed, but it stays. "You've had more years with him than I have."

"I was here."

"Because of him?"

He thinks it over. "No," shaking his head, "I came back because of my wife and my son, but mostly because I didn't know where the hell else to go. He was here. He was still the guy that came and took us away from the nuns that day, remember?"

"Yeah, sure I remember. He was great."

"You don't walk away from a man like that. I couldn't, anyway."

"I didn't walk away," she protests.

"I didn't mean that. He didn't want you to stay here. He knew you weren't for this place." He gestures at the town below them. "He's so proud of you."

She turns her head away. Yozo is so much easier to deal with when he's being the bad boy. This plain, honest man before her is hard, so hard. Gia suddenly recalls his face, as a young child, at the supper table with her family, looking from one to the other, looking tiny and scared, as though someone would at any moment grab his food away and tell him to leave. That is the face she is seeing again.

"If we could measure loss," she finally says, "yours will be greater."

"No," he answers. Then he thinks it over, and says, again, "No."

She doesn't know what to say, and they are both silent, looking out at their hometown in the valley below them. The leaves are changing, the sky is too blue, the light is crystalline, and she remembers that everyone here is insane. "This town is nuts. Everyone in it is nuts."

"I know." He nods. "I used to think it was the water. But the water's not good anymore, so now I think it might just be something like the Bermuda triangle, or one of those crop-circle places in England. Maybe some aliens are using it for something, a dumping ground or something."

They sit in silence for a while, and then she asks, "Why don't you ever go home, Yozo? Is it that bad?"

"Well, it's not great, but it's not terrible, either. Christine and I are at a point in our lives that, well . . . well, she doesn't care if I'm around or not. She's busy with her life, and, you know."

"Do you cheat on her?"

"Do you really want to know?"

"Yeah."

"Sure. I have. Right from the start. But not really, not anymore. It's too risky and, honest to God, I don't have that kind of energy now. What about you? You fool around when you were married?"

"The first time, yeah, but that was just, well, a big mistake. He fooled around more than I did. The second time, no. Even if he had lived, I wouldn't have."

"You gonna live the rest of your life without a man? I can't buy that, Gia, really I can't."

"There's a man I see more than anyone else. He's a judge, divorced, a little older than we are.

One time he said to me, did it bother me knowing that he was probably going to be the last man I ever slept with?"

"Oh, that's good. He said that to you?"

"Yeah. I sat and stared at the wall for about five hours."

"Then?"

"You'd like me to say that I went out and boinked some other guy, wouldn't you?"

"No, that'd be too predictable, and you're anything but predictable. I'd say that you just decided that you're going to live a long time."

She looks at him. "No, I went out and boinked an old friend. I've already outlived one husband. It's overrated."

He cringes. "Sorry. You think you'll ever get married again?"

"No. I'm too old. Have you noticed, Yozo, how this getting-older thing works to our advantage? How if you don't want to do something, you can say you're too old, and you get away with it?"

"The shit part," he says, "is that no one argues about it with you. When was the last time someone said you're not too old when you said you were?"

She thinks this over. "Yeah, that doesn't happen, does it? It'd be nice if it did, but I guess," she shrugs, "we're getting old. Older."

"Well, older or not," he leans forward, "it was even better than I expected, Gia."

"Thank you, Joe."

• • •

Whatever are their sins? he wonders, sitting in the dark, listening to the gentle, girlish voices of the women in black, the women with the indescribably soft skin on their hands and faces, the only parts of their bodies he has ever seen. What do they do that would bring them to me? What do they see when they turn out their small lamps?

"Bless me, Father, for I have sinned," the tiny voice begins, and William Cunningham, S.J., wonders on. How old are you? Why did you give it all up and come inside here, where there is nothing but you and your sister nuns and your devotion to God? What scared you so badly that you turned away from the world? Did you go away from something, or did you go to something? What do you want in this life? Where do your thoughts go when your mind wanders? What do you miss? Did you ever experience enough of life to miss any of it?

"I had impure thoughts," the voice says. "I felt anger. I was impatient. For these, and all my sins, I am truly sorry."

I wanted to take the clothes off a beautiful woman over an old grave last night. I wanted to touch her, to taste her, to get lost in her, so lost that I might never find my way back, and that would have been good, too. Then I wanted to kill her, to feel my bare hands snap the fragile parts of her fine neck. Then I wanted to kill myself.

"Impure thoughts," he repeats. "You must not

allow yourself to surrender to this weakness of the flesh. Only evil will follow."

"I know." The small voice, he wouldn't have believed it, gets even smaller, and he is momentarily ashamed of himself. Add to my sins, he thinks, that I am a bully.

But that is why he is here, inside the cloistered walls of the Sisters of Saint Cyprian. He comes here once a week, to hear their heartbreaking confessions and to say Mass; he rotates the singing of the Mass with six other priests in the area. When he woke up this morning, after only a few hours of fitful, exhausting sleep, he thought of his time with Gia the night before in the cemetery, and, reaching for his morning rigidity, he took what pleasure his memory, scant and frustrating as it was, afforded him. His recall was kind to him, alone in his long, narrow rectory bed, as he and the woman from long ago carried the act to its final, explosive, blessed end, and so did he, alone in his long, narrow rectory bed.

Shaken, he showered, shaved, gulped instant coffee, and drove quickly to the convent. It had been years, years, since he had allowed himself such a weakness of the flesh. As he drove, he realized that he couldn't wait until the next time.

"For your penance, say three Hail Marys," he says. "Now, make a good Act of Contrition."

There will never be forgiveness for me, he thinks, knowing that he will seek out one of his brother priests for a General Absolution, the kind that is given by one priest to another who doesn't care to enumerate his sins. There is no contrition. I am not sorry. I'll never be sorry.

"I firmly resolve," the nun recites with such feeling, "with the help of Thy grace, to sin no more and to avoid the near occasion of sin. Amen."

The near occasion of sin. Last night, he thinks, that was a near occasion of sin, and I wish it were nearer.

"Father?" The nun's voice is a little different, a bit demanding. "May I go now?"

"Sure, go, sure," he tells her, slipping for only a second. Why do I do this? Why do they come into this box to tell me their pitiful little failings? Why do they even think that I can do anything about it?

He is tired, he knows, and he is cranky, like a child. We are all children, he ruminates, kept so by the lives we have chosen. Never to have the responsibility for our own actions, never to have the choices that ordinary people make, never to have anything but the guilt and the shame and the terror that we will be found out.

I wish I were a nun, he surprises himself with the thought. It would be nice to be soft and pliant and helpless, turning to the Good Father for absolution and redemption and forgiveness and penance, having given up all pretense of adulthood. Why do they do it? he wonders again.

The answer comes to him in an intuitive burst that is not entirely welcome in the small, dark wooden box. He starts to sweat and pulls at his Roman collar.

They do it because they like the whip. They want to be punished. They can go on only if they know that they will be held to some impossible standard and found wanting. They must always fail, and they must always be punished. They like the whip.

And I am the whip.

Gia and Yozo are riding around the town, while he points out how various landmarks have deteriorated.

"Over there, remember the drugstore? That was the only building in town that had an elevator. Remember when we used to go to the movies on Saturday and then go ride the elevator? Three stories, up and down. We were goofy kids."

"No," she demurs. "We were imaginative. This was a good place to grow up."

"I brought lunch, back there." He points at the Rover's backseat. "Want to have a picnic?"

"A picnic?" She looks out the window and idly thinks, I don't know one of these people walking on the street. I used to know everyone who walked on these streets. "Sure, the weather's still warm."

"Want to go to the Greenie?" He smiles at her.

She jumps in her seat and turns to him. "I'd love that."

"You got it, honey," he says. "Call Barbara." He hands Gia the phone.

"Like old times." Barbara's smile is a sight to behold as she slides into the backseat. "A picnic at the Greenie. We used to build a fire up there, and toast hot dogs and marshmallows and swim in the public water supply. God, that dam was gorgeous, and what else?"

"We used to drink beer there, too," Yozo adds. "Lots of beer."

"Brewskis," Barbara says. "Rock-a-cha-chas. Hand grenades. Those little Rolling Rocks."

"Remember how nicely we used to lob them into the woods when we were finished?" Barbara reminds him.

"Why do you think they were called hand grenades?"

"You know, Yuengling beer is now real big in San Francisco. It's a yup favorite." Gia is speaking of a beer brewed in a nearby town.

"They're shipping so much of it out there," Yozo tells her, "that we can't buy it here."

"The oldest brewery in America," she recalls. "Remember the brewery in town? We used to go there at lunchtime, and they'd give us free beer. We weren't even old enough to drink, and we'd have beer for lunch."

"Bullshit, Yozo," Barbara says, watching as he turns off the road onto a cluttered dirt path, "you don't honestly think we're going to walk into the Greenie the way we used to, do you?"

"Oh, Jesus," Gia says, "it must be two miles through the brush. At least two miles." She turns and faces Barbara. "We used to walk that far? Hike that far?"

"Carrying food and beer," Barbara adds. "No, thank you. I'll have my sandwich here, if you don't mind." She opens the cooler resting on the seat beside her.

"Aw, bite me, you lazy witches." Yozo grins and slams it into four-wheel drive as they bounce and bump their way into the woods, back to where they once celebrated their youth, when they didn't know what youth was.

"I'll be right back," Yozo says as Barbara and Gia descend carefully through a thick stand of birch trees to the concrete edge of the huge dam.

"It's just the same," Gia says. "It's the first thing in this town that hasn't changed."

Barbara stands beside her. "Did we really swim in here? I wonder how deep it is?"

"We swam in it, we peed in it, we groped each other in it. No wonder I sometimes feel more amphibious than I should."

Barbara laughs. "You got felt up here, remember?"

"Artie Lancaster, the new boy from Philadelphia. He groped me in the water. At first I thought it was an accident, and then he did it again. Then we kissed. So romantic! I thought I had bumped into an underwater log. It was him." Gia shakes her head. "I made a big mistake, not laying that boy when I had the chance. I wonder where he is now."

"He's the police chief," Barbara tells her. "Trust me. You don't want to have sex with him anymore."

"Were we the only virgins in our class when we graduated, do you think?" Gia asks.

"I think so. It was you and me. I hadn't really

gone all the way yet. That didn't happen until I met Eddie."

"You were a virgin when you got married?" Gia is thrilled. "Let me get my camera."

"No, we did it before the wedding. But," she holds out her left hand, "after I got the ring."

"That's a nice stone." Gia lifts Barbara's hand closer to her face. "You did all right." For a second she thinks of kissing the back of her hand, just to see what she would do.

"Yeah, I did great. You hungry? I'm hungry." Barbara turns and slips into the birch stand.

Gia stays and watches the water, dark blue under the October sun. She hears Barbara call out for Yozo once, twice, and then, louder, a third time. She climbs up the short slope to find Barbara with the cooler of tuna sandwiches, cold-cut hoagies, bags of chips, plastic bags of cookies, containers of cole slaw and potato salad, and, in another cooler, packed with crushed ice, a twelve-pack of Diet Coke.

"He's gone," Barbara says, "he took the car and left us here. *Sonofabitch!*" She runs to the entrance to the clearing. "*Yozo, you rotten sonofabitch! Get back here!*"

A phone rings in the cooler where the food is stashed. Gia picks it out and answers it. "You mad at me?" Yozo asks.

"What the fuck, Yozo?"

"You girls need some time alone, that's what I think, so I'll be back in about, oh, let's say about four o'clock, all right?"

"*Motherfucker!*" Barbara screams.

"She's not taking this little surprise too well, is she?" Yozo asks.

"Enjoy your last afternoon on this earth, you prick asshole cocksucker," Gia says, and disconnects. Then she walks down to the edge of the dam and hurls the phone into the water.

"You want tuna, or this one, I think it's turkey—no, it's just meat, lunch meat. You want this?" Barbara asks.

"I'm not hungry. Get me a Coke."

Barbara hands Gia a can, across the broken bricks of what once was an ice house, a turn-of-the-century structure where large blocks of ice, cut from the Greenie dam, were stored and then broken up and sold to icemen. Gia can still remember, ever so faintly, the iceman in his wooden truck, it was orange, stopping at certain houses in her neighborhood. The kids, they used to sneak up behind the truck and steal slivers of the clear, smooth ice, and run away with them. Ice so clean, it looked like diamonds. Ice like she'll never see again on this earth. She remembers how it tasted, cold, clean, like forever. It tasted simple.

Barbara tosses the hoagies back into the cooler, pulls out a bag of chips, holds it up for Gia, who shakes her head; Barbara throws it back. Then she snaps open a can of Coke and lights a cigarette. "I like your hair that way," she says. "Is that a perm?"

"Why do you let him hit you?"

"Oh."

Her exclamation is so simple, so short, like a puff of air, that Gia knows it was genuine.

"I know you don't want to talk about it, but I do. Yozo thought he was doing a good thing, leaving us here, but I don't," she admits. "I wish he hadn't done it, maybe even more than you do. But here we are, and after he comes back, we don't ever have to see each other again. I'd just like to go away knowing exactly why my oldest best friend lets her husband hit her."

"It would have been a lot better if you hadn't wrecked Eddie's Packard."

"Yeah, I know, but, you know, somebody beats up my old friend, I get pissed. It's a failing of mine. Apparently, everybody else just takes it in stride."

Barbara delicately sidesteps the issue Gia has just tossed at her. "So you just rushed in to take care of me, didn't you? Big strong Gia, taking care of weak little Barbara."

"No, it wasn't that at all. I—"

"That's just what it was. You don't know anything, but you put yourself right in the middle of someone else's life and you try to take it over and you just end up making it worse."

"I'm sorry."

"Yeah. Sorry. Thanks."

"It's not me trashing the car that we're talking about," Gia persists. "Why, Barbara? Why?"

Barbara is silent.

"I guess that's the way it is, huh?" Gia leans back against the old bricks, warm from the autumn sun, not entirely unhappy to be sitting beside the Greenie, something she never imagined doing again. "Well, as long as I'm pissing you off, I might as well tell you that it's not a perm, and that this is how it dries right out of the shower, without my doing anything to it. All the gray came in wavy. I had straight hair until I went gray. So, there you are."

"See," Barbara says, "it's awfully hard to deal with perfection. We don't get a whole lot of it around here."

"I was your best friend."

"That was a long time ago, Gia. Why don't you just take care of your business here and go back to California and go on with your perfect little life? That's what you're going to do anyway."

"Perfect, huh?" That's when she starts laughing. "Yeah, I guess with your complete lack of knowledge about my life, it would seem perfect to you. Christ Almighty, have you gone through your life just knowing all this stuff about people, without ever bothering to get the specifics, or the facts? Do you just decide things about them, and then proceed as if what you made up is real? Is that how you've lived your life, Barbara? Must be easy. Easier than getting to know real live human beings, dealing with their complexities, their randomness. You just decide what's what, and you go on. Which one are you, the White Queen or the Red Queen?"

"You see, that's the kind of crap you dish out. I don't even know what you're talking about."

Gia sips her Coke. "And through the years you

managed to grow really stupid, too. Good. It's not like you wasted your life."

"Fuck you."

"Fuck you."

They sit silently, fortunately around the corner of the icehouse foundation from each other, so they don't even have to avoid each other's looks. Finally Barbara says, "This is really dumb."

"Yeah."

"You're scary."

"Yeah. So I've been told."

"Don't you care?"

"I don't know what it means. What I could do about it. I know lots of people who aren't afraid of me."

"How come you never came back? I mean, even for a visit? When I used to see your uncle around years ago, I'd ask him how you were, you know? He'd always say you were fine. Sometimes he'd tell me about visiting you."

"It didn't work out that way," Gia says. "You live in California, all your East Coast relatives come to visit you, not the other way around. It was good for Tony and Francie to bring the boys out, it got to be a regular thing, years went by. Barbara, except for my cousin's funeral, I never even thought about coming back here. Decades go by," she observes.

"You're just going to leave, so why should we bother?" Barbara asks. "And you won't come back."

"Indeed. Why should we? I'm so tired. In case you've forgotten, I'm in the middle of a deathwatch. Although," she looks up at the blue sky, "this isn't exactly how I envisioned it."

"I'm sorry about your uncle."

"Yeah, well, the natural rhythm, life, death, all that. It's the next step."

"But you're really close to him."

"Yozo's closer, I think. It's harder for him. Why aren't you and Yozo friends? I thought, with the two of you in the same town, you'd be close, like before."

"No, no," Barbara laughs, "not like before. You didn't know, Gia."

Gia's head rises, serpentlike, above the crumbling edge, to look over and to face Barbara. "You and Yozo?"

"In high school, well, yeah, sort of."

"We all hung together, what?"

"No, there were times when we went off, just him and me. Down to his neighbors' cabin, down the valley."

"And?"

"And. He used to go down on me. It was great."

Her head is all the way up now. "But you said Eddie was the first."

"He was."

"Ohmygod. You did it to Yozo. I did it to Willie."

"Everything but."

"You blow him?"

Barbara is adamant. "No. What kind of girl do you think I was?"

"Me neither."

"Jerk him off?" Barbara asks, her hand making a familiar gesture.

"Sure. If there was lots of Kleenex."

"But no all the way."

"No, not with Willie."

"So, who was your first?"

"A guy I met in Rome. An American student. From Cornell. No big deal. I was ready. He was spending a year there, studying the Renaissance. He had an *appartamento* not far from where I was staying, and we spent a lot of time getting to know each other, talking about doing it, setting it up. God, we spent hours and hours at the *caffe*, planning my deflowering. He was just a year older than I, nineteen years old. He was terrific. We had a great dinner, with wine, then went back to his place, he had candles everywhere, Andy Williams on the stereo, more wine, and you know, I think back, it was just the most amazingly romantic night. It was just how you want to relinquish your virginity. He was gentle. He was careful. He was just perfect. I went home the next morning, and I never saw him again. He called, but I never called him back."

"What was his name?" Barbara asks.

"What else? Joe."

"Yeah, of course."

"What was your first time like?" Gia asks.

"It was great. I had my own apartment. It was just a little bit of a place, but it was the first thing that was all mine. I had it fixed up nice. I was happy living there. I tried some roommates, but I could afford to live by myself, and I really loved it. I started taking some courses at Rutgers. I was gonna save up and go full-time, maybe in a couple of years.

"Then I went to a dance with some girlfriends from work, there were some guys from the Army there, from Fort Dix, and Eddie was one of them. He was so handsome, Gia. He was just the best-looking boy I had ever seen. I had dyed my hair red, and he really had a thing for redheads. We danced all night the first night we met, and then he sent me flowers at work the next day, and he called, and we started going out. We had been dating for about two months, and it got pretty hot, I mean, really hot, but we didn't do it. I wanted to, but he held back. And then he proposed, down on one knee and all that, gave me the ring, threw me down, and I finally had my way with him."

"God. That's the All-American engagement sex story, isn't it? Was it good the first time?"

"Not as good as it had been with Yozo. That boy, let me tell you, had an amazing tongue."

"Yozo?"

"Yozo. I don't know why Chris isn't nicer to him."

"What's the story there?"

"He's a dickhead. She's put up with his dicking around, all over the place, and she just got sick of it. She's kicked him out a bunch of times, I don't know how many, but he's a rich man, so she always takes him back."

"She'd get a bundle if she divorced him. I don't know if Pennsylvania is a community property state, but I don't get the feeling that Yozo would be cheap in a divorce, do you?"

"Cheap? He'd rather pay to have her killed than pay her."

"Yeah, well, I've seen that in my job. Guys who start out saying, 'Give her whatever she wants,' and by the time we're in the home stretch, they're fighting over the paper towel holder in the kitchen." Gia lifts herself up to the edge where Barbara is sitting, and reaches behind her for another Diet Coke. "You want another one?"

"No, I'm okay."

"I once had a client who was ordered to pay temporary support to his estranged wife. This was not a poor man. The judge told him to pay her seven dollars a week. By the time it reached this point, I know the judge hated both parties. I even hated my own client. Seven fucking dollars a week, right? What does he do? He orders me to appeal it. I had no choice.

"Guess what? It's reduced to three dollars a week, and the judge calls me into chambers and tells me if I don't get a settlement worked out between these anklebiters, he's gonna rip me a new asshole. After that court session my client sits in my office, paying me five hundred dollars an hour, crying his ass off because he has to pay three dollars a week. Figure that."

Barbara smiles. "They're dicks. No doubt about it." She lights another cigarette.

"Yozo? Really?"

"You want to know all of it?" Barbara looks

cocky, and Gia realizes that she is with her old girlfriend again.

"I want to know whatever you want to tell me."

"That's a safe answer. You're a diplomat, too,
huh?"

"No, I just don't want to scare you anymore."

Barbara looks at her for a long time. "That was
the perfect answer. You sure are perfect."

"Fuck you."

"That was a compliment."

"Excuse me, I'm a little touchy."

"Yozo is the father of my daughter. He doesn't
know it. Don't tell him."

"It was the happiest time of my life, before my wedding," Barbara begins. "I had quit my job in Jersey,
given up my apartment, and moved back home. I
took a whole month just to plan the wedding. With
my mom. We had fittings, and got the hall and the
caterer, and picked out the flowers, and got all the
bridesmaids' dresses made, and shoes dyed to
match, and everything. I dreamed about this wedding my whole life, and it was going to be everything I ever wanted.

"Six days. Six days before the wedding and
Eddie's brother, who was supposed to be his best
man, came down with the measles. So he was out
and here's Eddie, who's from Ohio and he doesn't
know anybody here, and he has to find somebody
to be his best man.

"So, I'm walking down Coal Street one day on
my way to my grandmother's house, and I'm almost

in tears because we already have Jackie's tuxedo and we have to find a best man and I don't know anybody since I've been gone from this town too long, and I hear a man calling to me from his car driving down the street. It was Yozo. I hadn't seen him since graduation. He was funny, I just kept walking and he said what are you up to, and I said I'm getting married on Saturday, this was like the Tuesday before, and he said that's good, do you want to go out with me, and I said, I told you, I'm getting married on Saturday, and he said, yeah, I heard you but what are you doing tonight?

"So I got in his car and I just started crying, telling him about the best man and everything and he said, I'll be the best man, and I looked at him and he had been in the Army and all and he had filled out some, so that he'd be about Jackie's size, and I said why don't you come back to the house with me and try it on, so we went back, and nobody was home and we had a couple of beers and nobody was home, you know? I guess I was just so grateful to him, or maybe it was something I had always wanted to happen, but I just didn't want him to be the first, or something. I don't know. I was so scared, and he said he'd never say anything, and he didn't. And I didn't. He was the best man, we had our beautiful wedding, and I was so happy.

"Wouldn't you know it, though? The guy we hired to take the pictures messed up, and we never got any wedding pictures. It was like God was going to make sure there wouldn't be any pictures of me and Yozo. So, I was real careful on our honeymoon—we went up to the Poconos for a week—but when we went back to Jersey, and Eddie started back to work and I was just gonna be a housewife, and I started with morning sickness, which I thought was the flu, or that I was just tired or something from all the excitement of the wedding, but I didn't get better, and when the doctor told me that I was pregnant, I immediately knew it wasn't Eddie's. It had to be Yozo's.

"When Andrea was born, she looked just like him, blonde hair, just like him. I told Eddie that I had been a towhead when I was little, but that was my sister. I showed him her baby pictures, and he never questioned it. He even picked her name. Before she was born, he told me he had had a dream that I had had a girl and her name was Andrea. And she was always his favorite. The boys were all right, as far as Eddie was concerned, but there was never anyone like his little girl.

"Who isn't even his little girl.

"She's so much like Yozo. Headstrong and selfish. She wants what she wants and she wants it, like, yesterday. She was the one who got married the night of her junior prom. We didn't know she was already pregnant—she had had an abortion in tenth grade, but I never told her father, I mean Eddie, about that—and she had decided not to waste the dress. Can you imagine that kind of thinking? Who does that remind you of?

"So now she's loaded down with a kid of her own, they live in this teeny-tiny trailer, he's barely making enough to support them, since he's not a very good mechanic, she works sometimes, but mostly she doesn't. Sometimes I look at her and think that maybe she's not even mine.

"You know that I could never tell Yozo. He's too unpredictable and I didn't want to get into that. It would have ruined my life, and my marriage, so it was better just to go on. You're the first person I've ever told about it, and I know you won't say anything. It would just cause so much bad trouble. I don't want him to know. You won't tell, will you?"

"How the hell do you live here all these years with that kind of secret?" Gia speaks softly, slumped against the bricks.

Barbara, who has been lighting cigarettes, one from the other, laughs without smiling. "Guess," she mutters.

"You drink. He doesn't hit you. You drink."

"It's not that bad. I'm clumsy. He doesn't hit me. Eddie's a good guy. He deserved better."

"Sonofabitch. You and Yozo have a kid. Oh, Christ, wait! That little girl is Yozo's granddaughter!"

Barbara nods. "I'm already planning to keep her away from little Joey. I really don't want both of Yozo's grandchildren dating each other."

Gia covers her face with her hands. "I don't fucking believe you." She drops her hands and grabs Barbara's arm. "It was Yozo. It was always Yozo, wasn't it?"

Her old friend looks away from her. "Six days," she says. "For those six days I thought I would lose my mind. I wanted to call the wedding off, I wanted to go with Yozo, and I couldn't. I was afraid. He was such a goofball then, he didn't have any kind of future, and Eddie had a job in Jersey, it was gonna be secure for us." She almost laughs, but makes only a sour sound. "I was wrong about that, too. His plant closed, we ended up back here."

"My God," Gia says.

"You know how different we are," she says to Gia. "You want to know?"

"I'm not sure we're that different," Gia says.

"I've never been on a plane," Barbara tells her. I've never been anywhere but Pennsylvania and New Jersey. You take planes like you're getting in a car, don't you?"

"Well, no, not hardly."

"I wanted so much. I got nothing. I really thought I'd go back to college, maybe get a teaching degree. You know what I loved? Literature, American literature. I think I maybe would have been a good English teacher. But I couldn't do it. There was a time when Eddie wanted out. I got so scared. I didn't love him anymore, but what was I gonna do without him?"

Gia looks at her friend for a long time. "Can I have a cigarette?" she finally asks.

"You don't want this." Barbara places her hand over the pack.

"Oh, yeah, I really do," Gia assures her. "If you're smoking, I'd better smoke, too."

She lights one, coughs, gags, and stubs it out while Barbara laughs. "You've lost your talent."

"I'm worse than you," Gia says.

"How are you worse than me?"

"In terms of screwing up your life, I win. Not only do I win," she pokes Barbara's shoulder gently, "but I get the prize, because I fucked up not only my life, but the lives of four other people." She holds up her hand. "Five, count them. Five. Maybe there'll even be more someday. I win, Barbara.

"When my husband died, it's almost sixteen years ago now, he left me with his kids. The boy was twelve and the girl was five. The first thing I did was to adopt them. They really wanted me to do that. Well, Cameron, the boy, did. Nancy didn't really understand about her daddy being dead. But their mother had died when Nancy was just a little girl, sort of like mine did, and there I was, mother to two kids going through an impossible situation.

"It was rough, we had some bad times, but we got through them. Or so I thought. I was too young to understand that a parent's death leaves permanent damage. I thought if I could just get them to a certain age, they'd be all right. I was young. I was stupid. All the shrinks, all the therapists, all the money, and I overlooked the most obvious truth. That it never goes away.

"When Cameron turned fifteen, he got a little wild. I expected that. He was a big, tall kid. His father had been tall, six foot four, and Cam looked just like him. That caused me more heartache than I realized. Nancy favored her mother, she was fair, but Cam, he was his father's boy. I think, just to protect myself, I built a certain distance between me and the boy. I didn't really want to fall into some Oedipal or Electral Greek thing, even if I was his stepmother. I just didn't want to see him. It was too charged. I should have sent him off to boarding school or something like that, I know that now.

"Now. When it's too late.

"I had the facts-of-life talk with both of them when they asked, just like the books and the doctors say. They both understood sex and all its consequences, or so I thought. Shit, Barbara, even today I don't understand the power of sex, but there I was, so sure that I had equipped these kids.

"So, one evening Cam, who is fifteen and very handsome and very bright and very precocious and very dangerous, comes to me and asks me to buy him some condoms. Without even thinking about it, I say to him, If you're old enough to fuck, you're old enough to buy your own condoms.

"Good wisecrack, huh?

"In my whole life, if there was ever one line I wish I could take back, that's it.

"He stormed out. I thought it was just a teenage boy stud thing, you know, carry them in your wallet. Today, kids have condoms, you can get them at the corner store or anywhere, but thirteen years ago, it wasn't yet like that.

"I never thought to ask him if he was having sex. I never even thought of it. I had put that distance between him and me, and I think maybe I didn't want to know. Me, the liberal, the humanist, the free thinker, the stupid stepmother.

"When his little girlfriend came with Cameron to
meet me, I found out two things: she was fifteen,
too, and she was five months pregnant. Her father
was a judge, wouldn't you know it? Devout Roman
Catholics. She wore uniforms to school, for Christ's
sake.

"There was never even any kind of civilized discussion. Her mother had to be sedated, and her
father just looked at Cameron and said, "You're
marrying her, and you're going to stay married."

"He had just turned sixteen. It was the most
barbaric act I ever committed, signing that consent form so that he could marry her. I can still see
his face, his eyes, looking at me with such betrayal
and fear. All I wanted to do at that moment was to
scoop up John's boy, my boy, and take him away,
and, Barbara, I should have. I should have. But I
didn't.

"Nancy couldn't understand where her brother
had gone. They had grown so close, he was her protector, her big brother. The judge and his wife fixed
up a little apartment for them in their house, and
that was the end of it. Caroline gave birth to a little
boy. He was born with a heart defect. For a month
or so, it was touch and go.

"Do you know that I never went to the hospital
to see that baby? Not until he was discharged.

"I thought, if he died, I might get John's son
back. I was wishing a baby dead. You cannot get
lower than that.

"Caroline got pregnant again right after they graduated from high school. She had another boy, he was perfect. Jeremy and Justin. My husband's grandsons. Cameron started college, dropped out. Her parents and I bought them a nice little house in Berkeley. They're still there. My stepson paints houses, when he works. Mostly he collects unemployment and watches TV. He comes to visit me sometimes, at the office, when he wants money. He comes there instead of to the house because he thinks he can embarrass me into giving him more. I give him everything he asks for, sometimes more.

"Caroline used to call, invite me to lunch. They were delicate times, a young girl and her husband's stepmother. We tried, but it didn't work. I kept thinking, I gave him to you, honey. I handed him up to you like a guard turning a prisoner over to an executioner.

"His sister never forgave me. Cameron told her the whole story. She left as soon as she graduated from high school. I got tuition bills and credit card bills, but I never got a Mother's Day card. She's a senior at Berkeley now, but I'm not sure what her major is. She hasn't been home for four years.

"Caroline watches TV, that's what she does. The boys are beautiful, but little thugs, undisciplined and common. I'll keep practicing law until I die, just so that I can be around to get them out of jail when they're arrested. And they will be. They will be. Maybe then I'll be able to have some kind of relationship with them, the grandsons."

• • •

By the time the Rover pulls into the clearing, they have cleaned up the empty Coke cans. Gia has taken it upon herself to pick up after Barbara; she finds all the cigarette butts, there are lots of them, and dumps them into the bag with the empties. The sun is getting low in the sky when they walk slowly to the car where Yozo waits for them.

He keeps his window down as they approach, an act of brazen good faith, and smiles broadly at them. "Good. There are still two of you. Good." He guns the engine. "Toss the coolers in the back and jump on in," he tells them.

Barbara gets in the front this time, and Gia sits in the center of the backseat. Yozo watches her in the rearview mirror. "So?" he asks.

"We had a good time," Barbara says. She turns, smiling, to look at Gia, and says, "It was good girl time."

"Yeah, it was. You were right." Gia pokes his shoulder. "You did all right."

"What?" He looks wary. "Why are you being so nice?"

"You got one right for a change," she tells him. "You're just not used to it. You thought we'd be mad. We're not."

"What are you gonna do?" he asks, not believing them for a second.

"Take me home, Yozo," Barbara commands. "I'm tired, and I've got a headache. I haven't had this much fresh air since the last time I was up the Greenie."

"That shit'll kill you," Gia concurs. "I want to

shower and change and go to the hospital. You see Willie today?"

"No." He throws it into reverse and backs up, heading out on the path. "I beeped him a couple of times, but he didn't call back. What happened with you two last night, anyway?"

"Oh, we had lots of sex up the cemetery. Like the old days, you know? He's probably just resting. I don't think he's been laid in a long time."

"No, what, I mean, what? He was weird last night."

"We had some things happen. Things that don't concern you. Can you leave it at that?"

"Yeah, but I don't want to."

"Oh, God!" Barbara gasps. "That potato salad! Oh, God! Stop, Yozo, stop now!"

He brakes just as they approach the main road, and Barbara jumps out, staggers away from the car, back down the path they just came over, bent over, holding her stomach. Gia looks out over Yozo's shoulder. "Go get her, Yozo," she orders him, "she's sick."

He leaves the engine running, and Gia climbs over into the driver's seat as Barbara does a neat twist around Yozo as he reaches for her and makes her break, running faster than Gia would have thought she could as she jumps into the Rover, and they peel out in reverse, leaving him standing there, in the woods, as they both throw him the finger from their respective windows.

Yozo watches them disappear backward down the thickly branched path, and then smiles as he takes out a cell phone and calls his garage, telling one of his countermen exactly where he is and how to pick him up.

Gia calls her law firm and spends more than an hour catching up with what she has missed. Her absence does not seem to have caused major damage to her clients, which leaves her just a little unnerved, but mostly relieved.

Her answering machine at home has a few calls from other single women she sees from time to time. There are no messages from her stepchildren, and only one from the judge she's seeing, saying hello.

When she hangs up, her room in Tony and Francie's house is dark. It has turned to night again. Gia looks over her shoulder, out the window, at the town's lights glistening in the valley below. It looks to be such a dark night. She turns on a lamp.

Willie Cunningham places the heavy leather volume back on the shelf in the rectory library. She'll get a kick out of that, he thinks. I'll bet she's never seen it, or if she has, she won't remember.

Finally, he thinks, finally I have something to show her. Something no one else can show her. His heart pounds. He sits heavily behind the desk and reaches across it to turn on the light, but then his hand draws back, and he sits still, because tonight the darkness seems to suit him.

"What are you doing home?" Christine Walenticonis asks her husband, who has just silently entered the family room, where she sits watching something on cable. "How come?"

He stands before her. "Where's Joey?"

"He's in Wilmington for a couple of days. He took the baby, remember, to see his mother?"

"Ah, yeah." Yozo sits beside his wife on the red leather sofa. "You look nice."

"You been home at all this week?" she asks.

"Not much. Tony's dying, and Gia and Willie and Barbara and I have been spending most of our time at the hospital. I've been sleeping at the store."

"How is he?"

Yozo shakes his head. "Not good. It won't be long."

"I'm sorry. I know how much he means to you."

"Yeah. Well."

They watch the huge-screen television in silence for a while, until Christine says, "Do you want to invite them over for dinner or something?"

"No, that's okay, it's not necessary."

"I could make something nice. It'd be nice, Joe."

He puts his arm around her shoulder, like he used to when they went to the movies. "Maybe one night, then," he tells her. "Thanks." He holds her a little bit tighter, and his hand slides down to her breast.

"Don't even think about it," she tells him.

The yearbook from their junior year smells just a little of mildew. The basement had flooded one spring, after an especially snowy winter, and some water had gotten into the storage room. She turns the stiffened pages carefully. Look at us, she thinks. Look at us. All that teased hair. We look like we're wearing hats.

There is the picture she's looking for. The four of them, part of the pep rally committee, performing some kind of skit, what they used to do in the auditorium in front of the whole school on Friday afternoons before the evening football games. It is the only photograph of all four of them that she has ever seen. We should have taken more pictures, she thinks, but that is the observation of the middle-aged woman, not the teenage girl who never thought that, more than thirty years hence, she would be wishing there were pictures.

"It's simple. He doesn't want anybody in there except his wife and kids. How hard is that to understand?" Gia snaps at Mella, finally enjoying whatever brief power Tony has bestowed on her. Gia is physically blocking the door to Tony's hospital room, and Mella, vast, bellowing Mella is crying, something that looks alien on her, and shouting at Gia. Her granddaughter is trying, without success, to comfort the old man.

"He's my kid brother," she hisses at her. "Who the hell do you think you are, telling me what I can't do?"

Tony is wrong, Gia realizes with a start. She moves aside. "I'm sorry," she says to her aunt, who rushes past her into the room.

Gia lifts her eyebrows and nods at the young woman, who is looking solemn and scared. "Dying is for the living, too, you know? Come here." She holds out her hand to the young woman.

They turn and enter Tony's softly lit room, where Francie, Joey, Lenny, and Mella surround their husband, father, brother. Tony sees Gia enter and closes his eyes.

This is it.

The boys are crying, holding onto each other. Francie stands to Tony's right, holding his hand, looking so frightened. Gia recalls how she looked across the kitchen table when she faced Mella down; her brown eyes are swollen now, but dry, as though she has no more tears. But she does. Gia knows she does. She can feel Francie's fear as she puts her arm around her. She married him when she was just a young woman, and she has never been alone in this world. Her sons will be there for her, but she is about to be left behind by the only man she has ever loved.

Gia thinks of Yozo. "Excuse me," she says to her family, and slips out to the hallway, to the nurses' station, where she calls him and tells him to come. Tony wanted his family tonight, his close family, and that means little Joey Walenticonis. Yozo says he's on his way.

The nurses look at her as she leans across the counter to hang up the phone. They know, too. They look away when she meets their eyes.

Back in the room, they do something that seems so odd, yet, Gia thinks, it might be the price we all pay, at some time, for loving someone: we wait for him to die.

She has nothing left to say to Tony. He knows everything he ever needed to know about her, and even when she wasn't as good as she might have been, he loved her. He took her as his child, he took his godfathering seriously, and he gave her all that she needed. He and his father, her grandfather, loved her so well that nothing, not even the evil Mella, could ever stop her. And he knows that she carries them both inside her, in her blood, in her thoughts, in her heart. She is the one, she knows. His sons will carry his name, and Gia carries his spirit.

"I will love you forever," she bends and whispers into his ear. And she remembers bending over another man, already dead, and whispering the same words.

The door behind her opens, and Yozo enters, tears streaming down his face. His father is dying, too.

In the strange fellowship of those soon to be left behind, they all embrace, Yozo, Francie, Joey, Lenny, Mella, Mia. He turns to Gia last; the two old friends are beyond arms around each other, yet still he reaches for her, and she is relieved to be in his grasp. For this one final time she can let Yozo be the strong one.

Then she feels him shaking, and she holds on tighter.

That's all right. Gia can be the strong one one more time. It's Yozo.

As it gets later, as Barbara looks around the house, she thinks about the lemonade she mixed up the day before, and she goes to the refrigerator, gets out the plastic pitcher, goes into the cabinet below the sink, where the cleaning stuff is kept, and from the row of bottles and cans farthest back, behind the garbage disposal, she pulls a bottle of generic vodka, the cheapest the State Store sells. It's a quart, it costs next to nothing, and it tastes pretty good in the cheap, powdered lemonade she likes so much. The plastic tumbler is tall and holds about a pint; her kids used to use it for punch in the summers, when they played out back, jumping in and out of that great aboveground pool Eddie put up for them.

She goes to the window behind the sink and looks out at the black night. In the sunlight of her memory, she sees the swing set, the jungle gym, the kids running, wet and skinny, their perfect little bodies jumping from one thing to another, their hair dripping in their eyes, laughing, laughing so loud, so hard. They were brown and slippery and gorgeous. My kids, she thinks. My kids.

She pours the vodka into the tumbler until it is half-full, tops it off with lemonade, and as she gratefully sucks in the first gulp, she closes her eyes to the sunlight that only she can see.

Tossing and turning in his narrow rectory bed, Willie Cunningham fights to obliterate the pictures he sees when he closes his eyes. They are too seductive, though, and he can't help watching; the pictures move slowly across his mind, and his hand reaches down.

Dear God, please.

But he watches. In the dark, alone, under the

heavy wooden crucifix nailed to the wall above his head, he watches and he moves, his lips silently make words he has never said out loud, the pictures go faster, and then he rises up, in a final act of surrender, he rises up as if to meet his lover, and when he sinks down again, he knows that it was his last time.

"He's hanging in there," the doctor tells them. "It's weak, but it's there. Why don't you go down and have a cup of coffee?" he says. "We'll keep someone here with him. Go ahead."

"I'll stay," Gia tells Tony's wife and sons. "You've been here a long time, go ahead. Yozo, go with them, go on."

She pulls up a chair, she sits beside him, she strokes his hair—he is already gone from her, but it is nice to touch him. He looks like his mother, she thinks, and she knows, wherever he is now, he is dreaming of her, the one he loved so. He is coming close to his brother, Gia's father. He will soon meet his father, her grandfather. They are waiting, her cousin Peter, the young nephew he loved, her *zia* Maria, her godmother, his sister, they are waiting, and Gia knows—her eyes fill with tears as she thinks this, for her Catholic training will never let her go—they are moving toward him even now, in her time, in their own, eternal time, with their arms open to him, and Tony, for all that he scorned, like his father before him, the man who taught them only to believe in themselves, Gia knows that Tony is lifting his arms to greet them, too, the ones he loved, the ones who love him still.

Then she notices that he has stopped breathing. A weird rattle comes from deep in his chest. If she hadn't been leaning over him, she might not have heard it, and he breaks wind in the weakest way.

Just like that, she marvels. You were here and now you're someplace else.

And then she realizes that a terrible mistake is about to be made and that she can stop it.

She flies out of his room, yelling at the nurses, "Where are the stairs?" They point, and, thank God this is such a little, small-town hospital, Gia runs down only a couple of flights before she smashes through the cafeteria doors and yells at the only occupied table, "Come quick! Come now! He's going!"

She's back in the room—it is no longer Tony's room, just the room—before they rush in, Francie in the lead, panting and flushed, and Tony is still warm as Gia watches her bend over her husband and burst into tears. Gia waits a heartbeat or two before she says, "Thank God you got back in time."

"Thank God," Joey, at the foot of his father's hospital bed, says, and makes the sign of the cross.

"Just in time." Gia sighs.

Francie looks up. "He's gone," she says quietly.

"He waited for all of us to be here," Gia notes.

"Thank God." Francie crosses herself, and since it seems the thing to do, Gia does, too. When she looks up, Lenny is smoothing his father's hair, crying, and she realizes that Yozo never came in. She goes out to the hallway and sees him disappear onto the elevator. His grief tonight is private.

She goes down the stairs once more and meets Mella, Mia, Tessa, Angelina, Gar, and Rosa, standing in the cafeteria.

"It's over," she tells them.

The aunts burst into collective wailing, just as she expected. Gar stands beside his wife but doesn't move to comfort her. The aunts stand apart and cry alone, and there is no touching. What odd women they are, Gia thinks. Tessa dabs her daughter's face, but Mia is not crying. She is watching her mother's aunts, too.

Gia's *padrino* died tonight. She lied about his death. She covered it up.

Somewhere in eternity, he is proud of her.

Willie steps off the elevator, in priest garb, flushed, a purple stole around his neck, flying as he rushes to Gia's side and scoops her into his arms.

"Are you all right?" he asks, his eyes searching her face.

"I was with him. He just died. No nothing. He just died."

He holds up a prayer book. "I have to do this," he almost apologizes.

"I know," she says. "Life goes on."

They fall onto him, one at a time, only Lenny holding back, curiously defiant, almost as though his father's rebellious spirit has already seated itself in his older son; Willie comforts them, mumbling the words he has used so many times before, thinking of all the nights he sat here with the old man who now lies dead before them. "He died in a state of grace," he tells the survivors. He lived in a state of grace, Willie thinks, moving to his own tune, always true to his own code. Would that I could be such a man. He feels his face flush.

"You understand, I know, that the sacraments are for the living. There are prayers for a time such as this, with Tony already gone, that's what these prayers are for."

The reading that Willie will now give to Tony's family, the Angels of Death, his brother-in-law, his sons and his wife, the niece and her daughter, everyone but Gia and Yozo, is one he has carefully selected for this night. Long ago, so long ago, it seems, when he realized Tony was not going to get better, Willie took it upon himself to find that passage in the Gospel that would be his own personal good-bye to the man he had loved like no other in his life. His prayer for the man who had shown him how to be a man, even if Willie had not always lived as Tony thought he should. We are both men, he prays to the dead man. I'll never be as good as you, but you helped me to become a man. For that I'll pray for you for the rest of my life, and I'll love you forever.

"From the first letter of John," he begins. "'We have come to know and to believe in the love God has for us. God is love, and he who abides in love abides in God, and God in him.' This is the Word of the Lord."

He makes the sign of the cross on Tony's still warm forehead, and prays, "Lord Jesus, our

Redeemer, you willingly gave yourself up to death."

You never went willingly to your death, Tony. You fought as long as you could, and you waited until everyone was here, just like long ago. Good for you.

"So that all people might be saved and pass from death into a new life."

My life without you will be new. No one to insult me, no one to call me il colletto, the collar, so disrespectful, so perfect, so utterly without pretension or piety in the presence of someone some call a holy man. God, I'm going to miss you.

"Listen to our prayers, look with love on your people who mourn and pray for their brother."

I will always love her for you, Tony, and I'll do my best to watch out for her. I can't do much. I'll help her through the funeral. Maybe that's all I can do, but I'll make sure she knows she has someone a little bit like you, someone who will always love her.

"Lord Jesus, holy and compassionate: forgive Tony his sins."

I know, you never sinned. You told me more than once during our dark nights in this room.

"By dying, you opened the gates of life for those who believe in you: do not let our brother be parted from you, but by your glorious power give him light, joy, and peace in heaven, where you live forever and ever. Amen."

Willie takes from his coat pocket a small flask and sprinkles holy water on the body. He can feel the collective air leaving the lungs of the family members, the relaxing as he takes off his sacramental stole and stuffs it quickly into his pocket. Now he is just another man in a Roman collar and black shirt. He embraces Francie again, Francie whose eyes have never left her dead husband's face. "He's with God now," Willie whispers.

"I know." She finally closes her eyes. "Thank you, Father."

Francie collapses in tears, and her sons take her up in their strong young arms. Willie then knows that it is all right for him to leave.

There is a woman outside, in the hallway, and she might be waiting for him.

"He's at peace now," Willie says because, Gia understands, he doesn't know what else to say to the hollowed-eyed sentinel he finds just outside the hospital room's doorway.

She gives him a long look. "There was never a moment in his life when he wasn't at peace." She glances up at the ceiling. "He was always so sure of himself. So sure that he knew what to do. And, you know, he was always right. If he ever fucked up, I don't know about it."

"There's more than a little of him in you."

"Thank you. Right now that's the kindest thing you could say to me. Are they going to be all right?"

He nods. "They have the mechanics to tend to. Phone calls to make when daylight comes, clothes to select, things like that."

"What do people wear to funerals around here? Do they still get dressed up?"

"It's pretty casual now. You can wear whatever you want."

"Willie, Yozo was here when he died, and then he split, just took off. I want to talk to him. Do you know where he is? Did he go home, do you think? Can you find him? I think he might be taking this harder than any of us."

Willie rubs his eyebrows. He had planned on stopping by Yozo's house on his way back to the rectory. He wanted to clear up the night before, he wanted to apologize to his best friend, and tonight he wanted to be the one to bring him the heartbreaking word of Tony's death. He feels vaguely cheated, and instantly ashamed of himself. When Gia looks at him, he suddenly sees how old she looks. This goddamned night, he thinks.

"I know where he is, I think. We'll find him."

"It's locked?" she asks as Willie fumbles in the dark to get the key in the big brass lock on the church's front door. "Aren't these places supposed to be open twenty-four hours a day?"

"Yeah," he says. "There'd be nothing left inside if we did that. They'd strip the place cleaner than a school of piranha."

"Well, how would he get in here?"

"He has keys."

"He has keys?"

"He has keys to everything. I was once with him when he let himself into the state police barracks. I don't ask. I don't know." He swings the big door open. "Go ahead."

The candlelight is strong enough for her to see Yozo seated in the middle of the third or fourth pew.

He has taken off his baseball cap, and she notices the lovely glow of his bald head amidst the soft light. She slides into the pew beside him. Willie sits behind them.

"Nobody should lose two fathers in one life, but you have," she says to him.

He doesn't seem surprised to see them, didn't even turn around when they came in. "I never really knew the first one," he says. "I felt that one more for my mother. This one, boy, it hurts. I thought I was ready, but I didn't know it would hurt like this."

"When my husband died, one of the things that kept coming back to me was, I had so much more I wanted to ask him. It was like, it was so incomplete, our time together. That made it so hard, that there were going to be things I could never find out from him. I don't feel that about Tony. I asked him everything. Did you?" She leans forward, looking up into Yozo's face. "Did you have more to ask him?"

He is silent for a while. "No." He is quiet again, and then he says, "I don't want to be the grown-up. Now I have to be."

She sits back in the pew, folds her arms across her chest, and slides her suddenly freezing hands into her armpits. "I never thought of that."

"See?" Yozo says.

"We've been adults for a lot of years, kids," Willie offers. "Tonight just made it official."

Yozo almost looks over his shoulder. "You do your thing?"

"Yeah."

Yozo nods. "You were there?" he asks Gia.

"No, out in the hall."

"I lit a candle for him," he says.

"You lit all of them, didn't you, Joe?" Willie asks, and that is when she notices that banks of thick white glass-enclosed pillars are ablaze to the right and to the left of the altar, and behind them, to the left of the confessional, to the right of the stairs leading to the choir loft. She counts the rows—ten—and then she counts the candles in each row—twenty. While they were still at the hospital, Yozo was here, lighting eight hundred candles for his beloved Tony.

"Yeah," he says. "It looks nice, doesn't it?"

"They're three dollars a pop, Yozo."

"Yeah, send me a bill."

Willie taps the back of Gia's head. When she turns, he is smiling, and he winks at her. He's fine, Willie is telling her. "I'll have to clip a little extra out of the collection plate," he says.

"He'd have liked this," Gia says.

Yozo finally looks at her. And he smiles. "He'd love it."

"He does," Willie whispers behind them.

"Can we just sit here?" Yozo asks. "Everybody's gonna be talking for the next few days. I'd like to just sit here and be quiet. Can we do that?"

"You want us to go?" she asks.

"No, I want us to be here. But quiet."

She starts to say, that's the hardest thing for us, but thinks better of it, and instead she gives her old friend the one thing he now wants.

Willie reaches over and runs his hand over Yozo's head, and Yozo nods, still looking straight ahead at the altar, and Willie knows he has been forgiven, that they are as they were before yesterday's hard night, and he reaches to touch the shoulder of the woman sitting in front of him, but he stops his hand, because he realizes that, at this moment of grief, he wants nothing more than to touch her, and he knows that if he does that, he will forget his sadness, his loss, the old man who just died, and Willie doesn't want to forget all that, so he draws his hand back, and they sit, alone, together, three old friends united in loss, sitting in a candlelit church, knowing that the dark night outside belongs to anyone but them.

FIFTH DAY

Yozo is in the family room when his son returns from his trip to Delaware. He holds his breath as he turns to greet the young man, and then releases it in a noisy, relieved hiss. His son is carrying his grandson. Always, when the boy takes the baby to visit his mother, Yozo is sure she will keep the baby, and that not so incredible scenario is the one, he knows, that will take his breath away and he will never get it back.

He holds out his hands, and his son says, "Nice to see you, too, Pop."

For a second Yozo thinks he misheard, and then he snaps his head back and forth, hefts his sleeping grandson's head onto his shoulder, and says to Joseph Walenticonis, Jr., "What did you just call me?"

"Pop. I don't know, it just came out. You mind? It feels right." Yozo's namesake, from when he began to talk, always called his father "Joe," always. It was the family joke.

"No, that's good. Give him here."

"Sure. He's gonna wake up soon. He'll need everything." The boy swings a huge stuffed bag from his shoulder and drops it on the couch. "I didn't mean any disrespect, you know?"

"I know." Where, Yozo wonders, did he learn a word like disrespect?

"Yeah." The young man grins at his father just as he slips out the door. "So long. Pop."

Is there a connection, she wonders, between the contaminated water and the absence of natural fibers in this store? Could that combination account for the madness of the people in the town?

"Polyester's real big here, isn't it?" Gia asks Barbara, who is across the rack from her in one of the big anchor stores at the Anthracite Mall, a huge place five miles from town, the place to which Barbara brought her when the walls of her uncle's house started closing in on her. Friends, distant relatives, people from the grocery store, they filled the house with their good memories and their home-made dishes and their kind gestures of respect to Francie and to her sons. It was, after a while, more than Gia could bear, as though each kind word about Tony made him even more lost to her. Their sympathies codified his passing, and she was not ready to have that happen. Barbara had appeared with a big, rectangular Pyrex dish of lasagna and, after one look at Gia, told her that they were going shopping.

Barbara grins. "Have you noticed that teased hair never went out of style here? The women here knew if they just dug in with their bouffants, they'd be back in style again. And see? I read *Vogue*, I know how chic we all are. Of course, around here, that's pronounced 'chick.'"

Gia pushes the clothes. An odd smell rises from them. It is a scent from another time, but its origin doesn't come to her, so she lets the thought go by. "I'm not going to find anything here. I have a long gray skirt, and a blazer, and boots. Won't that be appropriate?"

"You'll be better dressed than anybody. I just thought you'd like to see what our finest store looks like."

"I'd have to go to Philadelphia or New York to shop." Gia is amazed.

"We used to take the kids to New York for weekends, take them to a show, go sightseeing. Phillie, too. They grew up a lot more street smart than we were. Well, than I was."

"That's good. My kids were city kids. They were pretty young when we moved to Los Angeles, and they had to learn a lot about handling themselves. It's a different world there, and when we got back to San Francisco, which really is a big small town, they were older, but they were also a lot more worldly, which made me happy. I didn't have to worry about them, at least on that score." She turns away from the clothing rack. "Let's get out of here."

"You hungry?" Barbara scampers behind her.

Gia pauses. "Are you fucking crazy? Were you in the same house I was?"

"Yeah, but you didn't really eat anything."

"Before you got there, I ate everything. I don't even want to think about the clothes I have that aren't going to fit."

"That's the only part of getting older that I hate, that the weight doesn't come off the way it used to."

"Are you kidding? You're as slim as you were in high school."

Barbara lifts up her bulky sweater to show Gia a bulging belly, bracketed by those clumps of fat graciously known as love handles.

"Jesus!" she exclaims. "That's scary. Your fly is open, by the way."

"Oh, yeah," Barbara zips up, "that's another

thing about getting older. You can't really dress yourself right anymore."

"You ever go to aerobics classes or anything like that?"

"Do you?"

"Sometimes I sit up while I read the sports pages."

"We're not the type," Barbara concludes.

"If you ever gave up smoking, do you think you'd pack it on?"

"If I stuck food in my mouth as often as I stick a cigarette, and I probably would, I'd be four hundred pounds in a week."

"You're a good little obsessive."

"Thank you. It's good to be good at something. Come on. Let's sit over there."

Barbara leads them to a bench in the middle of the mall walkway. There are four benches, forming a square, and in the center are ficus trees, under an arching skylight. At the corner of each square are industrial-sized ashtrays.

"The concept of a nonsmoking mall hasn't reached this place yet, huh?" Gia asks.

"Nonsmoking, noneating. Try to put those rules in effect, and they'll take your head off. Look around."

There are senior citizens seated on the benches beside and behind them, and the ones who aren't eating something out of a cardboard or plastic container are smoking cigarettes. Old men with their bellies and ill-concealed scrotum hanging heavily between their spread legs. Old women with dyed, teased hair, Supp-Hose and sneakers, wide-leg polyester pants, and brightly printed complementary overshirts, big sizes. Almost all the old people have gnarled hands, but they look comfortable and healthy and happy and prosperous. Not wealthy, not terribly bright, but these, she reminds herself, are people who worked all their lives in factories of one sort or another, and with that thought she remembers what that smell from the clothes rack in the department store reminded her of: Yozo's mother.

I don't even know her name, Gia marvels. She was Yozo's mother. Mrs. Walenticonis. She can't quite recall her face. She remembers her crying at his father's funeral.

"What was Yozo's mother's name?" she asks Barbara. "Her first name?"

"Jeez, I don't know. Missus?"

"I don't know, either."

"What made you think of her?"

"Back there. The clothes. Yozo and I, when we were still in grade school, we used to go to the dress factory to wait for his mother after we got out of school. We'd get out at three-thirty, and she worked at Rainbow Modes until four. Do you remember that place? It wasn't too far from my grandfather's store? No? I'll show you where it was. But sometimes we'd go upstairs, where all the ladies were sewing. Row after row of sewing machines, and the ladies would call to us and they seemed so happy to see us. They used to say that we were boyfriend and girlfriend, and, well, I loved that, but it embarrassed

the shit out of Yozo. And we used to go to where his
mother was, and she had this bin of clothes on her
left, in front of the machine, and as he'd walk up to
her, she'd reach over the bin, her arms, you know,
and hug him and kiss him. Then she'd wave to me.
It was so nice. We would just go up there to tell her
that we were waiting for her. Then we'd go back
downstairs and watch the cutters, with their big
overhead cutting machines, and they'd be laying out
the patterns and cutting through all these thick-
nesses of material.

"And that was what I smelled back there. The
material. It still smells the same." She is amazed at
the clarity of her memory. "There was a horn that
used to sound at four o'clock, and we'd wait at
the bottom of the steps, and his mother used to
come down, punch her card in the time clock, and
then we'd all walk back to his house. She'd fix us
something to eat, but I think about how that
house was now, and it was so small and so sad. I
guess there wasn't a whole lot of money. And that
was while his father was still alive. But how much
money did they make, him in the mines, her in the
factory? Still, she fed us after school whenever we
wanted. She was nice. I can't remember her face."

"She was pretty. She had long light brown hair,
like in a pageboy, but real soft. She was thin, I
think she had something wrong with her. She was
so thin," Barbara repeats.

"She drank." Gia looks straight at Barbara.
"She drank. We always knew that. Yozo knew it.
We used to find her passed out on the floor some-

times, and we'd drag her up on the couch, or on the bed if she was upstairs." Gia hesitates, and then plunges in because it is still the same day that her godfather died, and there is very little that she has left to lose. "Didn't your kids ever have to do that with you?"

Barbara flinches, her eyes widen, and a quick flush appears on her cheeks, as though she has actually been slapped. "You don't leave anything to the imagination, do you?"

"We don't have to pretend."

"I'm not gonna do it anymore." She glances at Gia and then lights another cigarette. "I'm not gonna do it."

Gia keeps her fast mouth in check. This is the first time they've addressed Barbara's drinking directly, and she doesn't want to screw it up. Holding her breath, she says, "Do you know how you're going to do this?"

"By not drinking." Barbara is resting her elbows on her knees, her face in her hands, and she doesn't look at Gia as she says, "I started it and I can stop it." She swings her head around and looks up at her. "Don't you think I can?"

"I think you can do anything you want to do," Gia answers honestly, for she still believes in the goodness of her old friend, that this is still the little girl who came to her to share her milk.

"I have to ask you something," Barbara says quickly, and Gia realizes that she is trembling more than usual. Gia's hand rests on her back, and she rubs it in small circles.

"Yeah, go ahead."

"If I moved to San Francisco, do you think you could help me find a job?"

She hesitates only a second before she says, "Yeah, you can type, you can learn how to use a computer, and I can find something for you at my law firm. It's a great place. Big, lots of very good, very interesting people." She starts to say something else about the firm, and then, realizing that she sounds like a job-fair recruiter, stops, licks her lips, and then says, "What prompted this?"

"Life. Death. Old friends. You take a look at yourself, at your life. You hate what you see. You think about ways you might make it better. Maybe I should have left Eddie for Yozo, but he was already gone, into the Army, married to Christine, then she had his son. What could I do?"

Gia closes her eyes as she continues to stroke her girlfriend's back. This is how we get old, she finally understands. We begin to see the lost opportunities, the things we might have done better, the things we should never have done, the things we didn't do. She remembers when they came to tell her that her husband was dead. Her first words: I wouldn't have missed him for the world. Gia has not led a life of complete regret, of missed opportunities, but her knowledge of loss, that knowledge binds her even closer to Barbara. Ultimately, it is all about loss, what you had, what you lost, what you never had, what you lost.

"Don't look back," she cautions her friend, for now she can begin to be what she truly is—a divorce attorney. This is the easy part, she realizes. "What about your boys?"

"They were never mine," she says. "It's as if Eddie spit and those two boys popped out of the ground. They don't even notice that I'm there half the time. The three of them will be better off without me."

Yeah, Gia thinks, I guess having a drunk mother slopping around the house doesn't provide the ideal environment for mother-son bonding. "Think about this, though, all right? How would it be if you quit drinking and stayed? Maybe you got your own place, your husband goes to counseling with you, you both find out why he slaps you around and why you let him."

She sits up and stares at Gia with such intensity that she is certain for an instant that she's going to slap her, hit her, hurt her. "Have you ever known when something's over? That too much has happened? That it can never be fixed? That's what this is. That's why I have to go away."

You can't take it, Gia thinks, working to keep her face expressionless before her friend's sudden anger. You don't want to stick around to see the damage you've done. Your daughter pops out kids with a bum, and you've probably made your sons into the worst kind of woman-hating males. And now you're going to split and leave it behind, like something you dropped on the movie theater floor.

"My godfather died early this morning. I've buried a husband. I've divorced one. Yeah, I think I know a little bit about when things are over," Gia says slowly. "This isn't a contest, Barbara, who's had the harder life. I'm not questioning your decision. I'm just trying to make sure you've thought it out."

"If you hadn't come back . . ." she starts, and then shrugs, and lights another cigarette.

"You can stay with me until you find your own place. I've got a big house that used to have kids and their friends everywhere, but that's been over for some time now. There's lots of room."

"I'll smoke outside."

"By the time I get back, San Francisco, I have a feeling, might have declared itself smoke-free, indoors and out." Gia looks at her. "Oh, and you've never been to San Francisco! Oh, my, I'll be bringing the city a virgin. It likes that," she jokes.

"Do you think I could go back with you, when you go back?"

Gia blinks. "Barbara, I'm going back right after the funeral, probably the next day. I don't have anything to stick around for. I'm not in the will, and Joey and Lenny can take care of everything else. Willie, too, for that matter. Actually, I think Francie will handle all of them, but," she shrugs, "don't you think that's just a little precipitous? I mean, don't you want to take some time to talk to your kids? Say so long to your granddaughter? Your friends?"

"I want to go now," she says.

"I think I'll need some time to settle back in before you come." Gia is firm. "I'm with you on this, if this is what you want. I'll do everything I can. It's just going to have to be my timetable, okay?"

"Don't wait too long," Barbara says. "I feel like my life is just going to start, and I want to get on with it."

"What about Yozo?"

"Yozo's yesterday," she says, drawing deeply on her cigarette.

"We all are."

"I wish I could tell him everything, but I can't. He's someone else's husband. I should have told him when it happened. I should have let Eddie go and live his life, I was just scared. Jesus, Gia, I'm still scared."

"I won't let anything happen to you," Gia promises. "I'll make sure you're taken care of. This isn't hard. The only part I worry about, Barbara, is how you might sabotage yourself. I can't do anything about that, but I'm going to want you to see someone when you come West, a shrink, that's got to be part of the deal."

She grimaces. "I don't need a shrink."

"Yeah, you do. You've drunk away most of your adult life, you get yourself beat up for I don't know how many years, and now you're abandoning your family. Those are big things, Barbara. Big things, and no matter how easy I can make your life in San Francisco, those things are going to stay with you. You might change, but your behavior won't. And I'm not going to be part of that crap, not if it happens in my backyard."

"I think you're wrong."

"Then don't come."

"It has to be your way or not at all?"

"Yeah, because, listen to me, you've done it your way all your life and it hasn't turned out too well. I don't buy into this big popular concept of victimhood. Sorry. You drank because you wanted to drink, not because it's a sickness or a defective gene or anything like that. If you knew that your drinking was causing problems, you should have stopped. I know it would have been hard, but it could have been done. That's it. There's no discussion, there's no equivocation, there's no negotiation, because, frankly, I've been at this more than twenty years, and I've learned some things. One of the things I've learned is that people don't change. They get older, they just become more of what they were, that's all. People don't change."

"You don't think you've changed?"

"No. I just learned a lot. I haven't changed. And neither have you. You're still my girlfriend, you always will be. We've just both been through some stuff. That's a good thing to call our lives, isn't it? Some stuff."

"We can smoke in public now, and we own houses. And Yozo had hair."

"And Willie wasn't a priest."

"Is that giving you any trouble?"

"More than you can believe, but," she feels an odd kind of sad, "the idea that Willie will sing my godfather's funeral Mass is a whole lot more effective than, say, oh, a ton of saltpeter."

"We have changed," Barbara says, "whether you want to admit it or not."

"I know," Gia admits. "I know."

"Her name was Regina," Barbara says.

"What?"

"His mother. Her name was Regina."

"Oh, puke." Barbara spits when they see, from the driveway, who is out on the deck. Tessa is sitting next to Yozo on the swing, and Willie is deep in conversation with Lenny and Joey. Tessa is talking and Yozo is laughing.

"It looks like he's having a good time," Barbara says in wonderment.

"She can be really funny," Gia recalls. "She can tell awfully funny stories about the old neighborhood."

"I guess everybody has at least one redeeming feature, huh?"

"I read once where Hitler played the harmonica. I'll bet those Nazis did all kinds of dancing around while the Führer played, but when the harmonica music ended, he was still a maniac and a monster and they were still Nazi fucks. She's still Tessa."

"I remember reading that Hitler had a canary. Do you think, when the American troops came in and found Hitler and Eva dead, was the canary dead, too, or did all that take place to the sound of a canary singing?"

Gia looks at her. "You know, you think strange things."

"Maybe canary suicide. A little cyanide pellet in his birdseed?"

"Okay, they see us. Let's go." Gia gets out of Barbara's car.

• • •

"Where's your mother?" she asks the boys.

"At the funeral home," Joey replies.

"You didn't go with her?" Gia is surprised and not pleased.

"Mella went. They can do it."

"Aw, Joey, it's your father," Gia scolds.

"She didn't want us to go," Lenny tells her. "She only wanted Mella."

Lenny tries to help his brother. "Mella knows how to do all that stuff, clothes and stuff."

Barbara nudges the small of Gia's back, and she sees that she is pointing, with her chin, at Tessa and Yozo. Yozo winks at Gia. Tessa is looking intently at him, ignoring their arrival.

"How are you doing?" Willie asks.

"I'm okay, just tired. Really tired. Probably like everybody else. I'll catch up when I go home."

"I'm surprised you haven't gone back already," her cousin chirps, not turning her head to look at Gia.

"You want a drink?" Willie asks.

"That," she tells her old boyfriend, "would be wonderful."

"You like to get out when it gets difficult, don't you?" Tessa won't stop.

"Come on," Yozo says to Tessa, and puts his arm around her shoulder.

But she is not going to stop. Gia can see her losing control, just like when they were kids, and she sits up, as if readying herself for the attack she knows will come.

Willie is standing beside her, handing her a heavy glass. "After five P.M.," he tells her, "Lenny insists we use crystal and linen napkins. No more plastic and paper."

"Some members of this family are more civilized than others," she notes, and sips what, to her astonishment, turns out to be a pretty good single-malt scotch. She looks at Willie. "Your private stash?"

"Your uncle and I went through quite a few bottles of that stuff together." He smiles.

"Nice." That's a lovely picture he's just put in her head, him and Tony drinking and arguing. Like her grandfather and Father Pietro, both now long gone. So long gone.

She drinks more and slides back on the chaise longue. Willie moves her legs over and sits beside her, facing her. He pats her thigh, and then his hand rests on her knee.

"I took her to the mall," Barbara announces. "She didn't buy anything. Surprise!"

"Yeah, leave it to Gia to go shopping," Tessa grates on. "You can't even stay to help clean up. You knew Francie was going to the funeral home this afternoon. Why couldn't you stay?"

Barbara starts to say something, to defend Gia, but then, as if she can hear her friend's thoughts, closes her mouth and glances at her.

"*Mordimi*," she tells her cousin in Italian. Bite me.

"No wonder your husband killed himself. It must have been worth it to get away from you."

The crystal glass catches Tessa just above her left eye, and she screams as the blood begins to flow. It is going so slowly, Gia thinks, and the sound is so faint. There is also no glass in her hand. Willie has grabbed her wrist, but it is too late. Yozo is standing between Gia and Tessa, who, Gia notes from a very quiet place, continues to scream. Barbara is dabbing Tessa's cut with a bunch of linen napkins.

"It's not bad," Barbara tells her. "You don't even need stitches. Just a butterfly."

"How would you know, you little asshole?" Tessa snarls. "My God, you fucking monster, you! Throwing glasses!"

Gia's heartbeat hasn't even increased, she notes, and there is none of that adrenaline that she has come to associate with waking up from bad dreams or dealing with her family. She is as calm as she ever has been. Willie laces his fingers in hers and holds her hand tightly.

"Three kids and emergency rooms," Barbara answers. "You learn fast what needs to be stitched and what doesn't."

"Mia!" Tessa howls. "Mia! Come here! I'm hurt!" She is screeching to the bedroom windows that are just above the deck. Mia sticks her head out.

"What happened?"

"This fucking crazy *puttana* threw her glass at me! Get down here right now! I'm gonna have a scar!" She then bursts into tears.

"I should have aimed for your throat," Gia calmly tells her. Willie squeezes her hand.

Barbara is pushing pieces of the glass away with her foot. Lenny appears with a broom and some newspaper. "Just sit down over there." He nudges the wounded Tessa out of his way. "Let me clean this up."

"I'm bleeding, you little fuck, get away from me!" she shouts at him.

"Fuck you." He tosses the broom down at her feet. "Clean it up yourself."

"No, Lenny," Willie tells him. "You do it. You don't want your mother to come home to find this." To Gia's surprise, Lenny turns back, picks up the broom, and begins sweeping around his howling cousin.

Mia appears, and Yozo gives her an up-and-down look and a smile. "Here," he says to Tessa, "sit down here, they'll take care of you now."

"Don't leave me!" Tessa clutches his upper arm. "Please!"

Yozo leans over and whispers to her. Her frantic expression drops, and a smoothness comes over what can be seen of her face. Her mouth opens, then closes. As she stares at him, his eyes narrow. Yozo looks at Barbara, tilts his head, and Barbara and Yozo come to stand behind Gia and Willie.

"This isn't bad," Mia is saying. "It won't even need stitches."

"What did you say to her?" Barbara whispers to Yozo.

"I told her that when she fucked with Gia, she fucked with me, so she had best just go fuck herself."

"That's a record, isn't it?" Barbara inquires. "For using the word fuck in one sentence?"

"Let's get out of here," Yozo says, and without a backward glance, the four get up and leave the deck, leaving Gia's wounded cousin, her daughter, and Gia's godfather's sons, who are emptying crystal shards into a big plastic bag as though they did it every day.

What she hates most, what she knows she will see when she opens her eyes, is the way they will be looking at her. That hideous combination of pity, revulsion, and curiosity that she grew to hate after John died, the look that he might have left her with if she couldn't so clearly remember his last look at her. She was still in bed, they had just made love, and he was dressed, looking so big and tall and handsome as he bent over to kiss her, and tell her what he knew would be his final message to her: "I love you. You're such a good person, you know that?"

His suicide note was a lot more detailed.

So, when the Range Rover stops, and she feels the parking brake catch, she opens her eyes. Willie is still holding her right hand, Yozo and Barbara sit in the front seats and don't turn around. They are parked, naturally, beside the Cicada Mountain hospital, where Tony died, where they were all born. "Look at how nice the town looks from up here," Yozo says.

"You can look at me," she says. "It's okay."

But her old friends are not doing what the others did. The ones who turned out to be strangers to her and John and the children were the ones who asked her such questions as, "Will his insurance still pay up?" and "I guess you won't be able to have an open-casket viewing, will you?" They were the ones who wanted to get close to her just so that they could hear all the details of how he took the gun, lifted it to his right temple, and pulled the trigger. They wanted to know that there wasn't as much blood around him as you might have expected because, as a homicide detective kindly, but super-fluously, informed her, his heart stopped beating as soon as the bullet hit his brain, so there was no pumping action and therefore very little blood. They were the ones who wanted to see the blood, get just close enough to see it, maybe to dip their fingers in it, just a little, and then run off, run away, so that whatever monsters caused this horrendous act would not chase them. They wanted to get close, but they didn't want it on them.

They wanted to be able to tell their friends all about his death, how well they knew him, how close they had been to the couple, how unexpected it was, how sick he must have been.

They wanted to be able to gossip about her and John. Ultimately, what his death came down to was dinner-table chatter among strangers.

Her oldest friends are looking at her, straight-on and clear-eyed. "What do you want to know?" she asks them.

"You don't have to say anything," Willie says. "You know that."

She looks from one to the other. She cannot believe that their lives, all the years they have been apart, have led them here, to this place overlooking that small town where they grew up together and away.

"Would you like to know how perfect it was?" she begins.

"The first time I ever laid eyes on John, he was in the doorway to our legal clinic in the Haight. I had double-parked, and he was looking to see whose goddamn car was blocking him. He took up the whole doorway, and the light behind him made him look bigger than he actually was, but when I came out of my office and saw him, all I remember was that I clearly thought, this is the rest of my life.

"Later, after everything was over, someone asked me something about him, and I said that even if I had known at that moment how it was all going to end, I would have gone with him anyway.

"My three partners were there, and I told them to take care of the rest of my appointments for that day. I walked outside to where this tall man was waiting, and I said, 'Today's my birthday.' He said, 'Really?' And then he kissed me. Just as I had planned. I moved my car, with him in it, to the Stanhope, and that night he asked me to marry him. I did, but not for a few months. He had two kids, his wife had died of heart disease, and we both wanted to make sure that I knew what I was getting into. It didn't matter. I fell so hard and so surely in love with him, none of it mattered.

"Have you ever known that you've found your other half? That up until you meet that person, you didn't even know that you were missing a part?

"Life was so simple. I had the practice, he was a prominent and successful businessman, the children were thriving, we were good-looking and rich and happy.

"Maybe we were taunting the universe. I just thought we were lucky and happy.

"It wasn't easy with him. He was as volatile as I was; he was eighteen years older than I, and had been a CEO for a long time, so he was a lot more used to getting his way, but I matched his experience with my energy, and we had battles. Lots of them. It was a tempestuous and raucous marriage. It was wonderful.

"The slide began when someone made a move to take him over. No, I didn't say it wrong. He saw himself as his company. They weren't trying to take over the company, they were trying to take John over. It went on for months, he stopped sleeping about four months before he finally died. He lost weight, he looked awful, and nothing I said or did could reach him. He never stopped being wonderful with the kids, he was as attentive as his time allowed, but I could feel something in him slipping away. At the end, I knew he was spending Friday mornings running the business and the rest of the time fighting off the takeover. His employees had formed a stock-ownership plan, they were going to buy the company, but the day before he killed himself, their financing failed. All his banks pulled out on him in the face of the takeover's success.

"He had bought the gun a few months before. He had told me about it, how he felt creepy, even with the security guards, alone late in his office. I thought it was a good idea. This takeover business had gotten completely out of hand; there had even been death threats made, so I had stopped working for a while and had a bodyguard. So did the kids. It was a hell of a thing.

"I look at all these mergers and takeovers now, and they're so routine, and I wonder, what was he fighting for? What was the purpose?

"His note, it was left so carefully where the police would find it, said that he was so sorry that he had disappointed so many people. He never disappointed me. I still wonder if he knew that.

"He killed himself in his office, late on a Sunday night. I had turned the phones off because I didn't want the kids to wake up. Also, we had been getting a lot of crank calls, and no matter how often we changed our number, we still got them. So, people from the company came to the house and woke me up around one in the morning. It was funny, I was reaching for the front door when I got this strange feeling. I still can't describe it, even now, but when I opened the door, these were people I knew, I said to them, 'He's dead, isn't he?'

"They said yes, and I invited them in. I went into the kitchen to put on some coffee, and when I came out, I asked them how he had died. I was betting on a heart attack or a stroke, so I wasn't really prepared to hear the words 'self-inflicted gunshot wound.'

"His people took me to his office, something I insisted they do, and I saw the scene. I still wish I hadn't. He killed himself on the couch where we had made love more than once. The police were so kind. Then I went home, and sent everybody home, and called Tony.

"His son was twelve and his daughter was five when John killed himself. I think the worst thing I've ever had to do was to tell them about their father. I waited until morning. It was the longest night. I found a cigar butt he had left in an ashtray out in the garden. I sat and chewed on it and watched the sun come up. I didn't think it would. It was incomprehensible to me that the sun could rise without his presence on this earth. I watched the trails of planes taking off. I saw Venus out on the horizon. I wondered if he was a star yet.

"Cameron, his boy, when I told him and his sister that their father was dead, got angry and hit the wall. His sister got upset with him and tried to hit him, and we all three ended up in a pile on the floor, crying and holding on. I couldn't answer any of their questions. There was only one that mattered, though—why? All I could tell them was that their dad got tired and lost his good judgment.

"Later that morning, Cam got John's dirty clothes hamper and took it into his bedroom. He kept it there for a long time. He was wearing his father's soiled clothes when he was alone in his room. I let him do what he had to do.

"His sister, Nancy, was younger and confused. She kept asking if Daddy was still dead. We got through the funeral, and when we went home, she

ran up the steps and into the house, and all over the
place. I found her on the third floor, sitting outside
her father's study, crying. She had expected him to
be there when we got home, just like he always was.
That was when I knew we would have to go away.
That was when I moved them to Los Angeles.

"I had gone to college and law school there,
and I still had a lot of friends in L.A. There were
good people for me and the kids to be with. That
was a comfort to me, too, because I planned on
killing myself as soon as I could figure out all the
details. It was the only way I knew of getting rid
of the pain and being with John again. But somehow time went by, and life went on, and the kids
got bigger, and their questions got easier, and then
it was time to go back home and I had forgotten
to kill myself.

"My law partners were waiting for me. I went
back to work full-time right away. The kids
turned John's study into a place where they went
when they wanted to be alone. They did their
homework there, and eventually it became just
like all the other rooms in the house, there was no
more mysticism about it, and then they grew up,
and, I suppose, so did I.

"Of all people, my ex-husband made the most
sense of the situation for me. I ran into him one
day in Venice, and we had a beer and talked. He
had mellowed, but he still wasn't anyone I wanted
to be married to. It was nice to be able to check
that out. I told him what had happened to John,
and he gave me some great advice. He said not to

pay any attention to the people who would keep telling me that it was going to be all right; it's never going to be all right again, Mark said. Not in the way you've known. But you'll get used to it, and someday it will be a new kind of all right.

"Doesn't it just figure that in the last conversation I have with my ex-husband, the idiot made the most sense of anyone?

"There isn't a day that I don't think of John. I don't miss him quite so much anymore. Or maybe I've just gotten into the habit of missing him. I don't know."

They are all smoking, She doesn't remember lighting up, but it tastes grand, and so she takes another drag. Willie and Barbara and Yozo are all still looking at her, Barbara with tears on her cheeks.

"So matter-of-fact," she says, "the way you tell it."

"It's a long time ago," Gia says. "In a strange way, it's lost its edge, believe it or not."

"With all due respect," Yozo says, "John was a fucking asshole."

"Yeah, I'd have to agree with that," she says. "He was wrong to do what he did, but if that's what he had to do, well . . ." She shrugs.

"You make your peace with it any way you can," Willie says. "Would you like to have a Mass said for him?"

"You would do that?" Her old boyfriend praying for the soul of her dead Jewish husband. "That's nice."

"What was his whole name?"

"John Harold Farbman."

Willie smiles. "Not of the faith, huh?"

"He thought he was," she counters.

"I'm sorry," Barbara says.

"It was a long time ago. I don't mean to sound flip or anything, but time does have a way of helping round it off."

"No, I mean that I'm sorry that I just assumed that everything had," she reaches for a word, "that you had everything easy. I didn't know."

"Tony came out for the funeral, but I don't think there was a lot of conversation back here about it, and I sure as hell don't think they told anyone outside the family. His death was written up in *Time* and *Newsweek* and all the big papers, but the company did a good job of keeping my name and the kids' names out of the stories." She stubs out her cigarette. "You couldn't have known."

"Your cousin Tessa is an evil woman," Barbara says. "She must be punished."

"She was dying to nail me, one way or the other. It's always been that way, ever since I was a kid. She just hates me, she's out of her mind on the subject of me, and she can't help herself."

"If your cousin comes to me for confession," Willie says, "I could give her a penance that would make her head explode."

"It's a start," Gia says.

"Want to see your baptismal certificate?" Willie asks. "Want to see your grandparents' marriage certificate?"

"Where?"

"I found these remarkable volumes in the rectory attic. They were packed away. They're big, leather-bound books with all the baptismal certificates, marriage certificates, documents of confirmation, all sorts of things, going back almost to the beginning of the century. Your father's baptismal certificate, your godfather's confirmation. You want to see them?"

Yozo backs the Rover away from the edge of the mountain.

"What's that smell?" Barbara asks.

"Horny priest," Yozo offers.

"It's what's left from the incense at Mass. It seeps through. I like it," Willie says.

"You really live here?" Gia asks.

"You still can't get used to it, can you?" He is amused.

"Being here with you is weird. The last time I was here, Father Pietro was the priest and you and I were going steady."

"Welcome to middle age," Barbara says. "Are they the books you were talking about? They're beautiful." She opens one and starts to sneeze.

"Dust," Willie says. "You allergic?"

She nods and, sneezing, turns away. "I'm going back into your office," she says. "I'll wait there."

Now it was just the three of them.

"Look," Willie carefully turns to a page where, like many others, pieces of paper are sticking out, "here's your baptismal certificate. There's your uncle's signature. Here's your First Holy Communion certificate. You were six, going on seven." He looks at the date, May 1952.

"We all were," Yozo says.

"And here," he reaches for another marker and carefully turns the heavy, dusty pages, "this is your Confirmation certificate. Christ Almighty, your aunt Mella was your sponsor?"

"She was?" Gia leans over. "There's her signature, Carmella Scarpino Scognamillo. I don't remember that at all."

"Your middle name is Maria?" Yozo looks closely.

"Oh, yeah, wait, I remember. I took my godmother's name as my confirmation name, and she was supposed to stand up with me, but she got sick and Mella was the stand-in. I forgot that."

"Remember that part where the Bishop slaps you?" Yozo says. "Does anybody else remember getting whacked really hard?"

"Only you, Joe," Willie says. "Here's Tony's baptismal certificate, I think. Is that him, that name? Is that the right one?"

"Oh, yeah." Gia is grinning now, enjoying this. "I forgot. That's him, all right. My grandfather had his heroes. Anatole France was one. That's why he named his son after him."

"Tony's name is Anatole?" Yozo sounds dazed. "Anatole?"

"I had forgotten that," Gia says. Smiling up at Willie, she adds, "I guess that's proof that I'm a third-generation anti-cleric."

"Gia, did your aunt know that that was his real name?" Willie asks.

"I don't know. Why? What difference does it make?"

"Well, she ordered those little prayer cards we give out at the funeral Mass, and she wrote his name as Anthony."

"He probably never told her." She shrugs. "It's okay. We all know who he is. Was," she corrects herself. "Where's my father's baptismal certificate? He was born in 1914."

"Here." Willie hands her the document. She can't make out the names of his godparents, the ink has faded so. "They baptized him just before Christmas. He was born in early December. God, this is so strange." She runs her hands over the old paper. "I don't feel a thing. He was my father."

"Your grandfather and your uncle were your fathers," Yozo tells her. "They were here."

"Yeah," she sighs. "And now we're here, looking at old holy papers." She looks up at the men. "How did we get here?"

"How doesn't matter," Yozo tells her. "We're together. That's what matters." He nods toward the office door. "What do you want to bet Barbara's smoking in the church." Yozo opens the door and leaves the rectory office.

"Ah, Jesus," Willie says as Gia gently closes the big leather book.

"Thanks," she says, glancing up at him.

Willie looks at her in the soft light of his desk lamp, and he knows that this is the moment, no matter how many years he lives, this is the moment he will remember. This is how she will always appear to him, no longer a young girl but a woman, grown and gray, tired and sad, a real woman, not the gossamer image of his youth. And he will love her even harder then. She came back, she became real, and, with all her imperfections and regrets, she moved even deeper into his heart.

"Tell me again why we're doing this." Barbara huddles against Yozo in the dark autumn chill. He slips his arm around her to keep her warm. She coughs relentlessly, a function of her having run out of cigarettes earlier in the evening, and there has been no opportunity to run home and get another pack. All the stores are closed, and have been since nine P.M.

They are following the light thrown by the flashlight carried by Willie, who leads them through the cemetery that belongs to the Annunciation Church, locally known as the Irish church. It is where Gia's grandfather, as well as her father, is buried. Willie rousted the pastor at Annunciation and went through the cemetery map on their computer, where they found the old grave.

"Gia feels this strong need to visit her father's grave. Look," Yozo says, "if you weren't tramping through a cemetery in the dark, looking for a grave of someone you never even knew, what would you be doing? This is fun. We might even find it before dawn."

Gia takes Willie's arm as he waves the light from one grave marker to another.

"It's like when we were kids," Barbara says. "Why do we always end up in cemeteries? In the dark?"

"I don't know. If I owned this property, I'd put up condos. It's got the best view of the town, do you realize that?"

"The cemeteries and the hospital. Yeah, they built them up on the mountain. All the prime real estate goes to the sick and the dead."

"Maybe mid-level. Maybe town homes," Yozo muses.

"Who's gonna sell you a cemetery?" Barbara asks.

"Who ever thought I'd buy my high school?"

"Here it is," Willie calls. They are just a few feet behind, and they all take their places, like basketball players around a foul shot, two on each side, as Gia kneels with the flashlight and tries to read the tombstone's inscription.

"It's completely worn away," she tells them. To Willie, "Are you sure this is it?"

"This is the row and the number, yes. This is it, Gia. Here." He takes a piece of paper and a pencil from his jacket pocket. "Let me try something." He and Gia switch places, and, holding the paper against the stone, he runs the pencil up and down. "Look." He shows her what has emerged.

"G–I–A–N . . ." she reads. "Gianno. It's him."

Willie and Gia rise. There is a silence. Then Willie begins, "Our Father, Who Art In Heaven," and softly Yozo joins in, then Barbara.

After the "Amen" Willie, standing in the dark

beside a fifty-five-year-old grave holding the bones of the young man who lived long enough to father the woman who is standing next to him in the dark beside the old grave, continues to pray aloud, "Lord Jesus, our Redeemer, you willingly gave yourself up to death so that all our people might be saved and pass from death into a new life. Listen to our prayer, look with love on your people who mourn and pray for their beloved Gianno Scarpino. Lord Jesus, holy and compassionate, forgive Gianno his sins. By dying you opened the gates of life for those who believe in you: do not let Gianno be parted from you, but by your glorious power give him light, joy, and peace in heaven, where you live forever and ever, Amen."

"Thank you," Gia says. "That was nice. I wonder if he was an atheist, too."

"Let's listen for the spinning sound," Barbara suggests.

"He was only twenty-seven when he died," Willie says. "I don't think he was old enough to have lost his faith."

"Are you kidding?" Yozo asks from the other side of the grave. "Can you honestly imagine her grandfather or Tony ever really believing?"

"I think they did," Willie admits.

"I think you're nuts," Yozo says. "Did you know the same Tony I knew?"

"Where did Barbara go?" Gia asks.

"Here." Barbara appears out of the darkness. "Here." She places a basket of flowers on Gia's father's grave.

"From another grave?" Willie asks her.

"They weren't using them," Barbara says.

Yozo finds his son watching television in the family room. "Where's your mother?" he asks the boy, who points upstairs.

"She went to bed," he adds.

"You want a beer?" Yozo asks Joey.

"Yeah, sure."

"What's on?" the father asks the son, each settled into a recliner, each holding a cold can of Yuengling Black and Tan.

"It's a movie, *Shadow of China*. It's about this guy who gets out of the revolution and goes to Hong Kong and makes a bundle, but some of his enemies are gonna blow his cover about his past. I think he's in a lot of trouble."

"There's a lot of that going around tonight," Yozo says, and then sips, and belches. "Think that woke your old lady?" he inquires of his son, who replies with a burp of his own. Yozo notes, with some satisfaction, that his son's belch as yet lacks the resonance and fullness of his own.

"I'm gonna make an investment, Pop, and I want to know what you think about it."

This is new. His son has never sought out his advice for anything. He's getting older, his father thinks. He maybe can listen a little bit now. I wonder what I can tell him. Aw, shit, if it's about money, I can do this.

"I've seen the future of this town, and I'm gonna buy it," Joey says.

"What's that?"

"Funeral homes. You realize everybody around here is gonna die? You just always have business. I'm gonna get a mortician's license, and I'm gonna open up a string of funeral homes. Make them not so fancy, you know, make them like Price Club and Wal-Mart. I just talked to Mr. DiBello. He hired me. I have to go to school in Philadelphia for a couple of months, to get my license."

My kid, the funeral home king, Yozo thinks.

He'll make a bundle.

"You want a partner?" Yozo asks.

SIXTH DAY

She's dreaming that she's a little girl again, sitting in a horse-drawn cart, with her uncle Tony on one side of her and her grandfather on the other. They are stopped, watching a black funnel move across the distant landscape, but where they are, the weather is still and clear and warm.

It is not a dream, it is a memory that comes to her some nights in the guise of a dream. When Gia was almost four years old, her grandfather and uncle took her to Italy to meet the family of her dead mother. She remembers nothing of the trip except the small tornado, the freak storm that hit near the poor Calabrian village where they were visiting. Her mother's family wanted to keep her, she looked so much like their lost daughter, but Pop would have none of it, Tony told her years later. Money changed hands, as it should have, and the three pilgrims returned to the United States. Gia never went back to that village, and now, when she wakes up, the dream is telling her, she won't even be able to remember its name.

"Are you gonna let this happen?" A familiar voice comes from above her head.

"It's only a tornado," she says.

"They're making plans for a funeral," the voice says. "Are you gonna let them go ahead with it?"

She opens her eyes. Yozo is sitting on the twin bed across from hers. "I was asleep," she points out without lifting her head from the pillow.

And then, because she has just moved from that final instant of unconsciousness, reality comes to her, and she is jolted fully awake. Tony is dead. John is dead. It is the part of waking up that she has never been able to avoid, not since her husband killed himself. Sleep, heavily sedated sleep, was her only refuge then, but she quickly discovered that there was really no place to hide. There was that moment, just as she began to rouse, when the sheets felt smooth and perfect, the comforter, the pillows, even the air was just right, and then there was that shock: he is dead. He is dead. That was her awakening thought for years, and now, this morning, even before she wonders why Yozo is in her bedroom, munching on toast and drinking coffee, it is as before: he is dead. Tony is dead.

"What do you want first?" Yozo genially inquires. "Toast, juice, or coffee?"

Gia sits up, rubs her eyes. "I want the dead to be alive."

He looks at her. "Coffee," he says, and puts a mug on the nightstand.

"Does anybody in this town ever get to be alone?"

"You know what they're doing in the kitchen, don't you?" he asks. "You promised him."

"Promised what?"

"You promised Tony that you wouldn't let them take him to the church. You promised him that you'd have him cremated. You gonna weasel on that now?"

"Oh, God." She sinks back onto her pillow. "Did I tell you about that? He was nuts, Yozo, you knew him. He didn't mean it."

"Tony never said anything he didn't mean," Yozo insists. "You know that. Are you gonna turn out to be one of those scumbag sleazeballs who reneges on a promise? To your own godfather? I wonder how you're gonna live with yourself on this one."

"Fuck you."

"It was a promise."

"There'll be a funeral. It doesn't matter. Tony's gone. It's a body. It's nothing."

Yozo stands up. "You promised. You ought to be ashamed of yourself."

"You're making a difficult situation even harder, you know that? I loved him, he's dead. Do you think this is some kind of caper, some kind of adventure? An old man died, his family will put him to rest in the way they believe, that's it. It's how we'll mourn. When it's all over, it won't matter one bit where Tony's body lies."

"He was ashamed of himself, until the day he died, for not carrying out what his father wanted. Now you're gonna do the same thing. Shame on you, Gia. I had you all wrong."

She sits up again. "How'd you know that? That part about not doing what my Pop wanted?"

"We used to talk. He told me. He told me that he betrayed his father."

"Good. I'm glad you were so tight with him. With this little male-bonding thing that you were obviously experiencing with my uncle, did he also request of you that you take his ashes and put them into a water pistol and go to different homes and squirt deranged messages on their front windows? Did he ask you to do that, huh?"

"I wasn't to him what you were. But if he had asked me, I would do it."

"You know what?" She starts to throw off the comforter, looks to see that she's wearing a T-shirt and panties, and gets out of bed. "I give you the divine anointing that Tony gave me. Go. You go down there and tell those women what you're gonna do with their husband's, brother's body." She picks up the mug and sips. "I'll listen from up here. And when the screaming stops, I'll come down and I promise I'll give your remains a proper burial."

"You'll have to do it without telling them."

"I'm not doing it."

"You have to."

"Get out."

"You promised him." Yozo gets up and brushes crumbs from his jeans. "You promised him, and you're breaking your promise. It's better he's dead. He can't see this."

She sighs. "Go bust somebody else's balls."

"There's been no ball-busting here. You don't have any balls."

"Get out."

This time he leaves.

She drives around the town, with no destination, up and down streets she once flew over on her blue two-wheeler. There are too many empty row houses, some not even boarded up, just broken windows showing a frightening emptiness. This is the last time she'll come here, she knows. The town she grew up in is gone.

It vexes her, Yozo's scolding. She can't get away from it because he was right. Tony would be ashamed of her, and she still has enough Catholic upbringing left in her to believe that he is somewhere now where he can actually see her. That such a thought belies everything else she believes is of no matter to her now. She drives on, sure that his poor soul, which, the nuns inculcated in her, looks just like he did on earth, is sorrowful, and hurt, and disappointed.

Great, she thinks, now I'm afraid to die because Tony'll kill me.

She leaves the town and drives west on what she recalled as a simple secondary two-lane road, but which now is a four-lane divided highway. She pulls over and looks down at the roads she once drove, when she and Yozo used to sneak Tony's car out of the garage at night, roll it down the street, pop the clutch and drive, mostly backward, around town in the deep darkness, when even the town's cop was asleep in his cruiser. They drove backward so as to keep the additional mileage to a minimum, so that Tony wouldn't know what they were doing.

The Buick's radio, on clear nights, would pull in stations from Binghamton, New York, and Boston, sometimes Cleveland. Such far away places. They would park, always on an incline, listen to the music, and talk about their lives to come.

She can remember those times, she thinks, looking out over the smoky landscape, but she can't remember what they said. God, those mine fires are still burning, just like Yozo said.

Even though the fire is a terrible thing, she

rather likes the idea that it is still winning after all these years. It is the only thing that has remained unchanged since she left.

Fire. Even at the end there is only fire. Out loud she says, "Tony. *Addio.*"

"Father Cunningham is saying a Mass for your god-father tonight," Rosa tells her when she returns. "Will you come?"

"Rosa, I don't, you know, I don't," she stammers. "No, you go. I'll stay here tonight."

"Your problem," Tessa materializes like the mushroom over Hiroshima, "is that you don't know how to do what's right."

"Nice bandage."

Tessa looks at her, a long, hard look, and for the first time in Gia's life, she looks back at eyes that, she notices, are the exact same dark brown as hers. Italian eyes. There are a few seconds of silence. Wiser and wounded now, Tessa backs away, slamming the door as she leaves Tony and Francie's house.

Gia tries to remember the name of the flower shop that used to be on Center Street, but she cannot, and the house is empty, so there is no one to ask. She decides to go and find it herself. She has to find some florist and make arrangements to send a bunch of red roses to the funeral home, long-stemmed red roses that will be tied together with long white ribbons, and affixed to the ribbons will be shiny gold lettering, spelling out BELOVED UNCLE. She has not been gone so long from this small town that she doesn't remember the rules.

To her surprise, the florist is still where it was in 1963. "I got my prom flowers here," she tells the young girl behind the counter, whose eyes are testament to the fact that drugs have found their way to this hidden little spot in the mountains. Gia pays for the flowers, the girl tells her that they've received a lot of orders for Mr. Scarpino, and then Gia goes back to her rented car parked near the central intersection, gets in, locks the doors, although the streets this early evening are empty, and cries.

There is a point in the Mass when the celebrant says the name of the person for whose soul this Mass is being said, and when Willie Cunningham tries to say Tony's name, his voice cracks, his throat swells, he reaches for the altar to steady himself, and the tears flow.

In the back of Our Lady of Mercy Church, Yozo, kneeling, prays.

Barbara is sleeping, fully dressed, on top of her king-size bed when Yozo enters the bedroom, pulls off his shoes, carefully drapes his jacket over a chair, takes off his tie, slides his belt out of its loops, lays them both across his jacket, and then, quietly, gently, finds a comfortable place on the bed. She is sleeping on her side, he spoons himself against her, and when she rouses, she turns to look at him. She doesn't seem surprised to find him on her bed.

"I'm so tired," Yozo says.

"I know," Barbara says, and his arms around her, her hands holding his, they fall asleep.

● ● ●

"Well," Francie looks out at the assemblage on the sidewalk, "we might as well go in." She takes the steps as surefooted as a mountain goat, but on the third of six brick steps leading into DiBello's Funeral Home she slows, and on the next step she stops. Lenny, just behind her, wraps his arms around her, and she continues. The other family members are watching this, as if they were spectators and not players in this awful old tradition that once again this family must perform.

"I can't go in," Gia says.

"I'm here." Mia takes her hand.

"I just don't want to remember him this way, dead and stuffed."

"He looks kind of good," Yozo says, appearing behind her. Yozo has gotten taller, and his hair has grown back.

"Who are you?"

"Joe Walenticonis, Junior." The young man extends his hand. "I know, I look just like him."

"Jesus!" He is the young boy Gia knew. Nothing of his mother, as nearly as Gia can remember her, has appeared in this youngster's face. He is a duplicate of his father. "You sure do." She shakes his hand and introduces herself.

"I know who you are. I grew up looking at your pictures in my dad's yearbook."

"That wasn't me." Gia cringes.

"Hey, the sixties are cool, don't worry. Your uncle looks pretty good. You don't have to be afraid."

"How do you know?"

"I work here."

"Where's your dad, Joe?"

"I think at the garage. Excuse me, Mr. DiBello wants me. Go ahead in, I'll see you inside. Father Cunningham is coming by tonight to say the rosary." He slips away, going down the steps, almost concealed by the low hedge that circles the funeral home.

"Well, a corpse and a rosary. How can I miss that?"

"This is for Francie." Mia tugs her hand. And then she whispers to Gia, "I'm afraid, too."

Gia stays in the back of the big funeral parlor, and all she can see is the inside of the coffin lid and the shiny bronze casket. There is a huge crucifix overlooking the bier, and all of this is covered by flowers, baskets, vases, sprays, all for the dead, but really for the living. Gia recalls something she hasn't thought about for a long time: how she and her grandfather would go to the cemeteries and rescue the potted plants that had been left on graves. "They're only gonna die," he pointed out, and that was partly how her grandfather grew such beautiful flowers in his garden, the garden where she played, the garden she left behind, the garden she managed to bring Tony to before he died.

It is not enough consolation for her today.

"This is nice, isn't it?" Yozo seats himself on the folding metal chair next to hers.

"Don't start."

"You met my son."

"He's not your son, he's your clone."

"Wait till you meet his kid. There are three of us."

"Nice turnout, huh?"

"What are you gonna do, not think about it?"

She leans over, resting her elbows on her knees, and covers her eyes with her hands. "This is hard enough without you making it worse. There's not going to be anything except what my aunt Francie wants. That's it, Yozo. You can nag all you want, but this is it."

When she looks up, he's gone, and she doesn't even know if he heard what she said.

Rosa comes to sit with her. "He looks nice," she tells her niece.

"I can't, Ro."

She kisses Gia, fiercely, and then rubs the lipstick she's left on her cheek. "Then don't. He knows you're here."

Mella has taken the center chair in the front aisle of chairs, the nice upholstered ones, the ones for the immediate family. She is sitting in the chair which, rightfully, should be occupied by the widow, but, Gia is certain, only her own sudden death or dynamite will move her from that spot. Gia watches Francie standing at the head of the coffin, looking down so lovingly at the face of her husband, and then she reaches in and strokes his hair. That small gesture shames Gia, and she slowly, as if through a dense fog, moves to stand beside her.

From this angle it's not bad. His hands are waxy, clutching a rosary. Gia looks away and sees that the side of the coffin has a crucifix welded onto the trim. She can only imagine what's on the top of this casket. A diorama, no doubt, of Calvary on Good Friday.

"He looks so good," Francie whispers. "He looks so peaceful."

"Yeah, he does."

"I don't know what I'm gonna do without him," she says simply, and Gia's heart breaks for the old woman. She looks at Gia with teary eyes. "You went through it, and you were so young."

"It's never easy, Francie. No matter what age you are. You had so many more years with him, it's got to be hard."

"He was my life."

"I'm so glad he married you."

"So am I." She hugs Gia, and then she moves around her, and quietly says to Mella, "Move over one." After she is seated, she pats the empty chair and says, "Come and sit with me, just for a little while."

"Joey and Lenny picked out the music for the funeral mass," she tells her.

"Good."

"Francie, I've got to get some air."

"You go ahead, honey," her uncle's widow tells her.

Outside, Gia gulps and sweats. Yozo is on the corner, watching her. "You all right?" he calls. He is smoking a cigarette.

"Yeah. Now I am. Just got a little close in there."

"It's colder than a fuck in there, ain't it?"

She looks at him. "Please."

"Okay," he says. "You do what you have to do."

"Thanks," she says, grateful that her old friend will lay off. And then they begin moving closer to each other, and she is telling him about her drive earlier in the day.

"He always knew when we took the car," Yozo says. "He told me years later."

"He knew? How did he know? We mostly drove backward. I can still back up like a sonofabitch. There's not a parking space in California that I can't get a car into. That was good practice. How did he know?"

"Gas, asshole. That Buick devoured gas, and he'd find the tank half empty when he knew he had filled it up the day before. Plus, driving in reverse uses up a lot more gas than going forward."

"So he knew?" She begins to laugh. "God, he could at least have left the keys in it once in a while."

"Ah, but that would have spoiled the game, don't you see? He let us play. He trusted us and he left us alone."

"We were so smart."

"So was he," Yozo says.

SEVENTH DAY

They will take his body up the mountain later. First, they will gather at the funeral home for a last look, a last private good-bye, and then they will proceed to the church for what Gia can only imagine will be something akin to a papal funeral; then the pallbearers will pick up the metal box that holds the earthly remains of Anatole Scarpino and load it into a Cadillac built especially to carry the dead. That big black car will lead the procession up the winding roads she still knows so well, will take the hairpin turns that will bring them past the bakery where they stole those sticky buns on moonless Friday nights, through the sturdy wrought iron gates flanking the entrance to the holy ground that holds the bodies of the people who gave her life. Her mother, her father, her grandfathers, her godfather. There is no one left.

She stands at the bedroom window, looking out, and she is sad that it is such a beautiful day. The October sun is bright and the skies are clear, and the leaves have all turned out their finest colors as if today were a day that they, too, must put on a memorable performance. Her cousin Peter was buried on a day like this, and even though it was almost twenty-five years ago, she can still remember that the warm sun cut through her like a cruel knife. The trees in the cemetery were dazzling that day, too. She'll see Peter's headstone today. She's never seen it. Or his father's. She'll see them all today. They are all gone.

She looks at herself in the mirror. Gray skirt. Black turtleneck. Black boots. Gray and black plaid blazer. Black gloves. She can't remember packing any of this a million years ago when she left California.

Yozo is in the kitchen, wearing a handsome charcoal gray suit. Today he is a prosperous, well-dressed middle-aged man. "You look beautiful," he tells her.

"You look like a million bucks," she answers, brushing his cheek with a kiss.

He winks. "More."

Rosa is wiping down the kitchen sink with a paper towel, and crying. She is in a simple black dress, black hose, clunky black lace-up shoes with a kind of wide, stacked low heel. The kind of shoes her mother used to wear. For a small second Gia has a strong feeling that those may, in fact, be the same shoes she is seeing, her grandmother's shoes, but Gia does what she has to do, and in the finest West Coast tradition she takes a deep breath and lets it go, lets it go.

"You'll ride in the limousine with us?" she asks Yozo.

"Is that all right with you?"

"Remember the day he took us out of parochial school, when that nun hit me?"

"Didn't you hit her first?" Yozo teases.

"You spit on her. That was the day you became his oldest son, Yozo. God have mercy on your soul, but that was when you became a member of this family."

He leans close to her. "I loved your uncle, but they are all fucking nuts."

"When I go back, can you stay in touch with Francie and the boys? Can you and I stay in touch now, not like the last thirty years?"

"I'll be here with them. We have the same lawyer. It'll be all right." He looks at Gia for more than a couple of blinks.

One by one, they fill the kitchen, Francie, Ang, Gar, Mella, Tessa, Mia, Lenny, Joey, Rosa, Yozo. Danny DiBello starts calling out names, trying to tell them who goes in which limousine, and, as Gia would have expected, everyone stampedes him as soon as he starts talking. Ignoring his carefully written seating plans, they fill up the three black cars.

Yozo's son is their driver. He revs the engine. His father slaps the back of his son's head. "Cool it," he tells him, and the engine is left to its quiet, costly idle.

Their sad procession glides quietly out of the circular driveway. Yozo and Gia have the third car to themselves. They don't say a word, and soon the small caravan pulls into the reserved parking spaces in front of the funeral home. A group of onlookers stands across the street. "Who are they?" she asks Yozo.

"The professional mourners," he tells her. "They check the papers to see who died, find out where the funeral luncheon is going to be, and they show up for the free food."

"Luncheon? There's, what, a lunch?"

"No. Your aunt is having stuff brought in at the house. The store is fixing up trays and like that."

He knows this stuff. She thinks she should have paid closer attention, but she is already feeling herself leaving this place. It's as if she's on the plane, in line for the runway, just waiting to take off. When Tony stopped breathing, Gia started leaving.

"Okay, come on." Young Joey is holding the door open for her, and he gently puts his hand under her elbow as she gets out. It's a kind gesture, an old lady's gesture, and Gia wants to smack him. She sees Willie standing by the front door. He is in his black suit and Roman collar, holding a big prayer book with black and purple streamers fluttering from it. He doesn't smile when he sees them, but he shakes Yozo's hand and kisses Gia, a brief, polite, public kiss on the cheek.

She averts her eyes when they enter the room, and maneuvers herself so that she is behind everyone else. Yozo stands at the coffin, looking down at Tony's body. He stands there for a long time, until Willie touches his arm, and then he comes and sits next to her.

Willie's prayer is brief, and after embracing Francie and her sons, he leaves. Once again Danny DiBello starts trying to tell the mourners in what order they should make their final stop at the casket, and Gia slips out the rear door. Barbara is standing on the sidewalk. "I got here too late." She is almost breathless. "I didn't want to walk in on Willie's praying."

"He's really good at it," Gia observes.

"You all right?" She looks at Gia in the bright sunlight. Gia takes out her big sunglasses.

"Now, do I look completely L.A.?"

They hear the anguished screams coming through the front doorway of the funeral home. Gia recognizes Mella's voice, then Ang's, then another, she doesn't know whose.

"Here we go," Barbara says.

"They're too old to jump in the open grave, so I guess we'll have our scene here."

Yozo comes slowly down the front steps. "Jesus, your aunt Mella, she's a work of art."

"What?"

"She decided she wanted Tony's wedding band. Guess what happened then?"

"Aw, shit." Gia hears the raised voices, no longer anguished, just angry and sharp. "I wonder where my real family is right now, and what they're doing."

"It's almost over," Yozo says, glancing at his watch. "You want to say a prayer?" he asks Barbara, who surprises Gia by following him up the steps into the funeral home. One by one, her relatives come out, all of them crying, even Gar. A group of men in dark suits, Tony's employees from the store, are standing nearby, waiting for the signal to enter and to remove the casket.

Barbara appears in the doorway and falls straight down. No up-thrown arms, no staggering, she goes down like a brick in water. Somebody yells, a couple of the pallbearers come through the crowd on the sidewalk, and before Gia even knows she's moved, someone is pulling her away from Barbara's still form. She's being told to stay back by one of the burly men. "He's a paramedic with the Hookies," the Rescue Hook and Ladder Company, Francie tells her, looking around her at Barbara, who is now opening her eyes, pulling at her skirt, sucking in deep breaths, and then coughing as though she's going to blow lunch on these guys.

"I'm all right," she says, struggling to get out of their grasp. "I should have had breakfast. It's so warm." She waves her hand in front of her face. Two men help her to stand, and Gia grabs her arm.

"You want a ride home?" she asks.

"No, I'm fine." She wipes a streak of sweat off her upper lip. "I do that sometimes. I just don't eat when I should."

Gia realizes that she is sniffing her for booze, but gets only a faint perfume, something nice, and she is ashamed of herself. "In my house we always have breakfast," she tells her. "You'll get used to it."

She turns to look at Gia, and it is one of those moments, those timeless, incandescent fractions of a second that are destined to stay with you forever. She looks at her, eyes clear and blue, skin so smooth, hair shining in that October sun, and she smiles. For the first time since all of this sadness began, Gia sees her old friend Barbara, the little girl. And then she sees her newest friend Barbara, the grown woman.

Gia embraces her, because the openness of her glance, the simplicity of her gaze, they are more than she can bear. "It's all been worth it," she whispers to her, "to find you again." This time she doesn't pull away from her, and as the old girlfriends are holding onto each other, the pallbearers begin to bring

Tony's coffin out of DiBello's, and the sight stops Gia's heart.

There are eight of them, and they are all wearing white gloves, save one man, the man at the right front. Yozo is carrying Tony's coffin with his hands bare because, Gia thinks she understands, it is his way of being close to him one last time. That small gesture fills her with pain. Gia will go back, and not long after that, Barbara will follow, but Yozo will be here without Tony, and she hasn't even thought about how that's going to be for him.

The men slide Tony's coffin into the hearse; this time Yozo, Barbara, and Gia ride together in the third car, and, after Yozo asks Barbara if she's all right, they ride to the church in silence.

The small church is full when they enter, except for the front three pews set aside for family. The last time Gia had a reserved seat in a church was when she made her First Holy Communion. Come to think of it, it was also her last Holy Communion.

Tony's coffin sits in the middle aisle, before the altar railing. The place is filled with flowers, and Gia watches the altar boys come out, just as she remembered, to light the candles. The choir begins to sing a small, quiet holy song, something she almost remembers. A bell rings, a real bell, and the congregation rises. She follows their lead because she no longer remembers the protocol of the Roman Catholic Mass.

No matter. When Willie steps out onto the altar, he is wearing a black cassock covered with a simple white surplice. There are four altar boys flanking him, and when they all genuflect and then turn to face the mourners, she sees Willie's eyes searching her out. When he finds her, he stands still for a moment, looking at her, as if to say, Here I am, this is what I am, this is my destiny. He was the boy who loved her, and now he is the man who loves God. She smiles at him, and he, almost imperceptibly, nods his head, turns again to face the altar, and begins what must be the most difficult Mass he has ever sung.

It's so warm, young Joe turns on the air-conditioning in the limo. The four of them are silent. Barbara and Yozo are smoking, Gia is looking out the window as the funeral procession takes one last swing around the old neighborhood, past where Pop's original store stood, past the garden that was once Pop's, most recently Tony's, past the old Sons of Italy lodge, past the poolroom where girls were never allowed and past which they were sometimes afraid to walk.

"He taught me pill pool and eight ball in there," she points out.

"Me, too," Yozo says.

"It was a beautiful Mass," Gia tells Willie, who is still wearing his vestments and sitting very close to her.

"I felt him there," he says.

"Probably because you heard him trying to get out," Yozo says.

"Don't start," she warns.

"What?" Willie asks.

Yozo quickly fills him in on Tony's mad plan. "That's barbaric. He must have been very sick."

"This was long before he got sick," Yozo says, looking straight at her. "It was just what he wanted."

"Piss off, you know-it-all shit," is her feeble retort.

"Nice." Barbara looks past her, out the window. "Nice."

"I know, I'm sorry."

"No," she points at something, "nice."

Three cars in front of them, where the procession has just turned onto Main Street and is about to head north on the road that will take them up to the cemetery, the hearse is enveloped in a cloud of billowing black smoke. The driver has stopped, gotten out, and is looking at it. Danny DiBello rushes around from the other side.

"Aw, Jesus!" Yozo exclaims, opening the door, "that's a blown transmission. Cheap bastard gets his work done at some cut-rate clown garage." He slams the door and they watch him walk toward the hearse, which they can see now, some of the smoke having drifted away.

"Do you believe in the Devil?" Barbara asks Willie.

"You mean, do I believe that evil walks the earth incarnate?"

"Yeah, that."

"Yes, I do."

"Well, shit," Gia says, "anyone who ever met my aunt Mella would know that."

"Do you think this," she points at the disabled hearse, "is some kind of a sign from the Devil?"

Willie makes a playful punch at her shoulder. "I think it's a bad transmission, and I'll wager our friend will have a new contract by the time this day is over."

Gia is sitting in a puddle of her own sweat, and all the air-conditioning in the world won't help her. This is Tony speaking to her from beyond death. She has no doubt. He is putting a curse on her. Then she begins to shiver.

Yozo opens the door. "Just stay put. They're bringing another hearse, and we'll switch. I've got a truck coming, too. It'll just be a few minutes. Gia, you might want to go up there with Francie. She's pretty flipped out."

By the time the coffin has been moved into an identical hearse, a crowd has gathered, and Gia has even managed to say hello to a couple of high school classmates. This is the scene: a dead hearse, a dead body, her old boyfriend dressed up like a priest, none of the sisters, and that now includes Francie, are talking to each other because no one agrees with how Mella was treated at the funeral home when she tried to strip Tony's corpse of its jewelry. Apparently, someone took a swing, but Gia hasn't been able to nail down exactly who it was. Her money is on Rosa, who has an excellently developed forearm from all those years of teaching typing. It's always the quiet ones.

As she's getting out of the first limousine, she hears from the sidewalk, "Yoo-hoo, Gia Scarpino, do you know who I am?"

She is fat, badly blonde, and lacks front teeth. Gia is smiling, like an idiot. "Brenda Davies," she finally calls out. "How are ya? It's a shame about your uncle."

Gia nods. "Thanks," she finally manages to say.

"Do you know her?" She yanks on the appliqued sweatshirt of the equally large woman next to her. "She's visiting from Pittsburgh. Remember her?"

"No."

"Getouttahere," she says.

"I'm sorry. It's kind of a busy day here."

"Yeah, we saw that smoke. It's a shame. You burying him up here?"

"Well, we're trying to."

"You don't know me?" the second woman says. She has hideously dyed red hair, with matching eyebrows penciled in. Gia notices that they are both wearing leggings, and she wishes she hadn't.

Gia shakes her head.

When she says her name, her maiden name, Gia instantly remembers her. "Wait a minute," Gia calls to the women on the sidewalk, and goes back to their car. "Yozo, you remember that blowjob you didn't get at that dance when you were on student council? Well, who said there are no second acts in life?"

"Beverly Adamavage?" He looks interested.

"I think you should at least go and say hello."

"Go on," Barbara urges him. "A little blowjob while you're waiting."

"Dear God," Willie says.

Danny DiBello yells that they're ready to go, and Gia waves at her classmates, who vigorously wave back, and gets back into the car.

"I've got to get out of this town," Gia says to no one in particular.

"You know," Barbara tells her, "it's not like this when you're not here."

"Thanks."

"I can see one," Yozo is saying to her, "but two? Two breakdowns in a trip that's not even two miles? That's not a coincidence, Gia, he's telling you how pissed he is. Look what he's doing just because you're a weasel."

After the second hearse died at the first hairpin turn up the mountain, DiBello's was out of hearses, and now they are awaiting a station wagon, the one they normally use to transport the body from the morgue to the mortuary.

"What do you want me to do, Yozo? You think it'd be a good idea now if I went and opened the coffin, yanked Tony out, and, what, threw him over my shoulder and headed for the local crematorium? You know what? You know what I think? I think this whole fucking mess has been so nuts that if I did that, no one would even think it was odd! That's what's starting to scare the living fuck out of me, Yozo, and this whole thing has been miserable enough, from beginning to end, that I don't need you flying up my ass with all that you know is right and proper!"

"No room up your ass. You've got your broomstick parked there."

"That's it," Willie says, and leaves them to join Francie and her aunts in the first car.

"Are you happy?" she asks Yozo. "This is hard for him, too."

"Oh, good, now you're gonna worry about Willie. Well, guess what? Willie takes real good care of himself. Tony can't. He bet on you and you let him down. I hope you can forgive yourself."

"Oh, fuck you. Shut up."

"This is going to be a memorable funeral. They'll tell stories about this funeral for years to come," Barbara observes. "It'll be in the paper tomorrow. This will be front-page news."

"Yo!" Danny DiBello roars.

"It's not a funeral anymore," Gia says as they climb back in the car, "it's a goddamn roundup."

"If I was a betting woman," Barbara says, "I'd bet that the station wagon makes it."

"It better, because if it breaks down, I'm gonna dig a hole with my bare hands and put him in it and then I'm going back to San Francisco."

"I'd pay to see that," Yozo says.

"Fuck you," Gia says.

"Fuck you," he tells her.

"Correct me if I'm wrong," Barbara says, "but wouldn't Tony have loved all of this?"

Gia is taking her clothes out of her suitcase, but she is not back in her Pacific Heights house. She is still in the guest room in what is now only Francie's house. Barbara watches her from beside the window, open so that she can blow her cigarette smoke out into the night air.

"I didn't think Francie would want me to be there for the reading of the will, but she said she'd feel better if I went with them, so what else could I do? I've already seen his will, it's pretty straightforward, but she gets everything she wants right now." Gia hangs up her last clean pair of jeans. "One more day, one more week, I can't be any more tired than I am now."

"It's been intense," Barbara agrees. "Nothing personal, but I don't think you should come back here for a while. I don't think the town will survive another one of your visits."

Gia sits on the bed. "I'm never coming back, Barbara."

"Well, if you're gonna stay on a couple days more, why don't you come for dinner tomorrow night? Eddie's off and I'd love for you to meet my kids."

It takes her a moment, but then she says, "You want me to meet the kids you'll be leaving? The husband whose car I beat to death? The one who hits you? Do you really think that's a good idea?"

"Uh, well, no, I had forgotten about that."

"It cost me five large ones. I got off cheap, Yozo told me, and I think he was right. Barbara, I don't ever want to meet your husband. Plus, if you're coming to live in San Francisco, I think they're probably going to have some certain strong feelings about me. Even if it's after the fact. Thanks, but I don't think so."

"You're right. Maybe the four of us could have one last dinner together?"

"Look, Yozo's never going to talk to me again, and Willie is an emotional basket case. He started drinking at the luncheon, and I've got to tell you, he was pretty whacked when he left, so I don't think he's going to be up for a good-bye party. They'll both be glad to see me leave."

"Oh, I don't know about that. Yozo, well, he'll stay mad for a while, but then he'll be okay, and Willie, well, I don't think he's ever going to be over you."

Willie standing in front of the altar, looking for her, looking at her. Maybe she has a place in his heart. But he's where he should be, and it's all for the best. "It's time for me to go, Barbara. It's just gonna take a little bit longer."

"How about if I call you in a couple of weeks to see how things are?"

"Yeah," she puts some sweaters in a drawer, "we'll make our plans then."

"Are you still sure it's okay for me to come?"

"Do you still want to?"

"More than ever."

"All you'll be leaving behind is the place, Barbara. Everything else in here," she touches her chest, "will be the same. What about your father? He's gonna miss you, won't he? What are you going to tell him?"

She looks flustered. "No, I can't tell him. It's better that he finds out after I'm gone."

"Whatever. You know best. Now," she closes the

suitcase and slides it under the bed, "will you come
with me?"

"I know you didn't ask my opinion, but I don't
think it's a good idea, Gia."

"I have to do this."

"You don't. Tony's not there. You don't have to go."

"Bear with me. At least I can tell him I'm sorry."

"You're going to do this, aren't you, even if I
don't go with you?"

"I'd rather you went, because it's still a little
creepy, but if you don't want to, I understand."

"No, I'll go," Barbara says.

Her uncle's fresh grave is easy to find, even in the dark.
It is the only mound of dirt in that section. Danny's
boys have piled all the flowers around and on top of
the grave. Tony's name is on a wooden marker that
has fallen over, and when Gia kneels to straighten it,
she breaks down. Barbara kneels beside her.

"Don't do this to yourself," she tells her. "He's
not here. It doesn't matter anymore."

"I let him down. Yozo's right. I'm a weasel. And
I'm pretty sure Tony put a curse on me."

"You really think he put the evil eye on you? God,
you're getting to be just like your aunts. You've been
here too long. Look, you didn't let him down, you
did what you had to do. In the end, it doesn't matter.
Except maybe to Yozo. Let him sort it out. It's his
baby now."

"That reminds me. Are you going to tell him
about his daughter? Before you leave, I mean?"

"You think I should tell both of them?"

"As your friend, I'd say yes. As maybe your sort of lawyer, I'd say no. Later, but not now."

"I think I want them to know."

"Then the time will be right someday when you can tell them. You'll know when it is."

"I'm really excited about this," Barbara says.

"We're kneeling here, you know. In a cemetery again. We always end up here, don't we?"

"Yeah. How much longer do we have to stay?"

"That's a really good question. You know the truth? I mean, why I came here tonight?"

"What?"

"Because I had to make sure he wasn't walking out of the cemetery."

"Did you really think he might be?"

"Well, I considered it as a possibility, given my family and all."

"You're as crazy as they are."

"Yeah," Gia sadly admits, "I know. Come on, let's go. Thanks for coming with me."

"We're going to go to better places than this," Barbara says. "The good times haven't even happened yet."

By the time Gia falls onto the bed, it's after one A.M. The next thing she remembers is being kissed lightly on her cheek, and seeing Mia bending over her, saying good-bye. "Where's your mother?" Gia manages to ask.

"She's in the car, waiting for me," Mia tells her.

"Good."

"Can I come visit you, Gia?"

"Anytime you want, honey."

"I think I want to live in San Francisco," the young woman tells her.

"You come stay with me." Gia thinks of her house filling up again, and she smiles as she falls back into a deep sleep, barely conscious of Mia's lips brushing her cheek.

She rouses later, and sees that the sunlight is fading. She sleeps on, and when Rosa wakes her to tell her that there has been an accident, it is dark again.

EIGHTH DAY

Sunday nights suck. It was on a Sunday night that they came to tell her that her husband had killed himself, and it is on another, distant Sunday night that Yozo and Willie and Gia are speeding along an unfamiliar highway, in a state police cruiser, with lights flashing and siren blaring.

"Are you sure we're not doing anything illegal?" she asks. She's wearing the clothes in which she just slept around the clock, and Yozo didn't give her time to brush her teeth, so she is, of course, smoking one of Willie's cigarettes. All three are smoking now.

"Fuck 'em. We have the service contract on the staties' cars. If they stop me, they're just gonna give me an escort, so why the fuck shouldn't I do this?"

"What do you think happened?" she asks. "Was she drinking?"

"Eddie didn't say. He just said she had totaled her car, that they had revived her at the scene, and that she was at Good Shepherd," he recites. "That's all he said. I didn't ask him anything except did he want to meet me there, and that's when he said to bring Willie, and you. You ready to meet this guy?"

"Why did he ask for me?" she asks.

Willie is dressed like a priest, in black suit and white collar. He has a prayer book with him, and Gia doesn't take that to be a good sign.

"Maybe he thinks this is his chance to kick the crap out of you," Yozo says.

"Maybe he thinks having her friends there would be a good thing for her," Willie offers.

"They revived her at the scene. Does that mean,

like, that she was knocked out and they woke her up?" she asks.

Yozo and Willie exchange glances in the rearview mirror.

"Or does it mean that they got her heart started again?"

"I think that," Yozo says.

"This is really bad, isn't it?"

No one answers her.

Barbara's husband doesn't look at Gia when they enter the family room at Good Shepherd hospital. He greets Willie with a handshake and Yozo with an embrace, his children rising slowly behind him. She notices that Barbara's boys are both dark, like their father, and her daughter, Andrea, is fair, like, well, like her father. Barbara's kids, all three of them, have tear-swollen faces, and when Gia shakes Eddie's hand, he tells her, "If you think you owe me something, you do, but she needs you now. I don't give a damn about you or what you think."

Gia mutters a weak "All right," and then introduces herself to the kids. Andrea is taller than her mother, skinny like her mother was in school, and has oddly familiar green-gray-blue eyes. Hasn't anyone ever noticed this before? Gia wonders. The girl speaks clearly and seems kind of bright, in a cheap, trailer-trash kind of way. If she were Gia's daughter, she would lock her up before she'd let her out of the house in those skintight jeans and high heels, but she is not Gia's daughter. Nor is she Eddie's, but that's not the point right now.

Barbara's sons, Greg and Jamie, sixteen and four-teen, look down when Gia shakes their limp, damp young hands. The older one reminds her of his mother in his long face, his tawny skin, but the little one is pure Eddie Eckroat, a carbon copy of his father. They mumble their names and, as quickly as they can, scramble back to their plastic chairs here in the family room. A soundless television above their heads is showing something, but no one looks at it long enough to find out what it is.

Willie is gently tapping his chest with his prayer book, until she puts her hand over his to still it. He looks surprised, looks down at her hand, and stands very still while Eddie tells Yozo the story:

"I don't know why the hell she was on six twenty-five, but she must of been on her way home, she was in the northbound lane, and her car just flew off the road, they said it looked like it must of rolled three or four times. Almost a full tank of gas, too, so we're lucky it didn't blow up, and she was wearing her seat belt, but it wasn't enough. I was gonna get one of those dual-air bag vans, but she said her Oldsmobile was good enough. If she had an air bag, maybe this wouldn't've happened. They said she was dead when they pulled her out of the car, that her head must of bounced off the window a couple times before the car stopped rolling. Nobody can figure out what happened, maybe somebody coming from the other direction crossed over the double yellow line and crowded her off the road. She was doing about eighty, the cops said, but she never drove that fast. I don't know. I don't know."

"What did the doctors tell you about her prognosis?" Willie gently asks.

Eddie looks blank.

"What did they say were her chances of coming out of this?" Yozo asks.

"They didn't," Eddie says. He rubs his forearms with both hands. "I'm not too good about talking with doctors. I don't understand a lot of this stuff." He is looking at Gia. "I thought you could help here."

"Yes," it's like a horrible payment on his destroyed Packard, "yes, I can talk to them."

There are nuns here. They are nurses, too, but they are nuns first, as evidenced by the short white veils they wear on the backs of their heads. Sturdy white rubber-soled shoes, simple white blouses, and faintly striped pastel pink and blue skirts, no-nonsense nurse watches, and those strange, simple gold bands on the third finger, left hand, to signify that they are Brides of Christ. They move silently, just like the nuns from her childhood, but these nuns break a smile more often than not, and their voices are soft and soothing, not like the sharp, cutting voices of her grade-school nuns. The nun who pages the neurosurgeon for Gia is kind and, while they wait for him to answer his page, asks if she'd like a Coke or something. She can't ever recall a nun offering her anything earthly. She declines, looking at Yozo and Willie, who are standing several yards down the hallway from the nurses' station. Gia motions for them to come to her, but they stay where they are, holding their safe distance from the dangerous place she now occupies, the place where she will learn Barbara's fate.

When the phone rings, everyone jumps, and the nun tells her that Dr. Tolliver is on his way.

Tolliver, a tall, lanky, gray-haired, deeply tanned man, puts his hand on her shoulder and walks her down the hall into an empty examining room. "I think this is a little more private," he says, closing the door.

"She's gone, isn't she?" Gia says, just as she did the night they came to her door to tell her about John.

He looks relieved when he answers, "The EMT's are trained to get the heart beating. The emergency department doctor on duty had her put on a ventilator right away. We've done an MRI, all the necessary diagnostic protocols, but it's my opinion that she was dead before the car stopped rolling."

"She can't breathe on her own." It's not a question.

"No."

"How long can she stay like that?"

"Not indefinitely. The body knows when to quit." He bends over to look in Gia's face. "How close were you to her?"

"We grew up together. We hadn't seen each other in a lot of years, but we caught up with each other in the past week or so. She helped me out with, uh . . ." She is starting to have trouble breathing, and she faintly hears herself saying, "I can't feel my legs. Am I standing up?"

She is suddenly aware that Dr. Tolliver has her supine on the examining table, and he is looking into her eyes. "You didn't faint," he assures her. He touches her forehead, her hands, her cheeks. "You're a little shocky. It's to be expected. Are those guys out there your friends, too?"

She nods. "And Barbara's."

"You want them?"

"Yes, please."

She is sitting up before they enter, looking young and boyish and frightened. "Could you give us a few minutes?" she asks the physician. I can do this, she thinks, but we have to be alone. "Could you just wait outside?"

He leaves, and Gia feels the tears running from her eyes before she even speaks, and all she hears from a suddenly bent-over Yozo is the screaming cry of a wounded animal. Willie throws his arms around his oldest friend, and Gia sits there, on the examining table, without the faintest idea of what to do next.

"Dr. Tolliver," Gia reaches for Barbara's husband, who rises, rubs his hands on his pants, and extends his to the neurosurgeon, "this is Eddie Eckroat."

"Mr. Eckroat," Tolliver says. "Let's sit down here."

"These are our children," Eddie says, shaming her for not thinking of it, "Andrea, Jamie, Greg."

Tolliver shakes hands with each kid and then looks around, pulls up a small table, sits on it, almost knee to knee with Eddie, and tells him, in simple, deadly terms, what has happened to his wife. The kids don't change expression, and then Andrea starts crying. Gia sits beside her and puts her arm around the girl, who falls easily against the older woman. The boys lean toward their father, who is frowning.

"So, if she stays on the ventilator, her head injuries won't get better? She won't wake up?" he asks.

Tolliver glances at Gia as she strokes Andrea's hair. "Her injuries are very serious. Her brain has experienced a major assault."

"Brain dead," Andrea whimpers.

Tolliver turns toward her. "That's a layman's term." He says everything very quietly.

"That's," Eddie begins, "you mean dead. All of her. She's dead."

"Her body doesn't work without her brain," Tolliver says.

"Well," Eddie sits back, looks at his kids, "I guess we can go home now."

He's in shock, Gia understands, still feeling that cold, empty feeling herself. She has to keep reminding herself to breathe; it seems to be so hard to do here tonight.

Eddie stands up, and Tolliver rises, too. Gia didn't realize how tall he is; he looks down at Eddie, who's a good-sized man. "We'll come back to see her tomorrow," Eddie tells him, and starts to go around him. "Come on, kids," he says.

"Mr. Eckroat," Tolliver says, "what do you want to do?"

"I gotta get these boys to bed. She," he points at his daughter, "has a little girl she's got to take care of, and I'm working third shift tomorrow. We've gotta get some rest."

"Eddie . . ." Gia says.

"I know. I know about organ donations and all that, I know. But I can't do that tonight. Not tonight. If somebody doesn't get a kidney or something because I can't do that tonight, that's too bad. I can't do anything tonight except take my kids and go home.

"I know what has to be done, but not until tomorrow. I don't want her to die at night. That doesn't seem right," Eddie says, and Gia's heart begins to break all over again. "What time do you get here tomorrow?" he asks the doctor.

"Whatever time you want me."

"Yeah, well, I'll be here at nine. You two can figure out the rest."

"Eddie, are you saying—" she begins.

"Yeah, that's what I'm saying. We can't leave her like that. Don't make me say it."

"We'll take care of it," she assures him.

"Yeah, good, come on, let's go." He takes what remains of his family, and they leave.

"What now?" she asks Tolliver.

"I'll set up a meeting for you at eight A.M. with the hospital's administrator."

"Who is that?"

"Monsignor Flaherty," he tells her. "Nothing happens here without his consent."

"Thank you for everything."

"Are you going to be all right?"

She considers his kind inquiry. And then, to this perfect stranger, she says, "No, no, none of us is ever going to be all right again."

He touches her arm. "I am so very sorry."

"Are you really sure?" she asks, because she sees what is waiting for her and Barbara, and Gia will do anything, anything at all, to avoid the inevitable.

Again he says, "I'm so sorry."

"Them." She nods at the closed examining room door. "I have to go tell them. Excuse me." She walks away from the doctor, thinking that she should have thanked him, but she doesn't feel very grateful right now. Not very grateful at all.

Yozo stays with Barbara, sitting beside her in a cold little cubicle in Critical Care. She has been so badly injured, her face is a swollen, bruised, unrecognizable caricature of a human, and her head is heavily bandaged, huge, like some alien creature. She is hooked up to machines whose functions Gia can only imagine. She recalls Tony in his deathbed, waiting for the expected end of his journey in peace, with his self-administered pain medication, and then she sees before her this grotesque manipulation of what was once a living creature.

In a quick move Willie bends over Barbara's face, whispering things Gia cannot hear but knows to be prayers, and then he touches her forehead,

what was her forehead under the bandages, and
her cheek, and whispers something else, and with
his tears consecrating her face, he kisses her cheek
and stands up straight, asking Yozo, who is just
staring at her face, if he wants to come home with
them. When there is no answer, Gia and Willie
leave.

Willie seizes up on her outside the hospital, with
its big marble statue of Jesus beside the front door,
and goes all fluttery, claiming he doesn't know how
to drive the cruiser, which is why they are flying
through what remains of the night with Gia behind
the wheel of this Pennsylvania state police car, albeit
without flashing lights and sirens because she is sure
she does not enjoy the same immunity as does Yozo.

"You have to be there with me, Willie." She is
hectoring him. "I'm gonna do this, and you're
gonna have to be there to hold him up. I don't know
Eddie Eckroat, but I get the feeling he knows his
own mind real well. His decision to go home, to
take the kids, that was good, that was sound, like
he's not going to be forced to do anything he
doesn't want to do, but when he comes back tomorrow, and I'm assuming that he's going to tell them to
take her off the life support, I need you to be able
to hold on to Yozo. He's shattered. First Tony, now
Barbara. I don't know how much one man can
take."

"He's loved her from childhood," Willie says.

"Then why didn't they get married, why didn't
they get together?" Gia asks.

"She went away, he went away, Christine got herself knocked up, he had to get married, that was how it was in those days," he says.

She has no reply to that, not tonight, and she is suddenly aware that there are now only three of them, as two of them drive through the night.

NINTH DAY

The good Monsignor Cornelius Flaherty has coffee served in the quiet, well-appointed office over which he presides. A nun actually serves them, a quaint gesture Gia finds vaguely threatening. A huge crucifix hangs over the gray-haired, round-faced man's head as he looks over Barbara's chart. "This is just terrible," he murmurs, and Gia is relieved that she has stumbled onto a human being within this vast repository of medical paraphernalia and religious icons. While pacing outside his office, waiting for eight o'clock, she came across not one but two chapels on this floor of the hospital.

Willie sits still, stiller than she ever thought a person could be, beside her, in a comfortable leather club chair just like the one she occupies. The desk between them and the Monsignor is large and shiny and spotless. He uses a bronze head of the Blessed Mother as a paperweight, holding down a tidy, squared-off pile of papers.

"Well," he looks up, "you're the family's legal representative, is that right?"

"Yes."

"And you're from around here?"

"We're from the same town as Father Cunningham here," she nods, "where we all grew up. I live in San Francisco, but I'm here on, uh, because of a death in my family, when this," she stumbles, just a little, "when this happened. She is my oldest friend." There is a strange, unexpected dissonance here. Gia did not use the past tense. Barbara is not yet dead for her.

"And you're licensed to practice law in Pennsylvania?"

She is instantly wary. "I'm not actually practicing law here, Monsignor. I am trying to assist the survivors of my oldest friend."

"But in Pennsylvania you wouldn't be recognized as an attorney, is that right?"

She doesn't want to annoy the guy, but she is not going to back up when he tries to corner her. "No, that's not quite right. Just like the United States Constitution, courts honor a version of the full faith and credit clause, and I can be sworn in to practice in Pennsylvania courts for an individual matter. It's a procedure called *pro hac vice*."

"I see." He smiles at Willie. "It's always good to be educated on these little matters, isn't it?" He winks at Gia. She doesn't wink back. "Now, what is it the family wants us to do?"

"It's indicated on her driver's license that she wanted to be an organ donor in the event of her death, and the family wants to have the life support terminated in a manner consistent with organ harvesting," Gia explains.

"Ah-hah. Well, if that's what they want," he closes the lid on the chart and pushes it across the desk to her, "we'll need to have a court order to make this official."

She stands and picks up the chart. "That's a simple matter. I can have a motion in the proper court in a couple of hours," she says, offering her hand. His shake is properly solid. "Thank you for making this horrible situation a bit more bearable."

He smiles at her, showing no teeth. She turns to leave, and Willie rises and shakes his ranking offi-

cer's hand. Gia is almost at the door when she realizes Willie isn't behind her, and she hears Monsignor
Flaherty say, "Of course, we'll oppose all of this in
court." When Gia slowly turns around, she sees
Willie standing there, between her and the desk, and
she realizes he is not coming with her.

"What?" She is astounded, not so much by the
content of what he just said, but by the cold-hearted
treachery with which he just set up her and, by
implication, Barbara and her family. "What did you
say?"

"We embrace life, we do not end life here."

"So you don't do abortions, I understand that. I
even respect that."

"We don't terminate life support. She's in God's
hands now. We must follow what God has deter-
mined."

She goes reeling with the ironclad simplicity
and narrow-minded certainty of what the good
Monsignor has just said. "God's hands?" Gia
repeats, walking slowly back toward his desk, and
she swears she sees Willie flinch. "God's hands
started Barbara Eckroat's heart beating again when
they pulled her out of that car? *She left most of her
brain on the window, Monsignor*. She can't breathe
on her own. That's God's will, my friend, not some
tubes and the man-made interventions that have her
chest going up and down while air is shoved in and
sucked out of her lungs. God willed Barbara to die
in that accident, and she did. Man interrupted God,
and I'm here to help God get back His advantage.
What, exactly, is your problem with my acting as

God's handmaiden, Monsignor?" By the time she finishes this little closing argument, she is pressing her upper thighs against the front of his desk.

"That's hardly how we see it," he quietly says.

"Yeah? Well, thank God I'm here to set you right. We'll see you in court, then," she assures him, and heads for the door again. "Are you coming?" she asks Willie, who hasn't moved.

"No," Monsignor Flaherty informs her, "he's not."

"Willie," Gia says sharply, "it's Barbara, it's us. What?"

He seems to take a deep breath and, exhaling, grow smaller. "I'm sorry," he says, and she blinks in astonishment.

"Your oldest friends," she reminds him, furious that she has to say these intimate things before this monster of a Monsignor. "How can you turn your back on us now?"

"I'm sorry, Gia," he says. "We have different beliefs."

She stares, and then she laughs, more of a snort than a laugh, really. "You get to wear a collar and stay above all of us mortals. I guess that's better than thirty pieces of silver, you fucking Judas."

"That's enough, miss," the Monsignor warns her.

"Aw, fuck you, too, you sanctimonious Irish fuck. I'll see you in court, you prick." She amends her curse. "You pricks."

She slams the door so hard when she departs that she brings tears to her own eyes, and she will forever swear that the nun sitting outside the Irish monsignor's office collapsed, but Gia can't be sure, because she can't see, being blind with rage as she has never been before and hopes never to be again.

"What happens now?" Eddie asks her as everyone sits around the circular oak table in his kitchen, Eddie, Gia, Yozo, Tom Arminavage, Barbara's father, and Andrea.

"Well, you could go along with the hospital's policy and, I guess, just wait for her to pass away, but I know it could take a while, and there would probably be a lot of medical procedures done on her, but I don't think she'd be aware, no." Gia shakes her head. "Of course she won't know what's happening." She has never sounded so lame.

"I don't want that to happen." Eddie cocks an eyebrow at his daughter, who is chewing on her lip, bright tears standing in her eyes. She is seated next to Yozo, who needs a shave, his skin looks rough, everything about him looks damaged, but he does not seem to be out of it, as Gia had feared the night before. When she went to him, at Barbara's bedside, and told him what had happened up in the Monsignor's office, he wasn't surprised.

"What the hell else were you expecting?" he asked her.

"It's the nineties, you know, I thought maybe there was an infusion of humanity somewhere in that fucking Church."

"That fucking Church is mine, don't forget."

"You gonna fold on me, too?"

"No, I think letting her go is the best way, but if

you thought Willie would choose us against his
Church, you were living in fucking fantasy land. He
had no choice."

"He had a choice," her voice sounded brittle and
bitter, even to her, "and he made it. He had a
choice."

Yozo shook his head. "No, no. His loyalty isn't
the same as yours. His priorities, aw, shit, his beliefs,
I guess, are different than yours. You can't blame the
guy."

"Yes, I can," she told Yozo, standing beside
Barbara's bed in Critical Care, "and I do."

Now she turns to Eddie. "No," she says, "I
know."

"So, what do we do?" he asks.

"Well, I've talked to my colleagues in California,
and they're faxing me all the applicable case law
and statutory stuff on this matter here in Pennsylvania. I don't know a whole lot about this area,
but I suspect it's pretty well-settled law here, like in
other places, that if there is ample testimony that
the patient would not have wanted her life to be
continued artificially, the courts usually grant the
family's wish."

"Usually?" Eddie wants to know. "Not always?"

"Nothing in the law," she understands she has
to educate him, "is ever predictable, no matter how
simple they make it look on television. Sometimes
your outcome can depend on who or what the
judge had for lunch. I've learned never to take anything for granted. But I can go into that courtroom
prepared, and I promise you I'll do my best. I can't,

Eddie, honestly promise you that I'll be able to get you what you want."

"Yeah," he nods, while looking into the middle distance. "How about this? Why don't I just have her moved to a nursing home and have her disconnected there? I could do that."

Gia rubs her eyes. She has to keep fighting her worst impulse, which is to ask him if he beat her up one last time before she went driving wherever it was she went. "Uh, there was an outside chance, maybe one in ten thousand, that you might have been able to try that, but you would have been stopped, I'll wager. Now," she glances at her watch, "I'll bet you everything I have that the hospital has already filed a motion to have itself declared Barbara's legal guardian. That's pretty standard procedure in these cases, from what I've been able to glean so far."

"Can't you fight them?"

"It's not worth the effort. Judges, no matter what state they're in, don't like these cases, but they tend to grant the guardianship until the major issue, that of discontinuing, is settled. We won't prevail, but if you want me to try, I will. My advice is to let them do it and take them on at the next curve, which will be a hearing on your wish to have her removed from life support."

"So I have to testify that she wouldn't have wanted it?" Eddie asks.

"You and Barbara talked about it?" Gia is hopeful.

"No, but I think that's what she would have wanted," he says.

"Not good enough," she tells him, and her hopes begin to slip. "Did she ever talk about it with anyone?" She looks around the table, but no one looks back.

"I could say we did," Eddie offers.

"No." She may walk any number of questionable lines in her practice of the law, but she has never allowed a client to perjure himself intentionally, with her full knowledge and implicit consent. When she taught legal ethics, she used to wrap up her final class with this instruction: You are going to come up to situations that constantly question your personal and professional ethics. Your personal ethics are your own choice, and I have nothing to say about them. But as for your professional ethics, which are still my concern for a few more minutes here, I offer you, as a yardstick against which to measure whatever your professional decisions will be, this small circumstance: It is the ethical choice if you would still do it knowing that your mother was watching you.

"The judge wouldn't know," Andrea says.

Gia turns to her. "No, but I would, and you would, and your father would, and the fact is, if you don't know for a certainty that this is what your mother would have wanted, perhaps it isn't something she would have wanted you to do. Perhaps she would have had no objection to remaining on the ventilator until her systems closed down on their own." It is one of the cruelest speeches she has ever had to make, but she can't be any other kind of lawyer than the kind she has always been.

"So, what, then?" Eddie asks.

She thinks for a moment. "Let me study the case law. I still have to find out what court we'll be playing in. I'll have some answers for you by this time tomorrow. Until then I don't know what to tell you."

The doorbell rings, and Barbara's younger son calls from the front door that there's someone there for Eddie. "I got a call from the paper, they said they were going to send someone over. Is it okay for me to talk to them?" he asks Gia.

"Yeah. Just tell the truth, but don't say anything about not knowing what Barbara would have wanted."

"Got it," he says as he leaves the kitchen.

"So," she says to Barbara's father, whom she hasn't seen since 1963, and who appears to have aged very little during the past decades, "this is a hell of a way to meet again, eh, Tom?"

"Yeah, it's a hell of a thing."

"You look good," she says.

"I got some cold cuts and stuff in my car," Yozo says to Andrea. "You and your brothers want to help me bring them in here?"

After they leave, Gia says to Tom, "Did you and Barbara ever talk about, you know, about how, like when her mother died, did you ever talk with her about that kind of stuff?"

He waves her words away with his strong old hands, miner's hands. "Ah, the hell with it, it's all bullshit, anyway."

"Yeah, but did you ever tell her what you wanted if you, you know, if you went after your wife?"

"You mean, did I talk to my daughter about dying?"

"Yeah, about dying."

"My daughter was a goddamn drunk. I talked to her about football. The rest of the time she was too goddamn drunk to talk to."

"Tom," Gia swallows her incipient roar, "she's your daughter. She's just about gone now. Don't talk about her that way."

"I'll talk about her any way I want to. She was a waste. You gonna stick up for her now, huh, with your big mouth?"

Gia flushes. "That's your daughter. And, yeah, I am gonna stick up for her. I'm gonna do everything I can to make sure she's taken care of. That's what you're supposed to be doing."

He speaks in a low voice. "Don't you tell me what I'm supposed to be doing."

"You're upset. We're all upset. Let's not say things we might regret later."

She stares, incredulous, as he rises across the table from her and, shaking, raises his hand to her. "Don't tell me what to do, you little wop bastard!"

She is quick to her feet. "Don't you dare raise your hand to me, Tom. Don't you do that." Her voice is low and soft.

A hand seems to come out of nowhere, and wraps its fingers around the old man's shaking upraised hand. "Stop it," Yozo says.

Her mouth is dry, and her fists are clenched.

Yozo's grip on the old man tightens. "Son of a

bitch," Tom Arminavage mutters. "You can't do this."

"You'd better go home, Tom," Gia tells him. "Now."

Yozo and Gia stare at each other after the old man leaves, and then he looks down at the hand he recently had on Barbara's father. "Jesus," is all he can say.

Eddie comes back into the kitchen carrying a handful of papers. "What does this mean?" He hands them to Gia.

"I didn't know you could do this," she says as she looks over the documents. Her hands are still shaking, but no one seems to notice. "The hospital went into court and got itself appointed Barbara's guardian, all nice and legal, and they didn't even have to give you notice. Lovely commonwealth, Pennsylvania."

She looks up at Yozo and Eddie, while Andrea and her brothers carry in small trays of food. "This is going to be real interesting," she warns them.

She sits at her godfather's desk, in his office in the house, with only the banker's light on in the dark room. She has a yellow legal pad, covered with writing, a pile of faxed case law and statutes, and her grandfather's *Petit Larousse Illustre* on her lap. Its spine is missing, so she is very careful as she opens the front cover to find written, in pencil, in Pop's hand, "*Il miglio Italiano o geometrico e 1852*

metri, l'Americano e 1600 metri," and under that,
"*RIBAVT,*" neither of which means anything to her.

Inside the dictionary, in a separate section of pink
pages, her grandfather has left a penciled X next to
the phrase "*La mort frappe d'un pied indifferent.*"
She goes back to her high school French and, finding nothing in her memory, calls her law firm, where
it is only four-thirty in the afternoon, and asks to
speak to one of the international lawyers. In a second, a man on the line tells her that it means,
"Death kicks on the door with an indifferent foot."

"What does that mean?"

"I think," he says, "since death is usually de-
picted holding a scythe, he uses his foot to kick at
the door instead of knocking, and Death doesn't dis-
criminate, he comes for rich and poor, young and
old, and the like."

RIBAVT. Death knocking on doors. Who knows
what he had in his head? Gia rubs the cover, opens
it again, looks inside at the publication date—
1898—and thinks that the only person she wants to
ask for help is beyond her reach now. Tony.

What do you want me to do? she asks her lost
friend. Am I doing the right thing? Are you where
you can hear me? Can you tell me anything?

She has spent the afternoon reading the meager
number of opinions, all the while trying to recon-
struct anything Barbara might have said to her that
could lead Gia to someone, somewhere, who would
be able to illuminate what Barbara might have
wanted in a situation such as this.

There is no hope, she reminds herself. The damage is too extensive. Whatever she accomplishes, she's not killing Barbara, she's just trying to set her free.

This is the hardest night. When John killed himself, it was done, there was nothing she could do about it except to cope as best she could. When Tony fell mortally ill, Gia was with him, and so what if she didn't exactly honor his last wish? It's not like he made a lot of sense, she tells herself, but she knows the shameful truth, that she let him down, and now, with her oldest friend, she has a tragic second chance to do what is right for someone she loves. It may not soothe the sharp guilt she will always feel over her godfather's remains interred in consecrated soil, but it is all she can do now.

"Hi." Yozo enters the room quietly and folds himself into the overstuffed chair opposite the desk.

Gia waits for him to say something. The truth is, she is hoping he's here to tell her that Barbara has passed away, that there was a huge blood clot, or a power failure, one so massive the backup generators were blown out. The lawyer just wants to hear that her client is dead.

"Were you at the hospital?" she asks.

"No, I'm not going back there," he tells her. "I got some sleep this afternoon. How about you?"

"I've been reading the law. Pennsylvania's a tough state. Its statutes are narrowly drawn, and the courts interpret them very tightly. All the case law is against our position. It's very clear, without direct testimony, either from a credible witness or in the form of a living will or a health-care power of attorney, that the hospitals can do exactly what Good Shepherd is doing to Barbara. They can get her, and they can keep her. The religious issue is one way I might go, though, since I can't find anything on point here."

"How's that?"

"I would argue the separation of church and state. It's slippery, actually, it's specious, but I don't have anything else. I could say that the state has no right to interfere in how the church does its business, and while that sounds like I'm arguing on behalf of the church, I come in the back door and conclude that because of this invisible line that must be drawn, the state has no right to give the church legal guardianship in order to preserve what the church sees as its interests in Barbara Eckroat. I just keep plunking that separation of church and state string, and maybe I can find a tune the court will want to sing to."

Yozo smiles. "You were born to do this kind of stuff, weren't you?"

She smiles back at him. "Yeah, this is what I do best. I just didn't plan on doing it here. I don't know, Yozo. I don't know the courts here, and I'm on my own. I guess I could ask a local attorney to take it on, but I can't do that. I have to do this, you know?"

"Yeah, I know. What are you gonna do, put on witnesses and all that?"

"Like a little trial, yeah. I'm going to put Eddie, Andrea, I guess that's it."

"No," Yozo says, "there's someone else." He gets up. "You keep doing that, I'll see you tomorrow."

"The hearing is set for one o'clock," she reminds him.

"I know."

"See ya." She smiles up at him across the desk light, and she sees all his years in his face. Just as she saw them in the mirror today.

We're not kids anymore.

The Convent of the Sisters of Saint Cyprian is situated on what used to be the private estate of an Irish coal baron. It is two miles away from the town, far enough away to be private and apart. There is nothing between the convent and the town, no malls, no buildings, nothing. Harry Ryan bought up all the land back in the early 1900s, and now the good sisters hold title to all that stands between them and the secular world.

They have no phone, so Yozo arrives just before dawn and writes a note that he slips into the horizontal wheel, half of which is outside the locked stone gate. Turning the wheel so that his note is carried inside, he rings the bell and waits. He hears someone scurry through the courtyard to the wheel, feels someone reach into it, and then he hears the same footsteps running back to the main building, the house where Harry Ryan lived his life as a rich man and where now the nuns hide.

Wouldn't you just know it? he thinks as the first raindrop hits his sunglasses.

When the wheel is turned toward him, someone has written beneath his request a single
word. "No."

He writes on the back of it, "Please?", and
the process is repeated. Again, the answer comes
back, "No."

"It is a matter of life and death," he writes on
another piece of paper.

"Wait," the next note says.

A buzzer sounds, he pushes against the heavy
wooden door, and he is in the stone courtyard, looking around. A tapping sound leads him to the front
door of the mansion, oak, with a heavily thatched
panel about six inches square set about five feet
from the floor. He is instantly reminded of the confessional, where he doesn't go to confess but sometimes finds it a comforting place just to sit. He and
Willie have had some good conversations in the
confessional at Our Lady of Mercy, he recalls, and
he knows that Willie always waits for him actually
to make an official confession, but, honestly, they
both know that's never going to happen. Sometimes
they tell each other things, but it is never a confession, not between friends.

"What do you want?" A woman's voice, husky,
as though she needs to take a drink of water.

It's starting to rain harder, but Yozo is under a
wooden awning sheltering the doorway. "You have
a nun here, her name was Mary Ann Arminavage. I
think her name is Sister Anna now. She has a sister
named Barbara, and Barbara's very badly hurt. It
would help if I could talk to her, to Sister Anna."

"I'm sorry for the woman's injuries, but we do not talk here."

"Well," Yozo gears up his argument, "you're talking to me. I don't even have to see her. You could just put her where you are, and I could ask her some questions. Please?"

"I'm the Mother Superior. Sometimes, by necessity, I must speak. But the sisters do not. There are no exceptions."

"Look, Mother, uh," his eyes are burning, and there is a tightness in his chest, made tighter by the fact that Yozo is holding his breath, so afraid is he that he'll burst into tears, "her sister's life is in the balance here. Her soul, Mother, her soul. Her soul has to be set free, and we can't do that, she can't go, unless I talk to her sister. She's Catholic, Mother, it's her soul." He has a hard time getting these words out.

"We shall pray for Barbara," the Mother Superior tells him, and he hears a panel softly closing.

"*No!*" He slaps the door. "Don't go!" he shouts into the thatched panel. "Please?"

But there is only the sound of the rain hitting the stones in the courtyard. In this muted setting, Yozo stands in the convent courtyard, crying, and then he pushes open the heavy wooden door, the door that will lock when he lets go of it, then he turns back, looks up at the old mansion, and yells, "Mary Ann Arminavage! Hey! Mary Ann! Barbara needs you! Come on out! Please! Please!"

There is only the sound of the rain hitting the stones in the courtyard, and this time he lets the heavy wooden door lock behind him.

TENTH DAY

The first judge accepts her *pro hac vice* motion, and sends her to another courtroom, on a different floor, in the big old country courthouse where, she thinks, for no good reason, all their birth records are stored. Barbara's family is there, without her father. No Yozo.

"You'll wait out here because I'll be calling you as witnesses. We went over this, okay? There's no need to be scared or nervous. No one's going to do anything to make you feel bad or scare you," she is speaking mostly to the boys now, "because I'll stop them. All right?"

Everyone almost nods. Gia notices that they have all dressed up for this appearance, and their effort wrenches her heart. She is going into this unfamiliar court with a signed order from a downstairs judge permitting her to practice, these people are counting on her, and she doesn't know any of the rules. She doesn't even know who her opposition will be, although she noticed, on the order granting the hospital legal guardianship, that the firm representing the hospital is a collection of Irish names. She'll just go in and make like she knows what she's doing, and she knows that all her best arguments are going to be emotional, pure heart-wrenching stuff, so she's hoping that the judge has a heart.

She enters the ornate old courtroom, a wonderfully Gothic place, with dark wooden panels, an ancient chandelier above the center aisle, heavy wooden pews in the gallery, stained-glass windows, and thinks, I'm in a fucking church. She has never seen a courtroom like it, but then, she is a twentieth-century lawyer.

Taking place at the plaintiff's table, she goes to the defendant's table and introduces herself to the gray-haired man in the three-thousand-dollar navy blue pinstripe suit. "Gia Scarpino." She holds out her hand.

"Frank McGuire," he tells her. "Pleased to meet you, counselor."

"Yes, the pleasure is mine," she answers. "Is there any middle ground for us here?" she queries, looking for a compromise, something that will give her everything she wants, which has always been Gia's idea of a compromise. She can't imagine what there might be, but it is an obligatory question.

"No, our client, Good Shepherd, is very clear on its position. I heard you had a real go-round with Monsignor Flaherty."

"Go-round?" She pretends to think this over. "No, I don't think so." And then all that she has ever been in a courtroom comes back to her, and it is to harass and to annoy her opposition, to make her presence so goddamn irritating that they get flustered, make mistakes, lose it. "That was just a quick conversation where he made his position known." She smiles at Frank McGuire, who, she recalls, is one of the name partners, and who looks to be beyond retirement age. She wonders if he's doing this particular hearing as a favor to his friend the Monsignor.

"You're wasting your time," he tells her. "It's a very conservative commonwealth, with very conservative courts. Unless you have something I don't know about, you're going to be out of here very quickly."

You don't know about my mouth, she thinks, which will run you into the ground for as long as the judge will let me talk. But she looks down, her demure look, then looks up from under her eyelashes, and says, "I know. But it's a favor to the family."

"Well," he winks at her, and she knows she's pegged the old fuck right, "it won't take long."

"Thank you," she says, and returns to her table, where she places before her just a legal pad and a pen. She's made some notes about what her opening argument will be, and then she decides to pass.

The courtroom is empty except for the two lawyers. "You're from San Francisco, huh?" Frank McGuire says.

"Yeah." They've researched her in Martindale-Hubbell, the directory of practicing attorneys.

"That's a beautiful city. My wife and I went there on our twenty-fifth wedding anniversary."

"That's a good place to go for a silver anniversary," Gia chats back.

"You know what that town has?" He begins to instruct her about her home.

Lots of perverts, she thinks. "Hmmmmm?"

"Great restaurants."

"Oh, yeah, it's a real good restaurant town."

"I wish we could have gotten out to Alcatraz. We didn't go."

"I've never been," she says. "I hear it's really interesting."

"All rise," the bailiff, a hugely fat woman in a skintight brown uniform, sporting the first female comb-over Gia has ever seen, intones. "The court of the Honorable Alvin Sweet is in session."

"Okay, here we go." The dark-haired, round-faced man seats himself, and nods to both lawyers to be seated. Gia sits, and then rises again. "May it please the court, I have here the signed *pro hac vice* order just issued permitting me to represent plaintiff in this matter. As I'm not a member of the Pennsylvania Bar, this was necessary."

The bailiff hands the order to the judge, who looks down his bifocals at it—he's older than he looks, Gia notes—and says, "So entered. Welcome, counselor."

"Thank you, Your Honor."

"What have we got here? 'In the Matter of Barbara Eckroat' and Eckroat v. Good Shepherd." He takes off his glasses and looks at Gia. "Tell me a story, counselor," he says, and she senses that she might have stumbled across a smart, humane judge.

She stands and recites the facts, facing the judge, looking neither to her opponent on the right, nor the fat bailiff on the left; nor does she drop her gaze to the court reporter, who sits between her and the bench.

"Oh, that's sticky," the judge says. "Mr. McGuire, you have anything you want to add to that?"

"Only, Your Honor," he rises slowly and runs his thumbs under his sharply pressed lapels, "that my client believes that its position simply reflects well-established law and that its position is not only legally correct but also justified."

"Well," Judge Sweet says, "that's what makes horse racing. You've got an opening statement, Ms. Scarpino?"

"I think I just made it, Your Honor. The statement of facts, I believe, speaks for itself, both in terms of policy and the wishes of the family."

"All right," the judge says. "Mr. McGuire?"

"No opening statement."

"Oh, this is going to be easy," Judge Sweet says. "You have a witness list?" He looks through the petitions before him.

"No, sir," she responds. "I have Barbara Eckroat's husband and children available out there," she points toward the doors behind her, "and I'll call them one by one."

"It's your turn, counselor, so go ahead."

"Edward Eckroat," she tells the bailiff.

It's three up and three down.

She puts on Eddie, Andrea, and Greg, and after eliciting from them their testimony that their mother would never have wanted to be on life support if there was no hope of recovery, after demonstrating that her designation on her driver's license that she wished to be an organ donor was ample proof that she did not wish to have her life artificially prolonged, due to the fact that organs deteriorate when the patient is kept on a ventilator, after questioning each of them, and doing the best she

can to air what they thought their wife and mother
might have carried in her mind, Frank McGuire
stands up and asks them three straightforward questions:

*Did you and your wife/mother ever discuss a sit-
uation where one of you might be in an accident
that would leave you unable to survive without
mechanical support?*

*Did your wife/mother ever tell you that she
would rather have her life ended than be kept alive
on a ventilator?*

*Is your testimony that you don't actually have
knowledge of what it is your wife/mother really
would have wanted in this situation?*

He demolishes them, in a quiet, polite way.
Andrea and Greg leave the courtroom in tears. Gia
has only Jamie, fourteen years old, in the hallway,
and she does not want to subject him to the same
cross-examination.

She is thinking that it is time to get up and pitch
her best bullshit, the bullshit of her life, when she
hears footsteps behind her, and Yozo, leaning over
the wooden railing that separates the gallery from
the lawyers' well, pokes her back.

"Hey!" Judge Sweet calls. "You can't do that!"

"I'm sorry, Your Honor," Yozo says, "but I have
some information for the lawyer."

"Any objections?" he asks McGuire, who shakes
his head. "Go ahead. But don't do that anymore."

Yozo leans even farther across the railing, and
Gia shoves her chair back toward him. "What?"

"You have another witness," he tells her.

"No, I'm not going to call the kid. It's not worth it."

"Not Jamie. You have another witness."

"Who?"

"Can I get the next witness, Your Honor?" Yozo asks.

"Sure," Judge Sweet says.

"I'll be right back," he whispers to Gia, and scoots down the aisle, sticks his head out the courtroom doors, and then stands back as Father William Cunningham, in full priest drag, enters the courtroom.

Gia stands and looks at Yozo, who seats himself in the last row and, smiling, nods at her, and then at Willie, who is taking the oath, his left hand on the Bible. "So help me God," he assures the bailiff, and then, sober-faced, sits down and looks at her.

She feels as though she's been struck into stone. She glances at McGuire, who is busy with his legal pad.

Then, because Gia doesn't know what else to do except to be Barbara's lawyer, she stands, and approaches the witness box, and says, "State your name, please."

"William Charles Cunningham."

"Your address?"

"I live in the rectory at Our Lady of Mercy parish."

"And your position there?"

"I am the pastor."

"How long have you had that position?"

"Two years."

"Are you acquainted with the plaintiff, the patient who is the subject of this hearing, Barbara Arminavage Eckroat?"

"Yes."

"How would you characterize your relationship with Mrs. Eckroat?"

"We were friends."

"Long-time friends?"

"Objection. Leading." McGuire begins to earn his fat retainer.

"Sustained."

"How long have you known her?"

"Since we were fourteen years old. I met her in ninth grade. More than thirty-five years."

This scene is so surreal, Gia doesn't know what else to do, so she is automatically laying a foundation, but for what, she's not certain. It gives her a strange ache in her gut to think that Willie is here to perjure himself just so that she won't be mad at him anymore.

"Counselor," Judge Sweet prods her out of her confusion, "do you have any more questions?"

"Uh, yes, sorry, Your Honor. Father Cunningham, did there come a time when you had occasion to discuss with Mrs. Eckroat the matter of artificial sustaining of a life after an injury or an illness?"

"Yes."

"And when was that?"

"She came to talk to me after her mother died."

A warning bell tolls in Gia's head. "She came to you as a friend, not as a priest?"

"Oh, yes, she wasn't a member of our parish. I don't think she belonged to any church."

"Objection."

"Just answer what you're asked, Father. Let her ask you."

"Oh." Willie looks startled. "I'm sorry."

"No harm done," the judge assures him. "Counselor?"

"So she came to you, not in a priest-penitent relationship, but as a man and woman who had grown up together?"

"That's right."

"And what was the nature of that conversation?"

"Objection, Your Honor."

"Yes, Mr. McGuire?"

"I don't see how," he speaks slowly, glancing at his yellow pad, "it's that cut and dried that a priest steps out of his sanctified role without it having some influence on whomever he's talking to. I would recommend that the priest-penitent privilege attaches no matter what kind of conversation Father Cunningham is having, and it's just not that simple for him to step away from his calling. I would object that this whole line of questioning is improper."

Judge Sweet nods at Gia. "You got anything you want to say to that?"

"Mr. McGuire's reasoning would be, then, that, simply by the nature of his vocation, Father Cunningham would be precluded, say, from testifying about an auto accident he might witness, or an assault he might endure, simply because, according to counsel, Father Cunningham's every word to every person is automatically confidential, much as counsel and Your Honor and I all have taken oaths which place upon us the limitation of what we can discuss regarding our clients, but were we to follow Mr. McGuire's reasoning, I would be precluded from ever speaking about what I did, for example, in the course of my day, to anyone."

Judge Sweet is staring at her. "Was that all one sentence?" he asks.

"I don't think so," she says, and then she sees the court reporter nodding.

"Impressive. And, I think, on target. Overruled."

"Read back, please." She's lost her train of thought.

"'And what was the nature of that conversation?'" the reporter reads.

"Okay, thank you. And what was the nature of that conversation?"

"Her mother had just endured a long and painful death from cancer, and Barbara said that she would never want to die that way."

"So you talked about death?"

"Yes."

"What else did she say about it?"

"She said, if she was ever in a coma from which there would be no recovery, she would rather die. She said it would be just a matter of her body."

And then it comes to Gia in a blinding flash. Willie is telling the truth. Willie came here because he wanted to tell the truth. She almost loses her place again.

"Did you talk in any kind of hypothetical manner?"

"Yes."

"Did you two construct and discuss different scenarios?"

"Yes."

"What were they?"

"Well, one was if a person, if she had a really painful illness, and it was terminal, she said, Barbara said she'd just want to be able to die, not to be treated, except for the pain."

"Any others?"

"Yes."

"They were?"

"She said if she was ever in a coma, with no hope of recovery, she wouldn't want anybody to do anything to keep her alive."

There. Her case has just been made. Gia feels that same familiar, almost sexual rush she used to get in court just at that instant she knew she had connected with the jury or the judge, that the information had flowed in such a way as to take the law along with it, and it had been absorbed by someone who understood in more than an intellectual manner.

"Do you think her situation now is what she had in mind?"

"Objection. Can Father Cunningham read Mrs. Eckroat's mind?"

Gia says, "Well, at this point, obviously not. Mrs.

Eckroat has no mind. At least from a medical stand-point, which is all we're concerned with here today."

"Good one," Judge Sweet says, "but I'd rather have Father Cunningham testify to what he thinks, not what our plaintiff might have thought. Sustained."

"Okay," Gia continues. "Did you discuss a situation similar to the one in which Mrs. Eckroat is today?"

"Yes. It was exactly that. The car accident, the resuscitation, revitalization, actually, the absence of hope. That's what we discussed."

"And what was her position?"

"That she would not want to continue on an artificial life-support system."

"No further questions." Gia stands with her hand on the witness box rail and stares right into Willie's blue eyes. He looks back, even and clear-eyed and unblinking. Then she turns away, and Frank McGuire begins, but his questions don't go anywhere, and they all know that he is just going through the motions. He'll be able to present the transcript of this hearing to the Monsignor as proof that the Church's money was well spent.

"Closing?" Judge Sweet asks.

She is tempted. This would be a wonderful opportunity for her to show off in front of Willie and Yozo, to show them what she can do. But years of experience have taught her that with most judges it's best to let them do what they are going to do without pushing them from behind. If she stands up and gives her speech about what is right and what is moral and how he should rule, she must keep in mind that she doesn't know this guy, and she'll be running the risk of pissing him off. So, in her most restrained manner, she rises, and says, "The law of the commonwealth calls for my client to present clear and convincing evidence from a reliable witness as to what her wishes are. I believe Father Cunningham is a most reliable witness, and I believe his testimony is more than ample to support this court's ordering that Barbara Eckroat's life support at Good Shepherd hospital be discontinued immediately. Thank you."

Frank McGuire is in a position. Gia turns to watch him try to discount the testimony of a priest. He goes up one rhetorical alley and down another, but the only way he can snatch this case out of the fire is to call Father Cunningham a pathological liar, and since he didn't do that during his cross-examination, he can't do that now. So, poor old Frank McGuire flinches only a little as Judge Sweet tells them, as far as his court is concerned, the evidentiary burden has been met by the plaintiff, and he is issuing the order forthwith that Barbara's life support should be terminated.

"Stay the order, Your Honor, while we make an appeal?" McGuire asks.

"Counselor, do you really think there's been an error here, or are you jerking me around?"

Gia holds back a snicker. McGuire gapes.

"You have the order?" Judge Sweet asks her.

"Are a couple of handwritten lines acceptable, Your Honor?" She grabs her pen and legal pad.

"As long as they're legible."

Gia prints, in big, readable letters, "It is the order of this court this day that all artificial life support now being used to maintain the breathing of Barbara Arminavage Eckroat at Good Shepherd hospital be immediately disconnected, and her body be released immediately to her next of kin."

"Is that okay?" She hands it over the top of the bench.

"Fine." He dates it and hands it to his clerk, saying, "Two copies. One for each side. Hers needs to be certified. The court maintains possession of the original, all right, counselor?"

"Yes, sir." She is suddenly hollow inside. It's all beginning to go so fast. She turns around, and Willie and Yozo are standing behind the last row of benches, watching intently.

"You from around here?" the judge asks her.

"I was," she answers, "but I'm not anymore."

"About that stay, Your Honor," McGuire is at it again.

"Oh, counselor, I thought you understood. Denied." He signs one copy, then the other, then the original, and holds it up for the lawyers to see. He hands the copies to the bailiff, who gives them each one, Gia's being the certified one—she checks to make sure. McGuire thanks the judge and, without even saying good-bye to Gia, takes off.

"That's it?" she asks the judge.

"Good luck," he says.

"Thank you." She turns, pushes through the gate, walks quickly down the aisle, and tells Yozo,

"You have to drive now like you've never driven before."

"Let's go," he says, and the priest, the businessman, and the lawyer start running for the big marble staircase that bisects this beautiful old county courthouse in the county seat where they were born, which holds all of their birth certificates and where, soon, Barbara's death certificate will be filed, but not by the priest, the businessman, or the lawyer.

"You can't go in there!" the nun yells as Gia swings open the Monsignor's door.

"Watch this," she says over her shoulder, and, leaving the door open, she calls out to the startled cleric, who is already standing behind his desk, "Remember me, Monsignor? I'll bet you were just counting the seconds until I walked in here, weren't you?"

"I expected you."

"I'll bet you did. I'll bet that little old phone and fax have just been burning up with tales of my devilish handiwork, haven't they?" She tosses her copy of the court order on his desk, facing him. "As if you haven't already seen this. Let's make it official. Read it and weep, Monsignor."

He sits and adjusts his gold-rimmed glasses. "I'll need some time to study this," he says, just as she expected. He's trying to stall her while his lawyers attempt to get a stay from an appellate court.

"It's one sentence, pal." Gia counts aloud to ten. "Your time's up. Your turn is over," she tells him, grabbing the order out of his hands. She dashes out

of his office down to Critical Care, where Yozo and
Willie are waiting for her with Barbara's husband
and children.

"This is a court order," Gia tells the nun nurse in
charge. "It authorizes the disconnection of Mrs.
Eckroat's life support. We'd like this done immediately, and we'd like you to be there when it's done."

"I'll have to talk to . . ." She begins to pick up a
phone, but Gia reaches over the high counter and
takes the receiver out of the nun's hand.

"No. There's no more talk. We did all that in
court today. I'm not going to threaten you, and I'm
not going to try to force you to do anything you
can't, in good conscience, do. But we are going
down there," she points, "and we're going to turn
off her ventilator. If we have to tear the machine out
of the wall to release her, we'll do that. If you believe
that you can help us, we'd appreciate it."

"I'm sorry," the nun says.

Barbara's cubicle is bordered by white cloth curtains. The children are standing on the edge of the
adults, looking frightened.

"Do you want to kiss your mom good-bye?" Gia
softly asks the boys, who nod and slowly go inside
to where their mother lies.

"I don't want to go in there," Andrea says. "I
don't want to see her like that again."

"That's all right." Gia takes her hand and rubs it
between hers. "That's fine. Can you stay with the
boys? Take them upstairs or something?"

"We could go to the chapel," she suggests.

"That's good," Yozo tells her. "That's just right."

The boys are crying so hard when they come out that Gia fears something inside them will shatter. Perhaps it already has. She watches them get on the elevator with their sister, and Greg, the one who looks like his mother, gives a little wave as the doors close. Gia, who knows she has done a good job so far, has done all that was expected of her, has never felt more helpless in her life.

"The nurses won't help us," she says.

"I've looked at the stuff. I know what to do," Yozo says. "Is that okay with you, Ed?"

He nods stiffly. "Yeah. Is it now? Are you gonna do it now?"

"Yeah."

Barbara's husband disappears into the cubicle. Gia and Willie and Yozo all glance nervously at each other, listening for a sound. But there is no sound, and quickly, too quickly, Eddie Eckroat emerges, the saddest-looking man Gia has ever seen, she thinks.

"You're gonna think I'm no good, but you don't know anything about us. God forgive me, she was my wife, but our marriage, well, it hasn't been a marriage for a long time. She means more to you than she does to me, honest to God. I don't care what you think, but I don't care. She's dead, it's just machines now, and she's been dead for me for a long time. I'm gonna take care of my kids." He presses the elevator button. No one says anything. The silence seems to agitate him, and he keeps talking. "I used to love her, you know? She killed that. She killed everthing. And now she killed herself. I don't know. I don't know why she was out there or what happened in the car, but she was doing what she wanted to do, she always did. She didn't care about any of us."

The elevator doors open, and he gets in, presses a button, and, before the doors close, he turns his head away so that he doesn't have to face his wife's three friends.

Gia looks at Yozo, who is still looking at the closed elevator doors. "Can this possibly get any more fucked up?" she asks.

"Why didn't he let her go?" Yozo is talking to himself. "Why didn't he divorce her?"

"What difference would it have made?" Gia asks.

He looks at her. "I could have married her. I would have left Chris, I would have left all of it for her."

Gia gasps, and her eyes fill with tears, so suddenly, so densely, she cannot see, and she reaches first for Yozo, who is sobbing, too, but then she turns to Willie, who embraces her. She hears the sounds of lives colliding. She listens to that sad crashing until she hears herself saying, through the tears, "All these years. All that passion. What did we do? What did we do?"

"Don't." Willie's soothing voice cuts through her tears. "Don't. Nothing was lost."

"I'm sorry," she sobs.

"Don't," he says again. "You cannot know another's heart."

She looks up at his tear-streaked face. "I know your heart," she finally says.

"Yes, you do," he answers, and then she realizes that Yozo has stopped crying.

I love them so much. She looks at the men. I do know their hearts.

Barbara, she thinks, I love you enough to let you die.

Her godfather said good-bye, her husband never gave her a choice. She suddenly understands that to love is to say good-bye, again and again, and to know that the good-bye will always come, that knowledge, perhaps, is what makes love so sweet.

She wipes her eyes and takes a deep breath. She realizes that the three of them are holding hands, and the men are looking at her.

"Come on," she says.

Willie holds her left hand, the one that still wears Eddie's wedding ring, and he places it to his lips, kisses it, and then just holds it to his cheek. Yozo looks at Barbara for a second, then goes to a small panel off to the left of the bed.

He looks at Gia. "It's three switches."

She looks at Willie. He nods.

As soon as Gia hears the first switch click, something snaps in her, and she throws herself across Barbara's body, covering her upper body with hers, whispering to her as she hears the second click, "We're all here, Barbara. We're still here, all of us." And then there is the third click.

Gia stiffens and holds on tightly to her friend, as the cubicle falls into an instantly startling silence. The machines are stilled. Barbara's chest sinks, Gia feels it under her, and she waits, for what she is not certain, but she thinks something might happen, that she might feel the flight of Barbara's soul through her. It cannot end with just a silence. That doesn't seem to be enough, even though the silence is precisely what she has been chasing for Barbara these past days.

Barbara makes a strangling sound. Gia looks up at Willie. "It's a reflex," he tells her.

Then Gia feels Barbara rise up under her, and the strangling sound comes again, and Yozo shouts, "Holy shit! She's breathing!"

"No, asshole." Gia jumps up. "She's choking, get that tube out of her throat, goddammit, where's a nurse, oh, shit, how do you do this, don't let her choke, oh, fuck!"

Yozo swats Gia away from Barbara's body and, ripping the white surgical tape from her face, he gets the finest purchase on the plastic apparatus and starts, quickly but gently, in one smooth motion, removing the tube from her throat.

"Be careful, Joe," Gia prays. "Be careful, don't hurt her, be careful." Life has never felt more precious or fragile than it does at this moment. Gia watches to see that Barbara keeps breathing.

Yozo pulls the rest of it out, and Barbara coughs and vomits, and Willie slips his arm under her hugely bandaged head and lifts her up, just a little, so that she won't aspirate the matter into her lungs.

Her lungs. The ones that are filling and emptying without any help from any man-made device.

"Get a doctor," Yozo says, still holding the breathing apparatus, still looking at Barbara, who coughs again. Willie holds Barbara's head. Yozo shouts at Gia, "Get a fucking doctor, will you?"

Gia throws back the white curtains and breaks into a run, heading for the nurses' station she only, just a few minutes ago, just a lifetime ago, ran away from, and she is hollering, "We need a doctor! We need somebody! Help! She's breathing! Help!"

This time the nuns come running.

"The truth is," Dr. Tolliver is saying to the three of them in an office outside Radiology, on the third floor of the hospital, "that we really don't understand how the brain does what it does. Her scans, her injuries, they all look the same, but we're getting reflexes from her now, Babinski reflexes, deep-pain reflexes, and I'll tell you, I can't tell you why."

"Is she going to wake up?" Yozo asks.

"She's awake now. To put it in very simple terms, she's tired. Her brain has suffered a huge insult, and she's resting. Not sleeping as we know it, more like a twilight sleep. I won't mislead you, she may not come out of it, but there are cases where people do wake up."

"When they wake up, what are they?" Gia wants to know. "Is there a possibility that she can, you know, live a normal life?"

"Anything is possible from here on," Tolliver

says. "She might never wake up, she might and be impaired in any number of ways. Or she might recover. Like I said, the brain seems to do things that we cannot yet understand or explain."

Willie, who has been sitting quietly, listening, not asking any questions, but looking very pleased with everything that has happened, finally says, "Where I work, we call that a miracle."

LAST DAY

Yozo holds the ambulance's back door open and says to Willie, "You've got to tell her."

"Oh, that's not fair, Joe, that's just not right."

"We're going, she's leaving tonight, you tell her, okay?"

"Tell me what?" Gia crawls out of the ambulance, having kissed a sleeping Barbara good-bye. She spent the morning at the bedside of her girlfriend, spelling out in detail what had happened since her accident. Barbara had continued to improve these past few days, and the doctors have decided that she can get better care in a rehab hospital in Manhattan. Yozo, who, thanks to a motion by Gia and another quick court appearance, is now Barbara's legal guardian, has decided to take her there and he will stay with her. Last night he and his wife had their friendliest conversation in years when he told her he was leaving, and she, in the most amiable way, told him she wanted half. He agreed, and their lawyers will have an easy time of it.

"Tell what?" Gia asks again. "You gonna tell me something?"

"He is," Yozo answers, pulling her into his arms for one last embrace. "You're a hell of a lawyer, kid. You're really something."

"Take good care of her, Joe."

"Yeah, okay." He whispers in her ear, "Be good to him. You take care of him."

"I will. Stay in touch. Keep me posted. I'll try to get to New York in a month or so, all right?"

"Yeah, that'll be good." He kisses her hair, he kisses her cheek, and quickly he kisses her mouth.

"Gotta go." He slaps Willie's shoulder and climbs back into the ambulance, which pulls away, lights flashing, but no sirens, no peeling out, just another vehicle going to New York City.

"What are you supposed to tell me?" she asks Willie.

"What is this place?" she asks as they pull into a grimy parking lot at a gray place called Brutto's Foundry. It's about fifteen minutes outside the town, but Willie is driving her to Philadelphia, so Gia assumes it's on the way and there is something here he wants to show her.

Daylight is fading fast, winter is closing in, she notices the chill for the first time, and realizes that she has been here for a long time, longer than the few days it took her godfather to die. They walk across the parking lot, and Willie unchains the metal gate that leads into the foundry. "Whose keys?" she asks.

"Guess. He owns part of this. Come on." They go into a huge, hangarlike building, with bins everywhere, filled with orange-sized chunks of coal. "This is a foundry," Willie says.

"Yeah, so the sign said. Why are we here?"

He looks around, he wipes his brow, he walks away from her, and then he comes back. "Remember when Barbara fainted at Tony's funeral, before the procession to the church?"

"Yeah."

"When that happened, Tony's coffin—you know how they get it into that viewing room?"

"No, I never th

"Well, it's a hydrau

ies downstairs and everyth

coffin on the lift and they se

room. The same company who s

Yozo's garage does DiBello's."

"Yeah? So?"

"So, when Barbara did that, you know,

inside—I heard this whole story from Yozo, k

that in mind. I knew nothing about this, Gia.

Anyway, Yozo's kid was downstairs, and he hit the

button, and your uncle's coffin was lowered back

into the embalming area downstairs. This was while

Barbara was doing her fainting act. Yozo and his

son took Tony."

"They what?"

"And then they, uh, sent it back up, closed, you

know, and then we went to the funeral. Only Tony

was, uh, in a pine box back at DiBello's."

She is staring at him, and it feels as though she's

beginning to go blind.

"So you want me to finish?" he asks.

"Oh, I'd like that, a lot."

"Yeah, well, okay, well, after the funeral Yozo

drove your uncle's body, in the pine coffin, nice, it

was a nice box, to a crematorium right outside

Reading, and he was cremated that night, Gia. Just

like he wanted, so Yozo told me. You can get as

angry as you want, and you're probably going to hit

me and all that, and I don't blame you, but he

wanted it, and Yozo loved him, and he believed he

had no choice but to do what Tony wanted."

ught about it."
ic lift. They prepare the bod-
ing, and then they put the
d it up to the viewing
rvices the lifts at
I was
eep

ell me

yes with
ell me he

ever come
to the gar-
would want

to?"

"Well, the... is. Apparently, Barbara wanted to help, ... t a message for Yozo on Sunday afternoon that ... he was going to Reading to pick up the package. She meant Tony's ashes."

"Package."

"That's where she was coming from when she flipped."

Gia takes in all this new, mad information. "She was trying to do a favor for Tony."

"Yeah. And Yozo. And you. She knew how much he meant to all of us."

"So, where are his ashes now?" she asks.

"See, Gia, that's where the story gets funny." Willie is his most Irish, his most charming self.

"'Gets funny'?" Gia leans close to him. "You don't think this is pretty funny already, Will?"

"Well, ah, the car was totaled, and Yozo didn't really put the message and the accident together until after he had sent it off to be compacted—no, wait, don't say anything—and he didn't really tell them to hold on to it or anything, so it came here, to the foundry, and it got melted down."

Gia is looking at everything in the place except Willie. "So my uncle's ashes were in the car that got compacted and then melted down?"

"Precisely. They make them into these pellets, and the quality of the metal isn't real high-grade, so it's worked over and they melt these pellets down, and then they make them into barbed wire."

Gia is silent for a long time.

Willie says, "We weren't going to tell you, but when Barbara started to wake up and Yozo decided to go with her, well, the truth is, we flipped a coin, and it came up that you should be told, and I lost."

"You flipped a coin."

"Yeah."

She takes a deep breath. "So there are, what, hundreds of thousands of these things in here?"

"Yeah, they have these big machines that scoop them up and feed them back into the furnaces. It's closed now," he adds lamely.

"And Tony's in them?"

He nods. "Well, some of them."

"He's going to end up as barbed wire."

"Pretty much."

"So when Barbara was at the cemetery with me the night of his funeral, and she was saying to me, 'He's not here,' she really meant it."

He nods.

"And Yozo just kept bitching at me about not

keeping my promise to him during the funeral procession because, what, he wanted to look authentic?"

"Yeah, and it was fun for him."

She looks around. "Barbed wire," she says.

"I think he'd like it," Willie says.

"Prickly and dangerous."

She goes to one of the bins and takes out a pellet. It is cool and smooth and, in an industrial way, rather pretty. She puts it back.

Willie is watching her.

"And you're not likely to find it in a Catholic church." She faces him. "You did good. They did good," she says.

The two get into the car, and when they reach the road, Willie stops and smiles at her.

"We're all right, aren't we?" he asks.

They have years of separation behind them, and their time in the future is uncertain, but they know that they are sitting here, in the setting autumn sun's last light, as friends, lovers in a fine way that neither of them ever expected.

They had been, all four of them, on their separate journeys, and when they returned to that small town that was their beginning, they found the secret of their lives there. It was a simple truth, and it took them almost a lifetime to learn it.

Loyalty. Without loyalty, there is nothing.

She smiles at the man she will always love, the man who has always loved her, and she says, "Drive."